GOING HOME

RAIN TRUEAX

It's 1865 and the Civil War has just come to an agonizing end-- even impacting far off Oregon with its destructive divisiveness.

Oregon Historicals
Book 3

Going Home

is an original work of Rain Trueax.

ISBN: 978-1-943537-03-7
Paperback

Prepared and presented by:

Seven Oaks
Monmouth, Or.

Sign up for new release notifications at http://raintrueax.blogspot.com

 Created with Vellum

CHAPTER 1

June 1865 Portland, Oregon

Raine Stevens, along with the rest of the cast, walked from the wings to stand in the lights at the front of the stage. They took their bows, as the remaining gaslights were brought up to illuminate the auditorium. A sense of accomplishment filled her, as the audience rose to give them and Kirk Edmonton's exciting play a standing ovation. Even a few bravos rang out. She smiled at her mother, step-father, sister, and brother-in-law in the first row.

Russell Grayson walked up the aisle with a large bouquet of red roses, but her gaze was drawn from him to the back of the auditorium. A man, taller than those around him, stood watching her. His features were sharp. Tawny hair hung almost to his shoulders. He resembled, but no, he couldn't be Jed Hardman.

To clear her head, she looked back at Russell, who was now at the edge of the stage. It wasn't the first time she had been wrong in thinking she'd seen Jed. She knelt to take the roses from Russ. Smiling, she thanked him and rose, clasping them to her breast.

At the back of the large hall, people were beginning to stream out the doors. There was no unusually tall man among them.

Half an hour later, in her dressing room, her mother helped her out of her elaborate gown. With its layers of lace and silk, she would only wear something like it in a play. In slips, she sat at her dresser to wipe off the heavy stage makeup, while sipping from a glass of water.

"You've never given a finer performance," her mother said. "I should have brought Eli."

"And Laura," Amy added with a nod of agreement. "They would both have enjoyed it. They're old enough now."

"There will be other opportunities," Raine said, as she slipped into a simple, yellow dress and waited as her mother buttoned up its back. She felt full of nervous energy but was unsure how much was from the completed run of a play or those few seconds when she thought she had seen Jed.

"I liked your character," Amy said. "She was strong and willful, funny too. This is the first time I've seen you carry off comedy. I can't recall the writer's name, but he managed to insert humor into pathos. True genius to make an audience want to laugh and cry at the same time."

Raine perched on the edge of her dressing table and drank more water. "The playwright is Kirk Edmonton."

"Was he in the audience?" Amy asked.

"He came opening night and seemed satisfied with how it had gone. He wasn't here tonight. I agree about his gifts. His dialogue flows, feels real and yet as you said, can be funny and sarcastic. No wasted words. I always believe in his characters-- like in how he gave depth to Sadie and also the man she finally chose for her own."

"Well, you knew she'd get her way."

"They don't always, those strong, willful women," Raine said with a smile. "I should do a tragedy next time-- just to show the other side."

"And then at least my daughter won't be coming," Amy

retorted. "She isn't ready for more life complexity than needful. When our neighbor, Eunice died, it was upsetting for her, had her questioning life and meaning. She was more aware than the younger ones."

"All right, no tragedies for now." She didn't need them either.

"How is Fanny doing?" her mother asked.

"I haven't seen much of her since she came back from Eunice's funeral," Raine said brushing out her hair. "She is busy, living the life to which she was born, a large staff, a home to manage, causes to support, clubs to join. It was a huge loss to her though. No one will ever support her emotionally as much as her mother did."

"I thought we might see her and Horace tonight."

"They also were at the opening. The whole time we chatted, Fanny was trying to talk him into taking her to San Francisco for shopping. She's finding our stores less than exciting now that she has more money to spend."

"They say familiarity breeds contempt," Amy teased.

"I will not take offense... or try not to. I do what I can to keep my stores up to date-- with new styles for the ladies as well as the home. Some people though cannot be satisfied unless it came from a city more exciting than Stump Town."

"There are those who love the excitement of big cities," her mother agreed and then sighed. "I wish Belle lived closer, could see you in these plays. It disappointed me when, after college, she settled in Chicago—of all places. Why on earth there?"

"Perhaps you should visit her and ask." Pleasing parents wasn't that easy in Raine's experience. Her mother would like her living in Oregon City, but Portland was her home. While it might not yet be as cosmopolitan as San Francisco or Chicago, someday it would.

"She would no doubt be no less evasive than she is in letters," her mother said with that expression which told Raine she was thinking about more than she was saying. "But you are right, it's not my business. Besides, whenever I've suggested visiting, she writes that she'll be gone but will let me know a good time. She has yet to give me one."

"Family has never mattered that much to Belle," Amy said, not hiding her disapproval.

"That's not all her fault," Raine said, trying to be fair. "Being so much younger, she probably felt she grew up without the kind of closeness you and I enjoyed with only being a year apart."

"I give up, oh mighty peacemaker," Amy teased. "Let's forget her. Maybe next time we can talk St. Louis into coming with us. He complains that cities aren't for him, can't stand crowds, but he'd be so proud to see you in a play like this one—once he came."

"How is he?"

"Feisty as ever."

"Good," Raine said with a grin. "I'll be up river soon anyway and will try to see him then."

Listening to Amy and their mother talk about the children, the trip downriver on the steamboat, her mind was elsewhere and on those few seconds she had thought he was watching her. She had never told her family about Jed. Why would she, since there had been nothing to tell? Certainly nothing, she'd want them to know regarding her foolishness.

Maybe her feelings were tangled up in the Civil War finally ending. After Lee surrendered, she had thought maybe, if he had survived the fighting, he would return to Oregon. Except, a man, who had wanted to see her again, would have written. In four years he'd been gone, she'd received no letter. So many had died on both sides-- but more on the side for which he had fought, the South.

She turned back to the mirror, attempting to wrap her hair into a bun. Frustrated, she gave up and used combs to pull it back from her face. In the mirror, she saw herself, her mother, and sister reflected. She didn't have their black hair, but the three of them had fine boned faces and slim bodies. Raine's reddish-brown hair, a product of her father's heritage, was wavier than she liked. If she could have changed it to something smoother, more manageable, she would have. More silliness. Life was what it was. She wasn't going to be changing anything.

When they came out of the theater to where two tall men waited, Raine felt the warmth of a June night in the air. The street was well lit in front of the theater by its new gaslights. It was the kind of night, which might have inclined one to go for a walk down by the river. Unfortunately, that was a ribald area after dark, with bars and brothels spilling noisy customers out into the streets.

"We are going out to dinner to celebrate, right?" Matt, her handsome brother-in-law suggested. "You did right fine, Raine."

Before the others could answer, Russell Grayson, dwarfed a bit by the taller men, joined their party. "I would love to take you all to dinner," he said as he put his arm around Raine's waist. "You were superb tonight, my dear."

She didn't like his hand there but wasn't sure why it annoyed her. She recognized that she was in a mood, and so gritted her teeth with another forced smile. "It would be wonderful. I'm ravenous." She never ate before a performance. "How about Chinese? There is a wonderful restaurant only two blocks from here," she suggested.

Her stepfather, Adam sighed. "Seriously? No steak houses nearby?" She recognized he was teasing and only laughed when her mother pinched him and told him to be good.

As they walked off laughing and talking, Raine fought to match her mood to theirs. Perhaps all she felt was the letdown from another play ending. Maybe the weather was changing. Something was in the wind though, and it was making her edgy.

In the shade of the buildings standing back from the light, Jed Hardman watched Raine's party as they laughingly headed off.

"So go talk to her," Joshua said.

"And say what? Looks to me like she has a man."

"You don't know that."

Jed reached for the makings and rolled a cigarette. "I can see."

"What you saw was a woman with friends, one of whom put his arm around her. Not a woman who responded in anyway other than politely. My brother, you won't know anything until you talk to her. We pushed our horses for the last two weeks to get here. Now you want to just walk off?"

Jed grimaced. He didn't want to walk off. When had he become a coward? Maybe since a dream of the one woman had gotten him through four long years of war. Maybe the problem is he still needed that dream. When he talked to her, it'd be gone. All that would be left would be memories of a beautiful woman lying in a bed with her long hair spread out across the pillows, her slender arms reaching up for him.

Should he have asked her to marry him before he left? He didn't see how he could have. He had been called back to Georgia by a letter from his mother telling him of her illness and his brothers joining the Confederate cavalry. When he had left Oregon, he had not known if he'd make it back or be in one piece if he did.

Even before that, he'd not had a life to offer a lady like her. Jed possessed two contradictory dreams—his ranch in remote country, with Indian troubles nearby, and a love for a beautiful city woman, who lived too far away. He saw no way to bring them together, but Josh was right. He would have to talk to her.

From the looks of how she was dressed, the play in which she'd starred, she had grown even more successful in the years he'd been gone. She'd be even more unlikely to agree to life on a ranch in the middle of nowhere. Moreover, who was that man who put his arm around her? Was she married? Maybe with children?

Josh, his dark skin making his teeth show up even more as he grinned, said, "Argue it all out as much as you want, you won't let this one go. We both know it."

"Maybe or maybe not." He took another long drag on the cigarette, finding no pleasure in it.

"Let's get a drink," Josh suggested.

Jed nodded, even though whiskey wasn't going to do anything to make him happy. Josh was right also that he needed to settle it with Raine. If she was happy with someone else, he'd wish her well. Well, he'd do his damnedest to wish her well.

As they walked into a smoky bar, Jed wondered, not for the first time, what the attitude in Oregon was toward mulattoes, which would be his brother's legal definition for those who needed such boxes to label humans. Not that it mattered much what anyone thought, considering he and Josh were armed and a head taller than most of the men in the room.

They leaned on the bar until the bartender came over. "Two whiskeys," Jed drawled putting the money on the bar. The bartender looked at Josh a little curiously, but he and his brother were used to that. The drinks were poured with no questions.

"You boys are new around here," a bald man with a wide girth said as he moved closer to them. Jed took a sip of his whiskey without answering. "Back from the war?"

"And that would be your business?"

The man smiled. "Just trying to be friendly."

"Snooping into the business of other folks considered friendly these days?" Jed asked. He motioned to Josh for them to take their drinks to a table. The man followed and sat without an invitation.

"Just thought you might not know Oregon was in favor of freeing slaves."

"That so?" Josh asked with a cynical smile as he sipped his whiskey.

"They set this to being a free state before we went into the Union. Way ahead, then had to redo it. Of course, can't legally own land here."

"Who can't?" Jed asked.

7

"No colored folk." The man grinned slyly. "We're a real free state kind of folk."

"What's your game here, mister?" Jed asked.

"Friends call me Toddy. Todd Coen if you want to be formal and my game? Well let me think a minute on that one. It might be many things. You boys are new here, aren't you?" Jed took a long draw on his cigarette instead of answering. "Just curious. Always curious about folks... Uh what are your names so we can keep this more sociable?"

"Not saying we want to be sociable, but Jed and Josh."

"Guess you two are figuring I'd be one of those narrow minded types who'd block colored folk from their rights but no, I am not. What I am is a realist. I see the irony of life and can't help but observe it. Like the two of you."

"There's an irony to us?" Jed asked as Josh headed over to the bar and paid for a bottle of whiskey, bringing back an extra glass.

Coen smiled and said his thanks before he took a sip. "You two have Southern accents, strong ones. Georgia maybe?"

"Asking a lot of questions can prove dangerous—in some places," Jed said eyeing him coldly.

Coen grinned with real humor. Obviously, he didn't easily take offense. "Guessing since you just showed up, war just ended, likely you fought in it, and wanted out of the South after it lost?"

Jed contemplated punching him. It would actually feel good to hit someone... for a moment anyway.

Coen looked curiously at Josh and then back at Jed. "So you came north and brought your freed slave."

Josh laughed.

"Josh has never been a slave, Mr. Coen. He was a freeman from birth. And to stop more questions. He's my brother."

Coen laughed. "Well bless my soul. That's something else. So you fought for the north?"

Jed shook his head. "No."

"To keep slavery?"

"You are looking for a fight."

Coen laughed. "Not with a man your size. No siree. Just wondered is all."

"Well to satisfy your curiosity. I fought for the South. Josh and I were both in the war, in Jeb Stuart's cavalry until he was killed at Yellow Tavern. then under Wade Hampton until the surrender and our parole."

"You both fought for the South?" For the first time, their new want-to-be friend sounded surprised.

"We fought for family and state."

"I didn't mean to offend by asking."

"War is hell, stranger. It's even worse when you go into it knowing it's a lost cause, but I had family in it. Now all that's left of that is Josh."

"I still can't get over you fighting though for slavery given..." Coen's tone reflected his disbelief as he looked from Jed to Josh.

"Fought for a state's right to leave the union. Fought to protect our neighbors and friends from an invading army. My family never believed in slavery. They freed all the slaves as soon as they bought the land and could do it, but how the hell is it worth talking about this? It's over."

"Not hardly. The bad feelings still here. Hate is strong, son. People are strange; how one day they'll say one thing and then boom, the other side comes out. Dark and light. A lot of folks here won't take kindly if they find you fought for the South." His smile was wry. "Even more that you got a darkie with you."

Jed smile was glacial. "You are betting on the wrong cards if you think I give a damn."

Coen chuckled. "Nah, just figured you might need to know what you're up against back here."

"What's your work, Coen?" Jed smoked studying the man and wondering at his angle.

"Make it Toddy. Coen sounds too much like my father. I've done a bit of this and that. You name it. I've done it probably. Sometimes I write pieces for the paper."

9

"Hope this won't be one of them," Josh said with a grin as he sipped his whiskey.

"No, just was curious. Two big men like yourselves and now that you say it, I can see the resemblance, well it makes a man wonder about the story behind it—if the man's a writer anyway. What brings you to Portland then?"

"Business," Jed answered.

"And then you're moving on?"

"You do sound like a journalist," Jed said with a cold smile making it clear that'd be less than welcome.

"I'm not. I'm more a poet."

"Well, Toddy, who pries into stranger's business, I own a ranch, east of the Cascades, on the North Fork of the John Day River. We're heading there next."

"You didn't stop by there first though? Something more important here than there? Whole thing makes a body wonder."

"It's nothing for a poem." Jed's smile was the one some had said looked mean. He felt mean.

"Never know what might be. Poetry is nothing but painting pictures with words. Might be there is a poem or a lot of them in you two boys," Toddy said not looking intimidated.

"Well, you been giving me advice," Jed drawled, "now I'll give you some. Don't ask too many questions or you'll find yourself booted out of here."

Toddy grinned. "I'll remember that. So you going back soon?"

Jed put up one finger. "I had my reasons for coming here first. Among them, a need to go back there with supplies. I am not sure what will be left. Four years is a long time to leave a ranch."

"I suppose it is nosy, but how's it happen you have a place out there? Kind of unusual. That's pretty remote country as best I know. Not a place a man would find by accident."

Jed surprised himself by deciding to answer. Despite his nosiness, there was something likeable about Coen's persistence. "I came out in '59, bought it from a Frenchman." He didn't need to reveal the story of how that had come about. "He had been allowed to buy it as a reward for service, plus the fact it was wilderness. Not many wanted land out there. The deed is firm if that was your next question. He had built cabin and barns. I added onto the house, built corrals, stocked it with cattle. It was a good plan right up until the war interfered."

"You read about all the Indian trouble over there?"

"You are just a fount of good news."

"What Indian trouble," Josh interrupted giving Jed a look, which was answered with a shrug.

"Paiutes, Shoshoni, some others been attacking and hitting settlers, anywhere they can. Military being all back east, fighting the War, left an opening. Oregon formed what they call the First Oregon Calvary, but I look to see that disbanded now with real warriors back. When we get some professional troops over there, those honed in battle, it should straighten itself out."

"Oh yeah, professional killers, just what everybody needs," Jed said with a grimace.

"Hey, boy, that's what it takes sometimes."

Jed had known about the problems with Paiutes and Shoshoni before he left, but he'd hoped for the best. The Confederated Tribes of the Warm Springs were peaceable with their own reservation. He hoped that was still the case. He was counting on it.

If Coen was right and there'd been a lot of trouble in his region, he'd be lucky to find anything unburned when he got home. He wasn't even sure Grimes and Jessup would still be where he'd left them, supposedly looking after the property and cattle. If he was lucky, the cattle would've spread to the brush and be there to be rounded up-- instead of in a grizzly, wolf or Paiute's belly. At least, he had not assumed he'd be back quickly and had left money with a reputable lawyer to keep the taxes up to date.

"You didn't get much news about out here then?"

"Not a lot." A war is all about it.

"Hear about the gold rush over your way?"

Jed shook his head, wondering what else could go wrong. The

woman he had hoped would be waiting, even though he'd never asked her, looked to be taken. The cabin likely destroyed, cattle gone, and he'd have to start over. Now gold fever to take away any possible hired help. Perfect.

His brother grinned, obviously reading the disgruntled expression. "Well you have me, Jed."

"Not what I'd been hoping to offer you. A state that won't let you own land and maybe an Indian war out our backdoor. You want to head back to Georgia?" He shook his head.

"Hey, I didn't mean to be giving you all bad news." Toddy's smile looked concerned.

"I'd have had to find out sometime. Just a lot at once."

"It's not all that bad, Jed," Josh said. "I like the idea of a new start and want to see that land of yours. After all, you've been talking about it for four years."

Toddy stared at him. "You really went to war with him and fought for the South?"

"Where else'd I be?" Josh asked with a crooked grin.

"Damn. They let you do that?"

"You talk too much Coen," Jed said with an expression that said more questions were going to be out.

"Sorry. Just surprises me is all."

Jed wanted to stop thinking about any of it. "What kind of poetry you write?" he asked the older man.

"Want to hear one?" Toddy teased.

"Maybe after another drink or two," Josh responded with a laugh.

CHAPTER 2

The house quiet, the rest of her family apparently asleep, Raine lay in bed, tossing, turning, and most of all remembering. Why couldn't she let the memories go? It had been so long ago, and yet as if yesterday.

For years, she had held off the men who wanted to marry her. Where many men sought young girls, and she was well past being girlhood, there had been no shortage of those hoping to change her mind about remaining a spinster. It hadn't been hard for her to resist them. Foolishly, she had kept an image in her heart of how it could be with a man, how she had seen it be with Adam and her mother, with Amy and Matt. She had wanted that or nothing. Silly woman. Those kinds of feelings didn't come along every day. Except, the day came when they did.

She had met him in her store where he'd come in for supplies. "Howdy, ma'am," he had said in a rich Southern drawl, "Did I tell you that you're having lunch with me?" His smile had been a little crooked and very confident.

"I am not in the habit of dining with men I don't know," she'd responded tartly even though she had already known she would be saying yes. A hook, from long before he had walked into her store, had been set, waiting.

"That might be true, but you never met me before." Teasing, gray eyes had spoken to her. There had been that look in them, the one for which she had waited. It had been as though a flame ignited between them.

There had been no denying his physical attributes, wavy, golden brown hair, tall, muscular body, and a handsome, rugged face. However, it had been more than the physical. It also wasn't lust. She had seen that look in other men's eyes. This was something more, more than friendship, more than desire. It was a sort of inner knowing.

There'd been no need for him to court her or for her to play coquettish games. It simply was. Unlike so many women in her culture, she had never believed it necessary to wait for a wedding before being intimate with a man. The fact that she had no desire to marry didn't have to preclude sex. She had read about the famous courtesans of Europe. Women did not have to play by the old rules—certainly not women who could earn their own way. The fact that she had not had sex with anyone was only because she'd never wanted to.

And so, they had begun. The flame she had sensed was there ignited into an inferno that swept her away to a world she had imagined but never experienced or even expected she would. This had belonged to other women never to her.

She remembered every detail of the first night they had come together intimately. They had gone to dinner and back to her home. It wasn't her current home as she had moved up in the world since; but it was a nice home, not far above Portland's main business district.

"Want me to come in?" he'd drawled with his deep voice, which spoke of Georgia, cigarettes, and command.

She had wanted to tease him a little even though she'd known what this night was going to contain. "You want to come in?" she'd asked, her fingers lightly brushing over the front of his shirt.

His smile had been lazy and crooked, so sure of himself that she'd felt herself melting under its power, but she had wanted to play. He'd bent and lightly kissed her lips. "You have to ask me," he had said, pulling her tightly against his hard body.

"I won't beg." She had been cocksure and so wrong.

"Oh, but you will if you ask me in."

"Or you will," she had taunted as he bent and kissed her, first lightly, as he had before. Then his tongue pushed against her lips and into her mouth. Her body had seemed to come alive at the sensations that flooded through it.

He had lifted his head, those gray eyes intent on hers. "You have to ask, and you know what it'll mean if you do?"

"I do."

"Raine, you ever been with a man that way before?" he'd asked, a kind of assessment in his eyes.

"Of course," she had lied. "I'm not a girl."

Kissing her again, his tongue had teased at her lips. "You are lying."

"Damn how can you tell?"

His smile broadened. "Sugar, you don't even know how to kiss yet. I can teach you though. Want me to teach you?"

Between them had been almost an invisible cord that bound her to a man to whom it was never meant to be. He had taught her that she could explode with desire, beg a man, and drive him to the place where he would beg her.

For a month, they had met when they could, and each time the feelings had grown stronger. She had learned how to kiss, what it felt like to have a man's body totally possess hers, and then allow her to claim him in every way she could imagine and more than she ever had. That part was so good and only got better.

The obstacles were all there. She had let herself be possessed by him sexually but would not be owned. She could not see herself living a life on the edge of the wilderness, and he certainly was no man to come and live in the city running a store. It might have gone on longer except for the night he had come to her, his face hard, his expression grim. She remembered it all, every word they had said.

"What is it?" she asked knowing she didn't want to know.

He led her to the porch swing putting his arm around her shoulders. "You know the war has begun?"

"I saw that they bombed Fort Sumter, yes. I guess it can't be stopped now."

He sighed, and she saw the muscle jump in his jaw.

"You want to go?"

"Not want to but... I have family in Georgia, sugar. I got a letter from my mother. She is sick. My brothers, Geoff and Trevor joined up, leaving her alone."

"You will join up?"

"I don't plan to. It's a fool's cause. I need to go for her though."

"If you go to Georgia, you could be killed. The fighting won't stay in the North."

He had sucked in a breath. "It's a risk. I don't have an alternative."

She didn't either and yet. "How could you fight for the South feeling as you do about slavery?"

"I could fight for my family and protecting what is mine. I love my brothers. Slavery won't last whichever way this goes. If the North would have let it happen naturally, it'd be gone probably sooner than with this war. Only maybe ten percent own slaves and a lot feel like my family—that it's wrong. That damned book got folks all stirred up. They think it's like that all across the South, but it's not."

"You mean Uncle Tom's Cabin? It does portray a horrible view of slavery."

"I don't disagree when it's at the worst. Some have abused the practice. You know I don't believe in one man owning another. It's why my family has no slaves. We paid a wage, a fair wage for work done."

"Then how can you fight for it?"

"I do not plan to join up."

"You might be compelled."

"If I had to fight, I'd do it for my mother, my brothers."

"So you'd fight beside them?" She could hardly believe she had said that. Surely he wouldn't do that. How could he fight for slavery?

"Raine, I can't stay here and do nothing. I sure can't fight against my own kin."

"If you go to Georgia, you'll be sucked into the war. You and I both know that." She looked at his eyes and saw their inflexible purpose. He would go. She could not stop him, and he'd be killed. She had waited so long to find love, and she was going to lose it. No, that was wrong. She couldn't have held it anyway—too many differences to make it work.

"That is possible," he said, "but I'll do all I can to see it's not what happens. I have a lot waiting for me here. I hope part of that is you."

"So I should wait for you while you can't promise me anything, and you can't, can you?"

"No, I can't." He took his arm away from her shoulder and reached for the makings of a cigarette. When he had lit it, he said, "It wouldn't be fair."

"It's not fair that you are going to fight for something you don't even believe in."

"Raine, I believe in my family. My mother is back there alone. The last letter said they'd all left the plantation. Georgia is going to be a battlefield. She's left with just my youngest brother, Joshua."

"Your hired hands left too?"

He had nodded taking a drag on the cigarette.

"Why would they go?"

"They worked for her, but she wasn't family. They know what's coming. Georgia is in for hell. You know as well as I that the South is going to be torn apart by this war. It can't stand against the power of the North, not for long anyway. The workers left probably for safer ground. It's not like the plantation will have work or money to pay them until this is settled."

"You think the war won't last long?"

He drew again on the cigarette considering. "I don't know that either. It'll be short or a long drawn out agony."

She felt the tears starting, but she wouldn't beg him. It wouldn't do any good if she did. She wanted to though. She wanted to so much that her stomach hurt. "When will you leave?" she asked.

"It sounded like Mama was weak, sick. I can't wait. I have to ride by the ranch and then will head east."

She knew why he had come to her despite it adding to his difficulty. It had not been a traditional courting, but she supposed it was what he had been doing. Maybe it's what he had meant; but what could they have really done about it? Someday this had had to end. She had just hoped it'd be longer before it did. She had wished. Wishes were for fools.

"I suppose you will have to let the ranch go," she said surprised her voice sounded more level than she felt inside.

He let out a snort. "Not if I can damn well help it. I have a solicitor set up to pay the taxes and make sure the title stays clear while the country goes to hell. I will leave Jack Grimes and Bill Jessup to look after my place and hope it works that they do. Until I get back, I'll have them drive the cattle, most of them into the hills. I will round them up when I return."

"If you return," she said knowing her voice sounded bitter.

"There is that," he agreed.

"And what about tonight?" she asked.

"What do you want tonight?" His voice grew husky, the expression in his eyes had been tender as he'd reached out a finger to twist a strand of her hair around it.

She should have thought longer before she answered but she hadn't. "I want you to make love to me as though you were coming back," she said. "It'd not be smart though."

She felt his smile against her hair as he began undoing the braid, loosening her waves until they fell over her shoulders. "It's probably a little late to start being smart now anyway."

She managed a small laugh. "I suppose it is." She stood and took his hand as she led him into the house and to the bedroom.

That morning, when he left, before breakfast to get an early start, she didn't beg him to stay. She accepted that he had to go even as she wished he didn't. Would he have been the man he was if he hadn't?

Now as she lay in her bed, once again reliving all that had been and not been, she wondered if Jed had ever loved her. He hadn't said the words. He had never asked her to marry him. Had it been more than sex between them, had there been a deeper connection, as she had imagined, or had she fooled herself?

Would she have married him if he had asked? She didn't see how she could have. There were important differences in their lives, their goals, but he hadn't asked. She knew some of that had been the same honor that had made him go. He wouldn't bind her to him when he was unsure if he would return. She had no doubt that he had been pulled into the war. Maybe it killed him or crippled him as it had so many.

In the beginning, she had wished he had given her words before he left. Even that last night, when they had lain together, their bodies joined, skin slick with sweat, even then he'd not said he loved her.

When he had left, it was as though her heart had been ripped away. No, she mused with some bitterness, he had not ripped out her heart. For a long time, she had wished he had. Instead, he had left it in place, unfulfilled, but grateful a baby hadn't come from her rash actions. All these years later, she still felt pain at her mistake-- and she had come to regard it as a mistake. Perhaps she had learned from it. She could hope.

Dressed for work with a ruffled white blouse, gray skirt and jacket, her long hair braided and formed in a coronet around her head, Raine unenthusiastically wandered downstairs. She was happy to see, early though it was, Nancy Johnson, her all around helper with housework and cooking, had arrived and was in the kitchen with coffee already made and kneading bread dough.

"How'd you sleep?" she asked Nancy as she attempted to find some normalcy to escape the chaos of her mind.

What had triggered all of this thinking of him? Why did he suddenly feel so close? Just seeing someone at the back of the theater, who resembled him-- silly woman. It would never be him again. And if it was, she'd kick him out of her life before she had a chance to think twice about it.

"Kind of stormy last night," Nancy said, pounding the dough. "Think we're heading for a good blow. Clem says it's going to rain for sure." Nancy was married to one of the men, who had helped bring their wagon train to Oregon. Clem had settled in Portland to work for Jacob and Agatha Collins in their stores. It was then that he had met Nancy and love was born between two people who had thought themselves too old for it.

Raine poured her coffee hoping a jolt of caffeine would help clear her thinking. "I hope not another flood," she added to keep a normal conversation going. Portland, situated as it was on the Willamette River, always had to worry about its lower shops and homes being flooded. Fortunately, her home and stores were above the usual risky elevation.

"Could be. Lordy, this place does get the rain," Nancy, who had been born in California, moaned. In that, she and Clem were matches for how they enjoyed finding something about which to complain.

Raine sipped of her coffee. Shaking her head when Nancy offered to fix her breakfast. "I'll eat when the others get up," she said.

"Well just be sure you do, Missy. You're way too skinny."

To change the subject, Raine asked, "How were the children last night?"

"Good as angels... well except Rufus. Amy's littlest one, why he's gonna be a challenge, that boy."

"What'd he do?"

"It's not so much what he does but how he stirs things up." She chuckled. "He just gives me that look like his papa, and it makes a body's heart melt."

They heard the chaos starting on the stairs as Laura, Eli, Rufus, and Elizabeth headed down for breakfast. The four careened into the kitchen eager for something to eat and willing to tolerate hugs to get it.

"Are your parents getting up?" Raine asked, as she began frying bacon.

"They begged us to get more sleep," Laura said somberly, very adult for her being the oldest and trying to behave maturely for her almost ten years. "They said they aren't up to late nights anymore."

"They're younger than me," Raine reminded her.

"They don't seem it. You seem so young to me," Laura complimented while Elizabeth nodded with a thumb in her mouth.

Raine turned the bacon. "What'll it be-- oatmeal or eggs?"

Uniformly, they grimaced. "How about cinnamon rolls," Elijah suggested hopefully.

"No sugar," Amy said from the doorway. "You're all excited enough without that." She walked in and poured herself some coffee as she grinned at her sister and Nancy.

"No preferences given, so it'll be oatmeal," Raine said starting water to boil before reaching for the oats.

"That's no treat," Elijah complained.

"But it is sustenance," Amy said.

"Susta what?" Rufus asked

"Good for you."

"I don't like things good for me," Rufus protested. The four smiled when told there'd be brown sugar and cream to sweeten the deal.

As they ate, Raine and Amy sat at the table sipping coffee and nibbling on bacon. "When do you have to leave?" Raine asked.

"We can spend today if you'd like. We just have to get down to the docks early in the morning."

"I'd love today with you. Maybe we can go shopping. I'll take the day off."

"Wonderful. I would like more time here, but I feel guilty asking St. Louis to look after everything for too long. I wish you lived closer. I miss lying in bed and sharing our dreams."

She missed that too—although there was so much she couldn't share with anyone, not even a sister as close as any friend. Rather than saying all she was thinking, Raine said, "The stores make it hard to leave too. I have good help, but it's always something going wrong."

"How is Agatha? I figured not so good when she didn't come to dinner last night."

"She's up and down. She really does depend on Clem and me since Jacob died."

"Are you... well what about when she dies, will she leave the store and all to her kids back east? That's a terrible thing to ask, isn't it?"

Raine smiled at her blunt sister, but before she could answer, they were interrupted. "What does die mean?" Rufus asked.

"Just goes on like when Mrs. Lance died, remember?" Amy reminded him.

"I guess. I don't like it. You won't die, will you?" Rufus asked concern in his voice as he patted his mother's arm.

"Someday everybody does," Amy told him with a soft kiss on his cheek, "But it'll be a long time off."

As the children got back to eating and chattering among themselves, Raine said, "I own my own store, lease another, and manage Agatha's. I may buy the store I lease. As I began to make money, I invested in Portland's growth. Russell has been quite helpful with that."

Amy grinned. "He was certainly attentive last night. Has he asked you to marry him?"

"I have a good life as it is, Amy. I like my home, the comforts, freedom to go where I want, be in plays when it suits me, and have work I enjoy. I won't marry and have a man telling me what I can and cannot do. I don't have a reason to do so." She took a breath. "If that ever changes though, it won't be Russell."

"Does he know that? He seems hopeful to me."

"Yes, he's asked, and I have told him how I feel." Part of it anyway. "Whoever knows what a man thinks? I just can't see my being married. Any man would want me to cater to his needs and not be free to put my time into other interests. I like my freedom."

"There are some perks that go with it," Amy said with a slow smile. Raine knew how happy her sister was with Matt, but she also remembered how Amy had given up her own dreams for him. Her mother, after her father had been killed, had remarried, and with Adam, she had changed her dreams to whatever he wanted.

None of that was what Raine wanted for her life. She had her own dreams. She intended to follow them. Trying to help a man get his didn't seem like her thing. Maybe if it had happened when she was younger, it would have been different, but at thirty-two, she was set in her ways and happy to be an aunt and big sister. She satisfied any maternal instincts with her family's children.

She couldn't resist teasing Amy. "Maybe it's fine with you because you nearly suck Matt into you when you look at him.

Lord, the way that man's eyes light up whenever he sees you, well it is almost embarrassing." She giggled. "I just don't see that kind of thing for my own life. I am too busy for it anyway."

Amy sighed. "I just want you to be happy."

"I am." Or she would be when she managed to forget.

Their mother walked into the kitchen and went straight to Nancy who was now shaping bread loaves. "Need some help?" she asked.

Nancy shook her head. "Just you go get yourself some coffee and grab some of the biscuits I made earlier. You look tired."

"That's not tired. That's old age," her mother teased as she did indeed get the coffee, pouring a little cream into it. She sat down beside her girls. "You two work out the problems of the world?"

"We did decide it'd be fun to do something today with the little ones. Think you're up to that?" Raine smiled at the idea of her mother being old looking. At almost fifty, she still looked more like one of her sisters than her mother.

"I am, but let's not plan anything too ambitious for the children. Maybe next time we can come with enough time to spend a few days at the shore. They would love to see that. This time though, probably just playing here would be enough. They love your supply of toys."

"How about we all hit some of Portland's emporiums, the toy store, maybe an ice cream store... or how about the candy store?" Before she could remember that meant the out of favor sugar, she heard childish cheers.

"We might make an exception," Amy said with a smile that said she gave up. "It's not like an every day deal. Think you can behave yourself, Rufus?"

He nodded enthusiastically. "There really is a candy store?"

"Just one bit of rambunctiousness from you, and we're back here," Amy warned her son.

"What's that word mean?" he asked with a perplexed expression.

"What you do all the time."

The children asked to be excused and headed into the parlor and that box of toys. Raine enjoyed hearing their laughter and chattering.

"Rufus is a handful," Amy admitted. "I love him dearly, but that boy is always into something."

"Energy is good," their mother said.

"Easy for you to say with Eli being such a help around the house and wanting to learn. Rufus wants his own horse, did I tell you?"

Raine shook her head. "Six seems a little young for that."

"Of course, and that's what Matt told him, but he's pushing for it regularly. He's a little cowboy is what he is and not satisfied planting corn."

"You wonder about that kind of thing," their mother said. "I mean they do seem to have some imprints that you can't explain with logic. I know Elijah has been a lot that way since the day he was born. Determined and so like his papa."

"So, today we go shopping and maybe we can find something for each of them to take home as a souvenir of their trip," Raine said smiling as she thought how much fun that would be. "I know just the shop—and I think the band will be playing in the park if we want to listen to that."

"What are you four plotting?" Matt asked from the doorway with a big grin as he headed for coffee. Raine never saw him without thinking what a handsome man. It had been true even when he had not been more than a boy. Now, having come into his full strength and force of personality, a man in his early thirties, he dominated a room when he entered. It gave her joy to see that whenever he looked at her sister, that look of strength would melt away, leaving softness and love.

"We are all going shopping," Amy told him with a teasing smile.

"Good God, not me," he drawled. "I only do that when a gun's pointing at me, and I don't see no gun."

The backdoor to the kitchen opened and an older, wizened

man walked in. "Hey there, Clem," Matt said smiling and accepting the hug Clem always had for him.

"How ya doin', boy?" Clem asked as he also headed for the coffee pot sending his wife, Nancy, to start grinding more beans to make a fresh pot.

"Pretty fair. Got anything you can think of that'll get me out of shopping today?"

Before Clem could answer, Adam had walked into the kitchen quickly learning he'd be waiting for his first cup of coffee. Grinning, he and Clem shook hands. "You don't look older than when we worked together getting the wagon train across the country," Adam observed. "What's the secret?"

"Same as yores, I reckon," Clem said with a grin as he looked over at Nancy who blushed. Having them both working for her had all led to a comfortable situation for Raine when she set up her own home and business. A working relationship had evolved into a lovely friendship.

Adam watched the pot as it began to perk. "We could go for a ride today," he said.

"Up in the hills?" Matt asked with interest.

"Rent stable horses?" Clem said with doubt. "It's not like they ever have nothin' there but nags. I keep tellin' Raine here she needs two horses and a buggy, but she prefers to rent hacks. Need our own."

"And where would we stable them?" Raine asked. "This lot has no space for a horse. Keeping them at the livery would run into real dollars. Besides it'd give you more work when you are already busy."

Clem harrumphed but didn't carry the idea further.

"Well if not that, then it's down to the bawdy houses and bars," Adam said giving Martha a teasing look.

"You do that, and you better not come back smelling of some other woman's perfume," Martha said giving back as good as she got.

"Never a chance of that," he said bending and giving her a kiss that had the others looking away.

Clem snorted and said, "Just be careful if ya go down there."

"Of what?" Matt asked. "They water the whiskey?"

"Nah, it's the shanghaiing ya gotta watch out for."

"You're not serious," Adam said not letting go of watching the coffee and apparently willing it by force of personality to hurry up.

"I am dead serious. It's become right profitable down on the docks. They knock a fellow over the head or put something in his drink. He wakes up on a ship, and he's not a freeman no more. Owned by some sorry ba— excuse for a human, and no way to get free of it short of dying."

"The law does nothing about it?" Adam asked. Raine had noted he hadn't worn his badge on this vacation, but he was a good sheriff and would not be able to imagine a police force ignoring something like kidnapping citizens.

"It all happens down there where there ain't so much law. Lot of money in it. They get hardy lookin' young'uns, like you two." He grinned as he said it. "And the man's off afore anybody sees what happened or can get him back."

"That's terrible," Amy said visibly paling.

"It is, but it's also good for shippin', and those that sell the slaves. Right profitable market is what it is."

"Damn slavery in any form," said Adam riled but finally able to pour his first cup of coffee. He sat beside Martha.

"Wal, just make sure ya don't end up one of 'em. Riding into the hills, even on a livery horse would be better."

Raine sighed. "I suppose I do need to buy a good horse and pay the price to have it stabled. Times are changing and at first I thought I could do all I needed here, but a horse would be handy. Do you suppose the three of you could look around for something safe for me? It's not like I know anything about horses."

"Now that's the kind of shoppin' I can get into," Matt drawled with a grin.

CHAPTER 3

Since Jed had no idea what he would find when he got back to his ranch, he set out with Josh to first get breakfast, then buy all possible supplies. Rather than taking a steamship to The Dalles, he decided to go overland, which meant pack animals, two extra horses, ammunition, sacks of flour, beans, bacon, ham, and basic cooking supplies. From his ranch, the nearest towns of any size would be The Dalles to the north and Canyon City to the south. Either locale would be more costly than Portland if they even carried what was needed. After hearing of the Indian trouble, he had added to the list four of the newest Henry repeaters.

His liquid funds were in a Portland bank and one in New York City—gold and Federal dollars, not the Confederacy's now worthless currency. He'd have no problem paying for what he needed—at least not this side of the mountains. He wasn't sure about banks in Canyon City. What had gold fever done to that town?

He planned to put off contacting Raine until a day before he was ready to leave. Unless she was engaged or married, even if she turned him down, he would not give up on her, but first, he needed to know what he had to offer. He would only know that after he got back to his ranch.

On some levels, after years of war, of fighting and knowing his life was never safe, he had developed a kind of inner coldness, a detached sense of operating without his emotions. Whatever was required, he did it. He guessed that would prove handy now.

"Where do we head first?" Josh asked as they left the café, and Jed rolled his first cigarette of the day.

"Hey there, you two," a voice called. When they turned around, it was Toddy Coen walking hurriedly to catch up. "What you up to?" he asked with a huffing breath.

"Buying supplies," Josh said.

"I might be able to help."

Jed stopped walking and lit his cigarette. "Why?"

"Sounds like you'll be hiring. Why not me?"

Now that Jed hadn't expected. "My ranch is in wilderness. I don't even know what I'll find when I get there. It'll be hard work."

"Be good for me."

"And you can do what exactly?" He didn't try to hide his skepticism.

"Pretty much you name it, and I have done it. I can drive a team, ride a horse, cook, build fence."

"Cook, huh? How good are you at it?"

"Pretty fair."

Jed considered. A cook could be an asset. "It won't pay a lot. Room and board, plus a dollar a day unless you prove you actually can cook and then two."

"Sounds fair. I'll have you eating ambrosia."

"Hmph. You already told me it's going to be ugly over there with potential Indian problems. Maybe my cabin will have been burnt to the ground. Why would you want to step into that?"

Toddy grinned. "Adventure. I like the two of you. I've got nothing going on here and think I might like getting into this with you."

"I am thinking. You don't look like a man used to hard work." He pointed to Toddy's rounded belly.

"I don't have your height or muscles, I admit. What I can offer is I know things that can be useful and don't underestimate my staying power. You already said you're worried about finding help with gold fever drawing everybody's attention, and the Paiutes scaring off a lot of others. You need me frankly, and I am available."

Jed looked at Josh as he tried to decide. It was true that getting a crew could be difficult. "You got your own horse?" he asked as Josh nodded his approval.

"I do and can be ready to go whenever you are. I can also help you here by directing you to the stores with the best prices for what you need. So how about it?"

"You talk a lot," Josh observed with a grin.

"That's a bad thing?" Toddy asked as Jed chuckled.

"All right. We'll give you a try. If you make it across the mountains with us, you've got a job. If you don't, I'll pay you for the days you worked. Sound fair?"

"Optimum." He grinned.

They then headed for the shops where Toddy had said would have the newest rifles. In the end, Jed bought five Henry repeating rifles as he added one for Toddy, who had a sidearm but not a good rifle. He hoped his big gun, a custom 44 caliber Sharps, would still be at the ranch. While it had good stopping power, it wasn't what he'd want if he ended up being attacked by Indians, where having a string of quick shots could mean the difference between life and death.

As they left the store, Jed shook his head. "Kind of amazing. You can buy Henrys out here, but the South couldn't get them, couldn't have gotten the ammunition if they had. The North had them, and it was part of what won the war. This was more a war of attrition than battles. Finally we just wore down."

"I can see you don't plan to have that happen with the Indians on your ranch," Toddy observed, nodding his head toward the cases of ammunition.

"I am hopeful that I won't need it. I am not an optimist though and plan to take all the firepower I can bring. To begin, I am hoping we'll just be rounding up longhorns. If I got lucky, most are in the brush and trees. Short of killing them, the Paiutes and Shoshoni weren't likely to round them up. What the wolves, bears, and cougar didn't get should still be there. The miners might've rustled a few, but overall, I am far enough north and not in an area I'd expect much prospecting. I suppose it will have changed though and be changing faster from now on."

"Changes come, and yes, from the war, but also how men see opportunity. I can help you with a lot of things, Jed. Or should I make that Mr. Hardman now?"

"Jed is fine, and the ranch is the Hardman Ranch, Circle H, in case we get separated between now and then."

"I'll find it, but I won't get separated. How many cattle did you leave?"

Jed considered a moment. "We were running three hundred cows and four good bulls when I left."

"That could be a lot by now if they didn't get run off."

"As many as a thousand or down to nothing," Jed agreed.

"Do you plan to make a drive if you do have livestock to sell?"

"That will be down the road a spell. Before I leave Portland, I'll do some asking around for which way I'd be taking them—if I have any to sell." The way his life had been going, it was the safest way to consider.

He still had to buy horses, talk to his attorney and the land agent to be sure taxes had been paid, and that his land was still legally clear. Only then would he face the biggest question. Was she still there for him to court?

He remembered what she had looked like in the theater. Of course, he understood it was a play and makeup, but she'd morphed into a woman of exceptional beauty and grace. Obviously, with the theater and whatever other businesses she had going, she was a prosperous woman. Her name hadn't changed on the posters for the play, but that didn't mean she wasn't married.

He wasn't coming back a successful man. He'd fought on the losing side of a war. Although he had money, would have more when the plantation sold, he didn't know what he had in Oregon beyond ten sections of land, acres of grass, brush and timber staggered along the North Fork of the John Day River. It could take years to build it into a paying operation.

On many levels, he'd paid a high price for going to Georgia.

Already missing her family, after they left for Oregon City, Raine looked through the new cloth from the salesman from San Francisco. "Too expensive for our market," she said admiring the softness and fineness of the weave.

"Portland is growing closer to being cosmopolitan every time I come up here," he argued. "I think you'll find this will appeal to the ladies."

"Heavy gold brocade, and where would they wear it?"

"Balls."

Raine laughed. "In Stump City?"

"It's not that anymore. I see it becoming more sophisticated every visit. Miss Stevens, you have to offer what your competition does, or you won't be competing, but then you know that."

Raine looked at Sharon, her assistant. "What's your opinion on it?"

"It is lovely."

"Can't deny that. I guess we'll try four bolts but that's it. We'll see how it does. The brocade and three of the silk."

"Raine, my dear," Russell said as he entered the shop. "You were so wonderful on your performance the other night."

"Thank you, Russell," she responded to be polite. She was finding herself increasingly uncomfortable around Russell.

While true that he had been a help, what was he expecting in return?

"Has your family left?" he asked.

"Early this morning."

The salesman quickly wrapped up his business and left while Sharon got back to work on the books, all to Raine's regret. She remembered what Amy had said and wanted to be sure she and Russell understood the same thing about their friendship. Her refusals to marry him had not been a tactic but a final answer. She was unsure how to tell him that without it proving insulting.

When the door opened, she was still pondering the right words. As she looked up at the new customer, she felt faint. Quickly she pinched her wrist to try and wake up but the apparition was still there.

"Hello, sugar," he said, his tall frame all that she remembered with the broad shoulders and narrow waist, the horseman's hips. He walked toward her with that same loose-limbed walk that had melted her heart the first time she'd seen it. He pulled his hat from his head. He was cleanly shaven. His thick gold brown hair was worn longer than it had been. It had been him at the theater. She had felt his nearness ever since.

Russell gaped at the new arrival for a moment. "You know each other?" he asked finally.

Raine swallowed hard, trying to find her voice. Her eyes scanned over Jed for scars, any signs that the war had wounded him; but if it had, it was only in the hardness of his eyes, the stern set of his lips. "Yes." She was relieved to find she could speak normally.

"How have you been?" Jed asked, his gaze not leaving her face.

She bit her lip and then turned to Russell. "This is Jed Hardman. Jed, Russell Grayson."

The men looked at one another with unfriendly expressions and didn't either offer to shake hands. "You sound like a southerner," Russ said finally.

"You think?" Jed asked with an icy smile. He then turned back to Raine. "Can we have dinner tonight?"

"She had promised dinner with me," Russ said.

She was beginning to get her brain back in gear and said, "I did not, Russell, and yes, Jed, I'd like that. I am through here about... oh say six." What a tower of strength she was. Oh she'd get him out of her life instantly if he did return.

"Then I'll be back." Jed turned and strode out.

When they were alone, Russ sucked in a breath. "Who is he to you?"

"That's none of your business, Russell."

"I thought it was going to be."

"No, it was not. I have tried to make it clear to you that you and I will be nothing more than friends."

"I have thought there'd be more. Is the reason that southern trash?"

"You are being deliberately rude, Russ. Whatever Jed is to me is none of your business. I have work to do. Please excuse me." She needed to make very certain he understood the limits of their relationship. "I told you that I would not marry you, Russell. I hope you understand that was a final answer."

"Because of that Rebel?"

"It has nothing to do with Jed." She looked up and saw the anger in his eyes. That made her mad. He had no right to act as though she'd promised him more.

"It seems to me that you are showing poor judgment, Raine. If you are counting on that Reb, you are going to be disappointed."

She smiled through tight lips. "I'm busy, Russ. Hope you have a good day." He glared at her but stalked out the door. She saw he was livid, and she didn't care. She was not Russ's possession. Well she wasn't Jed's either, but it was only natural that she would want to hear how he was. That certainly couldn't happen in a shop with customers entering and needing service. Dinner made total sense.

Then she thought what a fool she was being. Dinner with Jed.

How strong would she really be? What had she been thinking? She'd said there'd be nothing between them if he ever returned. Well one dinner didn't make something.

"Miss Raine," Clem said as he came out from the back. "That shipment come in, the one Mrs. Collins ordered. You wanting it unloaded? Jerry didn't show up for work today."

"I didn't realize she'd ordered anything for here," Raine said wondering what day she had missed Agatha's visit.

"There was this peddler come by her house, I think anyways."

That wasn't going to be good. If Agatha started ordering from there and Raine from the store, they'd soon be in trouble. Perhaps it was time she separated herself from Agatha's store and concentrated on her own. She had the resources to purchase her leased store. Mulling questions of loyalty or the need to grow, she walked out to the loading dock to see what had been delivered. There were four large boxes labeled from San Francisco. Maybe it would be all right. Perhaps she was anticipating the worse.

When they'd gotten the first one opened, she knew she had not. Inside, carefully wrapped, were the ugliest porcelain statues she had ever seen. She had worried that Agatha was losing her grip on reality. This appeared to be the evidence of it. She tried to think what they could do with them. Probably refusal of shipment was too late. Sell them? She could not imagine who would buy such monstrosities.

Hoping the next three boxes would be more promising, she found more of the same. Someone had clearly taken advantage of an old woman's fading grip on reality. It appeared that she needed to write Agatha's children to see if they could deal with their mother's business.

The whole thing was giving her a headache as she went back into her office and made a note to set aside time to visit Agatha and discuss this. She added a reminder to stop by the nearby subscription library and return her overdue books.

By the time Jed returned, the last customers were leaving. She turned the sign to closed, pulled down the blind, and locked the door behind him to be sure no one else entered. She tried to think what she might say that would make this all seem less strained. Nothing suited.

She had questions and yet wasn't sure she wanted to voice any of them. In what important ways had he changed? Why hadn't he written? There weren't words for all she felt, as feelings surged through her, the likes of which she had never known until him.

She had to force herself to turn and face him. He had changed into a fine white shirt, string tie and a dark suit. "You look very nice," she said. How trite.

"You look more than nice, Raine. You've gotten even more beautiful-- if I thought that was possible."

"Thank you." She wondered if she was blushing. She felt strangely flustered. She wished she'd had time to change into something prettier. How silly. She had to get control of herself.

He looked around the shop. His gaze scanned past and immediately returned to the porcelain lion, with the garish rhinestones in its eyes and claws. "My God," he said as he walked to it.

"I know. Do you think you'd like it for your cabin?"

He smiled back at her. "Unfortunately, I think it'd shatter on the way over the mountains." He lifted it and looked at it more thoughtfully. "A lot heavier than it looks."

She laughed. "There are three more like it. Agatha ordered them. I am thinking even a sale won't rid me of them."

"Donation to a charity bazaar?" he suggested as he set it back down.

"That would be mean... to the charity."

"Couldn't have that."

"Tell me, Jed. How are you? How is the ranch?"

"I haven't been to the ranch yet," he said. She felt his gaze on her as much as saw it. Trying to get a handle on herself, she buttoned her fitted brown jacket and set a rather plain hat on her head. She was a plain brown wren-- not much of a beauty to keep a man faithful for four years. Perhaps he gave that look to all women.

She wanted to know how he had been, but she didn't want excuses for why he hadn't written. In many ways, they were two strangers, even as they knew each other intimately. So intimately, that her body grew warm just remembering what his had looked like when he was naked.

"So you really just returned to Oregon?" she asked to try and stop her wayward mind.

He nodded.

"I'd have expected you'd go there first," she said, turning off lights at the front door.

"No," he said as they stepped out onto the boardwalk. "So is the Pioneer House good with you?"

"It's expensive."

"It's a celebration," he said with a faint smile. "I'm back and didn't get killed. I saw your play. You have a real talent, sugar. So we can celebrate both, can't we?"

She smiled. "I'd like that." As they walked down the street toward the restaurant, she felt the tension between them and wanted to find a way to make it all more normal. "How is your mother?" she asked. She had no idea what was safe. Certainly she couldn't ask about the war. The lines in his cheeks, the shadows in his eyes, the timing of his return, all told her that answer.

"She's dead. I had just over two days after I got there. She and I had a chance to say a few last things."

"I'm sorry for your loss." God she hated this. He was a stranger, but she could not stop herself from thinking about the body under his dark suit, a body she knew so well. She had slept with him. She knew the touches that pleased him and wondered if he remembered her body as well or had sleeping with other women made his memories of her fade? Of course, there would have been other women. Why did she keep coming back to that thought?

She and Jed stopped, as in front of them on the boardwalk,

standing aggressively was Russell. His gaze on her, a smile that was not friendly on his lips. "Off to dinner?" he asked.

"A celebration actually," Jed said with a tight-lipped smile.

"Really? Of what?"

"You'll have to ask Raine later. Our dinner reservation is for now." He took her arm and tucked it under his, his hand on hers. "See you around, Russ," he drawled.

Russ's face showed his anger, but he kept his mouth shut, glaring balefully as they walked past him.

"He special to you?" Jed asked as they passed, not seeming to worry whether Russ heard him.

"He's helped me with investments, been a friend." She was beginning to wonder about that last. "But nothing more."

"Obviously, not his fault there's nothing more."

She didn't know what to say to that; so she said nothing and was grateful they had reached the restaurant.

The interior was softly lit by candles and a few of the modern gaslights. Their table had a nice white tablecloth and fine china as Jed held out the chair for her and then sat across from her. "I like being able to see you," he said, "not going to miss a chance to do it. Want a small glass of wine before dinner?"

"That would be lovely." She could actually use a big one. She felt her hand beginning to tremble and hoped it would be steady enough to hold the glass without spilling wine on her blouse. She wracked her brain trying to think of something meaningful to say, but all she could think about was how it would feel to be in his arms again. That would be a huge blunder. One she'd not make again. Following her inner desires had gotten her four years of yearning for what she couldn't have. Repeating the mistake would likely never see her free of whatever was between them.

"I was surprised you didn't stop at the ranch on your way here." That sounded normal. He was so handsome, his face one of hard planes, clear gray eyes, high cheekbones, and that sensual mouth. He had acquired no obvious scars. She wondered if he had them elsewhere. She didn't need to wonder if they were on his soul as she saw that in his eyes.

"I needed supplies," he said, "wasn't sure what would be left there. Been talking to some folks around town, and it looks like it could be rough around my ranch for a few years."

"The Indians?"

He nodded.

"The Oregonian has reported on some of the attacks. Shoshoni and Paiute, I believe, but wasn't sure how close that would be to your land, nor how much was exaggeration to sell papers."

"I'm not sure either. There had been some trouble before I left. I was told that when the cavalry was pulled into the war back East, it erupted."

"There was the Oregon unit formed to protect the miners and homesteaders."

"They likely did what they could."

"And the cavalry will come back now. Will the federal troops cause you trouble, I mean due to which side you fought on?"

"I have papers proving I was released. I'll keep them with me just in case somebody holds a grudge." He smiled without humor. She understood. The papers were the price of losing.

"I... well, I'm sorry. Not that the South lost. I think it was inevitable. You told me as much before you left, but that it ever happened at all. So many losses for both sides."

As they talked, Jed saw on her face and knew it was in his own that neither were saying words that came close to what was in their hearts. Was she angry with him for leaving? Did she have any feelings left for him? She wasn't the sort of woman to have slept with a man when she had none but what was left after four years? He had no right to ask, not with the situation so uncertain as to what he would find at the Circle H. He felt lucky even to be sitting across from her as they sipped their wine. She could have refused to see him at all. Just because Russ wasn't important to her life didn't mean there wasn't a man who was.

Ordering dinner and talking of meaningless things filled the space. More complicated words might've torn apart whatever fragile beginning was possible, blasting away any hope he could have for a future that included her somehow, someway. He knew that wasn't likely, no matter what had happened with his ranch. She had a life here. He couldn't fit into that nor could she into his. He knew it logically but not in his heart.

She was so beautiful with that delicately boned face and tonight her hair in a bun at the back of her neck, tendrils of curls slipping out to ring her face. She had a kissable mouth. He remembered teaching her to kiss. She had learned quickly. Had she since practiced on other men? He had no right to ask. He had gone and left her with nothing. If he lost her, it would serve him right. He had thought he had to go. He believed he still had done what was needed, but it didn't mean he didn't have regrets about it. If he'd never heard his mother's last words, his life might've gone very differently.

When they had eaten all they wanted, the waiter asked if they would like dessert, they shook their heads. The dessert Jed wanted wouldn't be found in the restaurant. Outside on the street, he asked, "You still live where you did?"

"I've moved, but you don't need to walk me home."

His smile was soft. "Tell me where you live."

It was a wonderful June night in Portland with the air soft, a light moistness to it and a faint breeze. The moon was coming up beyond Mount Hood, and it seemed to backlight the mountain with its glow.

"I missed this," he said, tucking her hand into his arm.

"Portland?" she said with her first teasing comment.

"Of course, being with you might be a small part of that and our walking like this."

"I also enjoyed those walks."

When they got to her house, he let out a whistle as he looked up at the two levels. "You have moved up in the world."

"It's an investment," she said, sounding a little defensive.

"It's a nice home. I like those trees. My cabin had trees behind it..." He stopped. "I guess I don't know if it's still there. With the Indian trouble, it's hard to say what I'll find. I will though rebuild if it's gone."

"It could prove dangerous if there really is Indian trouble. I guess your war isn't over, is it?"

He shrugged. "Maybe. Whatever happens though, I will be ready for it. The Circle H is a little out of the way. I am hoping that has protected it from the worst. I left two men there. They might still be." He knew that was a long way from a given.

"Well I hope it's all there and waiting for your return."

"You have a porch swing here too," he observed as he stepped up onto her porch.

"I brought the other one with me when I moved... Would you like to sit for a few moments?"

"I'd like that. Like old times."

"I often sit here and watch the moon rise."

He sat with his arm across the back of the bench, lightly touching her shoulder but not drawing her to him. He rocked it a little with his boot. "I'm glad you are happy with your life."

If she'd been dissatisfied, maybe they'd have had a chance; but as it was, it seemed any chance was long gone. She had created a very comfortable world with purpose and what he had to offer now was filled with uncertainty. He'd not have wanted her to come with him this trip, even if she had been receptive, which he doubted. In many ways, he felt her holding him at a distance. He'd lost his chance with her—only part of the price he had paid in going to Georgia.

"When do you leave?" she asked.

"Tomorrow. I have pretty much what I need. After looking at the options, we'll take the old trails across the Cascades before we cut down to The Dalles military road." He was talking to avoid having to say goodnight. He doubted she cared about what he was going to be doing. Maybe she wanted him gone.

"Will you be back?"

He looked down at her. Was that faint encouragement that she would ask? "I am not sure when, but I will be back. If the cattle are in the timber, I need to round up what I can find and make a drive to sell the bulls that my men didn't turn into steers. I can't make definite plans until I get there."

"Might you ship them to Portland?"

"Right now, it's looking like Baker City is going to offer better money. Too many cattle in the valley for me to get top dollar. With the Indian trouble, going east will be better. Maybe even some of those forts might want beef. The big question will be whether there is anything there to sell."

"Are you... going alone?"

"I'll have two men with me." He thought about telling her about his half-brother but that would lead to more questions. Emotionally, the last thing he wanted to talk to her about was family, the war, or the ranch. He wanted to take her into his arms, pull down that bun and carry her inside her house, find her bed and... But he wouldn't.

"I guess I should be going," he said after a long silence.

"Thank you for dinner. It was good to... see you. I am happy you got back safely, Jed. Be careful, please, with whatever you face over there."

"Thank you. I am glad also to see you are so happy... and doing well."

She hesitated but then said, "I wish... well I wish you well." He heard the emotion in her voice but didn't know what he could do about it. He knew what he wanted to do. He had no right.

He rose. "May I kiss you goodnight?" he asked.

"I think it's better you don't." Her smile was a mix of humorous and knowing. He couldn't deny she was right. One kiss wouldn't end it or solve it.

He took her hand and kissed her fingers lightly. "Goodnight, sugar." He thought maybe he was wrong and there'd be another time-- once he knew more what he had. No, he was being a fool. There'd be no other time. Their worlds simply could not come together.

"Goodbye, Jed," she said hurrying to the door and closing it.

CHAPTER 4

F eeling depressed at the hopelessness of any relationship with Raine, Jed walked toward his hotel. The district was not safe after dark, but he and Josh could never have rented rooms anywhere uptown. It was another of those nasty facts of life that he could either begrudge or accept, hoping the future would hold better. He crossed the street just shy of the block where he'd find their dive. Maybe he and Josh would go for a drink.

"Hey buddy," came the voice from the dark. He turned to look, realizing too late that someone else was coming up fast behind him. He twisted to meet the charge of the runner, slamming his fist into a face and blocking a down swinging club with his arm. Before he could draw out his knife, he felt something hard slam into the back of his head. There had been a third. The blow sent a shock of pain through his head and drove him to his knees.

He tried to get back on his feet, dazed but still conscious, when the next slam came against his head. He went flat out. Hands were on his jacket, pulling it from his shoulders, ripping open his shirt as those hands ran along his side and into his pants. He was being rolled. He might survive that and tried again for his knife. While one man grabbed it out of its sheath, the other roughly twisted his arms behind his back, lashing his wrists tightly together. His head was yanked up, and a rag was shoved into his mouth. Other hands used something to tie it in place, effectively gagging him.

This wasn't just a robbery. Damn, then what was it? He felt near to blacking out and fought to remain conscious, to find a way to fight back. A rag tied around his eyes, blindfolded him, and ended any chance he had of breaking away. He was shoved to his feet and forced to walk between two of them with the other behind to shove him if he stumbled. He had no idea where they were taking him but had no choice but to walk. When he faltered, someone slammed a fist into his belly.

"Walk, you son of a bitch," the man who had first spoken growled. "If you don't cooperate, we'll beat you so bad, we'll have to carry you, and even heavy as you are, it'll be worth it. Damn, I hate Southerners. Just give me an excuse, you bastard, any excuse."

He'd been taken like a green kid, and any option to fight his way out of this had long since disappeared. He'd have to let them take him wherever they were going. After what seemed several blocks, they told him stairs ahead. Holding his arms, they forced him down the steps. A basement. He tried again to wrench free, but even though he considered himself a strong man, against this, he had no chance. A door opened and he was pushed through it, forced forward. Another door opened, and he was shoved hard to land on what felt like a stone floor. He fought to remain conscious.

One of the men knelt beside him and removed the gag, but not the blindfold. "Don't bother yelling. Nobody except us can hear you down here."

"What's this about?" Jed managed to croak out.

"You wonderin' about that are you, Reb?" the man asked with a laugh. "I bet you are." Cords were being wrapped around his ankles, not that he had anywhere he could have gone if his legs had been free.

"Why are you doing this?" Jed tried again.

"Rebels. I hate Rebels. That's enough reason. I tell you what you're getting is no more than you deserve."

"You... know me?"

"Don't matter what your name was, buddy. It's now Clyde Jenkins and you're on your way to sea." He chuckled and stepped away.

Steps approached and then hands lifted Jed's head putting a cup to his lips. Water he needed water. With the first swallow, he knew this was something he didn't want. He tried to turn his head aside, but they held him, and he had to swallow or choke.

"Enjoy your sleep, big boy," the second man chuckled as what sounded like a heavy door slammed. At first he thought he was alone in the room and then he realized someone else was there, likely had been all along.

"Who are you?" he asked but got no response, just that sense he was being watched. Still dazed from the speed with which this had happened, the blow to his head, and now the effects of whatever drug had been forced down his throat, he felt himself drifting away. He had no choice but to surrender to the darkness closing around him.

Raine had slept restlessly and risen before first light, tired of lying in bed and thinking of what she and Jed had said, worse what they had not said. The knocking at her door was loud and insistent. Dressing quickly, she hurried down the stairs to see who could possibly need her at such an ungodly hour. She panicked at thinking something had happened to one of her loved ones.

When she swung the door open, she saw two strangers. "Miss Stevens?" the shorter of the two asked.

"Yes, is... is there a problem?"

"May we come in?"

"Not until I know who you are and what is going on," she said looking now at the face of the taller of two who stood back a bit. He was a very big, dark-skinned man. His expression was a mix of anger and worry in equal proportions.

"You had dinner with Jed last night," the shorter man said. "We hoped... thought maybe he spent the night."

"Jed? Jed Hardman?"

The man nodded. "I work for him. My name is Toddy Coen. This is Josh Hardman."

She looked again at the other man. Hardman? Then she saw, despite the dark skin, the strong resemblance. Jed had never mentioned coming back with a relative, but she was looking at one.

"Come in," she said, "but Jed isn't here. He did not spend the night. We had dinner; he walked me back but then left. I... what happened?"

"That's what we're trying to figure out," Josh said with a grimace.

She felt as though a shock had cleared her head of any morning fuzziness. "Someone doesn't just disappear," she said.

"Begging your pardon, ma'am but they can and do all the time. That's not going to happen to Jed though." Josh looked at her with a steeliness that was so much like Jed's that there could be no doubt of a close relationship.

"I wish I could help but..." She tried to think who she might know on Portland's police force. She wished Adam was closer. "I think you should go down to the police station and..."

Toddy Coen stopped her. "You think they aren't in on half of what happens in this town? Oh, not to say there aren't honest coppers, but how would we know who? Besides they'd take too long to get even started looking." He shook his head. "You live here. You have to know some are on the payroll for what goes on down there."

"Down there? Down where? Jed left here last night not long

after dark. He was going back to his hotel. Wasn't that the New Columbian?"

Josh chuckled. "You think Jed and I could check into a high end hotel? Not hardly. We were down on the waterfront."

She felt a shudder go through her. She should have had him stay with her. Sense or no sense, she never would have wanted him heading there at night. She might be naïve about what went on in the city, but she knew things happened and mostly down along the waterfront. Could he have been murdered for his wallet? She refused to believe he was dead. He couldn't have come so far, gone through the years of war only to have it end on a dirty street and for a few dollars.

"I'll fix coffee," she said leading the way into her kitchen as she tried to think through what they had said and put together what little she knew about the district along the docks.

In the kitchen, Toddy mumbled to himself, and the words she could understand were clearly the fears she herself felt. Men disappeared down there. That's what Clem had said. And then she remembered about shanghaiing. As if in an answer to a prayer she hadn't uttered, she heard Nancy at the door, and Clem was right behind her.

"My, you got coffee going afore me this time," Nancy said with a big grin before she looked at the two men sitting at the table. "Visitors?" she asked then.

Clem looked at them suspiciously. "These boys friends of yor'n, Raine?" he asked.

"They are here on a mission, I guess you could say," she said. "Clem, remember when you were telling us about the shang-haiing going on in Portland?" He nodded. "A friend disappeared last night on his way from here back to his hotel down along the river."

Clem looked at them with more concern. "Sorry to hear that. Real sorry. That's plumb bad news. I got to tell ya that's plumb bad news." He shook his head. "Might as well give it up right now."

"Give it up? Shanghaiing?" Josh asked his tone grim. "What the hell are you talking about?"

"You boys new to here?"

"I am." He nodded his head toward Toddy. "He isn't. You know about this, Toddy?"

Toddy groaned. "I should have thought of it myself. They grab strapping fellows like Jed and..."

"Sell them to ships," Clem said, the excitement in his voice rose. "They become slaves is what it amounts to. Slaves who never work it off, never get a chance to escape when in ports. They give 'em phony names, forge a signature, take away any identity they ever had. The ship captains don't give a damn about from where the men come. They are property. They work 'em until they die. If they won't obey, there's always the whip. Portland is the king of it on this coast. Some call us the forbidden city because of how much of it goes on."

"So..." Josh frowned, "Jed might already be on a ship headed somewhere, and we wouldn't know where?"

"Was he going to one of the bars last night?" Clem asked. "That's how it works with a drugged drink."

"No," Josh said. "If he'd been going to, he'd have got me first."

"This ain't the usual way then. Let me think a bit here," Clem said as he rubbed his forehead and sunk into a chair at the table. "Let's figure he got nabbed. No ship went out last night but one is due in today. We got a shipment coming in on it is why I know. It's the Calypso... Its captain is James, meanest son of a... pardon me, ladies. It's due to be docking this morning, which means they can't smuggle any men aboard until dark."

"Not a lot of time to find who got Jed and where he might be held... If that's what happened to him?" Josh clenched his fist on the table, still not touching the coffee in front of him.

"Who's this Jed to you, boy?" Clem asked.

Josh glared at him. "Who you callin' boy?"

Clem snorted. "Anybody yore age."

Josh relaxed. "He's my brother."

"He a darkie?"

"Damn you do rile me, old man."

Clem smiled. "Wal, just wantin' to know who we're looking fer."

"You knew him," Raine said. "He came to the house a lot four years ago."

"That tall cowboy with the Southern drawl?" Clem sucked in a breath when she nodded. "This is real strange then." He shook his head and stared out the window.

"Why?" Raine asked.

"Well sizewise, he's about what they'd be wantin' all rightie, but Hardman, as best I remember it, ain't a nobody. Not a common laborer. It's not the kind they usually grab."

"Then... he might've been murdered and not shanghaied?" Josh rasped, his eyes looking dulled.

"Didn't say that. Well if ya wanta find out one way or t'other, find somebody who knows the Tenderloin, the underground, and can get to your boy fast. If he wasn't knifed and thrown into the river his belly slit and filled with weights, there's no way they won't be loading him tonight. He's not the kind they want lyin' around here. Strange though. Real Strange. Nothing like I'd expect for the likes of him."

"Who might be able to help us find him?" Raine asked dreading what she was expecting to hear.

"Someone who works down there, who knows what goes on." Raine whitened. He could only mean one person. "Ya already know the answer. Miss Bernice."

She let out a breath. Bernice McDowell had traveled west on their wagon train. Since reaching Portland, she hadn't actually talked to her, as their paths would never cross, but Bernice's career choice had been no secret.

"You know madams. Wal maybe ya don't, but they have their fingers in everything. She'll know who the crimping crews are and likely the places they imprison the men until they can smuggle them onto the ships. If she don't know, she'll know who does."

"Seems to me you know a little too much about those houses," Nancy complained as Raine cursed, using a few words that she knew her friends had never heard from her. Clem was probably right. Bernice would know. The thought of talking to the woman again was repulsive.

"Just in case it applies, what is your history with this Bernice?" Josh asked. "It doesn't sound like friends."

"Hardly that," Raine said, her frown deepening. Asking a favor of her would be like pulling teeth. She had to do it. She couldn't bear Jed being imprisoned and turned into someone else's property. He'd die to break away, and it sounded like die was the only way he could get free without help. "I knew her coming west and all the sneaky and underhanded things she'd pulled then."

"She's not likely to want to help," Josh said, "if she has as fond of memories of you as you do of her."

"There are ways." She'd have to make a trip to the bank first.

Jed regained consciousness to find he was in the same straits as he had been when last he knew anything. Now, besides his head feeling as though it had been split open, he was sick as a dog. He forced himself not to vomit. He didn't want to lie in the stink of it. He tried to get hold of the knots on the cords binding his wrists. His fingers were too numb to do anything effective.

He heard the door opening, dreading what it might mean. Bad as this was, worse was possible.

"Ah you awake, huh?" said the familiar rough voice. He knelt by Jed's side; and by the sickening sweet smell, Jed knew he had the drug with him. "Thought you'd be out longer. Big guy like you likely it takes more."

"You have me tied. I can't get away... Don't give me that. It's making me sick."

The man chuckled. "You think I care, or that you get to tell me what to do? This is the fun of it for me. You don't want it. I can make you take it. This is just the first of many commands you will be taking—not giving." He slapped Jed hard across the cheek, snapping his head back.

"Say, Reb, how'd you like owning slaves? You are about to find out what it's like to be one." His fingers were at the neck of Jed's shirt. He felt them untying his string tie and then pulling it from the collar. "Might be I'd like me a tie like this one. You're used to find things, ain't you?"

The man then yanked hard on the shirt, ripping its buttons off and it from his shoulders. "Can't even keep a shirt on if I don't want you to. Fine fabric you had here. Too bad I didn't take that along with your tie. Guess you did have money, didn't you... before you became a slave that is."

"Whatever you're being paid, I can pay you more," Jed tried not expecting it to work as he felt the cold air against his now bare chest and shoulders.

"Oh yeah, you'd be out of here and then give me money. Sure."

"You could go to my brother. He'd pay you."

"Get it through your head. You're not going to pay anybody. You are going down." He put his hands over Jed's mouth and then squeezed his nose closed, effectively suffocating him. Jed bucked against the punishing hands, but he could do nothing to break away. Just before he blacked out, the pressure was released, and he gulped in air.

"See, Reb, you only get to breathe if I let you. I could kill you easy."

"I doubt it," he managed finally. "You have no product then, do you?" He knew taunting the man wasn't smart. It was bluster on his part to pretend he had any control over what happened next.

Helplessness was something he had never known, and it instilled a fear near to terror to realize how easily everything he had thought he had could be ripped away. His own muscles were useless, his wealth worth nothing in this situation. He gritted his teeth against giving way to panic. It was what this man hoped to instill; and if he could get any victory in this at all, it would be to hide his fear.

"You know, Reb, to be honest, I might like to take your money, or even something else from you." He ran his hands over Jed's chest in a way that was more disturbing then the pain earlier. "The thing is it wouldn't be healthy for me," the voice said with what sounded like disappointment. "Somebody important wants you on a ship, especially this ship. The captain is a special friend of his. He likes breaking in new slaves. Real special how he breaks them in."

Again he ran his hands down Jed's chest, this time to his belly, chuckling as Jed tried to move away from those probing fingers. "Hey, just get used to it. You ain't never again going to make a choice. You're just property now, Reb. You'll learn to do what you're told, how to please others, or the whip will teach you fast. The captain likes the whip almost as much as other things."

"You're... a son of a bitch," Jed managed, taking the blow to his cheek with barely a wince.

"I wish I could go along and watch," the man said with a chortle. "You're one mean bastard I'd like to see being broke. Soon you'll be on a ship. The drugs'll wear off, and then you'll find your real hell is just beginning."

"You talk a lot," Jed said dryly and got another blow for his trouble. There was silence and then a second or was it third person entered the room.

"Not so tough now, are you?" A new voice asked. It seemed deliberately disguised. He wondered if he'd heard it before.

A softer hand ran over his chest, tweaking his nipples as the disguised voice laughed. "Let go of him. I know you'd like to be the one, but no. He has a different fate in store."

Hands held his head while a cup was again put to his lips. He refused to open his mouth, but when his nose was squeezed shut, he was eventually forced to breathe and the drink was poured down his throat. In moments he was drifting off.

Strangely, he now felt like he heard more voices, arguing but he could understand nothing they said, and the mist was closing over before he could reason it out.

~

Although Raine wanted to go alone to Bernice's establishment, Toddy and Josh would have none of it. She did insist Clem stay at the house. Whatever this was turning into, she didn't want those two dragged into it. Coming to Bernice's would be delicate at best. She hoped the thousand dollars she had gotten in five separate packets of two hundred each, would help the conversation along. Bartering was something she was familiar with, but bartering for a life, this was new. She had no idea of the possible price. Had she brought enough?

They waited in an overdone parlor rich in tapestries and maroon colors with gold trim-- quite distasteful and hard to understand its appeal to male customers. The pretty girl who let them in went to fetch Miss Bernice as she called her. Raine looked around a bit curiously as she'd never visited a bordello. She guessed this was a high end one. Not cheaply done other than in lack of class. She had heard Bernice had found a profitable venture not long after she'd landed in Portland. Certainly, it was right up her alley from what Raine remembered of her as they traveled west. Given the apparent wealth here, maybe it'd take more than a thousand dollars to attract her interest.

As Bernice entered, she was dressed in a rich, yellow silk gown and smiling that wicked smile, that Raine remembered all too well. She might have no idea what Raine wanted but obviously knew she would never have come had she not needed something desperately. Bernice would take delight in refusing.

Then her eyes lit up when she got a look at Josh. Bernice had always had a thing for good looking men, which made her current profession understandable.

"So what can I do for you and your friends, Loraine?" she asked-- after the introductions and the offer of drinks had been politely refused.

"We believe that a friend was shanghaied last night. We want him back before he is off on the Calypso, which is docking as we speak."

"Not much I can do to help you. Sorry."

Josh spoke up then. "You will help, honey. You might be scared of somebody out there." His voice was even, the tones resolute. "You might even think that's the worst can be done to you. You would be wrong." His eyes were cold and menacing, sending a shiver down Raine's back. She believed him and saw Bernice did also.

"I have friends," Bernice tried to bluster.

"They'd never get to you in time." His hand rested on what Raine realized was the butt of a gun under his jacket.

Bernice's face whitened. Raine could see the wheels turning in her head as she considered the benefits and drawbacks to helping them.

"Please, we need to find him, and it cannot wait, Bernice." Raine hated to beg this woman, but for Jed she'd do what she had to. Bernice sighed and Raine could still see her reluctance to get involved. Raine knew her nature and added to the pot. "I'll pay."

"How much?"

"You going to help?"

"I don't know if I can." When Raine put up her hand in protest, she smiled with that same sly smile. "I mean it. I don't know if I can. I have heard nothing. However, I do have a friend and could ask what he knows. I can't promise until I talk to him. You wait here. How much is this worth to you?"

"Two hundred for you to bring him to us to talk. A thousand when we have him back safe."

"You have it with you?"

"I do."

Josh smiled then, a wolfish smile that she had seen on Jed's face. "And I also have a weapon to be sure it doesn't leave her hands until we have him."

She looked at Josh more closely. "What's this to you, handsome?"

"He's my brother."

"He's a Negro? I can't believe they'd take one right now at least, war just ending and all."

"We're half-brothers," Josh said.

Bernice sucked in a breath. Raine could almost see her calculating whether she could do this without it boomeranging back on her. "Two hundred up front?"

Raine nodded and handed her two one hundred dollar bills.

Bernice nodded. "All right, have some tea, and I'll be back."

When she had left, another girl returned with a tea pot and cups. Josh and Toddy would have none of it, but Raine poured herself a cup, amazed she could do so without her hands shaking. Jed, where was he? Would they be too late? Were they right and this is what had happened to him or had he been robbed and tossed into the river.

"I thought you knew all about this city," Josh said complaining to Toddy.

"Not like, in my condition, I had to worry about anybody wanting to shanghai me," Toddy protested pointing to his big belly. "I just never figured they'd try it with someone like Jed either. It's not just his size, but he doesn't look like somebody who could just disappear without someone coming after him. Wasn't he armed last night?"

"His knife, but he left the revolver behind because of what he was doing." He looked accusingly at Raine.

"People don't generally go armed into nice restaurants," she said defensively but wishing Jed had last night.

"How much faith you got in this whore?" Josh asked as he got up and paced around the room like a caged panther.

"She'll only do what helps her. So your threat might have helped our cause. If you're asking if I trust her, not as far as I could throw her, but I don't know anybody else down here who might be able to help find Jed in time." She couldn't bear to add if it was even possible. If Jed had been killed, if it was really too late, she'd never forgive herself for missing the moments she might have had with him. It couldn't be too late.

When Bernice returned, she had with her the tallest, most handsome Chinese man Raine had ever seen. He was not dressed in traditional Chinese garb, as she had seen so many, but wore dark pants, a white shirt, tie, and a revolver on his hip. Bernice had a frown on her face, obviously not happy about any of this, but she introduced them to Han Jei.

"You might know who has Jed Hardman?" Raine asked rising to stand in front of him. He had to be not much shorter than Jed or Josh, as she had to look up—way up.

"You are the actress."

She nodded. "I do the occasional play, yes."

"I do not know this Jed Hardman," he said with an educated polish that surprised her. "I would like to know more. Who are these two to you or this Hardman ?" He gestured beyond her to Josh and Toddy.

"I'm Toddy Coen. I work for Jed."

"And I'm Jed's brother. I will get him back or tear apart this and anywhere else behind what happened. If you don't believe me, well I hope you don't put it to the test." To Raine, Josh looked savage, his hand hovering over his revolver.

Jei wasn't easily intimidated and laughed. "As would I if it was my brother. Well it happens I do know the press gang, who likely was working last night, and where they generally hold their cargo."

The last word clearly infuriated Josh, but they needed this man, and so he held his tongue, which had Jei chuckling again.

"You find this amusing?" Bernice protested concern for her own skin written all over her face.

"My love, I find many things amusing but risking my life for strangers, not so much. How much did they promise you?"

"A thousand."

"Not a lot for what they are asking."

"You want more?" Raine asked thinking she would get it if he did.

Jei smiled. "I want nothing. We're talking of what Bernice wants. I will do this gratis because a thousand is nothing for such a risk. I would rather have a favor owed. Besides I like the looks of the big man there and most likely won't like what they would do to his brother." He looked back at Raine. "It might be best if you went home and waited."

"No."

He grinned. "I expected as much." He looked at Toddy and back to her. "I hope not just the brother is armed."

That meant they might have to fight their way to Jed. Toddy patted his pocket, and then Jei looked at her.

"I have a gun." She had tucked her loaded derringer into her pocket before they left her home. She had practiced with it but never expected to use it on a human.

"So be it then."

Jei led the way down the streets to a narrow alley. He pointed to a doorway at the bottom of a narrow set of stairs and then looked back at Raine and then Josh. "I cannot guarantee this is where he will be. It is, however, most likely. You do understand there are other possibilities for what they did with him?"

She gritted her teeth but met his gaze levelly.

"If the press gang is with him, this could be a bit unpleasant. It is, however, more likely that they left him locked in one of the rooms below, tied up, and drugged, waiting for dark to take him to the ship. If that is the case, this will be as you Americans say a piece of cake. We need to be prepared either way."

Raine looked at Josh who smiled and nodded. She shuddered, fearful at what condition Jed might be in. Was he suffering? She wanted to get to him and started to step forward. "You will wait up here," Jei said. "Let us know if anyone comes."

"How?"

"Shooting would be a good way." He smiled. "Take out one with it, if you can. We'll be right back for the rest."

She nodded. She pulled the derringer from her pocket.

"Not much of a weapon," Jei said with a grin.

"It makes a noise," she said managing what she knew probably looked like a sick smile. "If someone comes, I will scream and shoot. I will do my best to see that the bullet is not wasted."

Josh grinned. "Just be sure they aren't innocent," he said with the same husky tones she remembered so well from Jed. "The wolf has a good mate, I see," he added and then followed Jei down the stairs before she could say no such thing.

CHAPTER 5

When Jed woke again, he was bitterly disappointed to realize this had not been a dream. The reality in which he found himself seemed like a nightmare. He had to regain his senses and find a way to get free. If they put him on that ship, it was likely the only way he'd get off would be as a corpse.

Besides the nausea, and headache, his arms hurt from being wrenched behind his back. Though his hands were numb, he tried to make his fingers work. If he couldn't undo the knots that held him, it appeared he was heading for a worse hell than war-- something he hadn't thought possible. He cursed himself for not having been more aware, for letting this happen, as he fought the ropes, bringing renewed pain to his head.

When he heard the door to his prison opening. It was all he could do not to shrink back as he waited for the inevitable. Hands were on his body but instead of what he expected, a knife sliced through the bonds around his ankles. He was turned onto his side and his wrists cut free. When the blindfold was pulled away, he blinked trying to focus.

"What..." he croaked looking into a Chinese man's face. Was this a dream? He looked beyond the man and saw Josh smiling.

He tried to get to his feet but slumped back. "Sorry," he groaned. Josh bent to pull him to his feet. He fought not to faint.

"Watch it as we go out," he heard the stranger saying. "The idea here is that they won't be sure who got him. If they come back too soon, we'll have to kill them, and it won't end tonight."

Jed saw Josh had a revolver in his right hand. He stumbled and other hands took hold of him to keep him upright. Toddy. As hard as it had been to believe he'd been kidnapped, now he could hardly believe they'd come for him. He wanted to say something, but his throat was dry, his grip on consciousness tenuous.

It was at the top of the stairs, in the alley, when he saw Raine. She stood with a derringer in her hand and a smile on her face, tears in her eyes. He heard the stranger saying they would have to hurry, and the world slipped away.

Raine followed as Jei helped Josh and Toddy carry Jed from the red light district. "Where do we take him that will be safe?" Josh asked. Their hotel was not an option, at least if they didn't want to have to fight their way out. A quality hotel was out of the question with Jed in the condition he was and Josh with him.

"My home," Raine stated firmly. They looked at her but none challenged what she said, or her right to care for him, and so they managed the difficulty of carrying such a big man all those blocks.

When they got him inside, she directed them up the stairs to her bedroom. Josh's eyes held a question when he realized to where she'd taken them, but again, he didn't argue. His biggest concern was obviously his brother's safety.

When they laid him down, she asked, "Should we send for a doctor?"

Jei studied Jed's face, listened to his heartbeat before he said, "He just has to sleep off what they gave him."

"He has blood on his head. He had to have been hit hard and

bruises that look as though he was beaten. What if he has a concussion?"

Jei lifted Jed's eyelids, studying the pupils. "The men who did this know how to hit a man and not kill him. It's their business. His pupils don't seem badly dilated. I think it's mostly the drug. He's likely to be very sick when he wakes up and might sleep a day or two. Bed rest and liquids for a few days should have him back to himself—angrier, of course." He chuckled.

"I still think we need a doctor to check him," she protested.

Jei studied her. "We took him from very ruthless men. Maybe more than we know at the moment. This man is not one they would usually shanghai. Something else is involved here." He looked up at Josh. "You are both southerners?"

"We are and proud of it."

"At the moment, not all see it that way in Oregon."

"And that might be why they took him?"

Jei didn't answer. He looked back at Raine. "Do you have a doctor you know well?" She shook her head. "Then best no doctor. When we don't know who was behind this, the wrong doctor might endanger you all. He is a strong man. He will sleep this off."

Reluctantly, she nodded. They would have to do what they could, without taking the risk of bringing someone here while Jed was helpless to defend himself. Had his attack been random or had he been stalked? Could it have been because he was a Southerner? Did he have an unknown enemy? Until they knew the why of his kidnapping, she saw Jei's wisdom in keeping him hidden.

"You two must also stay here," she said turning to Josh and Toddy. "I have spare rooms. I know you won't want to leave until he's awake, and at least, until Jed is conscious, I will need you."

"You sure about that?" Josh asked, but when she nodded, he agreed. He then looked at the man who had gotten Jed out of the hellhole. "We owe you. We won't forget it."

"I didn't figure you would." He smiled wryly. "I'll be back

tomorrow night to see how he is, but will be coming in the back after dark. It won't be smart for me to be seen here. For awhile, they will be looking not only for him but for who helped him get away."

"Should I leave the backdoor unlocked then?" Raine asked

His smile was amused. "No need. Remember, if anybody comes around, don't let him be seen until he's himself again. Understand?" He looked now at Josh and Toddy who both nodded. He added, "And that means you two also keep hidden until the big man is himself."

"Why would it be safe then?" she asked trying to use logic on a situation that clearly had no logic to it.

Jei smiled. "You know the answer to that, don't you?"

She did. Then Jed would be back in charge.

While Josh stripped Jed of his torn and blood-stained clothing and got him under the covers, Raine went downstairs to find gauze, alcohol and a pitcher of water. She wished she remembered her mother's wisdom on herbal treatments and poultices, but she hadn't cared enough back then to think she'd ever need such. She had intended to live in a city where doctors were always available. What she had found herself dragged into had been beyond her wildest imaginings.

When she got back to her bedroom, Josh stepped aside to allow her to wash away the blood and dirt from Jed's face and the head wound. Not bleeding was good. She turned his head to pour alcohol over the gash, hoping that would protect it from infecting.

"You do care for him, don't you?" Josh said.

When her gaze met his, she looked away. "He is a friend."

She looked down at Jed and felt the warmth course through her whole body. It was a lot more than friendship. She looked up again at Josh who was watching her probably trying to judge her dependability. "He's lucky to have you for a brother," she said. "You saved his life."

He nodded. "We all did."

She bit her lip against saying more. "The bedrooms you two can use are down from this one."

"Thank you," Josh said. Toddy was tired enough that he only nodded and headed for one of the rooms.

"I will be easy to wake if you need me, Miss Stevens," Josh said, loosening his weapon in its holster. She took her own out of the pocket of her dress.

"It's Raine," she said, "and I'll watch over him while you sleep."

He nodded again with a satisfied smile at whatever he saw on her face. "I know." And then he left.

She put her hand on Jed's cheek stroking back his hair whenever she felt him grow restless. "You're with me. You're safe," she whispered.

He muttered something she couldn't understand. He seemed though to understand, as he slipped into a restless but sounder sleep. He would be all right. He had to be, and she would watch over him until he woke.

When it was dark, Josh and Toddy went to the hotel where he and Jed had been registered and checked out. When they returned, they told her they had taken a circuitous route back to be sure no one followed them. Jed continued to sleep off whatever he had been given. After a late supper, Clem, Nancy, Josh, Toddy, and Raine sat in the kitchen sipping coffee. She listened to them talk but mostly for any sign Jed had awakened. The back-door opening surprised her. Josh holstered his gun when he saw it was Jei.

"How did you do that?" Raine asked.

"If you ever need to know, I will tell you," he said.

"Coffee?" she asked, unsure if she would have any kind of tea that would suit him.

He nodded. "How is he?"

"Still sleeping." She handed him the cup.

Clem gave him a suspicious look but then asked, "You learn anything about why this happened? The more I think on this, the more I don't like it. They want ordinary working blokes, not important looking men and from what I remember of Hardman, he don't look unimportant."

Jei shook his head. "For now I know nothing new. It's quiet down there. Too quiet, which considering he wasn't where they left him tells me you are right. Something more was behind this."

"In other words, this happened for a reason and wasn't being in the wrong place at the wrong time," Josh said.

"You are astute. It will be interesting to see what your brother remembers. It is still possible, however that it was because he's a southerner. Feelings have run high on that issue. Rebels aren't popular in this state."

"Funny state," Toddy said, pouring more coffee into his cup.

"Will you look in on him again?" Raine asked. "You seem to know more about what is normal than any of us would after such a drug. Do you have any idea what it might've been?"

"Most likely chloral hydrate. It is dangerous in large doses, but these fellows know their business. They wanted him out, helpless, but not dead. There is no antidote, not that I know of-- if that was to be your next question. He just has to sleep it off."

"What if this is his head injury more than the drug?" She worried, not convinced they didn't need a doctor. Except Jei had been right. If there was no antidote, if the head injury was not endangering, a doctor could do nothing except possibly report to whoever ordered the attack.

Jei rose. "I will look." Raine led him up the stairs to where Jed slept but now more restlessly.

He lifted Jed's eyelid studying his pupil. "I doubt it will be long before he wakes. I suggest that he drink a lot of water, eat lightly for a day or two, and get out of Portland as soon as he's strong enough."

"He might want to report this."

Jei chuckled. "Lady, you do amaze me with your naiveté. If he stays here, he might find they finish what they started. Next time they might not bother with shanghaiing."

"You don't believe it was a one-time thing?"

Jei shook his head. "Could have been, but as your friend downstairs said, it's highly unlikely. Maybe someone didn't like it that he returned to claim his ranch."

"You know about that."

"I have those I trust. Your friend is very rich, but if his wealth was the reason, why no request for a ransom? He was being held where they hold the men before they are loaded onto ships as cargo. I don't have an answer, Miss Stevens."

She gave him one of her looks, which didn't faze him anymore than it ever had Jed. "It's Raine," she corrected.

Jei laughed. "Raine, just make sure he stays down for a day or two if you can."

"And how would I do that? He's not exactly an easy man to lead around."

"Use your imagination," Jei teased as he left.

"Like that would get him rest," she said to his back. He laughed again.

Josh appeared at the door, obviously having listened to be sure all was well. He stared at his sleeping brother.

"His color is better." She wanted to believe it. "He won't be easy to keep down. I know my brother. He'll want recompense."

She twisted her head to look at Josh. "You had a good education, didn't you?"

"The same as Jed's. We didn't go to college or anything, but we were taught by learned people. Our mother and father made sure of that."

"Your mother was free too?"

He laughed. "You want the mystery solved, don't you? How a colored man can be raised alongside a white as a brother?"

"It's easy to tell by your features, how you talk, that you and he are strongly related," she sat on the edge of Jed's bed, taking the cloth from the water bowl and washing his chest and shoulders, then his arms as they talked.

"Our mother was an unusual woman, Miss Stevens."

She stopped him. "I am Raine and refuse to answer to Miss Stevens."

He smiled sinking into the chair across from the bed. "All right, Raine. The woman I call mother is Jed's mother. She was a one of a kind lady. When I was born, my birth mother died. My father was, of course, Jason Hardman. Rachel Hardman knew all of it, but it didn't stop her from taking me to her heart as though I was her child. There aren't many women like my mother, and she was all of that to me."

"No, there aren't. She sounds very special indeed."

"Whether in the South or up here, yes, she was a tough lady with spirit and beauty. And as we grew up, Jed, he never questioned it either. I was his brother just like Geoff and Trevor. Now, they're dead, the first killed at Shiloh and the second at a skirmish without a name, the places that killed so many."

"I am sorry."

"Thank you. You know nothing would do but what he could come back here and get to you as soon as he could."

She felt tears come to her eyes. "I wish..." She wished so many things but none of them seemed possible. All that mattered right now was that Jed would live, and his mind would still be sound when he woke.

It was dark when Jed came to himself. Before, he had heard voices, understood he was in a bed, not that cellar, not still tied, not drugged, but it had all been as if through layers of fog.

He heard soft breathing alongside and turned his head,

without feeling as if his skull would crack open. Raine. She was lying, full clothed, with an afghan lightly draped over her. He just looked at her, remembering pieces of what had happened.

He felt weak, unable to think clearly. He reached out his right hand. His fingers worked. He saw abrasions on his wrists. It hadn't been a nightmare. He wished it had. He would have cursed if his throat hadn't been so parched.

He watched her awhile, her beautiful, long hair spread out on the pillow as he had dreamed of it so many times. He remembered then the last time he had seen her as he had turned and walked off her porch, looking back for one last view of that beautiful face.

No, that wasn't the last time. He remembered then seeing her in that alley, tears streaming down her cheeks but smiling at him before he'd let go and the world had been sucked away.

Her eyes opened as though she had felt his gaze on her. "You're awake," she said, reaching out her fingers to touch his cheek.

"So it seems," he said, his voice little more than a whisper.

"How do you feel?"

He considered that for a moment. He was hurting and still sick, but he was free and alive. "Not bad, considering how I felt the last time I woke up. Any water here?" He didn't want her leaving the bed but was grateful when she lifted his head and put a glass to his lips. He drank, stopped for a breath and gulped some more. His body felt totally dehydrated as though he'd never get enough water.

"They drugged me," he said. She probably knew that.

"Jei said it'll wear off but just take a few days until you're totally yourself again."

"Who... the hell is Jei?"

"He is the reason we found you. I think he took a terrible risk to do it too. We can talk about it later." She got the cloth and basin and began washing his chest again, working down his shoulders and then to his fingers. "Now you need sleep," she said as she finished with what she hoped had refreshed him.

"No, sleep is bad. What I need is you. I've dreamed of you over a thousand campfires, Raine."

She considered a moment as she put away the cloth and used a towel to dry him. "You need to rest and heal. There is time to talk of other things later." She didn't really want to say that, but it was wisest.

"Talk isn't what I want."

She had to laugh. "Jed, I swear there is nobody like you. You just woke up after one of the worst experiences I suspect anybody can have. Give yourself some time to heal from it." She stood up, but he grabbed her wrist and pulled her down beside him.

"Then lie with me. I know I am naked under this sheet, lie with me naked, sugar. I need you next to my skin, so that when I wake up... I don't find out I'm back in the war or worse that hellhole and on my way to a ship somewhere like they told me I'd be."

She knew that would mean they would sleep together soon, but she had known that from the moment she had feared he might have been killed. She would have him for whatever moments were possible.

She rose then. "You won't do it?" he asked, his voice husky. "I'd beg if that's what it'd take."

She began slowly unbuttoning her blouse, and then her skirt, letting it fall to the floor. She walked to the door and locked it. His eyes never left her as she came back and slowly unfastened and removed one undergarment after another. She took her time as she slid out of the last silky piece and stood before him naked. No man in this world had more a right to view her this way.

"You are as beautiful as ever-- more." He smiled. "At least we know part of me is working," he teased. His gray eyes had darkened with passion and she looked at the evidence of his arousal.

"You aren't up to more, not yet."

"All right—for now." He put out his arm and she crawled into bed alongside him.

"I need to be in your arms as much as you want me."

"I doubt that." He managed a smile. "In the war, I dreamed of this," he whispered against her hair.

"I thought of you too."

"Then I came back and thought I'd lost you."

"You won't lose me."

He smiled against her hair. "Then stupidly, I walked into a trap I couldn't walk out of." He brushed back her hair, kissing her temple.

"I couldn't let you go, not if there was any way to get you back," she murmured as she raised herself over him and kissed his chapped lips lightly.

"Well, it took you to get me out of that hole. I was careless. All it took was one stupid moment, and it was too late for me to do anything about it."

She kissed him again. "You couldn't have known."

"I should have known. I was a soldier. You learn about traps, about being attacked."

"But you'd left the war. Don't go blaming yourself for what others did."

He wanted to know how they had saved him but for now, she was right. He wasn't up to making love to her, nor to understanding how they had found him. All he could do was draw her against his body. He felt her tears on his skin.

"I was so scared," she murmured her words broken by the sobs she finally released.

"Me too," he whispered, on the edge of falling back asleep. He felt her clinging to him, holding him as tightly as he was holding her. He didn't know whether he really had her for other than the moment. The one thing he'd learned through this whole hell, the last four years of it, even the time in that cellar. The moment was all anybody ever had.

CHAPTER 6

They were both awakened at first light by knocking on the bedroom door. "Everything all right in there?" came Josh's deep voice, concern in it.

Raine would have jumped out of bed, but Jed held her to him. "It's fine," he said gruffly.

"Jed, you all right?"

"I will be if you get lost," he said. She heard Josh's laughter as he walked down the stairs.

"You are embarrassing me," she said. She felt his hardness against her and knew what he wanted, what she wanted. "You're not strong enough for this yet," she protested not wanting to convince him.

"So you will be on top," he whispered as he kissed her, his tongue delving deeply into her mouth. "I need you, sugar. I need you so bad. I want to feel alive again, and there is no way I know of that is better."

She kissed him teasing his tongue with her own and feeling her body heating up. It didn't take much after being against Jed all night. "What do I need to know about being on top?"

He grinned at her. He actually thought he was strong enough

to come over her, but the idea of her taking control appealed to him. "Why don't you find out," he whispered as he lifted her.

In moments, she was above him, his hardness against her softness. "Er uh now what do I do?"

His smile was a mix of amusement and desire. "What do you think?"

"Well... can I really?"

"Raine, do it without talking, or we'll both lose the ability." He knew that wasn't true of himself. Despite what he'd just been through, his long span without sex, his desire for her, the many dreams, he was going to stay rock hard until she took care of the problem. He began to wonder if he really could raise himself up and over her when she took him in her hand and settled herself properly in place. She looked adorably satisfied with herself.

"So now, move as it pleases you."

She began moving first back and forth and a kind of circling. "Do you like that?" she asked.

He groaned bringing his hands up to stoke her breasts and belly. He felt her soften, her skin flush. She shifted her hips taking him even deeper. She bent then and claimed his lips, delving her tongue into his mouth. He pulled her down to where he could suck on her nipples.

He felt the climax building within, fighting to keep from going off until she had attained her own satisfaction. "Oh my Lord," she cried, and it pushed him over the edge. A kaleidoscope inside began with a tiny pinpoint and blew up until it seemed to cover his whole body with a climax the likes of which he had never experienced as his body convulsed.

When he could think again, he saw she appeared as melted as he did. She lowered herself until she was beside him. "What was that?" she asked in a husky whisper.

He smiled against her temple. "I think it's proof positive you can do it that way."

She sighed and cuddled against him. "I suppose I should get up. You really certain this didn't hurt you?"

He laughed. "Sugar, you should know the answer to that better than anybody else in this world, and did you really think this was all?"

She looked at him with disbelief, but soon found he meant exactly what he said as they again made love, this time with slowness and deliberation, the feelings those of couples who knew each other's bodies and what it took to please the other. He had never known anything like it and knew he never would, not with any other woman.

"I dreamed of you hundreds of times," he whispered when she again came back to reality. "No dream was as good though."

She smiled and kissed him before sitting up. "You really do need to eat something," she said.

"Again?" he teased.

"You are incorrigible."

"I won't deny it."

She got up looking around for her clothing before she realized she had to find something else to wear. Everyone in the house obviously knew exactly what they had been doing anyway, but she wasn't about to enhance their impression.

"Where are my clothes?" he asked as he moved to sit on the edge of the bed as she found her undergarments. She wasn't really listening to him but instead was staring at the dresses in her cupboard. Normally she'd have felt she should go to work, but she wouldn't be doing that. The shops would sink or swim without her as she let a gingham patterned dress fall over her head and began buttoning it. Nothing was going to take her away from Jed until she had to go.

She realized then that he had struggled to his feet. "Wait," she protested coming back to his side. "You can't get up this soon, Jed. Really, you should lie in bed today and..."

He interrupted her. "Much as I'd like to do that, you with me, but I can't. I need to get up and move around. It's probably

73

what it'll take to finally remove this damned drug from my system."

"You won't leave the house though, will you?" She felt a shiver of fear at the idea of having him out of her sight.

He pulled on his black pants. "Sugar, I don't intend to let you out of my sight. Where is my shirt?"

"I am afraid whoever took you ripped it to ribbons. Josh went back to your room though and got your saddle bags." She pointed to the corner of the room.

"He's staying here?"

"It made sense."

She saw the effort he was making to remain standing. "I might have forgiven the kidnapping," he said, "but damn I hated those drugs they forced down my throat."

"Jei said it was probably chloral hydrate."

"I tried not to drink it. I went so far as to beg them not to. I felt..." He stopped and forced himself to take some deep breaths.

"You won't go after them, will you?" she asked uneasily. Now standing, with his sinewy torso bare, she wondered if they really had to leave this room. Silly girl. Of course, they had to get something to eat—sometime.

He looked at her as though he had read her mind, his smile faint but genuine. "No, but only because I doubt I'd find them. I have other problems more significant than them. But someday, when I have time..."

He walked over and squatted down by his saddlebags, pulling out an old blue shirt. He also picked up his Colt and holster, carrying both to the bed where he sat to pull on the shirt.

As he started to button it, she brushed his hands aside. "If you really have to cover up this lovely chest," she teased, "I should help you."

"I like your hands on my chest," he said as she deliberately brushed his skin more than needed to fasten the buttons. "I could almost forget I have things to do."

"You need to take it easy for a few days. I hope that's part of what you know you need to do."

He didn't answer but rose to buckle his cartridge belt and holster to his hips. Even though he claimed he didn't need it, she put her arm around his waist when they got to the stairs. "I can make it down some stairs," he protested.

"We had enough trouble getting you on your feet. A tumble down these steps would set us back." He grinned then, held onto the banister, and let her steady him.

In the kitchen, Jed could hear laughter, recognized Toddy's voice and even Clem and Nancy from when he had first met Raine. He had a hard time equilibrating himself to how normal this seemed after what had happened to him. Even having been in war and knowing how attacks happened, he still found it difficult to get his head around what had been done to him. He stopped and gave her a kiss on the top of her head before he pushed open the kitchen door.

"Well, it's about time," Josh said with a laugh as Raine helped Jed to a seat at the table.

"Good to see ya lookin' fit... mostly," Clem said sitting across from him. "You're a lucky man but reckon you know that."

"Coffee?" Nancy asked as she poured a cup.

It didn't sound appealing to Jed, but his stomach was reacting as though he'd had a bad hangover. Coffee would probably help. He nodded but sipped the hot brew cautiously.

Jed then turned to his brother and met Josh's level gaze. "I won't want to hear it, but I need to know what happened last night and how you got me out of there." Nancy turned back to the stove and began stirring what looked to be scrambled eggs.

"Well it wasn't last night for one. That was three nights ago that you were taken and two days ago that we found you."

"God. Damn them. I... they told me I was bound for a ship," Jed grated out through set teeth.

"What do you remember of it?" Josh asked.

Jed let out a breath, wished for a cigarette but remembered in time that Raine didn't much care for smoking in the house. He didn't have the energy to go outside yet. "I was on my way back to the hotel, probably a block from it and three... yeah, it was three men jumped me. Maybe if I'd understood what was happening in time, I could have... or maybe not. Anyway they hit me over the head, had me tied up like a hog. Then they... dragged me into some kind of cellar."

"Did they move you after that first time?" Toddy asked moving closer to the conversation and nodding as Raine refilled cups.

Jed shook his head wishing he hadn't, as it still hurt when he moved fast. "I don't think so, but they were drugging me from the start. I woke up once. They forced more down my throat."

"Did they give you any reason as to why they'd want you shanghaied?" Josh asked resting his hand on his brother's shoulder.

Jed shrugged. "The whole thing is confused in my mind now, but the one who did all the talking said he hated the South. I offered him money to let me go. He said somebody wanted me on that ship. He kept talking about me being a Reb."

"Could it be someone who wanted your ranch?" Toddy theorized.

"Who would even know about that in Portland?" But then Jed remembered they had bought all those supplies; so maybe someone had. He couldn't accuse the only one, of whom he could think to have a reason, as he was supposed to be Raine's friend. Besides, the man barely knew him. They had seen him that night on the street before dinner. It seemed unlikely he could set up an attack that quickly or even know who could do it. If it had been him, it meant he was ruthless at the least or a nutcase at the worst. Either worried him more for her than himself.

"So what now? You going to the law?" Toddy asked.

"I doubt it'd do much good," Jed said. "They kept me blind-folded, no names. I might recognize only one of the men's voices, and it sounded as though he was trying to disguise it. Going back to the cellar wouldn't prove anything about why or who. I doubt they leave behind evidence or have only one such place to use. No, it'd keep me here while it was investigated and who knows how long that'd take. I need to head for the ranch and see what's left there." He looked at Raine then. "I'll be back here though." His smile was determined. "Maybe I can do more about it then."

"So you'd leave right away?" she asked trying to keep her voice calm.

"No, not as soon as I'd hoped but sooner than I'll want. I have a few things to get set here first though... and will naturally need a lot of rest."

When she looked at him, his smile was teasing and so seductive that it'd have had her dragging him back to the bedroom if others hadn't been watching.

Nancy had the eggs ready, as Raine buttered the bread she had toasted in the oven. As they ate, she thought again how they had gone from a life and death discussion to a routine that seemed more part of what she had known as the real world. Except the real world wasn't all she had imagined. Then she remembered her concern about Agatha.

"Clem, how is Agatha?"

"Crotchety, mean as a buzzard as usual, and getting more and more weak minded," Clem said through a mouthful of toast. "Healthy enough though, I reckon. Just drive the rest of us nuts. That's what she'll do."

That didn't make a possible visit sound productive. She would put it off and spend her day around the house. She looked over at Jed and as their gazes met, she knew what she'd want them to be doing. Foolish woman. The real obstacles between them were as real as they had been four years earlier. The magnetic draw between them was equally strong.

"Tell me more about this Chinese fellow," Jed said as he pushed back his chair, "but before you do, let's go out on the back porch."

"To avoid us all hearing?" Raine asked knowing her voice had a trace of irritation. Good enough to help save him but not enough to hear his plans?

He grinned. "No secrets. You all come on outside. I just want to smoke, and you can't abide smoking in the house." He looked toward his brother. "Josh would you get me my makings?"

His brother went upstairs and soon Jed was outside in one of the wooden chairs rolling and lighting a cigarette, drawing in the smoke with a sigh of pleasure. The others had followed, Josh sitting on the back step, Clem bringing out a chair for himself and one for Toddy. Nancy stayed inside to clean up from breakfast, but Raine came and sat on the porch at Jed's feet. He put his free hand on her shoulder, stroking her neck a little as he smoked.

"Now who is he and why did he help you pull me out of that hellhole?" he asked.

"Han Jei, and I don't know his reasons for sure," Raine said. "We went to a woman I knew who is a madam down in the tenderloin."

Jed tilted her head up to meet his eyes. "You went to a bordello?"

"Clem thought, and it turned out to be right, that if she didn't know where you might be held, she'd know who would."

He sucked in a breath and glared at Josh. "And you let her go with you when you came to get me."

"I'd like to see who could have stopped her. Besides we needed her," Josh said with a grin. "We were with her, Toddy and me. She was in no danger."

"Tell me the rest," Jed said, teeth gritted.

"I knew Bernice from the wagon train," Raine explained. "She was not a friend. Isn't one now, but Clem told us that she was in the right business to know what we needed to find out. There would have been no other way, Jed."

He sighed. "And she did it as a favor to you?"

Raine gave a little laugh. "Not hardly. She doesn't like me

anymore than I like her, but Josh threatened her." She gave Josh a teasing smile. "And I appealed to her finer nature."

"She had one?"

"Well there were ways to encourage her to do the right thing —a combination of bribery and Josh's persuasion." She smiled at him. "She brought us Han Jie, who I think might be her lover."

"How much did you pay her?"

"I don't want you to pay me back."

"But I will." His tone brooked no argument.

"All right but it's silly. Just a thousand."

He let out an angry sigh. "How about the Chinaman? What'd you have to pay him?"

"His name is Han Jei," Raine reminded him at the same time Josh chuckled.

"He wouldn't take anything," he said with a glint of amusement in his eyes. "Said we'd have to owe him."

"Oh great." Jed drew in again on the cigarette. "All right. I am grateful. I know you got me out of hell, and it wasn't going to be better. I damn well couldn't have gotten myself out of it."

"Maybe, it wasn't your fault," Raine said. "Maybe you inherited an enemy."

"Which means?"

"Oh it's silly. Nothing."

"Might as well tell me. I probably already know."

"All right but just how Russ acted when we ran into him. I think it's foolish though. He has too much to lose to do something so illegal. And how would he know the right people to set it up so fast?"

"We'll let it go for now. I'd like to meet this Han Jei."

"He'll probably be back tonight. He is slipping in after dark to avoid being connected with your escape. He also suggested you lay low until you are able to defend yourself fully."

"He's right." Jed knew he was still dizzy, his muscles not strong. He needed to head to the ranch, but he had more fears now about leaving Raine. Except, it would not be safe at the ranch either, even assuming he still had a home there to offer her. Running his fingers through Raine's hair, he knew he wouldn't want to go. He was not meant to be a lapdog; so he would do what he had to do—but no sooner than he must.

"Are you going to tell me about what happened after you left Oregon?" Raine asked, brushing her fingers over Jed's lips as they lay in her bed, relaxed after an afternoon nap and again making love.

He let out a low whistle. "Do you have any methods to force my compliance? Possibly planning to torture it out of me?" he teased.

"Well I'd have to seriously think whether I had such tools in my arsenal."

"You have them all right."

"If you'd rather not talk about it, I will understand."

"We'd just be putting it off." He ran his hand down her slender arm. "You have a right to know. How about though you give me some time to think about it while you tell me what you did during those four years."

"Nothing very exciting." Her fingers moved to caress his nipple, not conducive to steady thinking. "I waited for a letter." She gave him an expectant look. "But, you know of course it never came."

"I didn't know what to say. That sounds like a weak excuse, doesn't, it?"

"Yes."

"I wanted to write, wanted to hear from you, but I had no idea if I'd live through it or in what shape I'd be in. I saw a lot of men killed or have limbs blown off."

"You know that wouldn't have mattered to me. I wish you had written, but I'll let it go. As for me, I worked on building up the business. When the time was right, I leased another, which so far has worked rather well even with managing Agatha's. I met a man."

"A man you were interested in," he said lifting her so that he could look into her eyes. "It was bound to happen. I didn't leave you with any promises."

"No, you didn't. Not to mention we both know we can't really work out a life together anyway."

He clenched his jaw, the muscle jumping. "I don't want to accept that."

"But it's true. Anyway I did meet a man, a very nice man actually."

"I hope not Russell."

"No, not Russ. His name is Kirk Edmonton. He's the playwright who has written now three plays I have performed in."

"He asked you to marry him, I suppose." He didn't really want to hear the answer to that.

"He has been a friend. No romance. We have interests in common with theater."

"Was Grayson jealous of him too?"

"I doubt it. He had no reason."

"Were there-- All right, I have no right to ask this."

"No, you don't, but there have been no men since you. I could have. You know I had every right to."

He was smiling, his eyes soft with tenderness. "You could have," he agreed, "but I am glad there wasn't anybody." He hesitated a moment and then said, "I want you to marry me."

"Just like that?"

"Want me down on my knees. I'll do it. Marry me, Loraine Stevens." She distracted him by running her fingers down his chest to his belly. It took so little for her to bring him back to an arousal, which the sheet didn't hide. "I couldn't ask you before I left. I didn't know if I'd be back. Now I have to leave again, but marry me before I go to the ranch. I want that decided for us."

"How could it possibly work? I am not about to leave Portland. You can't live here. We both know this is just an interlude for us."

"We know that?"

"We're adults, not children. We know it takes more than sex to make a relationship work."

"And sex is all we'd have?" She was turning him down. He supposed he should have expected it, but it hurt.

"I don't know that it's all, but how could we put a life together? I don't want to go to Eastern Oregon, to the wilderness. You don't want to live here, and there's more than that."

"Like what?"

"Well I don't like having anybody tell me what to do. I've been an independent woman now for over ten years, and I like it that way."

"What makes you think I'd be trying to tell you what to do?"

She gave him a look and a mocking smile. "Jed, seriously, you can ask me that?"

"All right. I'll let it go for now." He stared at the ceiling putting his hands behind his head as he considered what she had said. It wasn't simple.

"Are you going to tell me about you?" she asked.

That was even less simple. "As much as I understand of it. To answer a question you haven't asked-- there have been no other women. My life wasn't where it could have happened if I'd been of a mind. I wasn't. I only wanted you."

"You went straight to your mother?"

He nodded and frowned wishing for a cigarette. He gritted his teeth. "My mother was a strong woman."

"I've heard that. Josh told me some about her and how she took him in as her son."

He sucked in a breath letting it out. "She had asked me to get there as soon as I could, or it'd be too late. When I got there, Geoff and Trevor had gone to fight. As I said, the ones who had worked the plantation had left. Just Josh to take care of her. She rallied when she saw me as she had things to say."

"That was good then."

He grimaced. "Or not. She told me the lawyer had her will. She left it all to me, the land, the money, the house."

"None to your brothers?"

He shook his head and when she looked up, she saw his smile was bitter. "She had run things since our father died. She was trying to continue."

"What do you mean?"

"She left it to me to force me to hold onto the land for the family. She begged me to be sure my brothers survived. As the oldest, she said it was now my responsibility. She had never wanted me to come west, to buy the ranch from the money I'd inherited from my grandfather's will. He wanted me free to follow my dreams—wherever they led. My mother felt otherwise. In her dying, she thought she could hold me there and keep the Georgia plantation for future generations. She even suggested names of local women who I should marry."

"Oh."

He reached out and put his arm around her, pulling her against him. "She begged me to take care of my brothers. She said I had to promise before she could die in peace. She was in a lot of pain. Finally, I came to believe that she would lie there in agony until I agreed. I promised. Maybe I would have joined up anyway. I love my brothers, all three of them. I could never have fought against Geoff and Trevor. I don't know if I could have just gone back to Oregon and left them there without trying... Anyway, I can't say what I should have done. I only know what I did."

"Did you promise to keep the land too?"

He shook his head. "No, just to try to keep my brothers alive. I did try."

"I figured you had joined up when you didn't return."

"There were many times, over the next years, that I wished I hadn't left Oregon. War is hell, sugar. Worse when you don't believe in the cause and know you can't win. I didn't even want the South to leave the Union. Anyway no looking back with regrets. When Mama died, Josh and I buried her in the family plot. When I left to join up, he went with me."

"How did you find your brothers?"

"I knew they were with Jeb Stuart. Josh and I joined up there. For a while, the four of us were together. Stuart was one of my good memories of the whole thing. The only one. He was one of a kind. He recognized that Josh was no servant and treated him as an equal. Stuart's men would have ridden into hell for him, and we did."

"We read reports on the battles."

"Geoff was killed in one. I found Trevor's body after what amounted to a skirmish, not the kind of thing that would make a newspaper account. In the end, all I could do for either was see they were buried."

"After your brothers had been killed, you stayed with Stuart until the end?"

"Until his end at Yellow Tavern. Josh and I then fought under Wade Hampton. At that point, there was no leaving it. My only hope, and it was a slim one, was that I could keep Josh and myself alive. Nobody who understood economics or logistics had hope of winning anything. Then it was over. General Grant let us leave with our sidearms and horses."

He was staring at the ceiling. "Nobody who was in that war, on either side, the way it was fought, the insane loss of life, could think anything, but that there has to be a better way to settle things."

"Did you go to the plantation then?"

"Long enough to put the land in the hands of an agent to sell. I had shipped a few things out here after Mama died. When I went back, I only wanted my stallion. In the beginning, I had taken him into the battles. He was a true war horse, steady and brave, but I didn't want to lose him and arranged to get him back to the plantation. Now, he'll be the start of a new bloodline. Stubborn as Mama was, so am I and . My life is here."

"And now you face another war to hold onto your ranch."

"It doesn't seem men have much interest in living peaceably, does it?" he said trying to make his tone sound light.

"Maybe humans can yet learn a better way," she suggested running her fingers through his chest hair.

"It seems unlikely," he said with a bitter smile, "but we can hope."

"So again you go east and face the unknown."

"I have a lot invested in that piece of land. If you saw it, you'd know why I love it so much."

Now it was her turn to lie flat and suck in a breath. "I am not an explorer or a lover of the wilderness, Jed. I like the niceties of cities, building up businesses, modern conveniences, restaurants, theater. I had all I wanted of the rough life as we headed west."

"I understand that. No one should give it all up for another."

She managed a smile. "You don't sound like you believe that."

"Intellectually I do, but in my heart, I want you to think about it, about being with me, about how it'd be for us together. Give me some time there, and it won't be as rough as you're expecting."

"I'd be a long way from my family, from the things I know. I wish I could say I thought caring for you would be enough, but..."

"But it's not?"

"In the end, I don't think it would be."

"Marry me anyway, and we just wouldn't live together all the time. Not everybody does."

"It wouldn't be fair."

"I spent four years wanting you, thinking about you. I don't think any of this is fair to feel this way and not be together. We can work it out."

"When do you have to leave?"

"I have a few things to do first. I want to get you a better weapon than that pea shooter over there on the dresser; then teach you how to shoot it."

"I don't need another." She felt annoyed that his orders were starting so soon, even as she knew he meant well.

"I thought I could go out to dinner with you and walk back to my hotel. I don't want another nasty surprise involving you. You will let me do this. If you don't need it, then fine. I want to also get you a good horse and be sure you know how to ride it."

She sat up in bed. "Jed, seriously, weren't you listening to me? I thought about it when Adam and Matt were here but decided against it. I live in a city. I don't need to ride a horse."

"Sugar, you don't really know what you will need. I am going to be sure you have what it takes to protect yourself or run for your life if that's what you someday need."

She felt angry but suppressed it. If he thought he could order her around now, she could only imagine what it would be like if they were married. Instead of saying what she was thinking, she said the obvious. "Why wouldn't I go to the police for protection?"

The shadow of his grin flashed. "Do you know how much a police officer in your town makes?"

She shook her head. "Why does it matter?"

"Likely it's no more than $50 a month—maybe less. Do you know how much they make from looking the other way where it comes to shanghaiing?"

"I guess it'd be more profitable."

"Exactly. I would like to do some poking around town but being limited by this Southern drawl and being a stranger, I won't find out much. I hope Toddy will get more. I know there are bound to be good police officers. There always are, but before I leave, I want you to know who they are."

"You're expecting a lot for being here a short time."

"I have to do a lot. Something important to me is going to be here."

She felt a warm glow that almost covered up her irritation. He meant well. In many ways, she found it hard to believe how quickly he had returned, how abruptly her life had been tossed on end. Soon he'd be gone again. She doubted it would ever return to normal. That is if she hadn't gotten pregnant. She thought she was probably safe given the time of the month, but she wouldn't know for sure for a few more days. If he came in and out of her life, it was bound at some point that there would be complications. She wasn't ready to raise a child by herself... but what if it was Jed's baby?

"Your wheels are turning," he said. "What are you thinking?"

She lay back against him not ready to tell him her fears and doubts. Better he saw her as set in her ways. How would he respond if she got pregnant? Would it upset his plans?

"Don't argue with me about the horse and gun. I am set on it."

"Arrogant male," she responded working to keep her tone light. "Adam and Matt didn't find the right one for me. What makes you think you can?"

"Because I will. I don't want you getting an animal that will toss you. And one more thing, sugar."

"And that is?"

"Don't think I've given up on us either. Maybe it can't be yet, but I think we will work this all out. I work hard for what I want, and I'd sacrifice a lot to have you for my wife."

She didn't see how, but when he put his lips on hers, his tongue delving into her mouth, his hands on her body, she was in no mood to argue.

CHAPTER 7

I t was dark, and Raine was cleaning up after dinner, Josh and Toddy were in the living room playing chess, and Jed was sitting at the table when Jei appeared at the back door.

"Looking a lot better than the last time I saw you," Jei observed as he settled into a chair across from Jed.

"You a drinking man?"

"When it's good whiskey."

Raine went to the cupboard and brought back the bottle and two glasses. "Should I go get Josh and Toddy?" she asked.

"No reason yet," Jed said and then looked steadily at Jei. "I am told I owe you my life."

Jei's smile was satisfied as he took a small sip of the whiskey. "You'll pay the debt someday," he said with confidence.

"You seem confident about that."

"I am."

"How did you know where they were holding me?"

"Wondering if maybe I do a little shanghaiing on the side? Jei asked with a laugh.

"It would be one possible way."

Jei nodded his agreement. "In this case, it was not. Some

acquaintances do. They had seen you and been furious at the ones who took you. They had already come to me complaining it would bring an end to a lucrative sideline for themselves."

"Why?"

"You were not someone who could just disappear. They want a drunken logger or miner, a man who won't be missed. They did not believe that to be the case with you. Turned out they were right."

"So you had already heard about me before Raine's friend came to you?"

"As it happened, I had just heard and was still debating what to do about it when Bernice showed up requesting me to talk to a friend of hers."

Raine interrupted. "Hardly friends, please. We knew each other. That's all."

"Let's not play with semantics," Jei said. "At any rate, Bernice asked if I could help with a problem, but one that might prove dangerous. Obviously I could and decided I would."

"For your own reasons?" Jed didn't sound overly grateful or friendly toward Jei, which surprised Raine. He was right. He did owe him for his life.

"Yes, I had my reasons," Jei said without any look of resentment.

"Do you know the names of the men who had me?"

"I know the names of two, but I won't tell you. You going after them wouldn't help either of us."

Jed frowned with visible irritation. "How about telling me the reason they picked me out?"

"That's harder to figure. There are several possibilities for those, who would have such capabilities, but I see no reason for any of them to become involved in something that could turn dangerous on many levels."

"I obviously have concern for whether this will have repercussions for Raine."

Jei looked at her for a moment considering. "You fear Bernice would make trouble for her? I can assure you she will not." His smile was a hard one.

"My larger concern is whoever targeted me might target her when I am not here."

"I will do what I can to find the source of your experience."

Jed smiled. "Good enough. Thank you for what you did. I'd be on a ship headed for who knows where but for you."

"Possibly, of course," Jei agreed, "but your brother would have torn up the waterfront to find you. He might've saved you anyway."

"You are a good judge of character."

Raine knew it was true. She had seen that in Josh too. He was a strong man with an intense love for his brother. She was just grateful it hadn't come to that or a need for violence. She hoped it was over, but as Jed and Jei talked, she knew they neither believed it was.

"Well what do you think of her?" Jed asked as he rode up to the front of Raine's home on a brown horse.

"What am I supposed to think?" she asked looking a little skeptically at the bright-eyed mare.

"That she and you can be friends." He smoothly dismounted and put the reins over the post by the porch.

"That's not a sidesaddle."

"No, because you're going to ride her astride."

"That is not how ladies ride."

He grinned. "They do if they haven't ridden much and need to move out in a hurry."

"How would that work with a skirt?" She knew she was looking for excuses. Two things were going through her head. The first was he was trying to manage her life even if his intentions were good. The second that she felt uneasy at the idea of getting on any horse and riding anywhere. Josh rode up holding the reins to a big gray stallion.

"Which is why I bought you some more practical gear." He untied a sack from the back of the saddle. "Pants, a heavy shirt, hat. I had to guess at boot size but you can use extra socks if I was wrong. I had a pretty good idea of sizes—where it comes to you," he finished teasingly.

She gave him a pointed look. "I thought you weren't going to try to run things here."

"Sugar, this is for your own good. I did this for you because I had the expertise to judge horseflesh and get you a safe mount."

"I haven't needed a horse before this."

"I know you aren't taking me very seriously about this, but I have a gut feeling. When I do, I never ignore it."

"I don't have the same gut feeling." She folded her hands over her chest studying the mare.

"Are you scared of horses?"

She gave him a look. She didn't like admitting that she was frightened of anything. He handed her the sack, which she reluctantly took.

"She's been well trained. I can get you started on her and once you get used to riding, you will like it. Come on, sugar. Give it a try."

She frowned. "Is there a weapon in this sack?" She knew by its weight that there was.

"Hey, are you up to a challenge or not? You the lady who owns her own businesses, acts in plays up in front of a lot of people, crosses the prairies in a wagon?"

She resisted the urge to tell him that she felt he was overstepping. "You are determined."

Josh leaning over the pommel of his saddle laughed. "And when Jed is determined, might as well give it up, lady."

With a little moan, she did. "All right, but now? We have to do it now?"

"No time like the present. I want you to have a few rides under your belt before I have to leave."

With great reluctance, Raine took the clothing up to her bedroom, taking her time changing and wishing she could think of a legitimate excuse to avoid doing this. She wasn't scared of horses. Well, actually, she was, but she hated to admit that to Jed. Horses could be dangerous. Besides, she knew she'd have no reason to need to ride. She could take a stagecoach or boat anywhere she wanted and even the train was coming although the tracks were only in short sections for now.

As she put on the pants and shirt, she began to think about how the neighbors would feel about this get up. She took the soft felt hat and pulled it low on her forehead, hoping they would not recognize her if they did see her. Jed had included a lightweight coat that came almost to her knees. That helped some.

Why did it matter what the neighbors thought anyway? Well it didn't... not much anyway. She carried the belt, holster and revolver back downstairs. It was much larger than her derringer. On the porch, she wasn't pleased to see Nancy was watching the whole business. "You be careful now," she told Raine. Like she needed to hear that.

"Her name is Fancy," Jed told her as he stroked the horse's neck.

"She seems awfully large."

"She's a good size for you. She has nice legs, plenty of go, and a placid personality, not easily frightened."

"That's good?" she asked as she moved to the mare's side. "Hi, Fancy," she said unsure if you talked to a horse or not.

"Very good. Don't want a horse shying at every rabbit. Now just pet her on the forehead, look her in the eye, and let her see who you are."

"She won't bite me?"

"Nah, but you stay back from Midas."

"Midas?" She looked uneasily toward the tall stallion whose

reins Josh was holding as he leaned forward in his saddle and watched their byplay with a grin.

"He's got a little royalty problem—thinks he's a king. He's Andalusian."

"He is big." But then, even Fancy seemed big to her.

"You didn't belt the holster to your waist."

"Is that necessary? Good Lord, Jed, is that a rifle too?" She saw the obvious answer in a scabbard on the saddle.

"Raine, do you still think the world out there is all safe and nice?"

"I don't go out there."

"We can't plan everything. I want you prepared."

"You want me set up like a little army."

A quirk lifted at the edge of his mouth. "A very little one. Now let's get down to business." He took the belt from her, pushed the jacket aside, and fastened it around her waist. "You don't need to carry it all the time, but it's good to get some practice while I am here, be comfortable with its weight around your waist; so it's why I want you to wear it today. All right?"

She sighed with reluctance but nodded.

"Now then, do you know how to mount a horse?"

"I have been on one... a few times; so I have the general idea." The results had never been good but better not to dwell on that at the moment. She wondered if horses could sense fear. Doubtless.

"Want a boost up." His sexy smile said he wouldn't mind doing that.

"I can manage." She put her boot into the stirrup and swung her leg over the saddle managing to put her other foot into its stirrup. As she straightened, she felt as though it was a long way down.

"Now, don't put your foot all the way into the stirrup. Just the toe. If you do get thrown." He grinned at her look of concern. "Not likely to happen, but you don't want to get dragged now do you? Swing your boot out of the stirrup for a minute." He adjusted the length of each to be right for her.

She shook her head. She didn't want any of this. "Are you sure this is safe?" she asked.

"Nothing is totally safe, sugar," he said adjusting the reins into her hand. "Not even crossing a street," he teased. "Angle your toe up a little. Yeah, that's right."

She sighed reluctantly. All right, he was determined and maybe he was right. Maybe she'd even enjoy this. She did like his hands on hers as he showed her how to hold the reins. She put aside her misgivings over his ordering her to do it. "Now," he said, "feel your balance and use your knees, let go of the pommel. It will block you from feeling Fancy."

"I don't feel fancy now," she said trying to lighten her own mood.

Jed walked over to his stallion, took the reins from Josh and seemed to leap into the saddle. "We'll take it slow but pull on that right rein and turn her toward the road."

"Josh is going with us?" she asked recognizing for the first time that he apparently was.

"For today. I don't know this country and don't want to head out somewhere that might prove unsafe for you. He's our security." He gave his brother a wink.

She listened to his instructions as she gradually got the feel of the horse under her. Maybe this wouldn't be so bad... if they stuck to walking. She didn't think she could count on that. Jed headed them out the main road and then cut off on a side road that angled into the hills and timber. "We'll take it slow today," he said, "Maybe try a slow trot. Think you're up to that?" He instructed her a bit about how her seat would change for trotting and then told her to touch her heels lightly in Fancy's side and use the reins to give her the cues she needed.

"It isn't as bad as I'd expected," she said finally beginning to relax a bit. "It's pretty up here." She'd lived in Portland for ten years but never ventured into the hills.

"I'm looking for a good place to do a little target practice," he said reminding her that there was more to this than a pleasant little ride into the hills.

"Jed, did you learn something disturbing when you were out?" she asked glancing over, noticing how his eyes seemed always to be scanning the terrain.

His smile was tight. "I learned it the night I got taken. All isn't what it seems, and where it comes to you, when I won't be here, I don't want to take chances."

Wait, those would be her chances. She really didn't like his take charge attitude. She kept reminding herself he meant well, but it was more and more irritating to her. Was there real danger with which to be concerned?

"Should I talk to Russ about that night? I haven't seen him since."

He laughed. "Like he'd tell you if he had something to do with it? Not unless he knows about Bernice's involvement, and I am thinking she won't want that. Don't ask him anything. It's best he not see you as involved at all in getting me free."

"You talk like... well like he's a real danger. He's just a businessman."

"What do you know about him, Raine?"

"I suppose not much. I mean we've had dinner, of course. He helped me lease the second store and has been trying to get me a good price to buy it."

"How about his connection to the Collins?"

"I think he was instrumental in their first store too and for fair prices. He and I have met at various social occasions. He's never courted me. He's been a good friend... I thought."

"His choice on courting or yours?"

"Well, mine."

"So he wanted, probably expected more."

"I suppose so." She found with talking like this she was beginning to forget that they were riding horses. She almost felt at ease on Fancy.

Josh said, "Looks like that hollow will do for target practice,

Jed. Be a little down from the city; so won't anybody be hearing us."

"Good." They dismounted and loosely tied their horses to brush so they could eat on the grass below and then moved far enough away not to scare them. "It wouldn't scare Midas anyway," Jed said. "He does well with loud noises. In battle, he didn't hesitate or shy at all, but I am not so sure about Miss Fancy." His smile showed in his eyes. Raine knew he meant not only the horse but her by that nickname. Well she'd be more at ease with the revolver than the horse. She had fired her derringer.

Josh walked about one hundred feet into the draw to set up a paper target. As he walked back, Jed was explaining to her how it worked. "Just cock, sight, and pull the trigger. Nothing to it," he said.

"What is it?"

"A 36 Navy. Nice gun, easy to handle, not too heavy but it has enough power to count."

"You really think I'll need this?" she asked uneasy again.

"If you don't, then this isn't going to hurt anything, is it?" he asked with a faint smile, but his eyes were hard, determined.

"No, I guess not." So she spent the next hour shooting the revolver and then the rifle he had also bought for her, then watching the brothers shoot. Josh and Jed enjoyed competing with each other and kept moving targets back.

"That twig," Josh said with a laugh.

"Can't even hit the tree that far off," Jed teased, but he swung his up faster than she had expected. She squinted seeing that he had cut the twig off. Josh fired and cut it back closer to the tree. They were definitely a deadly duo.

"It's obvious you two don't need practice," she said before she thought.

"No, we've had plenty of that," Jed said smiling with no humor.

As they rode back to the city, Jed encouraged her to let Fancy go a little, and she found it worked. The horse even obediently slowed as soon as she pulled a bit on the reins. Overall she was feeling more at ease than she had expected by the time they got back to her home.

"You need to learn to saddle and unsaddle her but that can wait for tomorrow's lesson." He and Josh headed off for the stable as she walked into the house where Nancy greeted her.

"Mr. Grayson come by."

"He say what he wanted?" she asked uneasily as she headed up the stairs to change into something that didn't smell like a horse.

"Just needed to talk to you about something. Business sounded like. How was the ride?" Nancy followed her up the stairs.

"I might get the hang of it. I guess I could put a shed up here to keep a horse. Do you ride, Nancy?"

"Not me. I was on one once is all and it ran away with me."

"Were you hurt?"

"I rolled off and just got dusty. I figured that was enough. I'll stick to wagons, I will."

"Has Clem said anything about Agatha?" she asked as she poured water into a basin to wash up.

"Just you better talk to her. She's getting funny, he said. I think Mr. Grayson's been by there too. Stirring the old lady up is what I think."

"You don't think much of Mr. Grayson, do you?" Raine asked as she put on her slips before sliding a dress over her shoulders.

"No more'n I have to. There's something about him. Can't say what. Sort of weasely is what I'd say. But Clem says he's liked a lot by Mrs. Collins."

Raine sighed. She could not put off seeing Agatha. It was time to split their business interests. and she would happily help Agatha find someone else to manage her store. She didn't think it was going to be wise that they continue in their partnership—

especially not if Russ was influencing her. Maybe he'd like to manage Agatha's business. Then she wondered if that would be safe for Agatha. She realized with a start, that she was beginning to have Nancy and Jed's view of Russ.

Downstairs, Raine set about helping Nancy with dinner preparations. She actually had had very little interest in cooking but felt she probably needed to learn that too. That led to her deciding that, as soon as Jed left, she wanted to visit her mother. She knew things about healing herbs that she should write down.

She wasn't sure why she needed the information, but after Jed had been hurt and without freedom to use a doctor, she wanted to understand how to handle things should such arise again. Jed being Jed, that seemed pretty likely. She sighed as she realized-- if he did get hurt again, it wasn't likely to be with her anywhere near.

Before the roast, potatoes and corn on the cob was ready to eat, Josh and Jed had returned with Clem on their heels.

"When you boys leaving?" Clem asked as Raine poured them each a glass of wine, as Toddy joined them and they all sat at the table.

Jed let out a reluctant sigh as he looked at Raine. "I'm torn in two over this. I hope you know it. I guess we can't put it off much longer. We'll leave on Saturday."

That meant only two more nights. As she ate, she felt a sudden reluctance to waste a moment of that time with anyone else.

Jed looked at Clem, his expression serious. "I hope you'll be looking after her. You know what I mean."

"Hey, I can take care of myself," Raine protested before Clem could say anything.

"I don't like you living alone here."

"I've been living alone for a lot of years, and it's been fine."

"Things change," Jed said looking at Toddy with a grim smile. "I'm half in mind to leave Toddy here to look after you."

Now it was Toddy's turn to protest with a snort. "I want to go to the ranch."

"And I don't need a nursemaid," she retorted. "You are teaching me to shoot that gun, ride a horse. What are you wanting here? To turn me into a man?"

His smile softened as he looked back at her. "No, sugar, definitely I don't want to turn you into a man."

"Nancy, would you mind taking care of the dishes tonight?" Raine asked as soon as they finished eating.

"Of course, I don't," Nancy said with a knowing grin as the two left the kitchen.

Before they could head up the stairs there was a knock at the door. Raine reluctantly opened it to see Russell Grayson standing there with a bouquet of yellow roses in his hands.

"Russ," she said surprise in her voice as she reluctantly accepted the flowers. "I didn't expect you."

Russ looked over at her shoulder his eyes on Jed. "So I see."

She felt annoyed at the tone in his voice, which suggested he had a right not to expect a man at her home. Josh and Toddy walked in from the kitchen stopping as they saw the man at the door.

"What did you want, Russ?" she asked thinking she would get rid of him quickly. She laid down the roses.

"Invite him in, sugar," Jed said. She grimaced and looked back at Jed to see his humorless smile. "Want a drink, Russ?" Jed's tone was anything but friendly even if his words sounded that way. "You ever meet my brother?"

Russ walked into the parlor, ignoring the irritation on Raine's face. "I don't think I have," he said looking from the men back to Raine.

"Russ Grayson. Josh Hardman and this is Toddy Coen. He's working for me now."

Clem and Nancy had entered the room hovering at the door

obviously too late to escape the room, but the expressions on their faces said they wished it was otherwise.

Jed poured each of the men a shot of whiskey. He handed one to Russ, leaving Toddy, Clem, and Josh collect their own. Raine moved to where Nancy stood and urged her to come with her to sit in the parlor where they all found seats as the men sipped their whiskey.

"How have you been enjoying your stay in our city?" Russ asked with what almost looked like a smirk to Raine.

"It's been... a successful trip," Jed said his gaze steady on the other man.

"You staying long?"

"A few more days... but I'll be back."

"You are settling nearby?"

"Close enough to not have a problem getting here in a hurry if need be." Jed was offering no information about his plans. She didn't understand why he had invited the man for a drink. Was it to establish his own rights to be there, or was he trying to decide what kind of man Russ was? Distracting her from her pondering, Russ turned to her.

"Actually I had a reason for stopping by tonight, other than giving you the roses, which I know are your favorite flowers. Since you have company though perhaps I should come back another time."

"They are friends. Speak freely," Raine said.

"Well it's about Agatha. I don't feel she is well and cannot continue as she has been with her shop."

"Which means?"

"I will be purchasing it. Naturally I'd like it if you would continue to manage it. It's worked so well."

"I had already been thinking of not doing that, Russ, even if Agatha kept it. I hope you can find someone qualified, but it won't be me."

"I am sorry to hear that... Is uh this the reason?" He gestured toward Jed.

"No, it's not. I simply saw it a good time to move in other directions. The theater is taking a lot of my time. Two stores are plenty for me to manage."

"You will be doing more plays then?" Russ sounded pleased for the first time that evening.

"Kirk had mentioned he had a play he thought might be good for me," she said hoping that if he was building up any ideas about Jed, they would be redirected. Although she wasn't convinced Russ had had Jed kidnapped, she didn't know he hadn't either.

"Edmonton? Well that's very good. I will look forward to seeing that and..." He looked at Jed now. "Maybe you'll be back for her performance also."

"Could be," Jed said rising and walking over to the fireplace leaning his arm on the mantle as he sipped the whiskey. She saw that he was working to control his temper.

Raine looked from him to Russ. "Thank you for taking care of Agatha," she said, "as it takes a weight off my mind." She would be sure she went by Agatha's as soon as Jed left to be sure this was Agatha's intention also.

"Well," Russ said, sounding reluctant as he rose, "I suppose I should be going. I have the buggy outside. Would you men like a ride back to your hotel?"

"Don't worry about us. We'll manage our way," Jed said.

She was appreciative that he was not letting Russ know they were staying at her home. She was unsure how much damage that might do her reputation or her stores but better that Russ stayed uncertain as to the depth of their connection. Whatever Russ had to do with the attack on Jed, she no longer trusted him. As soon as he was out the door, she let out a groan. "I don't know why I ever thought he was a friend."

"You didn't like him buying out Mrs. Collins?" Clem asked.

"No, that's fine. She can't manage it herself anymore. Just it was his whole demeanor." She looked at Jed. "I wonder..."

He smiled and came over to take her hand and pull her to her feet. "You had a good idea right before he came to the door. Let's follow through on that."

Pressed against his body, she whispered, "You sure he didn't ruin the mood."

"Not a chance." He kissed the top of her head lightly and then said, "See you all tomorrow," as he led Raine up the stairs.

CHAPTER 8

In her room, Jed pulled her into his arms, his kiss long, his tongue moving around hers, urging her to put her own tongue into his mouth. "Mmmm," he said when he released her. "I have thought though there might be consequences to this. Unwelcome ones for you."

"You mean pregnancy?" she asked, running her fingers over his lips.

"It is the usual."

"It should be safe now. We do though need to figure out something for when you return... if you return."

"Oh, I will return."

"I guess there are things we could do to make it safer." She began unbuttoning his shirt, pushing it off his shoulders.

"Marry me, and it won't matter."

"Was that a proposal?"

"My second-- if I was keeping count."

She pulled his shirt off and took his nipple into her mouth, nipping lightly, feeling it tighten, as she knew her own was doing at his touch.

"We'd end up hating each other as one of us had to give up what we want. It's impractical and impossible."

"I don't like either word." His hands unfastened her buttons. Instead of letting her dress drop, he lifted it over her shoulders and laid it across a chair. "I want you, and I want you in my bed every night, Raine."

"You wouldn't be happy living in Portland, and despite you trying to turn me into an outdoors lady, I am not." She nearly added his bossiness was already making her irritated half the time, but she held off on it. He'd be gone soon. When he came back, if he came back, she'd set him straight that she ran her own life.

"Maybe you don't know all you are, but I won't argue with you about it. Right now you are better off here... That is assuming old Russ is as safe as you have thought."

She sighed as she began unbuttoning his pants. Her breath was coming faster as she pushed them down revealing his beautiful body and his total readiness for what she had in mind. Not bothering to pull off his boots, he pushed down the straps of her camisole and slips to puddle at her feet. Naked now except for thin pantalets, she walked over to the bed, leaving him to push off his boots, socks and follow. He laid her back on the mattress, leaving her only her stockings. She felt strangely more nude than if he had removed them.

His hands seemed to be everywhere as were hers on his body, all the sensitive, secret places.

"You are so ready for me," he said his breath coming faster as he pushed her thighs apart and began to use his mouth where his hands had been.

"Oh God," she whispered pulling him up and then guiding him into her. "You feel so good there," she murmured, running her hands down his back to his buttocks and pulling him harder against her. His skin was silky over the hard muscles. As he began to move, she lifted her hips to fit his rhythm. The next moments were lost in time as once again they found the cadence of lovers, the movement of the seas and skies, and finally the explosion that was the reward.

She wasn't sure how much later she came to herself recognizing they were still linked together and his body was again hardening. His eyes met hers as he again began to move. "You are home to me," he whispered, "and I will find a way to make this work for us. Somehow, somewhere, someway. I know it's not now, but it will happen."

In the morning, before they went for a horseback ride, Jed had another mission. "I heard of a breeder for the kind of dog I need. Want to come along?" Of course, she did.

"What kind of dog?" she asked as they walked west up the street.

"The breeder came by ship with the idea of bringing a tougher cattle dog to our country. You know a dog would be good for you too."

"I don't have a place for a dog," she said firmly.

"You live alone. A dog would give you warning if there was trouble."

"I'd have to fence my yard to keep it in."

"Tie it up for awhile. Some dogs won't leave their home once they get used to it being home."

"I'd have to walk it," she said thinking of a new objection. "I don't know anything about dogs. They bark too, might irritate the neighbors."

He laughed. "I am not going to insist. Just I think it'd be good for you." She liked walking with him, his arm around her and lost interest in doing anything but walking together.

"How big is a cattle dog?" she asked.

He put his hand down to around his knee. "Not much taller than that. If what I was told is right, these dogs will already be trained."

"Well I won't be getting one."

He hesitated a moment before he said, "I worry about you alone."

She laughed. "Seriously after you going off to war and now to a country with Paiute attacks regularly, and you worry about me?"

"When you go to war, you face an enemy you are expecting. I think you are taking life in your city too much for granted that it will be safe."

"I might have at one time, but not after what happened to you."

"There is another thing. In war you know your enemy. What if your enemy is a friend or a supposed friend?"

She sighed. "You mean Russell, don't you?"

"I can't prove it."

"I don't think he'd have ordered done to you what happened."

"He's been a friend to you. I know you don't want to think that."

"I will be watching though." She tightened her arm around him. "I won't assume I have been right about him."

"Good."

When they arrived at the modest home with a fenced pasture behind it, the breeder was the first Australian Raine had met, a tall, red-haired man named Austin Jackson.

"I'm a bit surprised ya heard of me," he said as he shook Jed's hand and nodded hello to Raine.

"The livery gave me your name. I am needing a tough cattle dog for a big job in rough country. Powell suggested your name."

"My dogs are tough, all right. What do you know about them?"

"Well I know the breed of cattle dog my father had in Georgia and that's about it. It sounds like these dogs have more toughness. The thing is the cattle I'll be going after will have been in the brush, fighting off wolves, grizzlies and every other predator. They'd laugh at a soft, polite dog."

Jackson chuckled. "Well these dogs," he said as they walked

out to look at the kennels, "were bred with dingoes. Know much about them?"

"Wild Australian dogs?"

"Exactly. Your cattle won't be laughing at my dogs. They are tough and won't take no for an answer. I have a question for you though."

"Go."

"Why are these of yours cattle in the brush, not getting regular care, for enough years to turn wild? If you're the kind of bloke who goes off and leaves his animals, ya might not be the man I'd want owning me dogs."

"I like that, you being a man who cares who gets your animals. Well you can decide it for yourself," Jed drawled, his southern accent even deeper than usual. "I fought in the Civil War on the side of the South. I came back when the war ended."

Jackson looked at him thoughtfully. "There a reason for that other than that drawl of yours?"

"My brothers were there is all the one I have."

"And you believed in the cause?"

"If you mean slavery, no I did not. Once you get into a war, survival is more the issue than causes."

"It's not like Australia has a lily white history in this matter; so I won't hold it against you. I supposed you'd be liking to see the dogs work?"

"I would."

Jackson went into the kennel and had a gray, white and black dog with a black circle around one eye when he came out. "This here is Ace and he's prime for what you'd be needing."

They walked out into the pasture where five steers were grazing at the opposite end. Jackson signaled to the dog and Ace took off in a flash, excitement showing in his movement and the gleam in his eyes as he left. In less time than it seemed possible, he had rounded them up and driven them back to the corrals by the house.

"Notice how he gives them the eye," Jackson said with pleasure in his voice. "He'll nip their noses if required. Cattle hate that."

"Impressive without a doubt. Of course, these cattle are used to going through the paces," Jed said as he leaned back against the corral fence and watched Ace work.

"I bring in fresh ones, but it's true, these aren't as tough as what he'd be facing out in the brush. You want to think about it?" He signaled the dog back to him.

Jed shook his head. "No, I don't have time for that. I'll buy him if we can work out a price. You wouldn't have a little female more aimed at a lady and for a home, would you?"

"I said I didn't need a dog."

"Happens, I have one," Jackson said with a grin as he called out, "Deucy, get yourself over here."

From the porch came a lovely little dog, smaller than Ace. Her coloring was reddish not black.

Raine knelt down and the dog came to her, nosed her and wiggled as she was petted.

"She also good with the cattle?" Jed asked.

"Not worth... anything," Jackson laughed. "She is scared of them, won't meet their eyes. I haven't been able to get her to bring back even a chicken. She's sweet natured though; and I'd have bred her to see if she could bring out a better son than she was, but so far, she hasn't taken. So she's not worth much to me at all."

Raine had been so sure she didn't need or want a dog, but this was truly a bright looking little animal with her pointed nose and alert eyes.

"If you don't want her, it's all right," Jed said as he squatted and looked the squirming little dog in the eye.

Raine sighed. "I shouldn't but... Yes, I'll take her... if we can work out a price."

They could and did. An hour later, they left with the two dogs on leashes. A dog was something she'd never imagined owning, but it would keep her company with Jed gone. She wouldn't need her for protection. She didn't look as though with her small size she'd provide much anyway. She did, however, seem to have a sweet temperament and took to Raine immediately.

By Friday night, Jed had taken Raine shooting and riding enough times that she was beginning to feel confident in her ability to handle Fancy and the gun. She had learned to saddle her own horse, understood how to deal with the stable for her care, and promised she would continue riding when she could find someone to go with her.

For all the things Jed had done to make her safer, she felt so annoyed she wanted to scream. He would never be the kind of man to let a woman make her own choices. As much as she felt the tension at his leaving again, of the risky situation in Eastern Oregon, the uncertainty of what he'd be facing, another side of her felt at last she'd have her life back. Even in the evening, he had said things several times that had her clenching her jaw against the retort she had been tempted to make.

As they entered her bedroom, he sat on the bed and looked up at her as she moved to her dresser. "All right," he said, "let's have it."

"What do you mean?' She didn't want to fight with him on his last night.

"You've been mad at me all evening. You think I couldn't tell?"

"So sensitive, aren't you," she said knowing her tone was snide.

She saw the muscle quiver in his cheek. So he was also clenching his jaw.

"You are trying to run my life," she said finally. "I know you mean well, but I don't appreciate it."

"I've tried to make you safer."

"I've done fine on my own."

"Have you?" he asked with a twist to his smile.

"What does that mean?"

"Russell Grayson and what about those porcelain lions?"

"Wait. You think some ugly lions mean I can't do a good job managing my businesses?"

"Did they sell?"

"Why yes, they did. So that proves they weren't such a disastrous choice."

He snorted. "Who bought them?"

"Actually two Chinese men came in, and they bought all four."

"Surprising."

"What does that tone mean?"

"Did it occur to you something was inside those statues?"

"Why would there be?"

"God, you are naïve," he said as he rose from the bed and walked to the window, staring out at the darkness.

She felt so furious it was hard to frame a cogent reply. "Tell me what you mean by that."

"Sugar, those vases were likely loaded with drugs."

She frowned trying to think through what he had said. "How could you know that?"

"I know the weight of porcelain. Those had something inside. What else would be worth bringing them up that way?"

She felt equal portions of rage that he would say such a thing along with a horror that he could be right. Had her business been used for smuggling?

"Why didn't you say something at the time?"

"It wasn't my business then."

"Well it isn't now either," she snapped. "I'm sure you are wrong." Only she wasn't. It would explain some other odd arrivals; but she'd been so busy thinking she was running a clean business, it had never dawned on her that anything was going on under the surface.

He turned back and tried to take her in his arms, but she pushed him away. "Jed, I don't want you to hold me tonight."

"Why?"

"Because. I'm angry with you, and I don't want to make love when I feel that way."

"It could be a long time before we can be together again."

Obviously being angry with her hadn't dampened his ardor even though it was clear he was angry also.

"It would be better if you didn't come back," she said finally.

"Why? Because I speak my mind? Because I tell you when you're not thinking clearly."

"That and beyond it that we cannot work this out. It's impossible between us. What we had is all we can have, and it's not working for me."

"All right." He took a deep breath and let it out. "I'll sleep on the sofa downstairs. If you change your mind..."

"I won't," she said stubbornly wanting to cry and glad he'd not be there to see her do it.

He picked up his bag, which had been packed, and went out the door, closing it softly.

She wanted to scream. She wanted to drag him back. She also knew this is how it had to be. She would have no man dominating her life. Jed would do it whether he wanted to or not. In the morning she'd manage to say good bye with a smile and a friendly wave. Tonight, she'd cry.

In the morning, right after breakfast, Jed was outside when Josh rode up with their horses and two pack animals. Ace had the energy of a working animal and was eager to take off. Jed stood by his horse, his arm over the saddle, gaze intent on Raine when she came out forcing a smile.

"You sure this is how you want it?" he asked.

She nodded, hoping she could hold back the tears until he left. "It's right for both of us," she said. "I wish you all the best. You know that."

"Yes, be happy, Raine."

"And please take care of yourself," she said. "I read something more about the Indian trouble getting worse."

"I've been through one war. I can handle another, if it comes to that. I hope it won't." She moved backward wishing she could throw herself in his arms, but it would only delay what had to be. "Can I ask you one favor?" he drawled.

"You can ask."

"If you have trouble here, you get word to me. If you need to leave Portland fast, head for The Dalles. Send word down with someone. I'll come for you."

"There won't be a problem."

"Maybe." He didn't sound convinced. "Take this too." He handed her a piece of paper. "It's the map to my ranch in case you can't wait for me to come. Don't lose it. Hire someone to take you though. Don't try to get out there by yourself. I know you don't agree with me about this. This is for just in case."

He was doing it again, trying to manage her life, but she held onto the paper. "All right," she promised knowing it wouldn't come to that. This was goodbye for them. She watched as he mounted his horse.

"I heard what you said last night. I do understand more than you think." His jaw was tight. "Know this-- you're important to me." When she said nothing, he swung Midas around and gave him a kick in the side to take off with Ace racing ahead and Toddy and Josh following.

Before heading for the ferry, Jed decided, for his own peace of mind, to have a talk with Han Jei. He asked Toddy and Josh to wait for him at the dock as he headed to the waterfront to learn where he could find him. His surprise came that his office was in an upscale building—not right on the waterfront.

Once ushered into the office with Jei, sitting behind a desk and rising to shake his hand, Jed quickly got to his purpose. "I am leaving Portland."

"Probably wise."

"Wise or not, I have to go. My ranch requires that, but I am concerned for Raine."

"Wise also."

"I am asking you to watch out for her as much as you can."

"I suppose, if I wanted to, I could do that... but why don't you take her with you?"

"Kicking and screaming all the way?" Jed suggested with a wry twist to his smile. He didn't find the image humorous.

"I suppose not. What makes you think I can watch out for her?" Jei asked with speculation.

"Because I know character. You are a man of power here, aren't you? It's what enabled you to find me."

"I have some meager amount."

Jed snorted. "At any rate, if nothing else, warn her if you believe she is in danger."

"That I can promise." He rose. Almost as tall as Jed, he reached out to shake hands. "You will owe me again," he reminded Jed.

"I pay my debts."

"I assumed that also." Jei grinned with more humor.

"You really going to leave her behind?" Josh asked as they arrived at the dock for the ferry that would take them, their horses, and mules across the Willamette.

"Like I had a choice?" Jed said coldly staring off toward the mountains.

"You've been four years gone. You could wait another week."

"She made it clear she doesn't want anything to do with me."

"That woman moved heaven and earth to pull your fat from the fire. She went to a woman she sees as an enemy to get to you."

"Likely would've done it for anybody," Jed said clenching his jaw.

"You know that's not true." Jed did not answer. "You should

have married her," Josh said.

"I asked. She said no."

"You dreamed of her all the way through the war and now you walk off without fighting for her." His brother's voice dripped cynicism.

Toddy, who had been listening without comment, said, "Better off without getting married. Wives always want something that a man can't deliver."

"You been married?" Josh asked as the boatman helped load the horses.

"Twice."

"Jesus Christ, you been a busy man, Coen," Jed said.

"Wow, two women." Josh's tone was dismayed. "I haven't had one. Not full time anyway. Not likely I'll find one out there either." He gestured toward the mountains. "Not going to be a lot of women in the wilderness where we're heading."

"Did I say it was just two. Two weddings though."

Jed listened to the two discuss women. He forced his own mind away, trying to think what he had to do at the ranch, anything but think about Raine. They fell into silence watching the east bank grow closer. Once over, they unloaded their animals, paid the ferryman and mounted.

"So how many women were there?" Josh asked.

"Like I'd be counting," Toddy said. "They all kind of blend together after awhile into one woman—who wants more than I earn, never is satisfied with who I am, always wanting change, nagging. Want you here. Want you there. Nagging is the absolute worst of it. Finally a man just says, that's enough, I'm gone."

"Two divorces," Josh said as the three of them rode toward the east.

Toddy gave him a look. "Did I say there was a divorce?"

"God," Josh said shaking his head. "What I really want to know is what makes you so desirable to women."

"I don't know-- except one thing. Whatever it was before they got me, it's not the same thing afterward!"

CHAPTER 9

Nancy agreed to look after Deucy while Raine packed her things for her trip to Oregon City. She stopped first though to speak with Agatha, not that she expected that to be pleasant even though it sounded as though Russ had managed to take the main weight off her without knowing it.

Agatha was sitting in the parlor when Raine was ushered in by her live-in help, Shirleen.

"How are you?" she asked as she sat opposite her on a stiff upholstered chair.

"Like it matters to you," the old lady chirped with a frown.

"Of course, it matters."

"You haven't been to see me in over a week."

"I have been busy."

"So Mr. Grayson told me. He said you had a man."

"That's hardly the case."

"You ain't getting married?"

"No, I am not. Russ was out of line even to mention such a thing. He certainly hadn't been told it by me."

"He tell you he is buying me out?" She gave Raine a sly look.

"Yes, he did. I hope he's giving you a good price."

"Like you care," she whined as Shirleen came back in with a pot of tea and two cups.

Raine debated how much to tell Agatha about her growing distrust of Russ's motives. Jed's warnings about the imported porcelain figures had just added to her feeling something was badly wrong with Russell Grayson's enterprises. Agatha was well out of them.

Saying anything though was likely not smart. Knowing Agatha, whatever she said was likely to go right back to Russ. She would have to hope the old woman was wise enough to protect her own interests. She would take the added precaution before she headed for Oregon City of sending a letter to James Collins, Agatha's son, to be sure he understood the situation without adding gossip that she couldn't prove.

"I am taking the steamship to Oregon City on a buying trip as well as to visit Mama. Want me to find goods for your store?"

"No, I'll leave that all in Mr. Grayson's hands now. The papers should be signed tomorrow."

"Did you get a fair price?"

"He wouldn't cheat me," she said with a confident nod of her head.

"Well... it's always wise to check several potential buyers and even a lawyer to be sure the price is right for today."

Agatha snorted. "Mr. Grayson's lawyer will do it for free."

"Agatha, that's really not very wise. You should have your own. His lawyer will be protecting his interests."

"Fiddlesticks. It'll be fine. You are just mad I am selling."

Raine smiled. That was her Agatha. "No, I think you're wise to sell and relax a bit. I will come by when I can."

Agatha studied her a moment then. "I... well I'll be glad of that, Loraine."

As Raine left, the two women hugged. She didn't feel comfortable with Russ anymore, but it'd probably be fine. He'd not cheat an old woman. Except if he had ordered Jed kidnapped, she wasn't sure what he'd do.

∼

Oregon City loomed out of an unusual, early morning, June fog. It seemed it was growing bigger every time she saw it. Some still thought it'd someday be Oregon's biggest city. Raine believed it would be Portland simply because of the obstacle of the falls above Oregon City, the cliffs that blocked easy development, and Portland's route to the Columbia and sea for shipping. Still one never knew.

When she disembarked, she headed for her mother's home. The walk wasn't that far, but she left her bags with the shipping office to retrieve later. She had brought along four bolts of rich material, some newspaper and magazine advertisements, with the hope she could inspire her mother or some of the women who sewed her designs to do something exciting that Portland would welcome. The salesman had probably been right. Portland was changing. Perhaps original ball gowns, inspired by the latest from San Francisco, would find a market with Portland ladies. Possibly even inspire a social change for the city.

At her mother's home, she sat at the big table drinking coffee, eating a muffin and listening to the latest news from the family. It all served to help her not think about Jed, about their argument, about where he might be.

"St. Louis seems to be fading," her mother said with sadness in her voice. "It won't be the same when he goes on."

"How old is he?"

"Not so awfully old. He's not even seventy. Maybe he's lost his zest for life or perhaps there is something wrong inside."

"He could come to Portland, stay with me, and see some specialists."

"We've suggested that. He has resisted that idea. If he changes his mind and is willing to talk to a specialist, it might be too late. You know how life is when you miss your chance." She gave Raine a look that she had seen too many times before.

Raine debated only a moment. When she had started for

Oregon City, she had believed it wasn't to talk to her mother about Jed. Suddenly, she knew it was. Explaining Jed though would not be easy. "I did have someone, Mama. It's ended but... well if you feared there'd never be anyone, there has been."

Her mother frowned. "Recent? Not that Russell Grayson, I hope. I didn't want to say anything. Well wouldn't have, but Adam had a few words to say about him after we left Portland."

"What?" she asked without answering the question.

"Portland has a crime organization. I guess you know about that."

"No, I did not. I mean, I know there are crimes that happen on the waterfront but... actually an organization?"

Her mother sighed and poured them more coffee. "There has not been enough evidence to bring it before the courts. And it's not just in Portland, but farther east in the state. Adam said that they appear to be coordinated by some sort of league or maybe an individual. The law has been looking for a connection that is concrete enough to do something. So far they have been too clever... or he has been."

"He?"

"It seems that your friend's name has been involved time and again. Some of his business enterprises look like fronts. The money that is flowing in cannot all be explained by his legal enterprises or should I say quasi legal."

"Russell?" Her mother nodded. "Why didn't Adam tell me when you were there?"

"Because, he's a sheriff and legally speaking there is no evidence. If there had been, there'd have been arrests. He only talked to Portland's police chief that last evening. Their discussion was private, of course." She sighed. "Even within the force there, not all can be trusted."

"Involving what kinds of crime?"

"Smuggling, robberies, even murders, and of course, the enslavement of men for ships that Clem explained that day. Too often, crimes like that are difficult to trace back to their source.

The thugs are caught, but they only know one level above them-- if that. People who might talk are killed, but Adam said he was told the one common thread appears to be tied to Grayson Enterprises. Eventually, they will tie it to him, and then they can move."

Raine rose and walked over to the window staring out through the trees to the river shining below. "I hate to think that but... Well I have had reason to wonder about Russell myself."

"I just thank God, that you're not in love with him."

"It might not be much better," she said with a small smile as she sat back at the table. Before she could find the words to explain Jed, Amy burst through the door and was hugging her.

"I was hoping you'd be here today. We had to come in for shopping."

"Where are the little ones?" She looked back at her mother and saw she was pulling mufflins from the oven. She didn't want to discuss Jed while Amy was there. Maybe she shouldn't discuss him at all.

"Elizabeth is with Matt at the store. Rufus and Laura stayed at the farm because St. Louis offered to stay with them. They didn't want the long wagon ride in and had homework to do anyway."

"How was he today?" Raine asked as Martha set about making more coffee.

"Better, I think. He seems to go up and down. I am not really sure what's going on. He says it's nothing."

"I was suggesting to Mama that he come up to Portland and have some tests—or even go to San Francisco for their specialists. Diagnosis and treatment is improving all the time."

Amy smiled. "He isn't likely to do either. He thinks it'll pass, and maybe it will. Mostly I think he needs something new to be interested in. As it stands, his adventures seem to be over. Sometimes old age seems sad especially for someone used to being so active."

"I will try to get up to visit him," Martha said. "Will you be staying for dinner?"

"No, we have to get back before dark." She turned back to Raine. "I am happy to see you again so soon. How have you been?"

From deciding she didn't want to tell Amy, Raine realized she very much did want to share with her sister also. She felt overwhelmed by the need to share Jed with her family. It made no sense since it was over and not a part of her future.

"Well, I was just telling Mama. I had someone in my life."

"Oh," Amy said, concern in her voice. "I hope it's not..."

Before she could go further, Raine interrupted. "You don't know him."

"Good. Not to say..."

"Yes," Raine said with a smile. "Not to say. His name is Jed Hardman... He and I met in 1861. It was only a month though before he left to go to Georgia."

"He's a Southerner?" Martha asked, modulating her tone with an obvious effort not to show disapproval.

"It's from where he came, and before you ask, he fought in the Confederacy."

Her mother sat down, concern on her face, but she said nothing.

"I guess... good people did that," Amy said. "If they hadn't read the newspaper articles about the... well, or Harriet Beecher Stowe, they might've."

Raine gave a little laugh. "Some fought who didn't have slaves nor believe in slavery and that was the case with Jed. He has a ranch out here, had it before the war erupted. He left because he got a letter from his mother saying she was alone and sick." She stopped asking herself why she was doing this. He was out of her life.

With their expectant faces, she needed to say more but how to explain something that she barely understood. She wanted them to know at the same time she didn't. She fought for the right words. "He... well he left to... take care of her or if she was well enough maybe he'd have brought her back to Oregon. It's not like he believed in the cause but..."

"You don't need to explain. I know how it can be," Martha said. "So he's back now and..."

"I don't need to, but I want you to understand. The long and short of it is he joined and fought alongside his brothers until two of them were killed. There is another brother, who is still alive."

"Who is still in Georgia?" Amy asked.

"Josh is here in Oregon now." She fervently wished she had never brought any of this up. How to explain. "Josh's father was Jed's father. His mother was... well, colored."

There was a silence. "Josh was a slave?" Amy asked finally.

"No. The plantation had no slaves. Jed's grandfather had freed them all. Workers there received salaries and were free to go or stay."

"Plantation. So Jed is wealthy?"

"I guess maybe. Not likely as much now as before the war. Josh's mother died with his birth. He was raised by Jed's mother as if he was her own son."

"Obviously she is a very special woman," her mother said.

"Was. She died shortly after Jed returned. You know, I think, despite what many believe here in Oregon, that there were good men on both sides of that conflict. Jed was one of those."

"So, let me see if I have this right. You are in love with him. But it's over?" Her mother smiled when Raine made a face.

She tried to think of words to explain why that was true. She was once again saved from answering when Adam, badge on his shirt, and still wearing his Colt on his hip, came in the back door. "I have to wash up. Glad to see you here, Raine. You too, of course, Amy." He kissed his wife's head, before he headed out of the room.

"Where's Eli?" Raine asked her mother.

"School-- although it's almost out for the season. Then I don't know what I'll be doing with him. That boy has so much energy."

"Before we get interrupted again," Raine said. "I don't even know why I told you about Jed. He has a ranch on the John Day River, miles from Portland, not an easy trip. I have the stores to manage. How would it work, even if there weren't other problems?" How could she explain that the sacrifices her sister and mother had made for love, she was unwilling to make?

Amy gave her a look but said nothing. Her mother smiled before she said, "We can talk more about this later. I think I hear Eli on the back step... He'll suck all the energy from the room, but we will talk again on this." Her smile broadened as her son entered at a run. "One more day," he yelped before his mother reminded him to go wash up.

When the three were alone, Amy pressed Raine's arm. "You know when people are in love, they can work things out."

Raine managed a laugh. "You are still so in love with your husband that you really don't have a clue that there can be barriers that simply don't make it work."

"I don't?" Amy said with a snort.

"It was different for you. You married Matt so young. You didn't have anything else you wanted as much."

Amy gave a little laugh. "Oh Raine. Tell me, do you love him?"

"Love isn't everything."

Her mother looked up as Adam entered the room, his weapon removed, badge gone, washed up, and a gleam in his eye that pretty well said it all. For some people perhaps love was enough. Raine knew she wasn't one of them. She and Jed had that gleam, but what they didn't have was a desire to live the same kind of life. She was right. It could not be, but that answer was not giving her any joy.

After Amy, Matt and Elizabeth had headed back to their farm and Adam had taken Elijah into the kitchen to do homework, her mother suggested she and Raine head to the garden to pick the last of the peas and carrots. Raine wished she had packed her boys pants, but pulled up her skirts and began crawling down the rows looking for carrots ready to be harvested.

"Tell me more about your young man, about the relationship you had with him before you decided you couldn't have one," Martha said as she sat on the dirt at one end of the row pulling weeds.

"It doesn't matter because it's over."

"Come down here, dear. We didn't come out here to pull weeds. We came out here for a talk, and I find such is always better in the garden where energy is growing around us."

Typical Mama, Raine thought, but she crawled to be closer. "So what do you want to know, but it really is pointless since it's not happening with him."

"Are you convincing me or yourself? Her mother smiled.

"Maybe both."

"Well, let's start with him. What is this man like?"

"I believe he's a good person," Raine said trying to think how to describe Jed. "He is honorable. Strong. From all I have seen, he tries to do what is right."

"Did you have letters from him while he was gone? Letters sometimes reveal a lot."

"No, he said he felt it would be unfair to hold me to him when he didn't know if he'd live through the war. I guess it was his concept of honor—the same thing that led him to go there."

"But then he was back."

"Yes. I always knew it wasn't possible between us. It probably wouldn't have gone further except, well that shanghaiing, it happened to Jed."

She had finally said something that brought a shocked look to her mother's face. "My God, and he was shipped off after just getting back from the war?"

"No, he got free... Actually I got him free after Jed's brother showed up at the house, telling me he was missing. The theory was that Bernice would be the key to finding him."

"Not the Bernice from the wagon train."

Raine nodded. "She runs a brothel on the waterfront."

"All right. that seems likely, And you went to her?"

"It was the only hope. There wasn't much time before the ship would be leaving with him on board. Then I don't know what we could have done to get him back."

"She never struck me as the helpful sort."

"Bernice is all about herself as usual. Between a threat from his brother and some money, she led us to a man who knew how to help. Han Jei. He was the reason Jed got away from the kidnappers."

"And the reason they chose him was..."

"My, you are quick to see the real issue. That is the question. He's not their usual target."

"All right," her mother sighed. "Tell me the rest."

"He had been drugged. It took some time, but he came out of it and... well one thing led to another."

"Youthful energy being what it is," her mother said with a smile. "And again without time to know each other first."

"Oh what does it matter? He's gone and won't be back."

"You're not pregnant?"

She shook her head. "No."

"So he ended it before he left for his ranch?"

"No, he wanted to marry me. I ended it. We had one thing going for us and that wasn't enough for a real relationship. Surely you see that, Mama."

"Of course. You chose to eat the frosting and skip the cake, then threw out the whole thing."

"What did that mean?" Raine asked with more than a little exasperation.

"In a healthy relationship, good sex is the result, not the only thing in it."

"I didn't say it was the only thing," Raine said defensively.

"Sweetheart, I don't want you to take this as a criticism. You know I am not a woman who goes by the rules—obviously. I am reading between the lines, but it sounds as though you and he jumped right into a sexual relationship without taking time to develop all the rest that makes for a lasting relationship. Now you tell me you ended it because something deeper wasn't there. How would you know?"

"What do you mean?"

"Loraine, I know you pretty well. The problem you are speaking about is not all about living in different places. I am hearing what you aren't saying."

"All right, it wasn't just that, but that's not minor. The thing is he wanted to run things. And I didn't want to do what you and Amy did. Give up everything for a man, any man."

Her mother laughed. "Is that what you thought we did?"

"It is what you did. I want to be independent. I don't need a man in my life and most especially don't want one telling me what to do."

"And you think that's what I do with Adam?"

"Isn't it? You gave up your life on the homestead for him because he wouldn't be happy there."

"My wonderful daughter, relationships aren't all that easy to see from the outside. You saw the spark we have. The spark that Amy and Matt have, but it's not all that is there. Why we live here isn't something cut and dried. While there is some truth that I left the homestead to come here, so he could be a sheriff. He gave up more to be a husband and father because the life he had led wouldn't work with a family. I didn't give up anything important to me."

"How can you say that? Your dream was the homestead."

"My dream was a kind of life. That can be had anywhere. I knew the elements I wanted in it. When your father asked to come west, I didn't really want that life either as such, but I believed I could make it good wherever I was, and I did. I had a dream too, but it was one that was flexible. I found the things that gave me joy, and I didn't have to make boxes to put them in."

"You think that's what I do?"

"Loraine, as my oldest, I know you as the practical one,

dotting all your i's and crossing every t. Sometimes that is good as when you made your business work, but it can cause you to miss the big picture."

"And I'm doing that with Jed?"

"I don't know that. I do know that love is not tidy. It's messy and deconstructs as much as it constructs. Then you put the whole thing together as something new. Just guessing now, but I think you went looking for things that would let you turn him down."

"Why would I do that?" she asked even knowing it was possible.

"Secure life. Comfort zone. Fear. I don't know. But consider this, you might've found that his life over there would suit you, and you'd find ways to do what you do in Portland. Or maybe he'd have given up the ranch and found something closer to Portland. I mean if you had wanted to try, you'd have found ways to compromise as Adam and I did."

"Then I agree. I didn't want to," she said with some resentment. Maybe she didn't fit the niche that so many others did. She wanted to find her own.

"Darling, love also isn't practical, and it does not fit into tidy slots," her mother said as though reading her mind. "It takes work, and when it's good, then the sex is the icing on that cake. You skipped the rest of it and thought the icing would be enough. You cheated yourself of the full experience."

"Oh, so I should just take off for the John Day River ranch he's got where he might not even have a cabin left as he said the Paiutes or Shoshoni might've already burned it?" she asked with frustration and a touch of irritation.

"Probably you don't need to go that far right now," her mother said with a smile, "but open your mind to the possibility. How about that?"

"I don't see how it is possible. I didn't know you had become a moralist about sex outside of marriage."

"And I am not. It's not the marriage that matters so much, not the piece of paper, but the relationship with that person that goes soul deep and is way beyond the good feelings when the sex is good."

"I'd be away from all of you if I went to his ranch," she argued. "I'd miss you—even if I thought I could live with his pushy ways."

Martha sighed. "And we'd miss you although you aren't as far from us as we were from our families when we left Missouri for Oregon."

"Your parents were dead."

"But I left where they were buried, all I had known, my friends, other relatives, and unlike your situation, I knew I'd never be back. Where you would be going, we could come, and you could visit. It's all changing so much that it'll be easier and easier."

"You make it sound so simple," she said tearing apart a piece of pigweed that she held in her fingers.

"It won't be. Neither would be having a real relationship with any man. More complex with him. His being a Southerner won't make it easy so soon after the war. Then there is the Indian trouble, well I have been reading about that, but what I fear is if you try to skip over the work of this relationship to something you think will be sweet, the sweet will sicken you in the end and not because sex is wrong. You just need to mix up that cake batter, put in the ingredients, then bake it, let it cool before you put the frosting on."

Raine laughed as she ripped the weed to shreds. "You make it sound like cooking and just a matter of following a recipe."

"There isn't one recipe. Sorry if I made it sound that way. It wasn't simple for your father and me. It's not for me with Adam now. It's work. It's constantly mixing in new ingredients. I remember my own doubts about Adam. More because I was older, older than you are now. I had gotten set in my ways too. I didn't know where going with him would take me. I'd be the last one to claim it's easy." She reached out and drew Raine into her arms. "Don't feel you have to decide all this right away. This is too important to your life."

"It's too late anyway," she said with a feeling of sadness at the knowledge. She had turned him away, turned him down. He would not be back.

"I don't know if it's too late with him, but you can develop more of you if that should be so. Then when the next right man comes along, you will be ready, not so frightened of what it might take, and instead look at what it might bring."

Raine thought about that. She didn't have the answers for any of it now. But she did have something else she needed and that she could get. "I have another thing I wanted to ask," Raine said as they both dabbed away tears.

"Go for it."

"It is a recipe. I'd like the names of some of those herbs. You know the healing ones. The ones I didn't think I'd ever need but now... Well, can we maybe discuss that, and you show me the right ones in the garden here and what they do?"

Her mother smiled. "I can, and I have something for you. It has waited until you asked. I wrote down all that I know, the dosage, the preparation. Each book was intended for one of my girls but only if they asked."

In the house, she handed Raine a small journal with drawings of plants and their uses. "I'll never learn all this," Raine said feeling perplexed at the little attention she had paid to flora.

"Take your time. Use the drawings, their descriptions and when you are in the woods or meadows, begin to look around."

"It looks confusing. Like I'd do better if you were beside me."

Her mother laughed. "I have an idea." She led Raine into the kitchen and opening a cupboard, she began pulling out sacks, considering as she went. "I'll give you some of my stores. We'll label them now. I did give instructions in the book how to gather your own and then store them, but this will give you a start..." She hesitated and smiled more broadly. "Just in case, you are going to a new place where the plants might be different."

Humming a little, she began filling small sacks and writing on them what was within.

"I hope I can remember all this."

Her mother handed her a cloth bag. "This is comfrey roots. They are good for wounds. Comfrey has been used for thousands of years. It will help reduce inflammation and heal. If you need to use comfrey, the leaves can be used also. I've dried and powdered the root. Sprinkle it on clean cuts... or worse."

"And I clean the wound how?"

"Alcohol if you have it. Get out any foreign material, pour it over it."

For the next hour, she was given a crash course in herbal remedies like willow bark to lower fevers and dried feverfew leaves to reduce headache pain. As her mother sacked some of each variety, she explained their use. "It's all in the book," she repeated.

By the time she left for the ferry, Raine knew she had given away her intent to herself as well as to her mother. Her path in life wasn't so set as she might have wanted to think. She needed to figure out what she really wanted. What was she accomplishing, and did any of it matter? When she had hugged her family good-bye, she knew only one thing. She was heading toward an unknown future.

CHAPTER 10

After four days travel along Indian trails over the mountain, Jed, Josh and Toddy reached the end of the timbered country, seeing ahead of them a new landscape. To Jed, it felt like coming home, but to the other two it was strange with junipers, rock formations, sage, and rivers in rocky gorges.

They camped that night in the rocky shelter of a grove of junipers. Ace was thrilled with the scents and circled the camp, always staying within voice range when Jed called. When they had the campfire going, Josh asked, "So is this what your ranchland looks like?"

Jed shook his head putting the coffee pot on the rocks at the edge of the flames. "It is a mix but a little is like this. There are meadows along the river, some of which I will need to expand for more winter graze. Then this kind of country until it gets higher, with the upper elevations covered with tall pines... or it's how it was when I left."

"What would change it?"

"Forest fires can. I have no idea what to expect after four years and no word."

"And the cattle will be where? Assuming there are any?"

"I expect them to be in the pines this time of the year. Grass is good there in the summer, cooler too."

"Assuming the wolves or the Injuns didn't get them," Toddy said watching the fire as he stirred the can of stew he had opened for their evening meal. Some cook, Jed thought with a smile.

"Mine are longhorns. They can fight off the wolves except the weaker or older. Calving is the risky time. They'll have done that a few months back where they can hide out in the brush, not the tall timber."

"You make them sound intelligent," Josh protested. "I don't remember cows being all that smart in Georgia."

"Longhorns are a different breed. They were born into country with predators and learned to deal with it. Ace is the one who'll have to learn to watch out for them." He petted the dog as he came over for a piece of a jerky.

"Jed, you always been an optimist," Josh protested.

Jed chuckled. "Maybe I was, but less so after the war and then what happened to me in Portland. But why not think positive and work toward what you want. That's all that gets a man anywhere." He wondered then if he had pushed Raine too much. Had he tried to dominate when he should have listened? It was hard for him to think about it objectively, given the pain any thought of her brought.

Toddy grumbled-- his words not distinct enough to interpret. "And your opinion is?" Jed asked as he poured them each a cup of coffee. He put his own down to roll a cigarette, taking a satisfying draw on it, as he leaned back against a big rock, one knee bent.

"Just this seems like a lot of work and even more uncertainty."

"Still time to turn around, Coen."

"I won't do that. I'd just like to see how we're going to do this. Just the three of us maybe in all that rough country bringing in cows that don't want to come with just a little dog."

Ace gave him a look that said he understood more than he should have about the putdown he had just been given.

"As I said, you can come or not. Right now, it's not that many days back and through safe country. Make up your mind."

"I will come. I'd just like to know it's going to work out."

Jed drew on the cigarette, pulling the smoke deep in his lungs. "I won't have a man with me who feeds disgruntlement. You either are with me on this, or you will be turning around—want to or not."

The rotund man sipped his coffee. "It's in my nature."

"I can live with a complaint once. Will even think about it. If it goes beyond that, that man is not going to be part of my spread."

"All right. All right. I'll work on it. But it's a genetic tendency, I want you to know."

Jed smiled thinking he had to watch his pushing where it came to not just Raine. "As for your concerns, well I have in mind picking up two men on our way."

"Miners aren't going to go to a ranch for less money than they can make digging for gold. You'd be wasting your time."

"Not to mention going out of my way. No, not miners. They are Wasco."

"Indians?" Toddy looked up with disbelief.

"Part of the Confederated Tribes of the Warm Springs now."

"I don't get it. Injuns are what we'd be fighting over here."

"Not all of them. They settled their differences with the government and worked out a good piece of land for their reservation. They are some of the best horsemen I know, not to mention know how to log if that comes to be what we need in building a new cabin. They've been rounding up wild horses and breaking them for a long time. Working cattle is second nature to them."

Toddy looked with disbelief. "How do you know all this?"

"Remember, this isn't my first trip to Oregon. I bought that ranch two years before the whole thing with the Civil War blew up. They'd ride through, sometimes looking for work. I hired the Kalama brothers. They might not be available, but they will likely know some who will. They won't stay all the time, as they have tribal obligations too, but they can be a big help in round-ups as well as drives when we get to that point."

"Bejesus. I never figured you'd thought this far ahead," Toddy said with disbelief but now a beginning smile.

"Why'd you come if you didn't?" Jed asked studying the older man.

"Didn't have anything better to do and to be honest, I thought at least, from what I've seen of you two, it wouldn't be boring." His grin broadened as he began to dish out the stew.

As they ate, Josh said, "What about Raine?"

"What about her?" Jed had just managed to force her from his mind.

"You just going to let that woman go?"

"For now. Not like I have a lot of choice. And since when did you get to be a romantic?" Jed shook his head.

"Not one, but I saw the two of you together. She'd make a good wife for you. She's the kind of woman a wolf needs."

"Maybe so but I wasn't the kind of man she needed."

"Come on. We could use a woman on the ranch, and you know it. You want to eat canned stew the rest of your life?"

Jed laughed but with little humor. "What makes you think Raine can cook? She had a woman doing it for her."

"Just a feeling I got."

"Maybe you're the one ought to head back and court her."

Josh gave him a big smile. "Might be, if you blow it, I will. Wonder if she likes the color black. We make good lovers. Wonder if she heard that."

When Jed glared at him, Josh laughed. "Don't worry about it. Somebody else will have snatched her up by the time I can get back there."

Jed was all too aware of that. She was a beautiful woman with a lot to offer a man. It was only amazing she hadn't already married. He didn't intend to tell his brother, but he knew he would go back. He would try again. Maybe find a gentler way to court her. He wouldn't give up until he knew he had to. First, he had to know if he had something to offer her.

~

Back at her home, Raine had brought back a lot to think about as Deucy jumped on her with delight at her return. "Down girl," she ordered, surprised when the little dog obeyed.

"I've been working on her obedience around the house some," Nancy said. "She's a prime little one."

"I've not had much experience around dogs, but she does seem sweet."

"How'd your trip go?"

"The ladies liked the fabrics, even those I wasn't so sure about," Raine said. "The dresses I brought back with me should find interest here once I get them ironed and can show them in the shop. Overall it was a profitable trip."

"How was your mother?"

"Busy as always."

"She's a prime lady too."

"That she is," Raine said as she contemplated again the things her mother had told her. "Mama gave me some of her herbal remedies and a book explaining how to use them and how to grow or gather them myself."

"She does know them. She suggested chamomile tea that sure helped my stomach," Nancy said.

"It seems to be a long tradition in my family with one generation after another teaching what they knew. I hadn't really thought I'd need to know any of it... until after this last experience."

"Can't hurt none, and it's not like doctors know it all."

Raine sighed. "There is so much to learn. I started trying to look at the drawings and instructions on the trip home. None of this comes natural to me."

"Maybe it wasn't for Martha either, but she just began earlier."

"She tried telling me. Oh well, I will see what I can learn. Some of it we can grow in the garden."

"You ain't got a garden," Nancy reminded her.

"Well I guess maybe I should by next year." That is if she was still here.

Nancy grinned but said no more as she headed for the kitchen to work on dinner. Raine sat in the parlor petting Deucy and thinking about the other things her mother had said, the ones she wasn't ready to talk to anybody about. Eating icing indeed, she rarely even ate sugary foods...

Going into the kitchen to help Nancy with dinner preparation, Raine knew she was doing it partly to avoid thinking about Jed. Had she really been trying to take a shortcut to something where there were no shortcuts?

With the Kalama brothers added to his party, Jed arrived at the ranch relieved to find the house and barns still standing. Coming out onto the porch, with a rifle cradled in his arms, was a heavily bearded Jack Grimes. His beard had turned white in four years. "Wal, I'll be jiggered," Jack said with a grin when he recognized Jed. "What all ya got there?"

Jed dismounted, stretching to get out the kinks after the long ride they had made their last day. "Jack Grimes, Toddy Coen, and this is my brother Josh Hardman. I think you might remember Joe and George Kalama."

"Shore do. Glad to see you all. Damn, it's been a long time, boy."

"I had a few things to do."

"I got a pot of coffee on, You all want some?"

"How about you unload the packs to the kitchen, and we'll

take our horses to the corrals. I won't let them loose until they are more used to it here."

"Dang, got any bacon with you? Been a long time since I had bacon."

"We do. Looks like you've been living on short rations. I sent money."

"I got it a few times but hard to get away with things as they been. Always beef to eat." He grinned.

"All right. We'll talk when I get back."

As he walked down to the barns, leading Midas, he saw that only one corral was in good shape. No cattle around the house or barns but that was to be expected. Two horses in the pasture below the house.

"You got a bigger house here than I figured," Toddy said as he unsaddled his horse.

Throwing his saddle over the fence, Jed looked up toward the house. "Guess so. I don't think much about it."

"More like a lodge, damnitall."

Josh laughed. "You should've seen the one in Georgia, and you'd know why he didn't think this one was much."

In the house, the first thing Jed to check required him to take the steps from the great room two at a time. Upstairs there was a walkway. At one end were two bedrooms, one for the master and one for the mistress of the home. He walked into the one intended for Raine, satisfied to see that the furniture he'd had shipped around the Horn had arrived undamaged. A door connected to his bedroom. On a simpler dresser, his mother's fine jewelry was in a box and nothing was missing. He went to his saddlebags and brought out a small box, which he put with the rest of the gems.

With some trepidation, he opened the floor to ceiling cabinet. Smiling, he saw the sword and its sheath. Folded neatly below was his kilt. Its plaid that of his clan. The sword had belonged to his great great grandfather and had been used in the Scottish war against the British. It was of the finest Toledo steel. He lifted it, hefting its weight and felt satisfaction at the feel in his hands. He had taken the risk to ship it around the Horn but had had concern over its arrival more than anything else.

Stripping out of his clothing, he put on the kilt and short boots that went with it. The day was warm enough that he didn't bother with a shirt. He picked up the sword and walked downstairs.

"What's up?" Josh asked as he came into the kitchen.

"A little ride. I'll be back."

"Want dinner?" Toddy asked not seeming surprised to see Jed wearing the kilt or at the sword.

"In two hours." He took one of the Henrys from beside the door and headed out to the corral for his stallion. Except for his desire to take the rifle, he'd not have bothered to saddle Midas. He trusted the sword as a weapon. He'd been taught from child-hood how to wield one, but at a distance, the rifle was a better protection.

Ten minutes later, he had ridden to the other side of the hill where he could see the river and his pastures. He ground reined Midas and taking his sword walked up the ridge. Sword in his hand, he knelt and looked to the sky.

"Whatever being rules this land, be it the one from my ances-tors or a new one," he said smiling as he considered his words. "I am grateful to return when I thought I never might. I am grateful for the stewardship I have been granted of this land. I will prove worthy of it. I claim this land in the Hardman name. I will prove worthy of that name and the heritage of this sword.

"While I live, I will hold true to the promise I have made. Land is sacred and the care of it is a responsibility, not a gift. I swear my oath to do all I can to be worthy of the land and my family past and yet to come, to all who rely on me for their lives."

He didn't end with the more traditional amen as he rose. He smiled though as he knew those on the other side understood.

An hour and a half later, sitting in his kitchen, Jed had changed back into pants, shirt and boots. He looked around the room. It was not in bad shape although it did look as though it was the home of a bachelor. Taking the coffee cup Jack handed him, he said, "Where is Jessup?"

"No good, didn't even last a year. He said he was taking off and hoped to get rich. Not like he will without working for it and he didn't much cotton to working when he could get out of it."

"He nearby then?"

"Said he was heading to Canyon City, ain't seen him in two years. Not sure though as seems like seasons go by here and hard to say how long anything's been."

"Any cattle still around?" He rolled a cigarette.

"In the hills. Mostly I seen 'em but ain't had a way to bring them down and maybe just as well. When the Walpapi or Shoshoni come by, they don't see nothin' and they ride on."

"I hear that might change," he said as he lit the cigarette.

"Heered that too. With the military back from fightin' that dang blamed useless war, most likely it'll heat up, all right. Lots of digging up the earth, wagons comin' and goin'. Makes the Injuns nervous. Don't much like more folks heading into their country. No siree."

"I thank you for sticking it out, for getting the goods I had shipped to The Dalles. I appreciate it. There will be a bonus for your loyalty."

"No need."

"There is on my end."

"This here's your brother, huh?" he said looking at Josh curiously. Jed grinned as did Josh, not surprised at the response. "And the fat one, him a relation too?"

"Hey, I'm not fat," Toddy protested. "Pleasingly plump they call this."

Jack cackled. "You call it what you want. I call it fat."

"Toddy signed on with us in Portland."

"You been to Portland first?"

"I had something to attend to." He wished that he had done better at the doing of it.

"Then you heard about the road agents west of us?" Jack asked.

"Only a little. What's that about?" Jed got up and walked to the window to look out at his land. It appeared, want it or not, he would have his own war to fight. At least this time, he had something worth fighting for, and it was a fight he knew how to wage. He wished he could say the same about winning Raine's hand.

"Just ruffians, holding up the stage and yeah, we got a stage line now, one of 'em goes by Monument, delivers mail even sometimes anyway. The dang blasted road agents seem to know when there's anything of value on a stage. Gotta have connections in Canyon City, The Dalles, or both."

"They come this far east?" Jed asked.

"Not anything here of value or wasn't nothing they knew about anyways. Nah, ain't seen 'em up here. But go into Canyon City or up to The Dalles, and you can see the hard cases. Dangerous yahoos, looking for trouble and finding it too much of the time. It ain't been easy while you been gone. Ain't kept things up like I should've. I done my best though."

"I see that. We'll start with the corrals, get the chutes back together and then find out what's up in the hills. Toddy here is going to cook, Jack."

Jack looked at him curiously. "You know how to cook?"

Josh laughed. "He knows how to open a can."

After supper, the three of them sitting in the parlor, Raine heard a knock at the door that had Deucy running in circles and her wishing she had kept her new pistol downstairs. Opening it, she saw why Deucy was so excited and that she had nothing to worry about.

"Hello, Mr. Jackson." She ushered Austin Jackson into the parlor and introduced him to Clem and Nancy.

"How do, folks." Jackson said, "And please, Austin. I just came by to check on how my girl was doing."

"As you can see, she's healthy and happy. Would you like a cup of tea?"

"Wouldn't mind if I do," he said as he sat in the parlor while Nancy hurried to the kitchen for the tea.

"Is your friend Mr. Hardman still around?" Austin asked.

"No, he's gone back to his ranch with Ace."

"Have you heard from him?"

"He hasn't been gone that long," she said. Austin smiled but said nothing.

When Nancy returned with a tray and cups, Clem turned it down and poured himself a shot from the whiskey bottle. "Unless you'd prefer that?" Raine said as she hesitated in pouring the tea.

"No, tea is good for me. So Deucy is settling in well?"

"So it seems. I love her."

"Good, very good." He sipped from the hot tea.

"Oh wait, do you prefer it with milk as the English?" she asked realizing she knew little about Australian customs.

"No, I like it black, just as it is."

She realized then as he watched her, the small talk he insti-gated that Austin Jackson had not come because of interest in how Deucy was doing. He was a handsome man. Lived nearby; so courting would not be a problem if it went anywhere. The problem was her feelings. Only one man interested her-- the one she could not have.

When the tea was gone, and he had run out of small talk, he left. Nancy chuckled. "You got yourself another admirer."

Clem added, "From what I hear of him, he's a good enough young fella too. You could do worse."

"I am not looking for a man," Raine said in a tone that she knew was defensive. "It's not like everybody needs a man."

"No, they don't but it's shore sweet at night when the bed is cold," Nancy said with a big smile as she looked at Clem.

"Not sayin' ya need a man," Clem said, "but ya turned down the Reb. Ya ain't getting' no younger, Raine."

"And if I didn't have a man period, ever, nada, none, I'd be just fine," she retorted.

"You would, gal," Nancy said, "but you that shore ya don't want one?"

Raine sighed. The world was clearly against her.

"Why don't we see what your palm says," Nancy suggested.

"You are joking," Raine asked with disbelief. "You can't seriously believe in palm reading."

"Wal, it's not like it's some kind of for sure thing, but it can sometimes surprise you with what your palm shows. Want me to look?"

She smiled. Since she didn't believe, what difference did it make?

Clem gave a disgusted look at the both of them as Raine moved to sit in the chair next to Nancy's and put her hand onto the table between them. "Ya gals are plumb crazy," he said

Nancy gave him a confrontational look. "Don't ya be makin' fun of what ya don't understand." She took Raine's hand into hers and began studying it.

"I ain't goin' to sit around watchin' this," Clem protested.

"So don't," Nancy said, "take Deucy for a walk and let me concentrate."

With a snort of disgust, Clem left with the dog on a leash as Nancy frowned and ran her finger along the lines. "Some say the right hand is what a body is born with and the left what they make of it. Mostly there ain't a lot of difference."

"How did you learn to do this?"

"My gram taught me. She was one of the fey ones if "ya know what I mean."

Given her mother, Raine knew that quite well and let her hands relax, as Nancy studied first one and then the other.

"You have a long palm and nice long fingers, dear, which means attention to detail. Probably why ya done so good at the stores." She chuckled then. "The Venus mount. Now some don't believe in reading mounts, that's that there roundedness here. It means an affectionate person, healthy sex life too." She chuckled as Raine grimaced.

"Your heart line, well it's well developed. All of the lines actually. Oh my."

"Something bad, Raine asked.

"Not bad just interestin'. Your fate line seems to say to me that you might face a conflict in life. You are a strong willed woman. Not that I wouldn't have known that without the lines, but your will is pulled two ways. Two different fates maybe."

"So no answers." That wasn't a surprise.

Ya know these lines can change through life. Might be someday it'll look different. Palm lines don't always stay the same. Let's look at the love line. Well that shows one strong line. A person like this might marry once or maybe never, but it'd mean one strong love and only one."

"Sounds self-defeating," Raine said dryly.

"I don't create them, miss, I just read them."

Raine giggled along with Nancy.

When Nancy turned to her other hand, she said, "Not that much difference, which means a woman living her dream to me. But... there it is again-- two dreams or fates. And one love."

"Well at least there was one. How many do you have by the way?"

Nancy giggled again. "Wal actually there's three of 'em." She showed Raine her hand. "I had two afore Clem; so I am figurin' he's the last."

"Clem would be glad to hear that." She wondered if she would ever have the opportunity to see Jed's palms and look for his love line. "Isn't there a life line also?" she asked remembering a smattering of what she had been told about palm reading.

Nancy pointed out her life line. "A plumb long one. Looks to me like you'll live to be an old lady." Given how he lived his life, Raine wondered what Jed's line would look like.

"How many love lines has Clem got?"

"I ain't looked at his."

"Why not?"

"He won't let me. Said it's foolishness and that was that."

"Said what was foolishness?" Clem asked as he returned to the house with Deucy rushing over to Raine.

"You know what," Nancy said. "You won't let me look at your palm to see how many women ya had and will yet have."

"Don't need no palm for that. I ain't had none until you and ain't havin' no more neither."

"Never?" Raine asked with surprise.

"Life I led didn't make for stayin' in one place long enough, not that I cared neither. Now, I got time to stay somewheres and found the right woman. Sure don't need no other."

"But what if there is no love line?" Nancy asked with visible frustration.

"Like ya'd want to know that?" Clem asked.

"Wal, no but better I'd be knowin' it than not, ain't it?"

"I don't hardly see how. Ya'd be mad at me for a month or more and no thing I could say would convince ya." He saw the sad look and gave it up. "Oh all right. Damnation. Hyar. Go look and cry yore eyes out."

Nancy smiled the smile growing broader as she studied the strong, weathered hand. "Lines most everywhere," she said with a gleam in her eyes, "but only one where it should be." With that she stood up and gave Clem a kiss.

Clem gave a sigh of relief. "Damn but I still don't trust that rigmarole."

"It's mostly for fun," Raine said.

143

"Ya just wait and see," Nancy told her as she lightly slapped her palm. "It's goin' to be true."

"It's not logical."

Nancy smiled. "Who said anything about logic?"

"It's what everything is based on. Why should those lines have meaning?"

"I don't ask questions like that, gal. But I believe in something more than us. A plan if ya want to call it that. Maybe the palm just lays out the roadmap."

CHAPTER 11

In the morning, before Raine had finished ironing the new dresses for the shop, there was a knock at her door. She set her iron safely back on the stove, hoping it'd not be Russ, and then wasn't sure that would not have been better, as at her door were two of her neighbor ladies, whom she had barely seen in all the time she had lived in this house. Their dour expressions didn't bode well for why they'd come.

"May I help you?" Raine asked as she ushered them into the house.

"We have a concern for our neighborhood," the apparently eldest of the two said.

Raine frowned. "I am trying to remember your names. Mrs. Sheffield?"

The woman raised her chin and proudly said, "Yes, I am Jane Sheffield and this is Bertha Myers."

"Has there been crime here or... " She thought then of the shanghaiing and worried that kidnapping had found their neighborhood.

Before she could ask more questions, Bertha Myers, said, "It's about your business."

"How does that impact the neighborhood? My business is downtown."

"The one you are conducting here."

She felt mystified. "Ironing a dress? I don't see how..."

Bertha interrupted her. "Your business with gentlemen."

"There is no business with gentlemen happening here."

"You can hardly tell us that. We have seen the men coming and going."

"Clem? He works for me at the stores." Actually she had to think about whether that would change with Agatha's business changing. Would Clem go to work for Russ? She'd talk to him. Surely though it didn't matter if Clem was in and out.

"Not him. The rest. It is obvious you have been operating a house of ill repute up here, and we want it stopped or you out of this neighborhood. There are children here!" Bertha Myer's voice had risen with her indignation.

"You must be joking. I am not operating any such thing," Raine said-- shock mixed with anger that someone could think such a thing of her.

"That many men can't be coming honestly. We saw the tall one just last night."

Raine sucked in a breath to quiet her annoyance. "He came to see how the dog he sold me was doing."

That caused the two to look doubtful for a moment. "But the rest. There have been way too many gentlemen here for an honest woman."

"And not all of them white."

"Ladies, if I may call you ladies, I have had friends visiting, which I might again but it is clearly not your business. To reassure your weak minds, there are no dollars being exchanged, nor do I have an assortment of lovers."

"You were in that play. Everybody knows about theater people," Jane Sheffield argued.

"Apparently everyone does not. I am in an occasional play but hardly doing it regularly."

The knock at the door interrupted the next thing the ladies might've said. When Raine opened the door, it was Kirk Edmonton standing with his hat in his hands, a fine suit on his portly frame. Not great timing but by now Raine didn't much care what the neighbor ladies thought. "Please come in, Kirk."

In the parlor, she turned back to the ladies. "Mrs. Sheffield and Mrs. Myers, this is one of those theater people—Mr. Edmonton. Perhaps you have read his books. Sorry you had to leave and can't stay to visit"

The ladies gave her a disapproving look but walked to the door. "Just remember what we said," Mrs. Sheffield said.

"For about as long as it takes me to close the door," Raine responded.

"The neighborhood improvement committee?" Kirk asked when she turned back to him.

"but, of course. Would you like a cup of tea?"

"I would love that."

He sat at the kitchen table as she poured hot water into the tea pot and then set a plate of Nancy's sugar cookies in front of him. "What can I do for you, Kirk?" she asked as she sat across from him.

He reached for one of Nancy's sugar cookies munching on it with a smile of pleasure. "I did have a request."

'You may ask," she said remembering saying the same thing to another man not so long before.

"I wrote another play, wonderful, wonderful interaction with the characters, of course. I would like you to read it for any suggestions you might want to add as I value your insights. You will be my leading lady, of course."

She poured their tea with a realization that many of her own answers were falling into place—none of which would she be telling him. "For the next few months, I'll be out of town, Kirk. I can't commit to another play right now."

He sipped the tea. "I can't imagine anyone else playing Regina."

"I'm sorry, but I cannot do it."

"Is it your gentleman friend?"

She felt a suspicion she didn't like. "My, gossip does travel fast. Where did you hear about such a friend?" She wished she had not mentioned her plans. Whom could she trust in this town? She waited for his answer, knowing it likely would be a lie.

"Well it was Mr. Grayson, if you must know. It was just a casual conversation. I barely know the man, but it came up when discussing the next play, I think." His smile was easy, confident.

Raine felt a little like a butterfly looking toward a gilded web. She had a sudden realization that if she kept flying as she was, she'd never escape what she was only beginning to recognize as a trap. Russell Grayson's tentacles frightened her, not just for Jed but for herself. Russ's help with her stores, the plays, his constant courting when she told him no, and Jed's kidnapping. Was it all connected? She had to work to school her features, as the thoughts raced through her mind.

"You have paled," Kirk said sympathy in his voice. "Are you feeling ill, my dear?"

"I do have a headache. Please excuse me, and I am so sorry, but don't count on me for your play."

"Perhaps in the fall?"

He was probing for information. All of it asked very innocently, but was it? She would not make it easy. "I like that idea but find another leading lady for this one, Kirk."

"No one can play Regina but you." His insistence convinced her she was right about there being more here than met the eye.

"I will be gone at least two months as I plan a small vacation mixed with a buying trip. I think San Francisco. There is always the future for plays."

As she closed the door, after seeing him out, she was sure he had been lying to her. About how much? Was he going straight back to Russell? If so, had he believed any of what she'd said?

Walking back into the kitchen to finish the ironing, Nancy came in the backdoor with a sack of groceries. "My goodness," she said as she set them on the counter. "Is something wrong? You don't look well, Raine."

"Nancy, did Russell Grayson ask you to work for me?"

"Why... why would you ask that?"

"I'm just trying to determine how far his web has spread."

"Web? What a strange word to use. And no. I barely know the man, except for him visiting you. Is there a problem?"

"No, I guess not."

"What is wrong, Missy?"

"I have a bit of a headache and need to lie down." She'd do the dresses later. She turned at the door. "I might be going out of town for awhile, Nancy."

"Might?"

"Will."

"Alone?"

"Do you talk to anyone about me?"

"Just Clem."

"Where is he today?"

"I think downtown. You want to talk to him?"

"Yes, tonight. Both of you."

As she walked up the stairs to her room, Raine knew a part of her life was ending. She had no idea what that meant. She still wasn't sure about Jed, but she was of one thing. Nothing was as she had thought. She needed time to think and that meant getting out of Portland. She would not go to her mother and Adam. She needed to get farther away from Russell Grayson. For now, that would not be San Francisco.

She would go to Jed's ranch. Whether she would stay there, she was unsure. She would follow her mother's advice though and find out if there really was a relationship possible between them. If Jed no longer wanted her, she would think what to do next.

She thought about her businesses and realized she needed to

meet with Sharon in the morning. Her manager was competent and could run things for a time at least. She also needed to talk to her lawyer. Slowly she began looking through her closet and dresser to determine what she would take if she had to leave more abruptly than she planned.

~

"Things are rather falling apart, Russ," Kirk Edmonton said as he entered Russell Graham's inner sanctum.

"What in blue blazes are you talking about?" Russ asked as he poured two brandies.

Sniffing the liquor appreciatively before sipping it, Kirk sighed. "She turned down the play."

"Did she give you a reason?"

Edmonton's smile was sharkish, the one Russell only saw when the two were alone. "She lied to me. She said she was leaving on a trip, maybe San Francisco."

"That could be possible."

"Could but was not. She stopped trusting me as soon as I revealed my knowledge of a gentleman friend."

"Why would that have caused her to distrust you?"

"Apparently my only source could have been you. I admitted it's where I had heard but pretended you and I barely knew each other. I could feel her immediately close down. She's naive but not stupid."

Russell frowned. "She's also not irresponsible. She is not a woman who can simply take off. She has business interests, which she has taken quite seriously. Short of selling, which will take time, and I'll make sure it takes time, she can't just go running off."

"I hope you are right, but how can you really stop her from leaving after she sells, if that seems to be her inclination?"

"I'm thinking."

Kirk chuckled, genuine amusement in his eyes. "No shanghai-ing, I take it?"

"Don't remind me of that. It was your idea that we do that instead of kill him as I wanted. If I'd had his throat slit, he'd be dead and out of the way now."

"The body might've been found."

"Not weighted down in the Willamette for the sturgeons to eat. You wanted him shanghaied to satisfy your own twisted objectives."

"Mine are twisted are they?" Edmonton laughed. "I'll admit this much. You were right. We should have just had his throat slit, but you made a mistake that night when you couldn't resist taunting him."

"He couldn't know it was me. I disguised my voice."

"Of course, impossible." Edmonton chortled.

"What about you touching him?" Russell jibbed. "Like that was so superior an idea."

"So we both made mistakes. Although a hand is not so recognizable as a voice. I just wanted to. Oh never mind, you'd never understand."

Russell snorted as he got up to walk around the room. "We're crying over something that cannot be undone," he said with his usual dislike for going back over mistakes-- especially his own.

"So what will you do with her? She would not be easy to kidnap. She has family, friends, a woman who is well known in the city, a father who is a sheriff."

"There are ways to control someone."

"Drugs."

"Not that I'd prefer that." He stalked around the room feeling angrier, as he thought about it. "I put a lot into her. Had it all planned how it would be, what a perfect wife she would make, intelligent, busy with her little projects and making a lovely front for my main enterprises. The perks of which would keep her busy. Now she's throwing it all over for a loser like that Reb."

"You think it's where she'd go assuming she gets away before you can do something to... er dissuade her?"

"That or to her mother's. Either way I will find her. She won't find letting my investments become worthless as easy as she thinks."

"Nothing unpleasant, I hope."

"Hopefully not for long. Perhaps just long enough to make her forget the bounder. I don't want to turn her into an addict," Russ said with a smile as he lowered himself into his seat, contemplating his brandy. "I also don't want to break her spirit, just make her amenable to my plans. She liked me before. She will again when she has no distractions."

"And the Rebel?"

"Him I would enjoy breaking, taking him apart piece by piece. Men like him infuriate me as they stride through the world as though they own it."

"You and I both know that he's a wealthy and powerful man or was before the war. From what I can have gathered by a bit of sleuthing, he still is quite rich with assets here, in Georgia and New York. A man like that could cause us real trouble if he were so inclined."

Russell laughed. "You just want to keep his body intact."

"There is that," he said with a chuckle.

"He has no idea of the range of my power. I captured him once. I can again."

"He won't be so easy the next time."

"That will make it more satisfying." He walked to the window staring out at the street below his office, the people walking by, the wagons carrying supplies. It all was so excellent, and he controlled a great chunk of it.

"I have to say this, Russ. Raine is just a woman. While admittedly a lovely one, is she worth all that you are putting into this?"

"Nobody turns me down."

"Forget him then. Concentrate on her."

"Hardly. Without him showing up, I'd have had what I wanted

from her. I gave her time. I didn't pressure. I thought all it would take was more patience. Then he came along and botched it all. He owes me for that. Besides he'll be back for her. I know his type."

"The Calypso is gone," Kirk said smiling.

"I want to see him suffer, not send him off for someone else to enjoy that. I can break him. I know I can. He fought for the wrong cause. I can stir up anger about that. I can make him wish he'd never been born before I end his miserable existence."

"Do you really know who you are dealing with?" Kirk asked finishing off the brandy.

"Say what you mean, Kirk."

"I am not playing with words here. Not only is he rich, but a physically powerful man who did just fight in and survive a long drawn out war."

Russ cursed. "Wars are the expected. What I want for him is what he doesn't expect."

"Don't underestimate him. It could be the end of many profitable ventures for us both."

Russ snorted. "He's one man. What can he do?"

"I don't know, but I believe to underestimate him would be a big mistake."

"Ha."

By nightfall, Raine has packed a small bag. When her stepfather, Adam, had taught her to fly fish, a sport he loved, and given her a three-piece bamboo pole with a few reliable flies, she had thought of it as a lark. Now she tucked it in its sack into the bag. She put her mother's journal of herbal remedies, and the small stash of supplies alongside the pole. She laid out coat, pants, shirt, hat, packed one dress, a jacket, two nightgowns, and underwear. She put her deeds, a copy of the certificate of her birth from Missouri, and her bankbooks into the bottom of the bag.

Her choices indicated the change she was expecting. Was she crazy? Was she imagining things regarding Russell? Would this all blow over? In case it didn't, she was ready for whatever came. Taking only what would be necessary, she planned she could come back for the rest.

In the afternoon, she had gone to her shops and talked to Sharon about managing her store. Her lawyer agreed to end her lease on the second store. With a non-binding contract, the most she'd pay was a penalty if no one immediately picked up the lease.

She was uncertain how connected anyone was to Grayson Enterprises, so she stuck to this being a buying trip, along with a small vacation. She told them both how much she looked forward to being in San Francisco again. From them, she went to the bank, withdrawing enough funds to make her buying trip sound reasonable. In the morning, she would buy two tickets-- one for San Francisco and the other on a steamboat bound for The Dalles.

After they had eaten, she asked Clem and Nancy to come into the parlor. "I am going on a trip," she said.

"How long will you be gone?" Clem asked.

"I am not sure. But will you two manage the house for me, look after things?"

"What about Deucy?" Nancy asked of the dog who sat at Raine's feet.

"I will take her."

"Can you?" Clem asked.

"Yes, I can. I will be back, of course." Raine could see they were uneasy at her vague plans, but she was reluctant to tell them too much. She trusted them, but at this point, she had no idea to whom they might talk. She didn't want anyone directed to Jed's ranch. She fingered the paper in her pocket. She still was unsure how she would notify him once she was in The Dalles.

"I would love to take you both with me," she said honestly, "but it wouldn't be fair. I think it's best you have as little involvement with me as possible right now."

Clem's face twisted into a frown. "Cuz you figure I am an old man, not able to fight."

"Why do you expect a fight?" she asked uneasily.

"Cuz I know where you're goin', lady."

"Please, whatever you think, don't tell anyone."

"Who the hell do ya think we are?" Clem asked with some irritation.

"I'm sorry. I didn't mean to insult you."

"You don't care that much for us then?" Nancy asked with some tears.

"I care. Look. Can I send for you later if I don't come back soon or if... I find somewhere to stay where I think you both would like? I don't want to leave you. You are family to me, but right now it simply isn't possible, as I am unsure where I will end up."

"All righty, then," Clem said. "We'll come when ya send for us. And take care, Missy."

"How soon will you go?" Nancy asked.

"I am not sure, but I think in a few days. And if anyone asks about me, I will be in San Francisco." She handed them the cash she had separated out for them. "This is just to tide you over. If this should be longer, I'll send more."

"We tell anyone who asks that it's a vacation?"

"And a buying trip for the store."

"It's not where you're goin' though," Clem surmised. "Nor to Martha's."

"No."

After they left, she sat in the parlor sipping a glass of wine and thinking her life had gone from secure and safe to so risky she had no idea what was real. She didn't have to leave. Russ should be no risk to her and yet... she felt he was.

Before she could take her musings further, she heard a knock at the door. It was too late for normal visitors, which made her cautious in opening it until she saw Han Jei. Seeing Bernice following him, she wished she had not.

Inside, Jei turned. "We are leaving town."

"Why?" She saw the resentful expression on Bernice's face. The blonde was wearing a riding skirt.

"It's not safe. I promised your man that I would give you a warning. I keep my word. It's not safe for you either."

"You ruined my life." Bernice glared at Raine.

"Bernice, shut up," Jei said shaking his head. "I swear, woman, I do not know why I took you at all."

"Because you love me," Bernice suggested managing a weak smile.

"Not that for certain," he said coldly.

"Where are you going?" Raine asked.

"East and not sure where yet. Just a long way from Russell Grayson's organizations," Jei said.

"When are you leaving?"

"We stopped on our way."

"So quickly?"

"Do you understand anything of him?" Jei asked.

"More than I did."

"Then you know why it's tonight. Things have come undone. He is a man who wastes no time. I also am that sort of man."

Raine thought of her own plans. "Do you have time for a glass of wine?" When they both nodded, they followed her into the parlor and she poured the glasses.

"I was thinking of taking the steamer to The Dalles, myself," she said as she considered what Jei had told her. "I am trying to let everyone think I am going to San Francisco though."

Jei took a sip of the wine and laughed. "You think it will take

Grayson any time at all to figure out where you went? He likely knows already you are planning to go."

Reluctantly she nodded.

"Tomorrow could be too late for you too. We are going now under the cover of darkness. I paid the ferryman to take us across and not tell anyone."

Raine made up her mind. "Would you take me?"

"Why should we?" Bernice sniped, "you're why we're going."

Jei smiled. "She is a foolish one," he said to Raine. "And has no clue that this was going to happen eventually anyway for me. Russell Grayson knew my power in the Chinese community. He brooks no competition."

"You should take me because I can pay you. I am assuming you need money for wherever you end up—to get resettled."

Jei watched her thoughtfully as he sipped his wine. "How long would it take for you to get ready? There is no time. I hope you understand that this is not a pleasure trip."

"I need a guide, but I know where I am going. I can pay. We can buy supplies on the other side of the river."

"I arranged for those," Jei said still seeming to be considering.

"Please take me. I think I know how important it is to go now. I can leave in half an hour. My horse is in the stable. Jed taught me to ride before he left, and I have a good rifle. I can shoot. I won't slow you down."

"I can't believe you are considering this," Bernice petulantly told Jei.

"Jackson's stable?" Jei asked.

Raine nodded. "She's there under my name and hers is Fancy."

"Get ready. I'll get your horse."

An hour later, having left a note to explain her hurried departure but not who was guiding her, blankets rolled to make a bedroll, rifle in the scabbard, her revolver belted at the waist, two full canteens, and her bag tied onto the packhorse Jei had, Raine was sitting on her horse. Deucy patiently waited at Fancy's feet as they crossed the Willamette on the ferry.

On the other side, Jei told the ferryman. "If you tell anyone you took us, your life will be the one at risk."

"Don't worry none," the bearded man said, as he counted his money to be sure it was the correct amount. "I got no use for Grayson neither." He looked curiously at the dog, Raine and Bernice but said nothing as they rode their horses down the road.

"You didn't mention a dog," Jei said without rebuke.

"She's my dog. I had to bring her."

"Hope she's not the barking sort."

"So far not."

"She one of those cattle dogs, Austin Jackson's been raising and talking up?"

She found herself a little amazed at the breadth of Jei's knowledge regarding what was in Portland. "I guess she wasn't very good at it. Jed wanted me to have her."

"So long as she doesn't bark."

"Which road will we take?" Raine asked as she found the riding she had done made keeping up with Jei easier than she had expected. She was worried some about Deucy, but if she found the dog lagging, she'd bring her up onto the saddle with her.

"Barlow Trail. You are heading for the other side of the mountains, aren't you?"

"You know where. He gave me a map and told me not to come alone. Although," she glanced over at the still pouting Bernice, "I doubt he expected who it might be with me."

Jei chuckled, feeling of his revolver. "He had more idea than you imagine. He is one who thinks ahead."

"Heading into the wilderness and a cabin with no luxuries," Bernice whined. "I thought I left Indians behind when we got to Oregon. And I don't like traveling with a stinky dog." She gave Raine a meaningful look, which meant the dog wasn't the only one she disliked.

"Bernice," Jei said, "you can turn back whenever you want."

"I know better than that," Bernice said.

"Then quit moaning about it or wherever you go, it won't be with me."

Bernice shut her mouth but glared at Raine.

Jei kept them riding even when Raine had been sure he'd stop for what was left of the night. He made one stop to hoist the tiring Deucy onto the pack horse where she balanced herself and looked around with satisfaction.

It was on the edge of the wilderness before he directed their horses into a grove of trees and said, "We'll take a break here."

"I am so sore." Bernice groaned as she stiffly dismounted.

"It was necessary to get this far. We had to be beyond where we'd be seen in the morning," he said as he took care of his horse, Bernice's and the packhorse. Raine took care of Fancy, removing the bridle so she could graze on what grass there was as she put a loop around her neck to avoid her heading back for the stable.

Jei handed the women each two large biscuits. "No cooking this time," he said. "Tomorrow we can do better."

When Raine sat to eat, Deucy again at her side, Jei pointed to the revolver and holster belted to her waist. "You are a lot better outfitted than I figured."

"I can't take credit for it. It was Jed's idea." She fed Deucy part of the biscuits, which she eagerly gulped up.

Jei nodded approvingly. "He expected trouble."

"I didn't think he was right at the time. Obviously I was the one who was wrong."

"The world is not always what we expect," Jei said.

"If he's so smart, how'd he get himself shanghaied," Bernice observed with a mean smile.

"Bernice," Raine said, "you really aren't doing yourself any favors with the constant snide attacks. What's that benefit you?"

"Always so smart and superior, aren't you Loraine?"

"Obviously not as I got into business with Russell Grayson. That was anything but smart."

Bernice snapped her mouth shut. "Well that was my mistake too," she admitted with a growl of frustration.

Jei leaned back taking a cigar from his pocket. "Grayson came to Portland with a lot of ambition and a willingness to grow his operation one way or the other."

"I gather he's been smuggling in drugs and my business helped him do it," Raine said with a sour taste in her mouth as she thought of it.

"You figured that out, huh?"

"Not me. Again Jed. Damn that man," Raine said with a grimace as she took a drink from her canteen.

"Damn him for being right?" Jei laughed. "Just like a woman."

Raine saw the illogic of her position, but it didn't make her less annoyed.

"So where are we heading?" Bernice asked.

"For the John Day country and Hardman's ranch," Jei answered before Raine could.

"I don't want to go to a ranch in the middle of nowhere," Bernice moaned.

"So you can go to Canyon City," Jei said. "Should be a good market for whores with the miners."

Bernice turned her glare on him. "I don't want to stay in some nowhere town."

"A lot of men there and gold, Bernice," he reminded her, watching her through the smoke.

"I thought we were going farther east."

"We were."

"That means we're not now?"

"First we take Raine where she's going, and then I'll decide. You though, you can stop whenever you want."

"You and I both know Russ has as much control this side of the Cascades as Portland."

"You know more about his operations than I expected," Jei said contemplatively.

"Customers tend to talk and so do the girls. Nothing that can be proven, of course."

Raine swallowed back her fear as she petted her dog. "Maybe Jed's ranch isn't far enough for me to go."

Jei's smile was hard. "It will be far enough."

"What makes you say that? I know that Russ arranged to have him shanghaied and that when he had no real reason to do it. It certainly won't be better now with me taking off as I did."

"That's true," Jei said. "Grayson put a lot into you, didn't he?"

"So it seems," she said tightening her lips. "I was such a fool."

"He's good at the act except when he wants to show his true colors and those who see that either are working for him or don't survive to talk about it. Don't blame yourself. He's a clever man."

"So why is it not dangerous for Jed that I go there?"

"Three reasons. One Grayson will already have targeted Jed. He will go after him with or without you. Two, you can give him warning which I doubt he needs it."

"Three?"

"Jed Hardman is a warrior. If Grayson has underestimated that because your Reb was taken off guard once, he will make the error of not understanding the man he's going up against. It will be to his eventual regret."

Bernice sighed. "This sounds like we're heading into a war. That's worse than heading into nowhere."

CHAPTER 12

As Jed headed into the hills with his brother and the Kalamas, he left Jack and Toddy to work on the corrals. Toddy had claimed he knew how to build fence, time would tell on that one. He was beginning to wonder if he'd been wise to bring him.

"Your land is pretty country," Josh said as a few miles from the ranch buildings they rode onto a promontory where they could see for miles. "How far does it go?"

"See that peak over there, it's north of that and then west to the ridge you see way in the distance. The North Fork flows through it to the south with small tributaries. It is good land and will be better as we clear some of the forests and plant better grass."

"You see any cattle on it?" Josh asked just as Joe Kalama pointed.

"A bunch over there," Joe said and grinned as Jed pointed out another small bunch to the north of them.

"We'll take it slow rounding them up. Ace, this is your job, got it?" The little dog ran circles around them in excitement.

"You really think he'll be any good at this?" Josh asked as they headed for one bunch while the Kalamas headed for the other.

"We'll know soon enough. He's used to softer animals. These longhorns are range toughened." He and his brother loosened their ropes. "They aren't used to men rounding them up either. So we also have our work cut out for us."

Most of the morning later, sweat running down his back, Jed with Josh's help and more and more from Ace had their bunch of twenty-five in the lower meadow where they would possibly stay while they went back for more. Before they left, the Kalamas arrived with fifteen more.

"Ace, you stay here and keep them in the meadow," Jed told the dog as he nudged Midas back toward the brushy slope where he'd seen four head.

The dog looked at him reluctantly when he was told again to stay but then headed back for the herd.

"It'll be good practice for him."

By late afternoon, they had gathered near to one hundred and fifty head. There would be more in the hills to the north but for now they had enough to bring them back to the pasture below the ranch buildings. Ace had proven better and better at handling the longhorns as he nipped at their noses and drove them back into the herd whenever one wanted to stray.

"I figure that's fifty bulls, about half of them yearlings or younger, and eighty or so cows and heifers give or take," Jed said as they moved them slowly back toward headquarters.

"Give or take," Josh agreed. "I guess that means some losses."

"You heard the wolves. We'll have to do some hunting to move them away from this ranch."

"I saw grizzly scat too." Joe Kalama said. "They like a calf as good as the next meal."

"We'll bring in what cattle we can, keep them closer to the barns. There is good grass down there. After we brand and castrate, we'll go after a few predators to see if we can make this country less attractive."

"You see any sign of unshod ponies?" Jed asked George.

He shook his head. "Rain three days ago though would have wiped that out."

"I suppose they are watching us," Josh said uneasily.

Joe Kalama grinned. "They ain't supernatural beings, brother. They don't know we're here yet." His smile disappeared. "They will though."

"So we'll get the cattle gathered as fast as we can," Jed said.

"No rest for the weary?" Josh asked teasingly.

"I'll make Toddy start carrying his own weight."

"That would be substantial," Josh said with a laugh.

As they began the climb up over the Cascade Mountains, Raine was grateful when again Jei leaned low from his saddle and scooped up the tired Deucy onto the pack horse. The Barlow Trail had been chosen as a lower route, but it still was hard going in places. The gallant little dog didn't give up, but it was clear she didn't have the strength to keep up with the horses all day.

"When can we stop for the night?" Bernice asked with a groan as she took a drink from her canteen.

"A few more miles," Jei said watching as a small party of wagons passed.

"How's the weather over there?" Raine asked a woman who had met her gaze.

"Went through a gully buster." The woman looked curiously at Jei then back at Raine. "You two women traveling with a Chinaman?"

"Obviously," Raine said with irritation.

"Lots of them over there," the woman said without a smile.

"Good," Raine said nudging Fancy to ride on past the wagons.

"Not very friendly people," Jei said when they were well past them.

"I suppose they are tired by now," Raine said trying to give them the benefit of the doubt.

"I swore I'd never get on a horse or wagon again," Bernice complained, "and here I am. I should have taken the ship south."

"You think you'd have gotten on it?" Jei asked with a smile.

"I suppose not. I still can't believe how Russ figured out my part in getting the Reb loose."

"Likely Jade."

"Jade? Why would she tell?"

"The same reason you helped Jed," Jei said. "Money. She was getting a little something on the side all along to make sure Russ got his share."

"That trollop," Bernice said with a grimace while Raine resisted the temptation to laugh. It wasn't actually that funny. When Jei had said Russ had wide reach, he obviously hadn't overstated it. Again, she castigated herself for being so naïve. Sharon might also have been on the payroll. She still trusted Clem and Nancy though but trust was wearing thin everywhere else.

"The other side of that meadow looks good to me," Jei said as he reined his horse to the right. "Back a little, and we can have a fire tonight. Do either of you ladies know how to cook salt pork and potatoes?"

"That's another thing I swore I'd never do," Bernice said with a groan.

"I do," Raine said. She had also sworn she'd never do it again, but she had learned well on the trip west. As Jei cared for the horses and Bernice petted the dog she said she hated, Raine built a fire ring and a small fire. Using the sticks that Jei brought to secure the pans, she started their evening meal.

As she worked, Raine was surprised to find she was enjoying herself. She had been so sure that only her life in Portland was rewarding. She began to wonder how long ago it had ceased being what she wanted.

When they ate, she fed Deucy scraps.

"You did well, Raine," Jei said as he lit a cigar.

"My mother. She taught me so many things." She thought of what her mother had said, when last they had been together. "She said I will be surprised at what brings me joy if I let it."

"Your mother is a nice lady," Bernice said surprising Raine.

"She is that."

"She's sure married a gorgeous hunk of man. I remember the wagon train and... oh never mind, it'll just make you mad again."

"It doesn't matter if Adam was attracted to you then," Raine said not liking to imagine he had been. "He chose my mother."

Bernice grinned. "I'd love to let you think he had been, but he wasn't. Actually I only had one affair on that trip west."

When Raine didn't ask who, Bernice smiled more broadly. "Can't you guess who it was?"

"No and don't care."

"Sure you do. It was..."

Raine stopped her. "Do not tell me. I swear, Bernice, I will yank your blonde hair out by the roots. I don't want your gossip and don't care who you chased down and finally won."

"Well it wasn't Matt. You know that."

"Yes, I do."

"It wasn't your father either."

Raine had to laugh at that. "Bernice, you are a joke."

"I have fun, Loraine. You are jealous of that. Like when I went swimming in the river without my clothing. You only wished you had my freedom."

"Bernice," Jei said in a voice that clearly said he'd heard enough female talk, "if you keep on, I'll be the one to take your hair, and it won't be pretty when I do."

Bernice gave him a shocked look. "You wouldn't?"

"Don't test me. I swear I am regretting taking you. A roll in the hay isn't worth the aggravation you cost. I had forgotten that. Don't make me teach you a lesson you clearly deserve." Bernice looked warily at him but for the rest of the evening, she kept her mouth shut.

Rolled up in her blankets, Raine did wonder what man on

that train had been so unfortunate as to have had Bernice's attentions. She wondered if Jed would be tempted by the lush blonde. No, he wasn't that kind of man.

Again she went back to what her mother had said. She didn't really know very much about what kind of man Jed was. She could not say she had left Portland to find that out. She had known she had to leave, but she knew there were other places she could have headed. She had been reluctant to involve her mother and Adam, but Adam was tough enough to protect them—not to mention his being a sheriff.

She could likely have gone to live in the homestead cabin her father had built. If she had wanted to go back East, maybe Belle would have liked seeing her, or she had family still in Missouri. Russ wouldn't follow her that far, she didn't think. But she hadn't done any of that. She had headed for the John Day country to find out what kind of man Jed Hardman was.

After three days of gathering cattle, Jed felt they had enough around the main house to begin branding and castrating-- roughly three hundred and fifty head, which was more than he had expected. Selling off the bulls to the forts or taking them to Baker City would leave him a nice sized herd given the complications he was facing with a possible Indian war looming. He had to add in the talk of road agents, which Jack kept claiming could shift to rustling-- if they thought it was profitable.

He had left Jack to work on the corrals when he was out bringing in cattle. One day he took Toddy, but found it wasn't worth what it took in energy to keep him going. Toddy hadn't done a bad job though on helping Jack with those corrals. Leaving him to that, he would be ready to go onto branding and castrating.

His own days had been as long as he could make them. Only when he fell into bed exhausted could he sleep. He kept thinking of Raine. He should have found a way to convince her to marry him. He'd lose her, and it'd be his own damned fault. First he rushed off to fight a war he knew could only be lost. Then he hadn't written to let her know that he was thinking about her. Finally he had showed up and demanded she accept him as he was.

Thinking back over his mistakes was actually easier than the other times he remembered-- the times they had made love. God, he missed her. There had to be a way to convince her they could work this out. Once things were straightened out here, he could go across the mountains to visit frequently. Maybe she wouldn't hate spending time at the ranch as much as she thought.

When he finished the branding, he would take a small herd to the closest forts to see if they were interested in fresh beef and then head back to Portland. One way or another he would convince her they had a future together. Maybe it'd be unconventional, but he was all right with that, just so long as he didn't lose her.

It had been years since Jed had branded cattle and the work was as hard as he had remembered. He built up the fire and used the Circle H branding irons he had bought before he left for war. A few of the cattle still showed that brand but many had been born after he had left. Two days of hard work had half the herd branded.

It was in the midst of the work, sweat running off his body, bloody from castrating, covered in dust, when he looked up and saw three horsemen and a pack animal coming from the west. Toddy had been in the house, supposedly fixing supper. They were all edgy enough about what might be coming, that Toddy came out with a shotgun.

Jed left the branding iron, grabbed his rifle and walked toward the riders. Halfway there he saw two were women. Three more steps and he saw one was Raine, Deucy ran straight for Ace who had seen what was coming before Jed. He felt enough shock at seeing her that he had to close his eyes and reopen them to be sure it wasn't a mirage.

"God," he said as he got to her, laid his rifle against a rock, and reached up to lift her off her horse. His lips closed over hers before she could say a word. It was long moments with her arms around him before he looked to see who the other two riders had been. Jei was standing leaning against his horse with a faint smile, and a woman with blonde hair stood just beyond him.

Swallowing hard and realizing he was filthy, covered in sweat, he let her go, expecting her to step away. She didn't. She tightened her arms around him.

"You said I could come if I needed," she said, tears in her eyes.

"I wanted you so bad," he whispered bending again and kissing her lips again. "I just didn't expect... God, what are you doing here?"

He looked again toward Jei; and although it was obvious, said, "You brought her."

"I was leaving Portland anyway."

"What happened?" He looked back at Raine.

"It's a long story, and it's been a long ride. Do you have space for us all?" Raine asked and looking beyond the barn finally to see the house. "Jed, I thought you said you had a cabin."

He smiled then for the first time he felt in weeks. "It isn't?"

She shook her head. "It's gigantic. And this is your ranch?"

"This is it."

The lodge was long and sprawling with a second floor, a long porch along one side, its setting nearly perfect with tall pines behind and lush meadows full of cattle out in front. "It's beautiful."

"You look tired. You all do. Go on in and get something to eat. How long ago did you leave Portland?"

"Took five days," Jei said as he led his horse up toward the house. Bernice followed with more enthusiasm now that she had seen the size of the home.

"Josh, take their horses," Jed said. As his brother led them off to the barns, Jed stopped on the porch. "I can't go in like this, and I have work to finish. I'll just brand those in the corral already. Toddy, you show them the rooms."

Toddy was still staring at them. "Which ones?"

"Doesn't matter... except for the one."

"I'd like to talk to you," Raine said.

He nodded then looked again at Toddy. "Show them where they can wash up. Make up the beds. Heat up some water. Didn't we have some roast beef left from lunch? Slice some bread to go with it."

Jei and Bernice followed Toddy in, but Raine stayed with him. "I have to explain."

"You're here-- that's enough. I don't know why or what you want but whatever it is, you can have it."

She smiled. "Can I watch you brand then?"

He laughed. "Aren't you too tired for that? I'd have figured you'd want to lie down."

"I found the trip more exhilarating than I expected. Surprising me too."

"I'll likely brand myself if you watch, but yes, come on down."

"So your cattle were here?" she asked. He picked up his rifle before heading back to the corrals.

"In the hills. We've spent the last week gathering." Ace and Deucy followed them. Ace eager to get to the cattle, and Deucy ducking behind Raine's legs every chance she got. "Overall the count has been better than I expected given four years on their own out here."

"How does Ace like being a cattle dog?" She thought how silly that she had ridden all these miles, and all she could think to talk about was the dog.

"He's taken to it."

"My goodness, they have big horns," she said as she finally saw the cattle he had in the corral.

"Hey there, sweet thing," Josh said with a laugh as he came up and she gave him a big hug, even though he was as covered in grime and dirt as Jed.

She laughed. "So now I'm a sweet thing, am I?"

"You are when you come here," he said with a big grin.

"Raine, these two are Joe and George Kalama. They are part of the Wasco tribe. I had hired them before, and they've been making the gather possible. Boys, this is Raine Stevens."

"Glad to meet you, Miss," Joe said bowing his head. George stood back but did manage a smile. "Don't mind him. He doesn't speak such good English," Joe said.

"You speak it so well. I am rather amazed," she said as she looked at the two handsome Indian men.

"Missionary school. Not by choice, I might add," Joe said. "George being younger avoided it and had to learn from me."

"It has to be handy to speak the language that is most prevalent," she said.

"French was handy too," he said with a flash of white teeth as he grinned widely. "Life changes though and maybe someday you folks will have to learn another language yourselves."

She grinned. "I don't want to interfere with your work but just wanted to see what this business of a branding was all about."

The Kalama brothers mounted their horses and flipping out their ropes, threw a loop around the head of one of the longhorn bulls. Josh, standing beside Raine, said, "When they aren't too old, they get castrated and branded."

She saw that Jed had built back up the fire and had several long irons down in the flames. The bull was dragged to him by a loop around his head and one hoof to pull him out flat, giving Jed the side of the bull he needed to put his brand.

She heard the sizzle of the hot iron as it burned the hair and into the hide. The bull was bellowing. "that has to hurt," she said uneasily and more concerned as the big animal threw his head around, and she imagined one of those horns going into Jed's leg as he was stretched out to hold the iron in the right place.

He stepped back. "This one's too big to castrate. Let him loose."

The operation proceeded that way as Josh moved into the corrals to let out the branded animals. When Raine saw one being castrated, she watched as Jed's bowie knife cut into the sac between the bull's legs, and then scraped away the vessels leading to its body. He threw the testicles into a bucket. She decided seeing that once was enough.

Toddy came down from the house with a tray that held a plate of sliced beef, sliced bread, and a cup of coffee. "I thought you might be hungry, ma'am."

"How nice, thank you," she said and took it knowing at home she'd have expected to wash her hands before eating. Out here that had become a luxury not worth a concern. "And remember, it's Raine," she corrected as she put together the bread and meat. She was hungrier than she'd been aware. "Where are Jei and Bernice?"

"She went to lie down. He seemed to be wandering around. Not sure what he was up to. That is one restless man."

"What do you do with those?" she asked pointing to the bucket of testicles.

Toddy chuckled. "Sure you want to know?"

"I had a feeling they were being saved for some purpose?"

"Fry them up and some like them very much. Mountain oysters, for what they look like."

She wasn't sure she was up to that much wilderness experience but maybe.

The afternoon went fast and finally the men had finished with all the animals in the corral, and Jed was walking toward her. He looked tired but satisfied. She was amazed that with the layer of blood, dust and sweat on him, she had never found him more desirable or handsome.

"I have to change clothes and clean up. Want to come with me?" he asked as he grabbed his rifle and a bag from the fence post.

"A bathtub?"

He laughed. "I could wish. You could wish. No, it's a stream that has a pool deep enough to wash up. Winter I'd have to do it in the house. I do have water in the house. Gravity brings it down and a spigot lets us fill a basin. Any hot water though comes from the woodstove. This season, I prefer the creek."

"If you have soap in that bag, I could do with some cleaning up myself."

"And you want to talk."

"I do... and Jed, talk is all I want to do." She gave him what she hoped was a determined look.

"Whatever you want. I'm just glad you're here."

She hoped he would continue to feel that way when she explained what she wanted.

CHAPTER 13

J ed stopped at a pool that had been naturally dammed by beaver. It had just enough width to take a half dozen breast strokes to reach the other side. The Ponderosa pines shadowed it with wildflowers and tall grass alongside.

"How beautiful."

"With the cattle farther from the house," he explained as he dropped his sack and kicked off his boots, "this has stayed pristine. It has a hot spring partially feeding it, keeps it warmer than you'd expect even in winter as it doesn't ice over."

"What are those flowers?" She pointed to a tall, spiky yellow flower on the far side.

"The goldenrod I know," he said as he unbuttoned and dropped his shirt. "Don't ask about the purple one next to it."

"Jed, what are you doing?" she asked although it was obvious as he began unbuttoning the front of his pants.

"Taking a bath." He smiled at her. "Come on in. It isn't exactly warm but not bad this time of the year."

Foolishly, she hadn't taken what he meant by a bath far enough. She had imagined a spit bath. This was not going to further her own plans. She swallowed hard watching him strip naked and step into the pool. If she had forgotten what a beautiful man he was, she was all too quickly reminded with the sun reflecting off hard muscles as he strode into the deeper part of the pool. He did have a bar of soap in his hands when she managed to get past the muscles to look that far.

"You aren't coming in?" he asked as he turned back to watch her with that smile that had seduced her from the first moment she had seen it.

"No, I am not." She tried to put a self-righteous tone to her voice, but knew it probably sounded weak and left no doubt what she was thinking.

"Sugar, you've seen it all," he said as he began to soap up his chest and arms.

She forced herself to remember what her mother had said about the frosting and the cake. This wasn't going to be as easy as she had imagined when they had been apart. It wouldn't just be about Jed's desires but also hers. "Where are the others washing up?"

"Not up here with you, if that's what you were wondering. There is a smaller pool below the barns. They went there most likely. We'll have privacy for that... er talk you wanted."

She looked away from the temptation as he strode back, handed her the bar of soap and then moved back into the deeper part of the pool to swim to the other side. "After a day like today, a little swim is good for loosening up the muscles," he said as moved to the goldenrod and picked one stalk.

Good God, she thought as she finally forced her eyes from his muscular backside as he swam back. Wash up, girl, she ordered herself and rolled up her sleeves. Taking the soap, she lathered her hands, her face but didn't go farther than the front of her chest where she had the top buttons undone. If she had taken off her clothing to join him, frosting would be all they'd be eating and likely she'd be unable to turn it around no matter whether it mattered for a deeper relationship.

As Jed dressed in the clean clothing, taking his time and in no hurry to cover up all that male flesh, she sat in the shade of the pine and looked at the pool. The rich turquoise color was so beautiful, so peaceful. It was hard to believe in a place like this that danger could be anywhere near. Yet his taking the rifle told her it could.

He came and lowered himself to his haunches in front of her. "It's hard to believe you are here."

"It came about suddenly. Very suddenly." She had no idea how to explain it, as some still seemed surreal. His smile said her coming had made him happy.

"Do you want to tell me it all now or wait 'til we go back to the house? It's clear you aren't here for the reason I had hoped when I first saw you."

"And that was?"

"Ready to live over here with me, be my wife."

She stared up at the blue sky overhead. "It's not that simple. I wish it was. I... well, I went to visit my mother after you left. It turned out Adam had learned more about Russ and the suspicions regarding his businesses. With a few other things coming into place, I came to realize Russ had set up all my so-called successes. You were right about how mine and Agatha's businesses were used. Considering what he likely had done to you, I couldn't stay there because I saw how ruthless he was."

He lowered himself and sat beside her, taking her into his arms. "I'm sorry for how that had to have hurt you," he said softly, his lips against her hair. "I know you trusted him."

"Well, fool though I had been, I do admit to myself when I am wrong. I had to leave. You had said I could come. I packed a bag to do that. I thought I'd take the steamship to The Dalles and figure out how to reach you when I got there. That night, Han Jei and Bernice came to the door. He said they were leaving immediately. He had come to warn me because he had promised you. I asked him to take me this far, and he agreed."

"Well thank God for that. I shouldn't have left you."

"You had to go," she said against his chest. "I had things I had to find out for myself. There's more to it, but anyway I am here."

"The way you are saying this tells me that you aren't here to be with me, or are you?" He leaned back to look into her eyes. His own were that beautiful gray, like a stormy sky. It made her want to melt into him.

"I am not... and I am. I know it will sound confusing but before I left, before I realized the whole level of Russ's duplicity, I had a talk with my mother. I told her about you, everything."

"You told your mother about me?" His smile had now changed to one of uneasiness as he reached into his pocket for the makings to roll a cigarette.

"Everything. I needed to talk to someone I trusted. I told her the problems that I saw as insurmountable. She told me that we had eaten the frosting without mixing up or baking the cake."

He gave a little laugh as he lit the cigarette. "Let me see if I get this straight. You told your mother all about us, and she wasn't pleased we had been making love?"

"Not so much that, but that we hadn't taken the time to develop a relationship first."

He shook his head. "Sounds like your mother should have met my mother." He stared out at the pool. "Did she suggest what we do now, or did we lose all chance to make it right?"

"She didn't exactly tell me that, but she got me to thinking. What if we began here... and we saw what we had in terms of relationship without sleeping together at all."

He smoked for a moment as he considered that. "It wouldn't be easy for me at least."

"It won't be for me either, but we can't really find out what's there if we hop into bed at each problem, can we?"

"So you want to come here and be like a friend, and it might be we find out that's all we can ever be if there are these big differences?"

She nodded. "Is that asking too much?"

He smoked a moment. "Can I think about it and tell you tomorrow? You've had longer to consider this than I have."

"Yes, of course. I hope you aren't disappointed that I came."

He reached out and took her hand. "Can I touch you?"

"Of course, just not, well, you know."

He smiled. "I am glad you are here. I had already been thinking how I could work out a way to get back to Portland. I had not given up on us, sugar."

"Then?"

"Let me consider your proposal. Tomorrow, I'll tell you what I think. Meanwhile let's go back to the house. I want to talk to Han Jei and see what triggered his own run from Portland."

Russell Grayson, still in a rotten mood from learning Raine had left town, looked up as his secretary ushered two roughly garbed men into his office. Her nose was out of joint at their lack of class. He usually dealt with such men away from his main office. It might have been a mistake that he hadn't done that. He appeared to be making too many of those lately. He ordered her to shut the door before he asked the two if they wanted a brandy.

"Got any whiskey?" Si Tubbs asked sitting in the overstuffed chair in front of the desk. He brought one booted foot up over his knee revealing the mud stuck to the bottom.

"Better for me too," Jace Walker said.

"You edgy about something, Jace?" Russell asked as he handed them each a shot glass of whiskey.

"Always edgy about something." Walker chuckled. "Stay alive that way."

"I have a job for you two."

"Pay good?" Tubbs asked as he swallowed the whiskey in a gulp and reached for the bottle to pour himself another.

"Doesn't it always?"

"Dangerous?" Walker asked still watching the street more than them.

"I'm not sure." One thing, on which Russell had always prided himself, was his judgment of men. His almost instant disdain for Hardman was making it hard to be sure if he was letting those feelings blind him.

"Tell us the deal, and then we'll decide if we are in," Walker said.

"I have several possible scenarios. You will have to play it by ear, but the first is the most important-- get hired at the Hardman ranch." He walked to the wall and pointed it out on a large map. "It's a cattle operation. Once you are in, you will get word to me and I will work out the rest of what I need from you."

"Pretty dangerous country over there," Walker said.

"The end goal is?" Tubbs asked.

"Naturally for Hardman to be dead but exactly how, that's where I would like to decide after I have you in place and know better the setup there."

They quibbled over the price but eventually it was agreed upon and they left on their way.

Five minutes later Kirk arrived, and he repeated his plan for him.

"My God, Russ. Those two?" He shook his head. "He will see them for what they are and then where are you?"

"No reason for him not to hire them."

"I told you not to underestimate him, but you are. The man was in a four year war. He survived it. He will be a judge of character."

"You have a better idea?"

"Forget him and her too. We have plenty to keep us satisfied here. We don't need to ruin everything for your idea of revenge. Let him rot over there in his wilderness or maybe the Shoshoni will get him." Kirk walked behind him, bringing his strong fingers down on Russ's shoulder and then neck as he began massaging.

"You are tense, my dear. This isn't working to keep dwelling on them."

Russell gritted his teeth and pushed Kirk's hands away. "That won't do it, you know."

"It does wonders for me," Kirk said with humor but moved away to sit in one of the stuffed chairs. "All right then, we better come up with something more apt to prove successful, where it comes to Mr. Hardman. Your men will be back, without being hired, and when they are, another plan has to be ready, one more effective than this one."

"There is something else," Russell said.

"And that is?"

"I learned that Bernice left town."

"Women like her are always leaving. Is it significant in some way?"

"I am not sure. It wasn't just her, but Han Jei."

"He had significant sway in the Chinese community if I recall. Were you planning to get rid of him?"

"I don't know how he got word of it."

"He is also one not to underestimate. You have any idea where he went?"

"My bigger immediate concern is that they have apparently been gone since Raine left."

"Do you have any reason to think it's connected?" He stared thoughtfully at the ceiling.

"I have no reason to think they aren't."

"You have become a bit paranoid in your old age."

Russell glared at him. "I am not old."

Kirk smiled placidly. "Dismissing the truth of that, I will do some investigating to see if anybody knows why they left. Are you sure it was at the same time as Raine?"

He shook his head. "Not for certain. Where it comes to Han especially, it's hard to get definite answers. The Chinese are so sneaky, but it was within a few days. She didn't use a ticket to leave unless she went under an assumed name. Why would she do that?"

"That she's smarter than you thought?"

"I always saw her as intelligent. I had someone check and she's not in Oregon City."

"That is interesting." Kirk headed for the door. "Let me see if anybody knows anything. Someone who might talk to a playwright rather than a gang boss."

"Nobody knows what I truly do," Russell snarled.

"Right." Kirk laughed as he walked out of the office.

As Jed and Raine entered the kitchen, his crew, all drinking coffee, looked up but said nothing. Jei was sitting at one end of the long table.

"Seems I owe you again," Jed said as he took a cup of coffee from Toddy and straddled a chair.

"I like having some men in debt, but in this case, your lady offered to pay me to bring her. You don't owe me anything."

"Not even for the warning?"

"Maybe that." He smiled. "Are you prepared for what's coming?"

"I doubt it, so tell me what you know."

Raine sat at the other end of the table from Jed not missing the avarice with which Bernice watched Jed. He would be like catnip to her, another of the men she always sought to entrap with her wiles. While she doubted Jed would fall for it, she thought watching how he handled it might be instructive on this business of getting to know him better.

"You understood I had to leave Portland?"

"For helping me?"

"A tiny part of it. Grayson wants power, and he doesn't like sharing it. I had too much pull with the Chinese community for him to tolerate my being in the same city with him, at least as soon as he felt he no longer trusted me. The word was out, and I listen to the heartbeat of the city to know what to expect."

Jed jerked his thumb toward Bernice. "What about her?"

"She was part of Grayson's network, but she betrayed him when she took money for helping with your rescue. One of her girls told Grayson. It was just a matter of time before he had her in the bottom of the Willamette River."

Jed rose and walked to the window staring out at the pastures below his ranch house. "This isn't much of a stronghold," he observed. "You think Grayson will come after Raine?"

"More likely you."

Jed turned with a tight smile. "I kind of thought he might. All right, what do you want now?"

"I'm thinking for now I wouldn't mind working a cattle ranch and being here when Grayson comes, or you go."

"Go?"

"After him because you will, won't you?"

"I have work to do here. There were thirty-one bulls too old to castrate, and I am thinking of driving some of them to Canyon City to see what the market would be there. One way or another I need to get rid of them as they will cause me nothing but grief here."

"Who looks after your place while you are gone?" Jei asked with some interest as he got out a cigar.

"I was thinking you might." He looked at Bernice more closely than for the first time. "Now you," he said, "what do you want here?"

"I was wishing I hadn't come," she said with a smile that irritated Raine, "but now maybe this would be all right if you don't mind that is." Her words ended with a cooing sound.

"Jei decides whether you stay as it seems you are his woman."

"I am nobody's woman... yet."

"Well then, if you stay here, you work. Nobody gets a free ride. That is except Raine." Jed smiled at her then, and the smile said it all. "If Jei has no say over you, she decides if you stay. I know you helped me, but I also know you haven't been a friend to her. If you can't be one, I'll be taking you down to Canyon City with the cattle."

Bernice gave him a shocked look. "I don't want to go there."

"You have a horse then, and you can go where you want. But if you cause any grief here, you're gone, want it or not." He looked at Raine then with that smile he only bestowed on her. "It's up to you whether she stays. Let me know what you decide."

Raine for once appreciated his take charge attitude and listened with some degree of surprise and pleasure as he laid out the work assignments for the men he had hired. The diverse crew was an unlikely one, and yet they seemed very natural for Jed's ranch.

When he came to her, he said, "I have to go out to the pasture to see how the castrated steers are doing. I'll be thinking though and get back to you on that proposition." He grinned as he walked out the door.

"He's certainly a pushy man," Bernice complained as she looked at Raine for support.

"It is his place," she said as she headed for the stairs to see the room Toddy said was to be hers.

Bernice huffed but didn't argue as she walked into what looked like a great room with a huge fireplace at one end. The furniture was sparse but the room looked pleasant enough and could be made more so.

Toddy led Raine up the stairway at one end. Along one wall was an open hallway that split the upstairs into two bedroom wings.

"This one is to be yours," Toddy said, as he opened a door to a spacious, beautifully furnished room with a large French door and balcony at one end. He put the pitcher and bowl with water onto a low dresser. "I hope you will be comfortable," he said as he left.

A door along one wall doubtless led to a second bedroom. She saw it had a key in the door to what had to be Jed's room. She swallowed thinking how easy it would all be to open that door, but is it what had gone wrong before? Too easy?

Her bag had been placed on the bed. She unpacked her dress, hung it in the wardrobe and put her other things into the drawers of a dresser made of oak and decorated with beautiful carvings. The fishing pole went on the top along with her mother's journal and the sack of herbs.

She sat then on the bed thinking how very foolish her idea to come had probably been. Jed must think she was insane to come so far and then deny what they both wanted. She kept remembering her mother's words and thinking maybe there was wisdom that would help her make something work that seemed so unlikely. If she truly understood who Jed was, would that change anything? She decided she would ask Jed if she could safely write her mother and let her know where she was. Or would that endanger them all?

She pulled off her dusty riding clothing, the pants, shirt. Using the water and a fragrant soap, she washed before dressing once again as a lady, with camisole, slip and finally the blue dress she had brought. It was one her mother had made her with a softly scooped neck decorated with embroidery. She smiled at the odd feeling of wearing the kind of garb she'd taken for granted all of her life. She spent some time at the mirror working her hair back up into a tidy bun before she walked downstairs to see the rest of the house. Might this someday be her home? It still seemed too unreal to imagine it possible she could be fit into this world.

Walking out onto the porch, she saw it ran the length of the house, had a few chairs for sitting in the evening and from it she could see the pasture below. In the distance, loomed a snow covered peak. She was unsure what it might be. Her whole landscape had changed as she couldn't see Mt. Hood at all or was it that it appeared different looking at it from the east?

When she saw the horseman below on the meadow riding like the wind, she smiled. She didn't need to see his face to know who he was. Jed rode so beautifully as though part of the horse. His stallion soared across the ground, with Ace left behind trying to keep up with the boss. Guiltily, she wondered for the first time where Deucy had gotten to.

Toddy came out with a glass and some kind of beverage. "Sorry no ice, but I make the tea with the sun and it's pretty good to drink."

She took it gratefully. "Where's Deucy?"

"Josh kept her from following you to the pool. He thought it might be best in case she got lost. She's quite taken to him."

"I suppose she's frightened. It seems so much does scare her."

"Yes, she doesn't seem to like the cattle much, but Josh makes her feel safe from what I can tell."

"Maybe she prefers men to women," she suggested sipping the tea. "This is delicious."

"I think she is looking for security. Like us all," Toddy said.

"It seems it will be in short supply for a while at least."

"Well, you never know. I try to think positive." He laughed then. "What am I saying? I never think positive. I just want to make you think positive."

"Thank you for that. Can I help fix dinner?"

"I have it pretty well in hand. Nothing special. Steaks and potatoes baking in the oven. Pretty much here the food stays basic with lots of it more than style."

Jed, who had unsaddled his stallion in record time, gave a big step up onto the porch. "That's a mighty pretty dress, sugar."

"Glad you like it as it's the only one I brought, and you're likely to see it a lot."

"I can buy you more. Canyon City has some shops. Not the quality you're used to though."

"Is there a way for me to let my mother know I'm safe?" It was a concern to her.

"Monument, about five miles from here, has a post office. It could have its risks though for you to use it."

"You think Russ would intercept the mail?"

"If he thought he had a reason. Road agents pretty well take what they want from what I've been hearing."

"I just fear my family will be searching for me. I left in a rush without much information to anyone."

"Then you need to write but don't put this ranch as a return address on the outside. You said you told your mother about me." She nodded. "Then try to let her know in a way that wouldn't tell anyone else."

"I can do that."

He leaned back against one of the posts, his gaze on her. "You like this house?"

"It's much larger than I expected. And beautiful. Like a lodge more than a house."

"Want some tea, Boss?" Toddy asked.

"Nah. You can bring me a whiskey though."

There was a bench at the far end of the porch; and when he had his whiskey, he led her to it. "With no windows behind it, this is a good place to talk without an audience. I don't need to wait for tomorrow, but you might need to think about what I want." The sun was just beginning to sink behind the mountain ridge to the west highlighting the mountains.

"And that is?"

"I want you to marry me. As soon as we can get down to Canyon City. I understand we won't be sharing a marriage bed until you decide it's the right time, but I want us legally wed."

"Why?" She should have been expecting this, but she had not.

"I have my reasons. They are not romantic. I don't need a piece of paper to know you are my woman. This is about business as much as love. I could wait to marry you until you decide and maybe we will do it again with your family there, if you finally accept me as your husband, but I have some concerns regarding this ranch and marrying you would solve them."

"What are they?"

"Josh can't own property in Oregon. If something happened to me, he'd lose this place. You as my wife could hold it. I know you'd do right by him."

"What would happen to you?" she asked feeling a cold chill.

"Portland convinced me I'm not invincible," he said. "Did Jei tell you that Russell Grayson is operating his illegal operations this side of the Cascades as well as that side?"

She nodded. "He won't find you here though, will he? Did I endanger you by coming to you?" That was intolerable.

"To the last question. No, you didn't. But what he did in Portland means he's not using rational thinking where it comes to me. He'll come after me eventually. If he didn't like me before, he likes me even less now. Grayson doesn't like losing, and he lost. He will move against me. I know how to fight, but I also know in any fight, life can be snuffed out by a fluke."

"You are scaring me."

"I don't want to do that. So what about it? Will you be my wife?"

"Would we have to tell people? I mean in case I really can't live it?"

He smiled at her, and she felt it all the way to her toes. "You saw that bedroom. What did you think of the furniture?"

It seemed an odd question. "It was very nice, special, good wood, more than I had expected."

"When I got back to Georgia, after my mother died, I boxed up some of the best pieces, especially a lady's bedroom suite, had it shipped around Cape Horn, to The Dalles. I directed the merchant there to send word to the ranch when it arrived. Jack took a wagon up to get it."

She felt amazed. "That had to be expensive as well as difficult."

"I wanted it for you. I wasn't even sure that I'd get back here, but if I did, I wanted that room waiting for the lady of this house as it had been for many generations of ladies on the Hardman Plantation."

"It is beautiful furniture."

"With a long tradition of women behind it."

"You didn't know I'd ever be here."

"No, and it seemed even more unlikely after I got back to Portland." He smiled. "I had not given up though and wanted a place for you if you did someday come."

She felt teary and amazed at the depth of his sensitivity, one of those things about which her mother had tried to tell her. She had had been so wrapped up in her own life, so drawn to him sexually that she'd missed all the rest of who he was.

"Sugar, there is a key in the door between the two rooms. A key on your side only. If the day ever comes that you want me in your bed, you will unlock that door. I can wait. And as for what we tell others, I don't care, but I want it legal, and I want the ranch protected for Josh and you if I don't make it."

She thought about it, about the horrible hole in her life if something happened to him. She would do whatever it took to prevent that.

"Should I go back to Portland and try to fool Russ into thinking he can have what he wants with me?"

He gave her one of those looks. "Are you out of your mind, sugar?"

"It makes sense, and maybe I can defuse this situation."

He laughed at her. "Fine, you do that."

"Really?"

"Sure, you head back there," he drawled with a smile she'd never seen, "and I'll tag along to hunt Grayson down and kill him even if it's right out on a street."

She managed her own smile despite not feeling much like it. She saw he meant it. "All right then I accept your proposal, Mr. Hardman. When would you like to put the legal to that?"

His smile changed and became as sexy as ever. "As soon as I can get this place shaped up. I'll give you a little time to get over the hours in the saddle. We'll take Jack, leaving Jei, Josh, and the Kalama brothers to look after the ranch and just hope they can keep Bernice out of trouble unless you want to take her along and dump her there."

"It might be safer for now to keep her here." She thought about Bernice possibly using information to buy her own safety. She did not trust her one iota.

"It is your choice. You will be the lady of this home. I will not try to pressure you about the rest but won't promise I won't try to tempt you."

She smiled. "Then it's settled. Could we take the cattle with us to Canyon City to try and sell them?"

"You aren't serious."

"I most definitely am. It seems if I am thinking about living on a ranch, I should get the hang of what that means."

"What do you know about cattle?" His expression showed his unease with the idea.

"How many men would you need to move them without me?"

"Just one."

"So any help I could be would be something, and if not, you could do it anyway."

"Minus worrying about you." His mouth quirked up into a semi smile.

"How many did you plan to take down there?"

"Maybe ten head. They won't be easy to move though to start at least. They are bulls and used to being wild."

"Are you taking Ace?"

"I was thinking about it. They are used to him making them mind."

"So there'd be you, one other and him. I might even be a help. You don't know that I won't be." He smiled. She had him there. "I think it's a good experience for me, and at night, I can fix the dinner over the fire. I know how to do that."

"That's a big plus," he admitted.

"How many nights would it be?"

"Not sure but depends on how well they move. From as few as two to four, I suppose."

"How can I know if this life agrees with me if I don't try to fit into it?"

He shook his head, but even before he said a word, she knew she had won. "All right. I still can't believe you really want to do this, but if you're determined..."

"And I am."

"You go dressed as a boy, keep your hair up in the hat, and when we get there, we can let the justice of the peace worry about what you are before we let him know." He grinned at the thought. "Did you bring any identification in case it's required?"

"Yes, as well as bank notes and cash. Need any?" this time it was her turn to laugh at his surprised look.

"What kind of woman am I marrying here?" he asked with a bemused smile.

"That's what you need to find out this summer, isn't it?"

CHAPTER 14

J ed and Jei sat out on the porch step. The other men were
playing poker as Raine and Bernice cleaned up after dinner
—much to Bernice's chagrin.

"You have a nice ranch. Don't want to offend you but how big
is it?" Jei asked as he smoked his cigar and listened to the bick-
ering in the kitchen and the laughter from the card players.

"No offense. Ten sections, not all in a block, lying along the
river and then up into the mountains to the north."

"So cattle and logging. No gold though likely."

"Hopefully not," Jed said rolling a cigarette and lighting it.

"Long way from home."

"Not as far as you. What took you out of China?"

Jei smiled reminiscently. The fading light accented his
features. "Wrong side of a war," he said.

"We have that in common then."

"You didn't leave Georgia though for that reason, did you?"

Jed smoked a moment before answering. "No, when I went, I
left behind three younger brothers. Mama ran it but they could
handle what was needed as well as me. I wanted the West. I had it
in my blood from being a child."

"Those fantasy books?" Jei suggested.

"More likely David Douglas and Lewis and Clark journals. I had read descriptions from those who had seen it. I had to see it for myself. Once I saw it, I wanted to own part of it."

"This is an unlikely place for a ranch."

"Not really. Good meadows, protected in the winter from the worst storms, year round river and a lot of little streams. It's a good place for cattle and nobody else here when I saw it."

"You bought it?"

"Yeah, from Jacques Aubuchon. He had come out here in the 30s. His grandfather had been a friend of my great grandfather. He was given the right to purchase a big chunk of land before it became a territory. He had a deed that had been strong enough to survive all those who wanted to remove such purchases. He built most of the house although I added on the second wing."

"So you knew him?"

"My family had also been in France for a few years, before they came to the Colonies. I don't know how much you are aware of the history of the Scots."

"A little."

"Picking the wrong side in a battle can make you leave a lot of places. We had been part of the Clan Buchan who picked the wrong side in the Jacobite uprising or the attempt to return the rightful king to the throne, depending on how you see it."

Jei grinned and poured himself another shot of whiskey. "I have had some of that experience."

"From France, my family crossed the ocean and made a home in Georgia where I was born. France got iffy also for Jacques. He had stayed with us awhile in Georgia. I liked him and he taught me a lot. When he left, he said I should come visit him. When I got old enough, I took him up on it. I liked this place a lot. It felt more like home than Georgia ever had. By then Jacques was thinking more about dying than living. He wanted to go home to France and he sold it to me. It actually helped to secure it since I was an American citizen."

Jei sipped his whiskey. "I can see you being a Scot. Is that why you sided with the South—past wrongs of your clans?"

"I don't look that far back. I got stuck in that war after a request of my mother that I would protect my brothers. I didn't do a very good job at it. By then it was too late to get out. I just had to try to stay alive."

"You probably could have bought your way out. You were a rich man. You chose not to."

"Your point is?" Jed asked blowing out the smoke and giving Jei a hard look.

"It's convenient to be rich."

Jed laughed. "That's been your experience, has it?"

"Actually, not so much."

"You want to go back to your home someday?"

"I would be executed if I did. When someone loses in China, there are no second chances. No amnesty like your country gave."

"Not always forgiving here either." He took a long draw on the cigarette.

Jei pulled out a long, thin cigar and lit it. "You are a fortunate man to have found where you wish to be."

"I consider myself to be so."

"No desire to go back to Georgia to be buried someday?"

"You are in a mood," Jed said with a chuckle. "I expect I'll die out in the brush here somewhere, and my carcass be eaten by the grizzlies and wolves for revenge on the numbers I have killed."

"Ah you begrudge animal predators like you do human," Jei observed.

"I might actually be more understanding of them. The long-horns held their own. If I bring in better breeding stock, it'll be more an issue."

"Your plans go far into the future for this land."

"I would not be here if they did not."

"And your lady, she will share them with you?"

"She will have to decide that." Jed smiled as he blew out the smoke. "Speaking of that how the hell did you hook up with the blonde?" He gestured toward the kitchen.

"I have rather been asking myself that question. We had been occasional lovers, of course. I took her because I felt sorry for what I knew would happen to her if I left her. We have no commitment to each other. She will go her own way when she finds something more profitable."

"For now, she represents a problem. If I force her off the place, she could turn on us. Not that I think Grayson has any doubts where Raine has gone."

"No, he has ways of knowing. When I began working in Portland, his network didn't appear to be as revolting or far reaching as it has become."

"Did you ever work for him directly?"

"No, but we had dealings. I saw him as an opportunist, amoral, dangerous but not all that I discovered he was. I thought there were many doing what he did. Turned out there weren't... or when there were, they were eliminated."

"Raine had no idea either, obviously."

"But you did. How?"

Jed thought about it before he answered. "He made it easier because he hated me from the start."

"Because he was in love with Raine?"

"Was he?" Jed doubted Grayson knew the meaning of love.

"Possibly not. She suited him as I suited him for a time. He takes what he can use."

She came out the door behind them, and with Deucy at her heels, sat on one of the chairs, holding her dress out from her perspiring chest. "Bernice is joining the card game," she said.

"Maybe we can lose her to one of them," Jed said with a laugh although he didn't find the situation humorous. Bernice was the kind of woman who would cause trouble wherever she was. Trouble he didn't need on his ranch. There was plenty waiting outside.

"Raine, you never told me how you figured out Russ?" Jei asked her.

"It was Kirk Edmonton. Do you know him?"

He nodded.

"My mother had told me what Adam believed regarding Russ, but at that point I had no idea how much he had manipulated all parts of my life. I guess I should have seen it when Jed told me he thought my business was a front for drug smuggling. I was still trying to work that through when Kirk came to the house. He wanted me in another play, which I had already decided I'd not do as I was going to come to Eastern Oregon." She smiled at Jed.

"I realized I had a more immediate problem, that didn't leave time for delay, when Kirk gave it away that he knew I had been involved with someone. Of course, I asked where he'd heard it. He admitted it was from Russ. He tried to make it sound coincidental. When he left, it came together. Not just my businesses were fronts for Russ but so was my theater career."

"That must've been hard to take, sugar."

"Not a great day, I admit. Fortunately, I had already begun to make some arrangements regarding my business and leaving a false trail. At that point though, I still didn't see it being a hurry. I did believe Russell's ruthlessness might turn on me when he saw no other way. That is when I packed my bag. Then Jei was there and the rest is, as they say, history."

"You didn't bring much," Jed said putting out his arm to encourage her to come to sit with him on the step. She hesitated only a moment. She liked sitting next to him where they touched even if only barely.

"I took what mattered most. The journal of herbal remedies my mother had created for me. My fly fishing pole and flies."

"What?" Jed and Jei said at the same time.

She grinned. "Hey, not only men can fish. Adam taught me, and he gave me a pole that could be packed. I figured I might need to get my own food and so..."

Jed shook his head as he put his arm around her. "You are quite a lady," he said hugging her to him.

"She held up like a trooper on the ride over the Cascades," Jei observed as he stubbed out his cigar. "Bernice whined the whole way, but Raine just kept at it. Even cooked at night. I was surprised and impressed."

"Well I had come over on the wagon train, you know," she said enjoying the warmth of Jed's muscular body. "My mother made sure all her girls knew how to do what was required to survive. The herbal remedies were the one thing I had never understood or even thought I'd need to."

"Your mama a witch?" Jei asked.

"Not at all," Raine retorted. "Well she does plant by the moon and with a full moon like this one, she might have some kind of ritual when she gathered herbs... Just purely practical, of course." She giggled.

"My mother believed in that kind of thing also," Jed said. "I hold nothing against women who can take a plant and know how to heal from it."

"Well I am not among them yet," Raine said, but I think I'll take the book with me to Canyon City. Might come in handy."

"You are going to Canyon City?" Jei asked with interest.

"We are taking a small herd. I would like you to stay here along with Josh and Toddy while I am gone," Jed said. "I'll take Jack."

"Before you go," Jei said with a somber tone, "tell me what look after means. There is that one thing we discussed. I can handle that if it turns up, but are you also expecting trouble with the Paiutes or Shoshoni? I heard some was going on down toward the Malheur, rustling stock."

"The few times they've been by, they haven't said anything according to Jack, but who knows. Better ready than regretting it later. The Kalamas will know better what their attitude is. Trust their take on it."

"Why are you going now?"

"We need to better understand the market. I will take fifteen bulls with me. Raine wanted to learn to drive cattle and talked me into taking her."

Jei laughed heartily. "That must have been very difficult to do." He laughed again.

"She has her ways."

"No spells though," she insisted squeezing Jeb's waist. "I don't think Mama has any, but I could probably check on it just in case I need some for getting stubborn men to see things my way."

"Spells?" Bernice asked as she and the men came out from the house to join them on the porch. "I always did figure your mama for a voodoo woman."

"Well she was not," Raine said firmly. "She just knows how to use herbs to heal... No getting rid of inconvenient women." She turned and grinned at the look of dismay on Bernice's face. "I have my own methods for that," she added.

Two days later, as they began moving the bulls, Raine quickly came to see what this job was going to entail. Jed had given her a whip, which helped to turn the big beasts. Nipping at their noses worked for Ace. As they moved out of the pasture, she was assigned the rear. It was least likely to have problems, but one bull did try to run toward her to reconnect with the main herd. Surprising both her and the bull, Fancy moved quickly to cut him off and the whip sent him back to the bunch now heading south. She felt lucky she had stayed on the little mare. Maybe Fancy was more cow pony than she had expected. She had left Deucy with regret, but the little dog didn't like the cattle and had taken a real liking to Josh. She would be safer at the ranch.

The first day they didn't make a lot of progress, but they did find a nice meadow with enough grass to make it easier to keep the bulls bunched. As Jed and Jack unsaddled the horses, she built a fire ring and then a small fire. Soon she had salt pork and potatoes frying over the flames. Coffee was perking on the hot rocks.

When Jed got back, he laid out her blankets next to his. "Where's your gun, sugar?" he asked.

"On the saddle, I guess."

"Make it a habit to bring it with you whatever you do."

"Whatever?"

He grinned. "Whatever. We don't know what's been going on down here. If we run into trouble, it might be a grizzly as well as a Walpapi. You need to be ready. Less apt to get attacked when you are."

"What's a Walpapi?"

"Northern branch of the Paiutes. This had been their land."

"Food is ready," she said taking tin plates and dishing out their servings. As they sat back eating, she thought it hadn't actually been a bad day. Not as hard as riding over the Cascades. "Will the trail all be this smooth?" she asked.

"It gets rougher. There is a ridge we cross before we drop down into the John Day Valley."

"This isn't the John Day Valley where we are? I am sorry but this part of Oregon I don't know much about. Except now that's it's beautiful with these tall pines and more grass than I expected."

"It won't all be that way. We are not taking the main road. This way, we cross a rocky ridge that's more sagebrush and juniper. Drier too." He leaned back sipping his coffee. The sky overhead was full of thousands of stars, none of which did Raine know their names.

"The air is so clear here," she said smiling at the picture of campfire, a man, with a long white beard, sitting hunched over eating while the younger man sprawled out, one knee bent up, supported by an elbow as he sipped the coffee.

"Your coffee is surprisingly good," he said with a smile.

"Coming across on the wagon train did teach me some handy

skills although I never was involved in herding stock; so this is all new."

"You done real good, Ma'am," Jack said as he set down his plate. "Plumb good meal."

"Thank you. You remind me of the wagon master who took us across. He had a beard too. Not so fine and luxuriant as yours, but a fine beard."

"You like beards?" Jed asked with a glint in his eyes.

"I would prefer your face stay clean shaven," she said reaching out brushing his check with her fingertips.

"Any special reason for that?"

"Several and we will not take the topic any further."

Jack chuckled. "You kept up fine for a female. Better'n I figured."

"Thank you, Jack. One thing I sure will sleep well tonight." About then she heard the howl of a wolf. She'd heard them before, but it seemed different sleeping out under the stars and with cattle nearby who depended on them for protection... or did they with those horns?

"How far away is it?" she asked as the wolf howled again, and then she heard a response from higher on the mountain.

"A few miles," Jed said, "and don't worry. They won't bother us. He's probably looking for a lover to sleep with tonight."

Jack chuckled. "Me, I never liked sleepin' with a woman. Picky they are, fussin' at a little snoring."

"A little snoring?" Jed asked with a snort. "Jack, your snoring would scare that wolf away."

The older man harrumphed a few times but rolled himself up in his blanket and promptly seemed to fall asleep, snoring came immediately afterward.

"I see you weren't understating his snoring," she whispered with a little laugh as she pulled off her boots.

"Cuddle up to me and I'll rub your back," he offered taking off his own. She saw him put his revolver under the edge of his blanket. The rifle was just beyond. Ace had curled up at his feet.

She supposed cuddling would be safe with Jack right there. She did like the idea of sleeping with him. "Did you tell Jack about the wedding?"

"Better not to. If you really want it kept a secret for now."

"And I do."

He put his arms around her, pulling the blankets over them. "I like this," he said. "Never had a woman on a cattle drive."

"Ah so a first for the mighty Mr. Hardman."

"With you, there have been a lot of those," he whispered as he rubbed her neck and shoulders, his rough hand feeling surprisingly good as he soothed muscles she hadn't realized were hurting.

"How many cattle drives have you done?" she asked curious about his experience now with this work.

"I can't count them all. We had cattle in Georgia. Devons, which also can have horns, not so long as these and not nearly as tough of animals. We had to move the herds sometimes, take them to the ships. Then once I got to this ranch, twice. Once bringing cattle in and then I had one chance to sell steers before I had to leave."

"Where did you sell them that time?"

"The Dalles. A little farther but a better price then."

"And you didn't want to do that this time?"

"One problem would be the possibility of road agents who might not mind taking a herd. Plus it is more likely Grayson would hear about us and send someone to the ranch."

"You don't think he will anyway?"

"Eventually." He kissed her neck.

"This way is more dangerous to the Indians, isn't it?"

"If it was a regular route. From what I have heard, most of the attacks have been south of us. I know it'll get to us, but better to do this as soon as possible for that reason. Don't worry about it. Ace would let us know if a stranger was approaching."

She wondered if that was true or was the gutsy little dog too tired to care, and Jed only told her that to reassure her.

"Are you a good businessman?" she asked turning and kissing his neck where the shirt was open.

"It's not my favorite thing, but I can work with numbers when I have to. My father taught me a lot about making a business work. He had taken what his family had built and took it further."

"Without slaves."

"Without. My great great great grandfather freed all the ones on his land as soon as he bought it."

"When did your people arrive?

"1748. It's a convoluted story."

"Tell me"

His name was Duncan Hardman. He saw what was happening, the doom ahead for the clans and the Jacobite cause. He sent his wife and two children to France, but in honor he could not go."

"And was killed?"

"No. He was though at Culloden, where so many died. Wounded, he escaped and got to France. He reached Margaret where she had found sanctuary with old friends, the Aubuchons. As he healed from his wounds, Margaret and he knew they could not return to Scotland, didn't want to live forever in France. Their only hope for a new life was in the Colonies. When he bought the land in Georgia, they set down roots, grew cotton, and within a year had freed all their slaves. Or so the story went."

"So you're Scottish."

"Amongst other things now—like most Americans. What are you?"

She had to think about that. "I guess English. Would that make us enemies?" She gave a little laugh.

"I think we could work out peace terms." He brushed her temple with his lips. "My people are practical. Our not having slaves was not just about morality but based on logic. My grandfather said Duncan told him that freemen work harder. It proved to be true as our land there prospered. There were a lot of south-erners who had no use for slavery."

"But didn't like colored people."

"I suspect some bigotry is part of human nature. Oregon, with all its pro-North sympathies has prejudices written into its laws."

"I guess it's fear of the unknown. Your mother was excep-tional to raise Josh as if he was her own son. They would not all have done that, would they?"

"Not there or here. She could have resented him for what her husband had done. She didn't put that onto a baby." He smiled. "She adored him from the start and maybe he was her favorite."

"Despite wanting you to run the plantation?"

"She was a practical woman."

She felt her eyelids growing heavy. She enjoyed watching the stars, smelling the wood smoke as it drifted upward, hearing the cattle grazing nearby. If it weren't for the worry of rustlers or warring Indian tribes, she would have liked this whole experience.

She woke once during the night, hearing Jack snoring loudly. She looked up to see that Jed was not sleeping. "Haven't you slept?" she asked.

"Best not to," he said with a smile in his voice as he ran his hand lightly down her arm.

"You need sleep too."

"I've had a lot of sleepless nights. I can manage."

"You hear anything out there?"

"No, it's quiet. I heard a deer eating off to the left, beyond some small creatures scurried around. An owl swooped down on probably a mouse. The full moon has them all busy."

She hadn't realized the moon was so full but saw now it was high in the sky and giving an eerie cast to the meadow and to Jed's face. He looked almost white in the silvery light. She supposed she looked the same. "I could stay awake while you sleep," she offered wondering if she really could.

"Nah. I'll be fine. Tomorrow we'll be in a better place where there are some rock canyons, easier to hear someone come up on us... not that I expect anything."

"You'll be so tired tomorrow though."

"I was in a war, remember. Sometimes we had to go several days without sleep. You get used to it."

"You are tough," she teased rubbing her hand down his arm, taking his big hand into hers, feeling the calluses and hard ridges. The moonlight was sufficient to see the lines in his hand. She remembered what Nancy had said about a love and life line. She held Jed's hand up to where she could see the palm.

"What are you looking for?" he asked not missing how seriously she was studying the lines.

She felt frightened as although Jed only had one love line, like hers, it didn't appear his lifeline was very long. She felt a shiver of fear.

"Don't anticipate the future, sugar," he said, kissing her hair. "It will take care of itself."

"Can you really live that way?"

"Sometimes."

Two days later they drove the herd through Tiger Town into Canyon City. "The cattle corrals will be here," he said, "and we'll have to find someone with money to buy the beef."

An hour later, her hat shoved down over her forehead to make it difficult to see her face, she sat on her horse as she watched Jed dicker with two men about the price for the bulls. They seemed excited at the prospect of fresh beef and soon a bill of sale and dollars had exchanged hands.

"Want a hotel tonight?" he asked.

"They have a hotel?"

"Shore do," he drawled, "bath tub too. I'd like to buy you some dresses but we'll have to be careful how we do it. Some more pants too. I've grown real fond of you in pants."

"You got a good price?"

"Fair price. We need to visit the bank too."

"There's more town here than I expected."

"Where there's gold, business will follow. Did you see the flour mill as we drove the herd in? We should buy more flour since we have been expanding our population at the ranch." He grinned.

"I wonder... could we go into a saloon?"

He looked at her with amazement. "Why?"

"Well as a young man, I could do that. As a woman, I cannot. I just was curious."

"Bank first, and then... All right, if you are sure."

She was; and forty-five minutes later, he led their way into the saloon off the main street. The air was smoky, the smell of beer and vomit in the air. He wondered how long she'd be good for. He had told her to use the strap on her hat to keep it on tight as if it came off, this could turn nasty. He wondered how far away the local sheriff was.

"This is interesting," she said forcing her voice to a deeper tone.

"You think?" he asked as he ordered two beers.

"The kid of age?" the barkeep asked looking at her with some doubt.

"Just barely," he said aware his Southern drawl had gotten some attention as soon as he opened his mouth.

The barkeep shrugged and set two lukewarm beers in front of them. She took a sip and managed to do it without making a face. She looked around the room. He wondered what she thought of the woman in a garish red dress sitting at a table with two men who looked like miners. There was a sizeable mirror behind the bar. Red curtains at the window looked as though they had not been cleaned since they were hung.

"You the cowboys brought in the beef?" the bartender asked.

Jed nodded, uneasily aware that he should have said no to Raine. A rough looking character walked down the length of the bar to stand next to her. "This here, your friend?" he asked adding a crude comment, as he looked at Jed with a sneer.

Jed ignored him until the man, taller than Jed, grabbed his shoulder and turned him to face him. "I asked you a question, Reb."

"And I treated it like it deserved," Jed said with a cold smile as he removed the man's hand.

"We just taught you Rebs a lesson. Maybe you need a refresher?"

"You in the war?" Jed retorted.

"No, why?"

"Just checking your credentials to find fault with anybody."

The man turned then to Raine and took hold of her arm. "This guy your special friend? I heard Rebs like special friends."

"I want to go," she said in a husky voice.

"You go ahead, kid. You sound like a northerner. Him though, he needs a reminder why the South was riffraff and lowlifes, wanting slaves. Any Reb deserves to be slaughtered, not paroled." He swung his fist as Jeb stepped back avoiding the punch.

"You're drunk," he snapped hoping he could yet avoid a fight. When the miner's fist was directed at him again, that wasn't going to happen, and he slammed his right hard into the man's belly, doubling him and sending him staggering backward.

A man who had been standing quietly behind him at the bar grabbed his arm as another man tried to get hold of the other. Jed wheeled, kicked out with his boot and sent the first man to the floor as his boot slammed into the man's knee so hard that he'd be lucky if it wasn't broken.

Fists were coming at him from all directions as he lashed out, feeling his own blows connect but some were getting past his defenses. He was staggered back against the bar. The gunshot shocked him as well as the man who had just punched him in the jaw.

"Let him go," an angry voice snarled. Jed looked and realized Raine had drawn her revolver and fired it into the ceiling. It was enough to cause the few men interested in a fight to stagger away. "Let him be," she growled still forcing a depth to her voice that he had never heard.

The men who had been interested in beating up a stranger were less interested in confronting a weapon in the hands of a boy who seemed quite willing to use it. "Hey, back off," one said as he grabbed the arm of his friend who now had the damaged kneecap.

Raine grabbed Jed's arm and pulled him toward the door. "It's time to go," she said again in that lower register.

Outside the night air helped clear his head. "My God," she said in her own voice as they walked rapidly away. "Is that the way it usually happens in saloons? Why didn't you warn me? I'd never have asked to go."

"I hadn't been here since the war either. But Southerners aren't popular in Oregon. I did know that," he said feeling of his jaw to try to determine if he had broken anything.

"You're bleeding." She touched the side of his cheek lightly where the skin had been split by one of the punches. "I'm sorry, Jed. I had no idea."

"Maybe they were suspicious because I had a kid with me for nefarious purposes," he drawled with a crooked grin.

"Hmmph, well you do," she said smiling now. "How about we find that hotel and get a bath."

"Together?" he suggested with a laugh that hurt his jaw.

He saw her think about that but shake her head. He smiled but didn't argue. "Write your letter to your mother, and we'll mail it from here—and remember what I said—no return address. In the morning, we'll get married, and head north right after."

"Married in pants?" she asked with an amused smile.

"Not quite how you imagined it?" he teased with an answering smile.

"I didn't think I'd get married but no, not as I would have imagined it."

"At this point, the sooner we get out of here, the better; so yes, in pants. You can have the dress next wedding. How does that sound?"

"Fine. Even better sounds a bath and a real bed. Where will you sleep?" she asked.

"In the room next to yours. I don't trust this town. If you wake up and hear anything, let out a rebel yell or better yet," he put his hand on the butt of her revolver, "kill the bastard."

She laughed. "Unless it's you, of course."

"It won't be me until the day you invite me into your bed." He needed to believe that day would come. He knew what he wanted. He just hoped someday she would, and that it'd be him.

CHAPTER 15

In the morning, when Raine walked down the narrow stairs, to what served as a lobby in the small hotel, Jed was waiting. He looked, as she did, cleaner, but they were both garbed for the trail. She had pulled her hair up into her hat but this time didn't have it pinned there. She felt she might be required to prove she was a woman beyond her certificate of birth.

"I have something for you," he said as he walked with her outside.

"I hope it involves breakfast." She looked hopefully up and down the dusty street to see if anything looked like a café.

"That comes next." He dug into his pocket and came out with a gold chain and locket. "It was my mother's. I brought her jewelry back with me. You can have it all when we get back to the ranch, but I wanted you to have this now. Today isn't meant to be the real deal for us. It's more of a business transaction, but someday I hope we have a wedding with all the trimmings." His smile showed his expectations. She hoped she would fulfill them. She still was not sure.

She took the delicate locket and studied the engraving of a

rose before she opened it. Inside were tiny photos of a man and woman.

"My mother and father," he said. "You can feel free to change the pictures to something you prefer if you wish."

"Even with the beard, he looks like an older you, but I can see Josh in him too," she said as she studied the images. "Your mother was beautiful, and I wouldn't think of removing them. It's an heirloom and beautiful. Thank you." She opened the clasp and handed it to him to fasten around her neck. She then let the locket fall between her breasts.

They ate breakfast at a tiny café where the lady doing the cooking also did the waitressing. "More coffee?" she asked as they had finished and were sitting back. Jed nodded. "Town's kind of quiet today," he said as he took a sip.

"Posse went south looking for a band of Paiutes stole some horses from a ranch south of here. Fools. Ain't likely they'll ever find 'em."

"You have a sheriff?"

"If you can call him that. Mostly he lays around when he ain't riling folks up to run off on a wild goose chase. Just shiftless is my opinion," she said with a twisted smile.

"Goodness, why don't you get rid of him?" Raine asked thinking of her own stepfather and what a good sheriff he made.

"I would, sonny, but I married the no count," the woman said with another grimace before she disappeared back into the kitchen.

It was all she could do to resist laughing. "You see there are reasons to be careful about getting married," she told Jed as she saw his own smile.

"Well, boy, I'll be real cautious about that," he drawled forgetting for a moment to watch that Georgia twang.

The woman came quickly from the back. "You one of those Southerners?" she asked with narrowed eyes.

"Years ago," he said. "Had to escape. Just not worth being in a place full of scoundrels. You know of land for sale around here?"

"Everybody wants to mine, and you looking to farm?" she asked with a friendlier look.

"I'll check at the courthouse. Thanks for the great breakfast."

Once outside, she said, "You feel even she needs to have a false trail laid?"

"Me being a southerner is not a commendation around here whether Grayson reaches this far or not. He might since they got the stage line running between here and The Dalles."

"Where's Jack?"

"He'll meet us a little north of town about noon. If he shows up."

"You doubt it?"

"Not really, but I had two men and one decided he'd profit more by panning for gold than looking after cattle. You never know."

"Hey, Hardman," the yell came from down the street, and a rough looking man came running up to them.

"Speak of the devil," Jed said as he turned to face the man. "Jessup. Find any gold?"

"Nothin'. All taken or in big mines. Who's the kid?" The man looked curiously at Raine.

"Your replacement. Lucky I brought him when I came back, wasn't it?"

"How'd you know I wouldn't be there?" he asked as he kept looking at Raine with curiosity.

"Just a lucky guess."

"I'd like to come back."

"Sorry I have all the hands I need now."

Jessup frowned. "I heard you brought in a herd. You and the kid?"

"And Jack?"

"He's older than me. I could do more for you."

"Except one thing."

"What?"

"Be trusted."

Jessup glared at him. "Someday somebody will take you down a notch."

Jed smiled. "But it won't be you today, will it?"

Jessup glared at him but walked off glancing back once more to look at Raine.

"Time to move fast," Jed said as he turned her toward the small building that served as a courthouse. "It should be ready for us."

"Witnesses and all?"

"Men here wear a lot of hats. Turns out the blacksmith is also the Justice of the Peace. He said his wife and daughter would be witnesses."

In the front office, a man wearing an official looking jacket rose from the desk and smiled. "Are we going to wait for the bride then?"

Raine pulled off her hat and let her hair fall loose. "She's here," Jed said with a grin at the man's surprise.

"Reckon I shouldn't be surprised. I'm Gabe Wilson and glad to meet you two young folks."

Two women rose from the back of the room. One older and plumper and the other young enough to be looking hungrily at Jed as he took off his own hat. Raine looked up at him thinking again what a handsome man he was. If that was all it took, that and lust, they'd have a great marriage, but it wasn't and because of that, she knew her mother had been right. They had to have more.

Justice Wilson spoke the words she had heard before only this time it was her turn to answer yes and repeat the ancient vows. "Do you have a ring," the Justice asked.

"I will get her one."

The Justice nodded and then finished the rest of the words that made them man and wife. Jed bent and lightly brushed her lips with his. Then the two women, one with more regret in her smile than pleasure, congratulated them. They signed the papers, which Jed pocketed.

"I'd appreciate it if you didn't mention this wedding to anybody," Jed said as he handed the man a $100 bill to pay for the services but also encourage forgetfulness.

"Don't worry. I ain't the talkin' sort. I'll get the papers sent in though; so it's official like you want."

Outside, her hair tucked back up under her hat, Raine tried to think if she felt any different but, of course, why would she. This wasn't a real wedding although it was as binding as though it had been.

"So what'd you think of Canyon City?" he asked as they rode north.

"It is larger than I expected."

"Instant gold will do that." His smile was crooked. "It's a lot wilder here than when I came before I had to go east."

"I did notice that too." Did you come here often?"

"For what?" He laughed.

"Shopping... or things."

"I haven't been much for towns." When he didn't say anything more, she looked over. "They never did do good by me," he added teasingly.

"You might be hanging around the wrong places." She lifted her eyebrows with a questioning look.

"Ah, so that's my problem. I need you for a guide to the right places."

"I pass on that," she said remembering her own poor choices, which had led directly to his problems.

When they reached Jack, who was sitting under a pine, they dismounted to drink from their canteens. "You see Jessup in town?" Jed asked as he rolled a cigarette.

"Seen him," the old timer responded reaching for a biscuit that Jed had brought from the cafe.

"Tell him anything about the ranch?"

"Nope. He sure had a lot of questions though. What do you figure he's up to? This is a right good biscuit. Jessie make it?"

"If she's the lady in the café, yep."

"She sure married a scoundrel with that no good they got for a sheriff."

"Easy to make that mistake," Jed agreed smoking with a thoughtful expression.

"Woman can cook like that, she could get herself any man she wanted," Jack said with a chortle.

"Jessup with anybody when you talked to him?"

Jack thought a moment. "Seems like he was. Two no-counts."

"Checkered shirt on one of them?"

"Yep."

"All right, likely it'll not be a problem, but we need to watch our back trail. I banked most of what we made from the cattle, but somebody might not know that."

Just when she'd been trying to relax and quit worrying, he had to go and say something like that. Then she thought about her own city. Safe hadn't existed there either. It wasn't the problem with places. It was the problem with people. She realized how good it was that Jed looked ahead and beyond. Another thing to his credit that she had not appreciated so much in Portland.

As they rode north again, she began to think about the real problem. Clearly it was not Jed. He was a man to admire and even now with the way his eyes scanned for movement both ahead and behind him, she knew he was a man to ride the trail with as she'd heard some describe it. But was she? That's what she had yet to find out.

The ride back to the ranch went fast. Once there, Raine took a few hours to rest but then set about figuring out what she had to offer to a life like this. Her first step was to walk around the outside of the house. Surprisingly, on the edge of a small stream, she found the remnants of what appeared to have been a vegetable garden. The deer and weeds had done a lot to take it over, but it had rhubarb plants, some herbs she didn't recognize, and a few fruit trees of indeterminate type. She would need tools and headed for the barn to see what was there.

Jed was at the corrals with a horse he had on a long lead. When he saw her coming, he released the horse and came to her. "Need something?" he asked.

"A hoe and shovel."

"For what?"

"You have a garden behind the house. Did you know that?"

He shook his head. "Maybe Jack does or maybe it's what was here from before I bought it. Wouldn't seem it'd be in very good shape."

"Not yet, but I think it could be. It's not too late to plant for a fall crop if I can get it worked up. I actually saw a rhubarb plant, which must've survived the winters. It makes a good pie." She smiled at his bemused expression.

"You sure you want to do that?" he asked but headed for the barn to find the tools she'd requested. With them, he also handed her a scythe. "When I finish with this mare, I'll go see what you've been up to."

"You're gentling her?" she asked looking at the lovely brown horse in the corral.

He nodded. "She's two years old. It's time she got used to being worked and ridden. You might need a backup for Fancy at some point if we did longer rides."

"You sure I wouldn't fail before she did?" she asked with a little laugh.

"I would have said that if you hadn't shown what you can do when we took the bulls to Canyon City. I was surprised to be honest. I expected you to want to stay in the house."

"As your mother did?"

"No. She was hands on. I just thought you'd want what you had in Portland."

"Well, I fit into what I needed to do for there. I thought I was creating that world. Turned out I wasn't, of course."

"Don't blame yourself for that," he said putting his hand on her shoulder with a soft touch that was more brother to sister than lover. "He wanted what you offered, and it wasn't just a pretty face. You are a classy, strong woman. I think that's what drew him as much as anything."

"Is it what drew you?" she asked genuinely wondering why from the time he had come into her store he had begun to court her.

His smile was gentle. "I don't know what it was. I just knew you were my woman. It was probably the whole package." He let his eyes roam down her body. "It's a pretty nice package," he said dropping his hand, but the twinkle in his eyes said everything.

"Yours is too," she said with one of her own smiles.

"In town, I asked Jack to buy some small sized pants when he was stocking up on the supplies. It won't be female garb, but it'll give you something to change into. That and a spare shirt are there too."

"Thank you, Jed. Where do I do washes around here?"

"In the winter, we heat it up on the stove and wash clothes in kitchen. This time of the year, we use the smaller pool near the barns for washes, especially when the clothes are filthy and bloody from the cattle work. Wherever you wash up, don't leave the ranch yard."

"Why not?"

"Last time I was up there, I saw grizzly scat up the ridge, evidently nosing around for some easy pickings." He pointed to a rocky bluff beyond the pastures. "That's just too close for comfort. I'll kill him as soon as I can find him, but until I get him in my sights, I don't want you wandering far from the house."

"Wouldn't my gun be enough protection?"

"Maybe with some more practice but a charging grizzly isn't something I want to think about you facing. Keep it with you... but stay close to the house even with it."

When Raine got back to the garden space, she was surprised to see Bernice sitting on a rock by the small creek, her head in her hands. "What's the matter?" she asked.

Bernice looked up quickly and put a snide smile on her face. "Nothing. Why would you think that? I'm just fine."

"Obviously you are not. What is it?"

Bernice turned away pursing her lips together into a hard line. "I am fine. I am always fine."

"All right. Have it your way."

"What are you doing here anyway?" The blonde sighed and wiped her eyes before she turned back around.

"This looks like a garden has been here. See that plant? Rhubarb. It would make a pie and it looks like it's not overripe."

"God, how do you know this stuff? Oh wait, it's your mother, isn't it?"

"And my grandmother. I used to visit her before she died. She always had a garden, even in winter. I know so little of it, but I can learn."

"My family never did any of that."

"I don't remember your folks on the train at all."

"Because they kept away from everybody. They were so superior, always knew they were the best and could care less about anyone who could not profit them."

"That's a shame."

"Not to them," Bernice said coldly. "Don't you dare feel sorry for me, Loraine. I despise pity."

"All right. Why don't you take that shovel. I'll take the hoe and we'll see what we can do about pulling up some of the weeds taking over this garden."

Bernice made a face but without a good excuse to say no, she sighed and took the shovel.

"Mama always says working in a garden is good for the soul."

"She believes in a soul?" Bernice asked as she fought to get the shovel into the ground. "This feels like clay or something is blocking me."

"I don't know about that. I think it's a phrase she used. Whenever she wanted to talk to me, give me a lecture or some wisdom, out to the garden we'd go."

"She sure got herself a hot husband. God, I couldn't believe it when I learned Adam Stone married her."

"This line of conversation is going to send you back to the house," Raine said with irritation.

"All right. All right." Bernice laughed but then her face turned sad. "I made a lot of mistakes, Loraine. I hate to admit it, but it's true."

"Welcome to the club."

"I don't just mean with Russell but everything. I hate to even say this but I took the easy road, and it didn't turn out so easy."

"You can always turn that around. That's what Mama always says."

"I think sometimes it's too late."

"I doubt that."

"You can do things that hurt others, and there is no going back."

Raine stopped trying to hoe and sat in the dirt. "All right. Tell me. You need to get it out. What is eating at you? That you were a whore?"

"Actually not that," Bernice said with another laugh and giving Raine one of her looks. "I see nothing wrong with charging for what men want."

"If not that, then what?"

Bernice sighed. "I hurt someone good. Someone I cared about."

"I can't give you absolution, you know."

"What does that mean?" Bernice sat down hard on the ground.

"Forgiveness."

"Well nobody can give me that."

Raine found it hard to believe she was having this conversation with Bernice, a woman she had disliked for years but maybe never really knew. "You can give it to yourself."

Bernice gave a snort. "You didn't even want to hear about it. You don't want to hear about it?"

"Did you murder someone?" Raine tried to think what could be so bad that a person would feel they never could be forgiven.

"No." Bernice rose and walked over to the little stream.

Raine gave up and came to stand with her. The stream was shallow-- little ripples revealed round rocks beneath the water. She reached in and found one that looked nearly round. "Tell me now. I won't give you either forgiveness or condemnation, but you need to talk to someone."

Bernice stared into the water. Sunlight was barely reaching the area as the sun headed behind some clouds. "Remember I told you there was a man on the wagon train?"

"Yes."

"It was my cousin's husband."

Raine felt a shock that went through her body. Jennie. Sweet Jennie and the loss of her baby. Her husband always gone somewhere to play cards only it wasn't playing cards. This was bad all right. Worse that she knew about it now. "William"

Bernice nodded.

"Did Jennie know?"

"No, or at least I don't think so. She never said anything to me. When they got to Oregon, William wanted nothing to do with me. I haven't seen her in all these years. I haven't wanted to see her."

"I had no idea. Well I knew Jennie was unhappy and William... I can't believe it in a way."

"Why because it's such a horrible thing to have done?"

Raine gave a little laugh of her own. "No, because he was such a... well pathetic little man."

"I thought... well he liked me. He told me he did. He made me feel wanted. You won't understand what that's like not to be wanted. You had parents who wanted you, sisters. Now even Jed. I had nobody. I kept trying to get love all the wrong ways." She glared resentfully at Raine but then sighed again. "I have lived a life of a fool. I even had my fortune told once, and it said I'd never know love. The woman was right."

"I wish my mother was here."

"Thank god, she's not." Bernice laughed again but without humor.

"I am thinking of all the wisdom she gave me over many years including not all that long ago."

"Like you needed that?"

"I always need that. Anyway what I think she'd say is what I am going to say. You have to learn to love yourself before you can truly love anyone else."

Bernice began to cry again. "What was to love? I was beautiful, but I soon won't be. Jei would drop me at any town where I could be a whore until men couldn't stand me and then what?" She shook her head as she stared blankly back at the stream.

"I can't help you learn to love yourself, but I know it's where this has to start. And you have choices besides being a whore."

"Like what? Marrying someone who will hit me when he's mad?"

"It doesn't have to be that way."

"Hah." Bernice glared at her again. "What do you know about it? Miss Goody-two-shoes."

Raine laughed, and Bernice looked at her with surprise. "You don't even know what that means, do you?" Raine asked her.

"It means holier than thou to me."

"It's actually from a nursery rhyme by Oliver Goldsmith and about a little girl who is very poor and has only one shoe. She gets two shoes and is so happy. If I remember right, she then becomes rich and shares her wealth with others."

Bernice cursed. "Leave it to you to come up with some positive way to see even that."

Raine laughed. "I wish my mother could hear you say that. She'd love to think it was true. Look, Bernice, I can't help you with this. I just know the answer is loving yourself, and there are ways to make money without marrying for it or turning to prostitution."

"Like what?"

"Cooking, sewing. Mother makes money from sewing dresses."

"Those haven't been exactly in my skill set," Bernice said with a reluctant smile.

"It's ironic," Raine said as she turned the small round rock over in her hand. "We might have that in common. Surprising as it'd be that we'd have anything. I've been feeling as though I may not have really loved myself either."

"You?" Bernice sounded truly amazed and for once the look on her face seemed authentic.

"Look, we are both looking for the same thing, I think—to feel better about ourselves. If you aren't doing that yet, you will have to if you ever want to find someone else to love you. Maybe we can find some of that—starting with this garden."

"Seems unlikely," Bernice said with a reluctant smile.

"About as unlikely as I can imagine but, we can give it a try."

"I won't like you. I hope you know that," Bernice said with narrowed eyes.

"I don't expect to like you either. Let's work on the garden though and let that take care of itself."

CHAPTER 16

R aine lay in her bed, Deucy sleeping at the foot of the mattress. Outside she heard an owl in one of the pine trees-- calling for its mate perhaps? She thought, as she had for the week since they had returned from the drive, how close Jed was to her. All it would take was opening the door, and she could be in his bed.

She remembered though her mother's words and was sure that despite her recognizing more and more the caliber of man he was, she still wasn't sure they could make a life together. She was beginning to believe the problem lay in her more than him. They had not yet put together the ingredients to bake that cake. What would it take to change that... if it could be changed.

She remembered the cryptic letter she had sent her mother from Canyon City. She hadn't signed her name but had simply said she was trying to see if she could put together a cake and not to worry about her. She knew her mother would understand. Whether she would worry, now that was another question altogether. She told her not to write and hoped she would understand the reasons why.

In the morning, Jed planned to take cattle to one of the forts south of them. He said he would be gone as much as four days. She had not asked to go. Jei wanted his own chance to try taking a herd, but that wasn't her reason. She needed time without Jed nearby tempting her to think about where it was going with him. She was his wife and yet she was not.

Surprisingly, she and Bernice had gotten along better than she had expected after their talk. She had no idea how seriously Bernice had taken any of it, but she seemed to be working harder do her share and not say offensive things. Perhaps her fear that Jed would make her leave was a factor more than any words Raine had said.

She wished she could just go and lie in the bed with him, cuddle as they had on the trail drive. It wouldn't end there though; so she stayed where she was, wondering if he also lay awake.

By first light, she dressed in the boy's pants, a loose fitting shirt and hurried down the stairs to the kitchen to help Toddy prepare breakfast. For once she had beat him and after letting Ace and Deucy out for a run, set about getting the stove fired up and coffee started.

She felt Jed's energy before she heard his step and turned to see him in the doorway, leaning against the jamb. He was wearing a work shirt, scarf at his neck, pants, boots with spurs, the ever present cartridge belt and holstered revolver. He looked ready for the trail, but his eyes said his mind was not on where he was going.

"You look pretty at the stove there," he said with a smile that was more sexy than it had a right to be.

"You look ready to leave."

"Not ready but willing. I don't ever want to leave you, sugar," he drawled. "I hope you know that. I haven't pressed you, but it's not because I haven't wanted to. I hope you can make up your mind soon about what you want."

She knew what she wanted. She just wasn't sure she was willing to face it. Maybe she was afraid. She managed to smile.

"You will be careful," she said as she went over to the cupboard for the bowl of eggs. Those had come from the small settlement west of them when Jack had last ridden over for supplies. She was thinking she should get some chickens and then knew that meant she was thinking of staying. Chickens would require building a chicken coop. She wondered if Jed would be willing to build one, or would he see it as silly.

"Would you like hotcakes?" she asked as she got out the ingredients and avoided addressing what he had said.

He smiled as he sat at the table, rolling and then lighting a cigarette. "Sounds good." His tone of voice told her he was disappointed in how she had evaded him. Jack and Jei entered the kitchen yawning and looking anything but ready for taking the bulls south. Josh came in right after them, with Bernice behind him. For the first time Raine wondered about that relationship, as Bernice and Josh had spent a lot of time together recently. Jei didn't seem to care. Was Bernice, however, heading for hurting another man?

By the time Toddy came in, everyone was eating, and all he had to do was sit at the table accepting his own cakes. The Kalama brothers came in from outside and shook their head at the food being offered. They had their own preferences for food and often slept out in the woods.

"That bear's been around again," Joe said as he accepted a cup of coffee.

Jed took another draw on his cigarette. "Where'd you see sign?"

"Scat and on the ridge and below it."

"That's too close." Jed frowned as he took another long draw on the cigarette.

"Maybe you gonna have to track him," Joe suggested.

"Damn, I wanted to get these bulls gone. The military came through Monument and sounded like the camps were ready for them. I can't take the risk though of the bear coming to the house."

"Not much you can do about it, brother," Josh said sipping his coffee.

"There is one thing. You take the herd to the fort. Jack knows the way. You and Jei should be enough. Joe will help me track the grizzly and put an end to him hanging around here. There was a dead calf in the woods two days ago. I didn't say anything because I wasn't sure who had done the kill. Grizzly, cougar and wolf all had been at the carcass. The tracks though were the size of the big silver."

"Why don't I go after him?" Josh asked looking uneasy at being the one to take the bulls to the fort.

"Several reasons, but the main one is I am the boss. You are taking the cattle. It'll be good for the soldiers to get the idea that this ranch has more than one in charge."

Josh snorted his incredulity. "Right, like I am in charge."

"You aren't yet, but you might be someday. You're taking the bulls, and I'm going to get us a rug."

Raine poured each man more coffee and felt a surge of fear at the very idea of Jed going after a big bear. "Couldn't we just let the animal go?" she asked trying to keep her tone neutral.

"Josh, get yourself ready," he told him as he took her arm. "You, come outside with me where we can talk this out."

On the porch, he took another drag on his cigarette. "I won't take the risk with Josh going after the bear. The only ones used to that kind of hunting, besides me, are the Kalamas."

"So they could do it."

He smiled but the expression in his eyes told her this was not going to be changed. "I have the responsibility, and I will be the one doing it."

"So can I go with you on the hunt?" she asked thinking if she was with him perhaps she could keep him from taking too much a risk or save him if he did.

He gave a little laugh. "You can't be serious."

"I could be a help."

"Grizzlies are undependable for what they will do. They are as likely to hunt you as you hunt them. I don't want you with me."

"Oh, then like you should do it?" she asked with some rising anger in her voice that she tried to suppress but couldn't quite manage. This was it. This was exactly what she had feared. He would do risky things and end up dead.

He considered as he looked out toward the cattle grazing below the house. "Raine, are you ever going to let us have a real marriage?"

"What does a real marriage mean?"

"One person has to make the decision in the end, after listening to the other. In one area, that might be you. In another me. You don't know anything about bear hunting, do you?"

He had her there. She shook her head.

"I trusted you to write your folks. I didn't ask to oversee what you said or question whether you needed to do it, did I?"

"No," she said feeling frustrated with where this was going.

"That bear is coming too close to our home and animals. I can't take the chance that one day he'll be out back while you're working in that garden you are doing such a nice job of renovating especially since you got seeds from the Sutlers in Monument."

She was not about to let herself be distracted, as he probably hoped, by the talk of her garden. "You seriously think the bear would do that?"

"Bears aren't supposed to hang around people's homes. Maybe he got into refuse somewhere. I don't know, but we can't have him here, and there is only one way to change that."

She sighed. "You will be careful, won't you?"

He smiled then and pulled her into his arms. "I have a lot of reasons to be careful."

"Why did you want Josh to take the bulls to the fort? It's not as simple as you said, is it?"

"Part of it, but part is I want him to have some time away from

Bernice. He's a young man with all the weaknesses that entails. She's working him."

"Maybe she really cares for him."

He leaned back and gave her one of his looks.

"It's possible, isn't it?"

"Which is why I won't say anything to him about it. I just want him to get some time away and maybe I won't have to.'"

"She could have changed," she said.

"True..." She could see he had his doubts, but at least he was open to that possibility.

"I know... She might not too," she said with a smile.

"You will have to take care of the place while I am off hunting, and they are gone."

"You plan on camping out there instead of coming back each night?" She didn't like that idea at all.

"Most likely in a tree near that carcass," he said with another of those smiles that melted her to her toes.

"Then don't fall out of it," she ordered.

His smile broadened. "You getting any closer to knowing what you want with us?"

"Maybe."

"What is it about me that makes you doubt me?" he asked with a touch of uncertainty in his voice.

"It's not so much you." Although she knew some was him. "It's me. Can I really live this life?"

"We can compromise on that. I told you I would. Right after we make sure Grayson is no danger to you."

She didn't like the way he said that, but she didn't try to argue. She only wanted to be held by him... oh and have him not go bear hunting.

When the herd had been gathered and sent off, with Ace along to help the three riders, Jed began getting together what he would need to go after the grizzly. He wanted his 44 Sharps with its bone crunching 375 grain slug as well as 44-40 revolver. He didn't plan to sleep on the ground and well knew the bear might go after him even in a tree. If he didn't see the bear soon enough, and it required close fighting, he also sheathed his hatchet to his belt.

When he saw two riders heading toward the ranch, he walked up from the barn. "Can I help you, boys?" he asked thinking he probably looked armed for bear, which he, of course, was.

"I'm Walters and he's Smith. We're looking for work," the bigger of the two said scanning beyond Jed to the two women now on the porch.

"Full up," Jed said sure these two wouldn't be hired even if he hadn't felt he had enough men.

"Sorry to hear that. We know cattle," the smaller man said with the kind of smile that Jed recognized as forced.

"Might be some ranches down on the Malheur need help," Jed suggested.

"Heard there's Injun trouble down that way," Smith said.

"That can be found anywhere. If you want to avoid that, head back to the Willamette Valley." He rested his hand on the butt of his revolver.

"We could use a meal," Walters asked.

The hospitality could not be denied. Jed nodded, stepped back and showed them where they could water and tie their horses at the corrals. A few minutes later, the two stepped onto the porch. "Pretty place here," Smith said. "You working a few cows?"

"A few."

Walters looked up with interest when Raine came out from the kitchen. "We have roast beef and bread," she said.

"Sounds right good, Ma'am," he said.

"Why don't you boys sit on the porch," Jed suggested unwilling to admit them to the house.

"Shore. Mighty fine here." They sat on the chairs and studied the buildings, smiling at Jed as they did it.

In the kitchen, Raine began slicing beef. Bernice came to her.

"I know that guy. He's worked for Russ. His real name is Walker that is if he wasn't using a phony there too." She looked pale. "The other one is Si Tubbs. They are both bad news."

"Jed seems to be aware they aren't to be trusted. Don't let them see you but please finish here, and I'll get my revolver just in case there is to be more trouble than he can handle." She doubted that... but on the other hand. She ran upstairs for her holster and revolver, belting them around her waist. Carrying out the food, she smiled and set the tray on the small table. "Want some coffee too?" she asked.

"We'd plumb appreciate that if it's not too much trouble," the man she now knew to be Tubbs said.

Toddy came out from the house with the coffee. "How you doing Si?" he asked.

"Si? My name's Jim... er Smith."

"Look," Jed said, now holding his revolver and pointed at them. "The game is over. Take the food with you but get out of here."

"What about the coffee?"

"That works for honest men coming through—not liars." He wanted to kill them. He felt he should kill them, but he'd done enough of that in the war to last him two lifetimes. He knew how. He just didn't have the stomach for it.

Whatever was in his eyes, the two men grabbed their food and mounted their horses. "Not a very friendly place here," Tubbs said.

"No, it's not," Jed agreed. "Hope I don't see either of you again as I'd figure you were back for trouble if I did."

"You talk tough," Walker blustered.

"There won't be talking if I see you again," Jed said coldly. "Now get out."

When the two had ridden out of sight, they walked back into the house where Bernice sat at the kitchen table. Toddy poured himself some coffee.

"So what do you know about them?" Jed asked them.

"Si is mean as a snake," Bernice said. "He beat up one of my girls once. Just for the fun of it. She said he laughed the whole time. After that I didn't let him back in. I don't know much about Walker other than he worked for Russ."

Jed felt frustrated but not surprised. Grayson would soon be told Raine was here. When Jei got back, they'd discuss how to be sure lowlifes didn't get this close again. Until then, he'd be taking no long hunting trips away from the ranch. He just hoped the grizzly would respect the brief respite and leave the area. He doubted it would be the case either.

"You want us to trail them and make sure they leave the area?" Joe Kalama asked as he and his brother walked up, rifles loosely at their sides.

"They'll at least go far enough to get word to Grayson for further orders," Jed said staring toward the distant mountains. "From now on watch out for Walpapi, grizzlies, timber wolves, and the human kind."

Joe chuckled. "I could kill those two now if you want. Bury them out there and not likely anybody ever knows."

"You been to war, Joe?"

"That a question I have to answer?" he asked with a glint in his eyes.

"Then you know what it's like to kill." It wasn't a question. "It's not something a man does lightly once he knows."

"It'll be how you want, but they might be back."

"They might." He looked up and met Raine's worried gaze. "Then we'll do what we have to."

That night, Jed and Raine sat on the porch bench to watch the sun go down as they found often was a good way to end the day. "You do expect more trouble from Russ, don't you?" she asked when she could resist the question no longer.

He was smoking but reached out and put his other arm around her. "Maybe not."

"Liar."

He grinned. "Now was that nice?"

"The truth then."

"Grayson will be a problem until he's dead." He blew the smoke away from her. "He's like that grizzly. They just can't let it alone. They have got to be king of the walk. The grizzly likely feels he had this area all his way. It's his by right of domain. He doesn't like anybody coming along to mess it up for him. Maybe a bigger grizzly, a mountain over, wouldn't let him go there when earlier he wanted."

"The grizzly at least acts by instinct."

He nodded. "Who knows why men do what they do. I saw enough of it in the war to recognize a lot of life doesn't make sense, not as we'd reckon it to be."

"Russ certainly doesn't."

"Do I act with logic?" he asked with the gentle smile that she had come to love.

"Not at all," she agreed. "A man using logic would not have come back for me."

"Oh I don't know about that. You do have a few qualities that might make fighting for you worth it."

"Dare I ask which ones?"

"Oh like how you fill out a pair of pants." His smile was sexy and teasing. "That shirt looks better on you than any man. Sexy as hell."

"Such a strong logical reason."

"There might be a few others."

"Dare I ask?"

"Headstrong. Complicated. Daring. Interesting. Smart as hell."

"Are those the pluses or minuses?" she asked reaching up for the hand around her shoulder and stroking the long fingers.

"Pluses, of course. You didn't think I'd be choosing a mate who was compliant, unthinking, submissive?"

"You wouldn't?" Just his voice was seducing her, and he didn't have to do anything. They could talk about the weather, and it would have her thinking of how it would be in bed. But she had to be sure this cake was ready for the frosting. More and more she thought of it that way. Be sure the whole package was right, and then add the ties that would bind them together. It was so tempting though to just reach for what she wanted. Tonight to go to his room.

"What do you think Russ will try next?" she asked to distract herself from the seduction she had in mind-- and that seduction wasn't Jed seducing her but one of her seducing him.

"If I knew, I'd block it," he drawled. "Like we said. He isn't acting like a logical man. If I was smart, I'd go to Portland and kill him right now."

"You couldn't do that."

"Oh but I could. But I won't. Like I said, I had a bellyful of killing. Senseless killing. This at least would though make sense." He smiled, and she knew he was teasing her.

"Maybe I am the one who should kill him," she suggested to match his teasing mood. "I could go into his office with my little derringer and..."

Before she could say more, he had bent and claimed her lips with his own, the kiss tender and sweet, not nearly as passionate as she craved. When he released her lips, she whispered, "Is that supposed to discourage or encourage me."

"Both. Encourage you to come to my bed tonight and discourage you from doing anything dumb with Russell Grayson. He's a wolf like those two he sent after me except they made sense. They do it for the money. He does it for the pleasure. You would not stand a chance against him, sugar."

"I don't know if I could kill a man anyway," she agreed, stroking his neck. "I don't want you to either."

"That we agree upon. How about the bed?" His eyes had that teasing glint that even in the last bit of the light from the sun was visible.

"It's not time yet."

"I like that... the yet part. Not the not part."

"I just want to be sure."

"I can wait. I waited four years. At least now I can hold you although I have to say it makes for some restless nights sleeping or trying to sleep while I think about you and what I'd like to be doing, while I remember what we did do." He ran his hand lightly down to her breast and circled her nipple.

What more might have transpired was hard for her to say because at that point Toddy and Bernice came out from the house and Jed moved his hand back up to more appropriate territory.

"She cleaned my clock," Toddy said with a grimace. "All my wages for the next month up in smoke."

Bernice grinned. "And I didn't even cheat to do it."

Toddy gave her a apprehensive look. "Could you have?"

"Of course."

Toddy sighed. "When do you think the boys will be back?"

"Maybe tomorrow or the next day. Depends on whether there was someone at Camp Watson who could authorize credits to pay for the beef."

"Credits?"

"Script. Promissory note. It should be good—good as the federal government anyway."

"You hold a grudge over the war?" Bernice asked directly speaking to Jed as was not her wont.

"Nope. It was a stupid war for the South to let happen. A lot of men died, and it could have been avoided by just ending slavery on command. The problem was the South wanted to do it on its own timetable."

"Slavery is an abomination," Bernice said, but it wasn't in an argumentative tone, more of a probing one.

"We agree on that."

"But you fought for the South? It doesn't make sense to me."

Jed smiled. "War doesn't make sense, honey. If you saw one being fought, you'd think it was even more senseless."

"What do you mean?" This time the question came from Raine.

"Rows of men line up and start shooting at each other. Whoever has the most standing at the end-- that side wins. Probably no wars make sense. This one though, the least of all as I saw it. Brother fought against brother and for what?"

"The end of slavery," Bernice suggested.

"Which had ended in the North and would have in the South," Jed said. "Southerners, most of them, and that included blacks, they didn't fight for that. They fought for their homes, their brothers, for a right to govern their own lives."

"But at least now the slaves are free," Bernice said still exploring this whole idea, which was clearly a novel one to her. "President Lincoln did that."

"He was as much a victim of this war as any of the soldiers. When he began it wasn't to free the slaves. It was to prevent secession. He didn't declare them free until two years into it and then more for the war than to end slavery."

"I still find it hard to believe Josh fought on the side of the South."

"Josh was a free man, born free, educated right alongside me. He chose. That's what freedom is supposed to be about. Like me, he fought for his home and family."

"And they lost two brothers," Raine added.

"But don't you think the colored people will be better off for the war?" Bernice asked.

"Better off is a vague term. Being free is better, but if you mean economically better, I don't know. I am not saying that there were not slave owners who were bastards. The system was wrong. But what comes next is a question. Not many were educated as Josh was. Some will be free to work as sharecroppers with no responsibility from anyone to pay them a fair wage or take care of their health as once they would have. We'll see how this free works out."

"But wouldn't you prefer to be free?" Bernice asked still obvi-

ously struggling with the whole subject as she sat in the chair
Toddy had brought for her.

"If I am. I mean are any of us?"

"My, this is becoming a very deep subject," Toddy said with a
little laugh.

"It's a strange world is all I can say," Bernice said.

"You just figuring that out?" Jed drawled.

Bernice gave a little laugh as she stared out into the darkness.
"It might be I am. Amazing isn't it?"

As the mosquitoes came out, it drove them into the house.
The card game resumed this time with Raine joining in as Jed
and the Kalama brothers discussed the next day's work in the
great room.

"That big old bear still hanging around." George Kalama
offered one of his rare comments.

"I'll go after him tomorrow, but I can't stay out doing it. I have
to hang close around here in case those two return."

"You still want us moving the yearlings to that high pasture?"
Joe asked.

"We should get what grass we can from there before the
snows start. And I'd just as soon they were farther from the
grizzly for now. Take salt with you and that will encourage them
to stay a month before they work their way back down."

"I seen Walpapi sign up there," Joe said.

"If they get one to eat, it's how it goes. If they try to drive them
off, we'll keep an eye on them for any noticeable movements. I
don't think they will find it worth rustling them, considering the
rough terrain and lack of potential traders nearby."

Joe nodded approvingly. "Next month me and George need to
go back home. Big doings happening. We'll be back though for
the winter if you still want us."

"I want you. Shall we start building a cabin here for you?
Something you like better than the house or barn?"

"Hey boss, I like that idea," Joe said with a grin. Us, we're not much for fancy houses like this one. Might wanta bring us a woman sometime too."

George chuckled.

"He's got a girl back there," Joe said with a conspiratorial smile to Jed.

"That would be fine. Place could do with more females. Pretty it up," Jed agreed as he rolled a cigarette.

"She might turn him down." Joe winked at Jed as George frowned.

Smoking, Jed said, "It's not all that easy to get a woman. Take it from me." He chuckled and looked toward Raine whose match-stick pile was growing.

"You got one, Boss. Just got to convince her about staying is all." Joe laughed with this time George joining in.

"That is the rub, all right," Jed agreed staring at the tip of the glowing cigarette and wondering why logistics of the ranch, a war, even managing dollars, that all came easy to him, but the logic of a woman had him at sea. He wondered what he could offer her, that he hadn't already tried.

The more he thought about it, the more he knew he didn't have a clue. He'd done all he knew to do. Instead he'd concentrate on getting that big silver. While it was more dangerous, had its own uncertainty, his heart wasn't so at risk.

CHAPTER 17

With Josh a day overdue, Jed had concerns that all had not gone well even as he knew the military had its own timetable for doing anything. He took off his shirt and set himself to chopping firewood for the winter as a way to burn off the energy from worrying not to mention the sexual frustration. Within an hour, he had sweat running off his chest and felt more relaxed than he had in weeks.

"We're on our way to take a bath," Raine said as she and Bernice walked up to him, towels over their shoulders.

"Where's your rifle?" he asked when he didn't see one.

"Surely we don't need it that close to the ranch," she argued.

The look he gave her was enough to send her running back to the house.

"I didn't mean to offend you the other night," Bernice said.

"You didn't."

"I just was curious. I haven't really thought a lot about the war. I mean beyond it was there, and men talked about it but me having an opinion on it wasn't required."

"I understand."

"I suppose you dislike talking about it, the killing you did and all."

He chuckled. "You can't help being obnoxious even when you're trying to be nice, can you?"

She smiled and gave a sigh. "I suppose not. Always talking when I should listen."

"I don't mind the talking and didn't mind the questions. People who haven't been in a war don't know what it's like. It's understandable they'd be curious."

"I had a cousin who went. He fought for the North. I don't think he wanted to go. He was conscripted."

"He survive it?"

"He was at Richmond when it fell. Yes, he did. By being drafted, he came in a little after the worse losses for the North. He wrote me, but... I haven't seen him in years. He got married as soon as he could, living in Illinois."

"Good." He watched as Raine came out of the house, running toward them with the rifle in her hand.

"Did you see a lot of action?" Bernice asked not letting the subject go and not stopping when Raine came up to them.

"Bernice, you need to wash your mouth out," Raine said as she took back her towel. "And you keep harassing Jed, I might be the one doing it."

Bernice gave her a crooked smile but nodded. "Sorry."

"You ladies watch the area around the pool, any sounds you hear that don't sound right, anything you see, scream to high heaven. Don't use the rifle unless you have to because you likely wouldn't get a second shot."

"Jed, you are trying to scare us," Raine complained.

"I am. Take turns bathing and whoever is out, keep the rifle in your hands. You know how to shoot, Bernice?"

"Not really," she said with uncertainty looking toward the woods as though expecting a bear to come charging.

"Then scream real loud. I haven't seen any sign of him this

morning, and I did go up that way, but you never know. Just stay alert for sounds. He's a hunter. He will come at you like one."

Walking up the trail toward the pool, Bernice said, "You really think he's going to be around?"

"The bear or Grayson?" Raine asked with a little laugh.

"Both, I guess. I am worried too. I mean Josh should have been back by now, shouldn't he? Suppose..."

"Bernice, you really have to control this habit of being insufferable," Raine said giving a little growl. "There's a saying my mother had—each day's troubles are sufficient... or something like that."

"You can live that way?"

Raine laughed. "Of course not, but I don't want your worries added to mine. Let's just get our baths, and then we'll both feel better."

Raine let Bernice strip and bathe first, holding onto the rifle and feeling capable of killing a bear if it tried to hunt them. She had a shell in the chamber but wondered what it would take to stop a charging grizzly.

When Bernice had come out, Raine stripped and took her turn with the soap and swimming across the little pool, remembering how it was when she had been there with Jed, how beautiful he had looked as he had swum and then stood up shaking off the water. She wondered how much longer she could hold out on going to him. Surely the cake was baked now.

As she pulled on her chemise and pantalets, she heard the first sound to make her uneasy. "What was that?" she asked Bernice, who still held the rifle.

"It sounded big whatever it was. Hurry."

Raine had on her pants when she heard it again and looked through the trees to see a huge bear approaching. "Scream," she yelled as loudly as she could. Screaming, the two backed into the water with the bear continuing to approach. She thought of grabbing the rifle from Bernice, but they were about ten feet apart. The water wouldn't stop the bear. Would it delay him enough for Jed to get there?

Then her fear rose as she realized what Jed would face. She screamed again to try to scare the bear away. Whatever they were doing wasn't working as the big animal growled and stepped into the pool.

Heaving for breath and standing now at the other edge of the small clearing, Jed put a bullet between his teeth to enable a quick reload. He yelled at the bear but it paid him no mind with prey within its reach. He had to distract the bear from the women. One quick shot wouldn't kill it, not from this angle, but it would turn the grizzly toward him. He fired one into its side, quickly opening the breech and slipped in the paper cartridge. Levered shut and primed the nipple. As he had expected, the bear turned toward him, enraged by the pain, and ready to kill the new enemy.

"Get to the other side of the pool," he yelled at the women, not letting himself look to see if they would obey.

He'd killed a bear before but never a grizzly, though he'd heard the stories of those who had. It was never easy. Some said even with a death dealing shot, they often kept coming.

He aimed for the eye but maybe the fast moving bear made his shot miss as the bear was on him. Its big paw swiped at his left arm, knocking the rifle from his hands as well as ripping his arm open with its claws as it threw him backward.

It was as though it was all happening in slow motion. With time his arm would be filled with agony; but in this moment of action, he felt nothing but the need to kill. With his right hand, he jerked the hatchet from his belt, swinging it with all his strength at the bear's skull as the big mouth opened wide and lunged for him again

His axe struck the bear solidly, cleaving into its skull right at the eye sockets, splitting its head wide open as blood sprayed everywhere. He heard a rifle shot as the bear began to collapse, taking him down with it as it landed on his right leg. It was dead. He was alive, or he hoped he was.

In another moment, Raine was at his side, her hands on the heavily bleeding wound on his left arm as she shrieked at Bernice, "Get Toddy and the Kalamas. Run." She bent over him. "I thought he was going to get you."

He managed a weak smile despite the now excruciating pain. "He did." He tried to push the bear off his leg but either loss of blood or its weight left him pinned.

"Lie still," she ordered. I need to make a tourniquet. I'll be right back." And then he felt something pressing hard against the jagged wound.

"I heard another shot," he gasped, trying to master the pain that was growing in agony.

"Bernice had the gun, and I had to get it from her when she totally froze. Then I had to get somewhere I could hit him and not you. God, I was scared, Jed."

It had all been too fast for him to know fear except that moment when he saw the bear going toward her. "It'll be all right," he whispered wondering if it would. He'd seen men lose their arms for less of an injury than his. His leg hurt where the bear's body trapped it. It hurt too. Was it broken?

"Where do you hurt?" she asked as she kept her hands on the gash to hold it closed. The bleeding was slowing, but he had lost too much blood.

"I'm trying to decide where I don't." He managed a smile and was glad to see her force one of her own. God, this wasn't how it was supposed to happen.

When he heard running on the trail, it was the Kalamas and Bernice with Toddy following and heaving for breath. "What'd you do to yourself, Boss?" Joe asked with a grin as he knelt to assess the situation.

"Well, we got the bear," he managed, trying to make a joke and gasping before he got to the last word. Fine hero he was.

"The weight of the bear is trapping his leg," Raine said. "Can you get if off? But be careful in case it's broken."

George moved down and giving a heave, shoved, but it took Joe beside him to move it. Joe made a quick slash of the grizzly's neck to further more bleeding. "Make lotsa good food," George said moving back to get hold of Jed.

"I can get up," he said as he assessed whether he could. His right ankle was twisted, he thought, not broken. Some good news if not a lot considering the arm. Damn, after going through the war with only minor injuries, was this now how he'd end up a cripple after all?

"Joe, can you take his shoulders and Toddy and George each a leg. Be gentle but carry him back to the house," she said as though he wasn't there.

"I can walk," he said wincing, unsure if he could.

"Your arm is going to take stitches. You have lost a lot of blood. Make it easier on all of us and let them carry you," she said in a tone that said she was willing to fight over this.

He groaned but yielded. He wasn't feeling all that great and with a gimpy leg it'd take a long time to get himself back there.

As they picked him up, Raine said, "Bernice, get back there and put more water on the stove. If the fire is down, get it going. We need boiling water and find that whiskey bottle if you can."

He fought back the cry of pain when the men tried to find a rhythm that would move him without unnecessary roughness. "You always this bossy?" he asked Raine when he could finally get the words out without a groan.

"Only when someone gets torn up by a bear," she said. She had not released her pressure on the gash in his arm. She was handling blood better than many men he'd known.

Once they had him in the kitchen, she gestured toward the table.

"Lay him carefully," she said. "Bernice, get the bag on top of my dresser."

Although he had nearly blacked out, he managed to voice his concern. "Think I'll lose my arm?"

She studied the wound where the claws had ripped his skin. "I don't think so. But we have to deal with infection. It made one deep gouge but didn't tear the muscle loose. When I start stitching, I'll know better."

"You know much about sewing?" he asked only slightly surprised at the way she had taken charge.

"This kind," she offered, bending and kissing his lips. "Trust me. I've been studying."

"Studying what?" he said biting back a groan.

She put her hands tenderly on his forehead. "There are no doctors nearby are there?"

"Not that... I know of."

She forced a more confident tone than she actually felt. "Then we have to go with what I know. When I visited my mother last time, she gave me a book of herbs and poultices with some basic medical treatments. She also gave me some bags of things she thought I might most likely need for healing."

He managed a tight smile. "You sure she's not a witch?"

"Not that I know of. Look, I watched her do this for others. This next hour won't be easy for either of us, but I think her herbs can prevent the infection which is the greatest concern."

He nodded, clenching his jaw. "All right." His head felt fuzzy, unclear. "I'm in your hands."

Bernice returned with the bag and Raine looked for what she knew she would need. "I think you should tie him to the table," she told Toddy. "The alcohol will be agonizing and then the stitching, well, not sure if you can hold him if he jerks up."

Jed didn't object when they took cords and ran them over his chest, then tied his left wrist to the table leg before they did the same with the right. If anything could save his arm, he would suffer it.

Raine put the needle and thread in a small dish before she poured alcohol over them. Next she approached Jed. "I have to pour this over the gash." He nodded. When she poured it, he jerked but did no more than utter a grunt. She swallowed looking at the wound, trying to see this abstractly and just something to be done, not her lover's body. She retrieved the needle. Holding the wound together, she began making the stitches she remembered seeing her mother do.

When she had closed the wound, she took the comfreys root and created a poultice, which she patted onto the gash. Operating more by instinct now than thinking, she found the willow bark, put it into a cup and poured boiling water over it. Coming back to the wound, she finally applied strips of cloth to hold the comfreys in place. She wasn't sure if Jed had lost consciousness, but his eyes were closed.

"Carry him to his bed," she told George and Joe.

Jed's eyes opened and he looked up at her. "It's over?"

She kissed his forehead to assess whether he had yet begun to run a fever. Such was inevitable. "For now," she said with another kiss.

"There are better places," he managed with a smile.

"And times," she agreed.

"I can walk upstairs," he said. "I think anyway."

"Save your strength," she disagreed as they untied him from the table. "You're going to need it."

Once he was in bed, she stripped him of his clothes and boots. She washed his body before she covered him with a light blanket, then sat on the edge of the bed with the tea she had requested Toddy bring up. "If you can drink this, it will ease the fever and pain," she said as she showed it to him. "But you won't like it much."

"I haven't liked anything... since I heard you scream about the bear," he said with another smile.

"You killed it though."

"You shot it too, didn't you?"

She nodded. "I saw the hatchet slice open his head as I fired." She helped him drink the bitter tea. When he'd taken all he would, she pushed his hair back from his forehead. "Joe and George are cutting the meat up for steaks. They say it's very tasty."

"You don't think I'll lose my arm."

She shook her head. "I won't let it. But it will take the poultices and maybe more alcohol or salt if it starts to infect. It will be a hard time ahead, for us both. You won't lose your arm."

He sighed. "I can't be laid up long."

"Josh and Jei should be back soon. The work will be taken care of."

He didn't say it, but that wasn't his biggest concern. Grayson's two thugs would either be back or report to Grayson. It was likely more would come with them next time. If not them, then the Walpapi. He looked at Raine with concern. He didn't know how long they had before it'd all turn bad. Where would she be safe? If he couldn't fight, could he get her somewhere Grayson wouldn't find her?

She bent and kissed his lips running her fingers over his bare shoulder. "I know what you're thinking. I should have never come here. I was why you got hurt, and now I'm what you're worrying about instead of healing yourself."

He managed a smile. "Whatever else I am thinking, it's never part of wishing you hadn't come. It wasn't your fault about the bear. We are just lucky it wasn't worse."

"I've been thinking about it. About where I might go that would keep you safe."

This time, despite the pain, his smile was more genuine. "You think he'd let me go if you weren't here? Not care about killing me?"

She pursed her lips together. "I suppose you are right."

"You know I am. Look, you work that witchy magic on me, and I'll get over this as fast as I can."

"You better. There are other things for us to settle." She felt his forehead again and realized he was beginning to run a fever.

The next two days were hard ones as he ran a high fever, seemed to be delusional at times, and fought against the pain. She replaced poultices, plied him with the herbal brew and kept getting him to drink water all the while fearful whether he would turn the corner or this would get worse. By the third day, he was at least sleeping more naturally. Mostly he slept, which was probably what his body needed to heal. The wound had not grown infected and the jagged tear seemed to be healing.

About the time she had been worried something had happened to Jack, Jei and Josh, they showed up, tired from the trail and not happy to hear any of what had gone wrong while they'd been gone.

"The federals made it hard," Josh said. "We told them that we'd take the herd to Canyon City if they couldn't decide. They said they had to wait for their captain. Once he got there though, it went fast.."

Raine poured them both brandies as she told them about the strangers and more details on how Jed was. Toddy and Bernice joined them as they all sat in the great room.

"Damn," Josh said looking worriedly up the stairs. "He going to be all right?"

"With time."

Jei stared into the brandy. "Who were the men?" he asked Bernice.

"Si Tubbs and Jace Walker."

Jei grimaced. "Did they see you?"

"She didn't go out. So not unless they were spying earlier or came back," Raine said. "The Kalamas said they haven't, so I guess they went back to report."

"Which means they won't know I am here either."

"No way they could unless Grayson has a contact at Camp Watson," Toddy said.

"How long before Jed will be on his feet?" Josh asked.

"About now," Jed said from the stairway where he had dressed and made it halfway down before needing to grab onto the banister for support.

"You should have stayed in bed," Raine protested as she ran up the stairs to give him support the rest of the way down.

"When I heard the riders come back? Not a chance." He did drop gratefully into the big chair. "Get me some whiskey, sugar," he drawled as he looked up at her with that lazy smile that drove her crazy when it didn't make her furious. She wasn't sure it would be good for him. With that stubborn look on his face, either she'd get it for him or he'd get it himself. She brought it.

As he sipped the liquor, he got the story again from Josh and Jei about the delay in the sale. "Who is this new captain?" he asked.

"Phillips."

"Rand?" Raine asked with surprise in her voice.

"Didn't tell me his first name," Josh said as he got up to pour himself a whiskey. "Tall guy, hard look about him? He's been to war from the looks of him, and he's back to run the operation out of Watson. He's got what looked like a company with him to do it."

"You know him?" Jed asked her trying to find a comfortable position and frustrated that he wasn't as recovered as he needed to be.

"He is a friend of my stepfather. They served together down on the Rogue, and then he came by a time or two to visit."

"Married?" He wondered how often the captain had actually come to visit, and how significant might those visits have been.

"Since I haven't seen him since before the war, I have no idea," she said with a smile as she moved to sit on the arm of his chair and surreptitiously feel of his forehead to see if he was again running a fever.

"That could be good to start seeing more action against the Indians," Jei said.

"Or it could stir things up to a red hot heat," Jed said thinking if he didn't lie down soon, they'd likely be carrying him back up the stairs. He felt frustrated at his weakness. This was not a good time to be debilitated. He moved his arm relieved that at least the muscles, while weakened, did his biding.

"Why don't you men get something to eat," Raine suggested. "And Jed, you need to lie down."

He smiled not minding her proprietary way of saying it and nodded. "We can talk later," he said to his brother. "And Jei, if you want to get out of here, with what's likely coming, you and Bernice, it's your choice. I would understand."

"I'm sticking around," Jei said with a tight smile. "But if you want to go east, I'll take you as far as a train," he said to Bernice.

She shook her head. "I didn't lose anything back there. I'll stay."

CHAPTER 18

Relieved to be lying in his bed again, Jed didn't object as Raine began unbuttoning his shirt. "Jei could take you too," he said as she eased it from his shoulders. "I could arrange for you to go back to New York City for a while. I have friends there—despite it being the north."

"I have no interest in going there."

"It might be safer for a few months." He hoped that's all it would be.

She brought a basin of water to the stand beside his bed and began washing his arms and chest, running the cloth almost seductively around his nipples, down his belly. He guessed by now anything she did would seem seductive to him.

"Who is this Phillips to you?" he asked even though he had told himself he would not.

"A friend of Adam's. That's all."

"He never came to see you in Portland?" That sounded jealous. He couldn't take back the words.

"A time or two but before I met you." She smiled as she dried his skin and then began unbuttoning his pants.

"Watch what you're doing there," he ordered aware he was already partially erect from her earlier touch.

"I won't damage anything... important," she said with a smile as she pulled off his pants, leaving him naked until she pulled up the blanket.

"I can undress myself," he protested.

"You could. How are you feeling?" She felt of the skin around the wound.

"Sore but not as bad as I'd expected given the nature of what happened. My arm seems weaker, but the muscles seem to be working. I have to give your mother credit for those herbs... your mother and you."

She sat back and watched him with the expression in her eyes that he couldn't read. "Do you want me to leave?"

He knew what he should want and nodded.

"Why?"

"It'd be safer. It is looking like we've got trouble coming at us from all directions."

"You don't think the military can take care of the Indian problem here?"

"While it's possible, I don't expect it that fast. There are a lot of places they can hide in these hills. I think this won't be over fast."

"Nor will Russell."

"No."

"Will the military be a problem to you also? I could talk to Rand, explain about you."

"Or you could not," he retorted. "I don't need anybody explaining anything. Not even you. From what I have seen, the military has no problem with those who fought against them in the War, most especially not career soldiers like Phillips. It's more the people who didn't go who are most of the problem on the times where there is one."

"I'm glad to hear that. I think Rand is a fair man. I hope you two meet."

"He'll likely be by if he is interested in you anyway."

She gave him a look. "I have no reason to think he's interested in me."

"You've held off giving me an answer about us," he said knowing he felt too sick and weak to be having this discussion. He needed to be on his feet, someone who could be a fit mate for her. As it stood, he was anything but.

"I wanted us to have time to be sure it was a forever thing, that we could work out a genuine life together, not one with one of us living one place and the other somewhere else."

"I suppose the bear attack convinced you this isn't for you if we can clear up the Grayson thing in Portland."

He could see that irked her. She rose with a rush. "I'll talk to you about this when you are feeling more yourself." With that she left the room slamming the door.

It opened again a few minutes later but to his disappointment, it was Jei. "I thought we need a plan. You look pale though. Maybe another time."

"I'd rather think about that then what just went out of here like a tornado," Jed said even as he knew he was weaker than he should be to do any cogent thinking.

"Grayson will send more men... or he might show up himself," Jei said as he settled into a chair by the window. "He won't fight fair. He also won't want just to kill you. You know all of that though, don't you?"

Jed did. What he didn't know was what he could do about it. It was a rotten time to get laid up.

"You two are idiots," Grayson said as he glared at the men he had sent to Hardman's. It didn't just anger him that they would be no use to him but even more that Kirk had been right. He was not going to find getting his revenge easy, but he was determined he would even if Kirk continually told him he was being foolish.

Foolish or not, he could not rest until he had gotten the best of the Reb, and shown Raine what a fool she had been.

"We told you the woman is there," Tubbs said interrupting his thoughts. "Doesn't that help? She acts like the lady of the manor too, I gotta say."

"Who else did you see?"

"Remember Toddy Coen?"

"Vaguely. Odd jobs but never worked for me, did he?"

"Wouldn't know about that. I seen him in Portland a time or two hanging out at the saloons, working odd jobs. Well, he's with Hardman. He likely is who told him who we really were and queered the deal."

Grayson sneered. Unlikely as that seemed, it was possible. More likely was Hardman recognized them for who and what they were. Kirk had been right. He should have sent more reputable looking men. Too late for that and now Hardman had a piece of information he would have preferred he not. Knowing who Tubbs and Walker worked for would give him no doubts that Russ hadn't forgotten him. There'd be no point in sending anyone else.

"In The Dalles they said over eighty cavalry troopers come in and headed out to work out of Camp Watson," Tubbs said.

"Where is that?"

"Off The Dalles Military Road." He went to the map on the wall and pointed it out.

"And Hardman's ranch is where from there?"

"Looked like he hired two Indian men too. I couldn't say what tribe though," Walker spoke up.

Tubbs pointed to where the house would be, not far above the North Fork of the John Day. "He's got a real nice place and barns up there. Never seen nothing like it even around here. He's got money is all I can say. House looks more like a hotel than a home."

"Ah." Russ sat back at his desk steepling his fingers as he thought of what he knew about the place. It was all coming back to him as he had met Jacques Aubuchon a few times before he left Fort Vancouver for the wilderness, taking a sizeable construction crew and his luxuries with him. Having earned favors, he had bought land in a wilderness. Before the gold was discovered, nobody cared much about it anyway. He had heard it had been sold relatively cheap when he lost interest as so often happened with men who had more connections than ambitions.

Russ stared at the map thinking about how the cavalry arriving would impact his operations. Their main concern would have to be marauding Indians, but they would also take an interest in stage robberies.

For some years, as it developed and the mines produced a lot of wealth, it had been a lucrative sideline with so little law and a transient population. He might have to change his plans for the region. Or maybe the military would only stay long enough to make it look better and move on. It certainly wasn't likely they'd enjoy being in the middle of nowhere if they had a choice.

Then he considered that what he really wanted was that ranch. Of course, Loraine to go with it. Maybe he'd keep her over there for his own pleasures once he tortured to death the man who had ruined his original plans for her. The only question was how he would make it all happen. When a letter was brought to him, he read it and groaned.

An hour later, Kirk came in the back way. "Learn anything?" he asked as he poured himself a brandy.

Russ told him what his men had learned.

"Were Bernice McDowell or Han Jei there?" Edmonton asked.

"They only saw Raine and Toddy Coen."

"I found out Raine didn't use either of the tickets she had brought. She left Portland without a trace on the same night Jei and Bernice McDowell also disappeared. Would Jei have taken either woman? He seems into it only for profit. On the other hand, someone got Hardman out of our trap, and those two could well have been the key to that."

"What would they have gotten from doing it?"

"And something always has to be in it?" Kirk said with a chuckle as he sipped the fine liquor.

"In my experience."

"How many men does Hardman appear to have? Toddy certainly wouldn't be much of a crew. I remember him from around town, soft and not interested in working harder than he had to."

"It's hard to say. That day it's all he saw, well and two Indian men."

"Hardman had a brother. If he wasn't there, then it means he was out. All right, let's send out feelers to Canyon City and the camps around there to see if Hardman or his outfit have been selling beef to any of them."

"Why would that matter?" Russ asked.

"If he goes out, then he leaves the place unguarded right?"

Russ nodded.

"So maybe we can make the sale of beef very attractive to him, high price, and when he goes, we take over his place and Raine. When he comes back, he won't have a lot of say on what happens next, not if he is in love with her."

"There is something more." He held out the letter.

Edmonton took it and read. "He married her," he said finally when he put it back down.

"That's what my source said." He cursed. "I can't believe she would do it. How could she choose that Reb?"

"There could be reasons." Kirk smiled with the look that told Russ he was thinking strategically as he did when writing his plays. "Their being married might not be bad," he said finally.

"How could it be anything but?"

"Let me get back to you on it." The shark smile returned.

After two weeks and tired of trying to cajole the slowly healing Jed out of his rotten moods, Raine remembered her fishing pole and the peace she had found on the river when her stepfather had taught her how to use a fly rod. Although she had not explored beyond the ranch house, with the bear gone, she should be able to do so, maybe head down to the North Fork and try her luck at catching a rainbow or two.

She realized as she looked at the trees at the edge of the lower pasture that it was edging toward fall with a few turning golden on their tips. Perhaps there would even be salmon in the river. She found her mouth watering at the thought.

Upstairs, she put her pole together, found a couple of flies that she thought looked like the insects she had seen flitting around the creek below the house, and grabbed her rifle she was sure Jed would insist she take.

When she walked back outside, dressed in boots, pants, and flannel shirt, Jed stopped doing push-ups to look at her. "Where are you going?" he asked in a terse voice as she headed down the steps.

She looked back at him, hard put not to lick her lips at the sight he made with sweat running down his bare, very muscular torso. It was all she could do not to turn around. "Fishing. What does it look like?" She looked at the pleading eyes of Deucy and said, "No, can't come this time."

"By yourself?" Jed asked rising to watch her with narrowed eyes.

"The bear is gone and I do have a rifle if you will notice."

"Any memory of the Walpipi coming to you?"

"Have there been any signs of them around us?" She knew if there had been, he'd have mentioned it. Still the Kalama brothers had yet to return and maybe nobody was actually out looking for tracks.

He shook his head, but she could see he still didn't like the idea of her going off by herself. Before he could come up with another argument, Bernice came outside. "Could I come? I never saw anybody fish." She ran back inside to change before Raine could answer.

Toddy, who had followed Bernice outside, looked at Raine's pole with interest. "You fish?" he asked with amazement.

"Do you think I'd have this if I didn't?" she asked. "You know how to cook salmon?"

"God, yes but you think they'd be in this creek?"

"I suppose it's possible, but if so they'd be spawning and too old to taste good, but I had in mind the North Fork which I only got to see when we crossed it to take the cattle to Canyon City. If the salmon haven't come this far yet, likely there'd be rainbows, who have never seen a fly, and should be easy pickings." She grinned.

"I don't like the idea," Jed said with a muscle jumping in his jaw showing his tension.

"I will be watchful."

"Me too," Bernice said who had changed into a pair of pants, boots and her own shirt in record time.

"Where's your gun?" Jed asked resigned to them going.

"I'll find it." She ran back inside.

"She's more likely to shoot me with it than any Indian," Raine complained.

Jei had been sitting at the other end of the deck and spoke up for the first time. "I have worked with her. She can shoot now."

Within five minutes, the women were down at the edge of the meadow and heading into the trees. Raine remembered the instructions to the river, stay west of the creek and avoid the bluff. She wished though that Bernice had stayed back at the house as the blonde was full of chit chat as she walked.

"When we get to the river," Raine said, "no talking and no swimming at least not upstream from where I am fishing."

"I'm just so glad to get out of the house that I'll obey anything you say, ma'am," Bernice said with a teasing tone.

"You thinking of leaving here?"

"No, not yet but I need more to do. Toddy does the cooking. You keep the house, and sometimes go out on the horse with the men to check or move cattle. What is left for me?"

"You don't like lying around?" Raine asked knowing it was a snarky question, but the habit of it was too engrained when talking to Bernice.

"Not hardly. I kept busier than you probably imagine being a madam."

"I know nothing about what a madam even does," Raine admitted. "How did you get into that line of work?"

Bernice laughed. "Not what you might imagine. I was not working in the bordello and worked my way up. I bet that's what you figured, wasn't it?"

"It would have been a logical assumption."

"Leave it to Raine to always be logical," she said with a wicked grin. "Well I got offered it not long after I had come to Portland. Yes, I like sex but not on demand. I won't say I never took a customer myself... but I never took one I didn't want to take."

"You didn't mind hiring girls though who were not so fortunate," Raine said knowing that would probably irk Bernice but not caring.

"That was the catch, of course. It requires not thinking much about that side of it. Although I made sure they had a safe environment, that no one abused them, that they received their pay. Some girls don't have a choice, you know."

"I suppose so. I admit there are not a lot of options for women to work."

"And I didn't have the Collins behind me to get me started into anything. There was no man begging to marry me. I hadn't been in Portland long before Russell met me on the street, asked me to dinner, discussed the possibilities for me, and pretty much that was the best fit. He liked the idea of a beautiful, showy woman out front. I fit his bill but made it clear as to my limits."

"Were you and Russ ever lovers then?" Raine asked as she saw the shine of the river ahead of them. Cottonwood and willows lined its banks with their yellow glow reflected in the deeper pools. To her excitement she saw a fish roil the surface, and it looked big enough to be a salmon. She headed up the stream looking for some rapids and the kind of setting Adam had taught her where the fish often waited for insects.

"Not with Russell," Bernice said. "Don't you know about him?"

She shook her head as she found the right spot. "What was to know?"

"Russell has his good looking male friends more often than women friends. I guess he likes both or maybe neither. I didn't find him appealing at all, and he didn't want me either. He wants a more ladylike woman on his arm. He needed a way to not be recognized for what he really was."

"And that is?" Raine asked as she loosened the fly from the pole and suggested Bernice stand away from where she'd be casting. She whipped the pole in the air to fluff the fly and then set it down by the small eddy.

"You really can fish," Bernice said as she gave a little laugh. "That was beautiful. I wonder if I could learn to do it."

"Probably, but not with this pole. Adam gave it to me, and it's sacred."

Bernice giggled. "My god, it would be. I still remember the first time I saw him. Matt is handsome but Adam, he's a god."

"Too bad they both got away," Raine said with a grin as she felt something take the fly and pulled back as she had been taught. Five minutes of playing it, she had the rainbow on the bank beside her, and slipped a willow branch through it's gills so it did not flip back into the water. This was a fishing paradise.

"I've reconciled myself to the loss," Bernice said admiring the fish as Raine caught them. "I need a new hobby. Maybe fishing could be it."

"These kinds of poles aren't easy to come by,"

"Drat. Nothing good ever is."

Raine cast again. This time with a little orange ball of wool yarn wrapped on the hook as Adam had showed her, to imitate the fish eggs floating at the edge of the stream. She flicked the line through the air three or four times before letting it drop naturally to what looked like the bottom end of a small pool. The water exploded as a large silver streak flashed across the stream nearly taking the pole from her hand.

"God damn, I won't lose my pole," Raine yelled as Bernice shrieked.

"Get it. Get that son of a bitch."

The fish was large enough to break her precious line if not her pole. Raine understood from the lessons with Adam that she only had one alternative. She jumped into the water, running down the shallows as much as knee deep, letting out line enough to keep the fish hooked until he or she wore out.

From the hillside, Jed and Jei had been watching the two women, their rifles at the ready. There was no way in Hades that Jed would have let them go down to the river alone. Although they had seen no sign of the Walpapi and maybe the cavalry would make quick work of this Indian war, even a lone warrior might find two beautiful women a temptation he wouldn't resist. Not to mention the miners wandering the hills possibly without a lot of moral turpitude.

"She really can fish," Jei said with admiration and a quiet laugh.

Jed glanced at him just as a shriek and some cursing yanked his attention back to Raine who had entered the river. When Jed started to lunge forward, Jei put a hand on his shoulder.

"Let her do it unless it looks like she's going to drown," he said with humor in his voice. "She's got it."

Jed marveled at the way she moved down the stream trying to hold onto the pole and not snap the line on the fighting fish. He had fished enough to know that if she let the line go slack it would all be over.

He loved fishing and seeing her get a steelhead was as though he could feel it himself. Nothing felt as exhilarating... well almost nothing. Seeing her totally soaked in the autumn sunlight, her nipples now pushing against the wet shirt reminded him of the other thing. He thrust the thought from his mind. Too bad his body didn't find it as easy to let go of what it made him want to do.

It was clear she'd never let that fish go as she ran ahead to a bend in the stream and a sandy beach on the inside corner. After playing it awhile longer, he could see her beginning again to try reeling the fish to the surface. Tired from the fight, it lay on its side as she drew it into the shallows, lunging forward to throw it onto the gravel.

She looked as exhausted as the fish as she flopped down beside it with a big smile on her face.

Jei grinned at Jed. "God, you got a real woman there."

Jed knew that. He'd always known that. It was how could he hold onto her, how could he keep her, that was his problem.

As they watched Raine teach the grimacing Bernice how to clean the fish she had caught, he and Jei sank back in the shadows of the forest, staying at a safe distance as the women walked back to the house. They would circle around and head back to the house from the other side, letting Raine think she'd had her afternoon on her own.

That night as they all enjoyed the salmon and trout, that true to his word, Toddy had deliciously cooked, the story of catching them had to be retold. Before the story could be embroidered or told a fourth time, Jack came into the kitchen. "Rider coming," he said as the dogs outside began to bark.

Jed grabbed his Colt and headed for the front door with the others right behind. When Raine saw the tall rider, she let out a yelp of pleasure. "Adam!"

He leaned forward on the pommel of his saddle smiling as he looked from her to the others. "Your mama's been some worried."

"But you weren't," she suggested laughing as he dismounted and took her into his arms.

"Maybe just a bit," he admitted as his smile disappeared, and he studied the tall man who had come to stand beside Raine.

"How did you find us?" Jed asked before Raine could introduce them.

"Stopped at Camp Watson first." He looked down at Raine. "You didn't give us much to go on."

"I told you I was fine. I thought Mama would understand."

"She did but then it got to be a month, and she was more concerned. I decided I hadn't been on a horseback trip for a while and offered to find you. She and Elijah are staying up at the cabin with St. Louis and Matt to keep an eye on things while I'm gone." The set look to his jaw said he understood something wasn't right about any of whatever had led her so abruptly to leave Portland.

"Joe can take care of your horse," Jed said beckoning Joe to take the gelding down to the corrals.

"Come inside," she said. "I caught a big steelhead today on your pole and there is some left."

"And this is?" he asked with a hard smile as he looked back at Jed, who had shoved his revolver into his belt.

"Where are my manners?" Raine proceeded to introduce all of them, then with her arm still around him, encouraged him back into the house.

After he had eaten, and Jed had poured him a whiskey along with one for the other men, Adam said, "This is quite the operation you have up here, Mr. Hardman."

"Jed... and yes, I am lucky to have found this place." He smiled, but it looked no more friendly than Adam's as the two apparently sized each other up. While she hoped they would be friends someday, at the moment that might be asking too much. Adam was protective of what Jed saw as his domain.

"Hello, Adam," Bernice finally said as she stepped forward. "Remember me?"

"I saw you back there. And yes, I do." He didn't add to it.

"Why don't you men take your whiskeys out onto the porch,"

Raine suggested. "It's a lovely night for sitting out and watching the stars."

"If we ignore the mosquitoes," Bernice said glancing around uneasily.

"That's what the candles are for," Raine said setting several in strategic spots hoping to draw the insects from them. Sitting on the rail, Jed rolled a cigarette.

"You got any extra tobacco?" Adam asked. "I keep quitting. Martha's always after me on it. Then I get out and want a smoke."

Jed understood that emotion and gave him the one he had just made. Adam lit it from one of the candles as Jed rolled another for himself. Raine sat to one side with Bernice as they sipped brandies. She wondered if Adam was angry at her not giving her mother more information thus worrying her. She got her answer without asking the question.

"You know Grayson is out to get you," Adam said taking a long draw on his cigarette. He was looking at Jed in the candlelight.

"It was a logical assumption."

Adam studied him through the smoke. "I have been putting a few things together. Grayson, who I didn't like when I met him. Then there was Raine leaving so abruptly followed by that enigmatic message. Word also came to me that he's been hiring more toughs."

"He didn't have enough already?" Jei asked with a grin as he smoked his small cigar.

"Not of the kind he wanted, it appears. The Portland sheriff sent me a message as he wasn't sure if my area was going to be a target. If he knew what was, he didn't say."

Jed reached down and lightly petted Ace as he smoked. "You came to warn us."

"I came to take Raine back with me where I can protect her," Adam said with a hard smile.

"And I can't?"

"You'll be lucky to protect yourself."

"Can't argue with you there but why should I trust that you can keep her safe?" Jed's smile was as unfriendly as Adam's.

Raine had had enough. "You two are talking as though this isn't my choice. As though you should work it out between the two of you."

"Isn't that how men normally think," Bernice agreed with a derisive snort putting her brandy aside.

"Well it won't be that way this time," Raine said. "I will decide where and what I do and don't need you two to work it out for me."

Adam laughed for the first time with genuine amusement. "And that choice would be?"

Jed was interested in that answer himself.

"When I know, I'll let you both know. Jed, will you see that Adam has a place to sleep. I am going to bed."

CHAPTER 19

With everyone in bed, moonlight highlighting the trees and patio, Jed sat out in a lawn chair smoking a cigarette, Ace at his feet. He supposed he should have decided what he needed to do but he had not.

"You not sleeping either," Adam said as he came out of the house, sitting in the chair beside him. He accepted the makings for another cigarette.

"Full moon does that sometimes," Jed said without looking up. "I'd have figured you tired after the long ride."

"Sometimes a man gets past tired."

"That too."

"They told me you killed a bear with an axe."

"Only after it got me," Jed said with a grimace. He put his left arm out, rotating it as was his wont whenever he thought of the tightness in the muscles from the injury.

"Last hit is the one that counts," Adam said. Jed could see his teeth flash in the moonlight.

"I'd have liked doing it right the first shot."

"Raine told me that you shot to distract the bear from her."

Jed smoked but didn't respond.

"So now how do you figure to do this with Grayson?" Adam asked after a few minutes.

"I wish I had a better answer for you than I don't know. He's not somebody a man can just kill."

Adam chuckled. "But you thought about it."

"I did. I also know he isn't a man whose hands I'd like to fall back into. Worse than that would be imagining him getting Raine in his control."

"It is why I came. Martha was worried, but I'd have not taken it so seriously, if I hadn't heard from the Portland sheriff."

"He tried to have me shanghaied. Actually he would have succeeded if not for Raine and Jei."

"And you figure it was Grayson."

"Can't prove it, of course."

"No, never can. I agree though. With him behind it, he won't stop—not his kind."

"If I had hoped otherwise, the two lowlifes who showed up here would have changed my mind." Their cigarette butts glowed in the darkness. "So you stopped by Watson first," Jed said finally. He was still uncertain exactly what Captain Phillips meant to Raine.

"I was actually heading for Canyon City. Rand is a friend. I found out there about the cattle sale. Saved me wandering all over the territory. He might ride by in a day or two. He's doing a circuit to assess where the trouble is coming from."

"Or now that he knows Raine is here?"

Adam chuckled. "He would've shown up anyway."

"Would he?"

"You sound jealous."

"Should I be?"

"Tell me something about you, Reb. I don't know that much other than you have this ranch, which looks like a rich man's toy. Is that all she is to you?"

"You think that because I came from the South or fought for the Confederacy?"

"I got nothing against you for that. Man does what he has to do. What I do wonder about though is how serious you are about my daughter."

Jed considered a moment what he should say. "I married her. Is that serious enough for you?"

Adam whistled in surprise. "She's not wearing a ring. Didn't say anything about it. What's up with that?"

"Her choice that it's a secret. I hope you will respect that."

"There are reasons for the secrecy?" Adam asked.

"Partly so she can do what she wants when this is all over... if it's ever all over. It was my idea that we marry, and she agreed on the condition that it be in name only."

"This is leaving me a little confused if you'll pardon my saying."

"There were reasons for the marriage that weren't romantic. If something happened to me, I knew she'd protect the property for my brother, Josh, who as a colored man could not own property in Oregon."

"Practical choice." He could hear the smile in Adam's voice.

"I had another that I didn't tell her. I hoped it would protect her from Grayson and if... I didn't make it through this, would protect her period."

"She's not pregnant then?"

Jed gave a short laugh. "She hasn't let me touch her since she got here. I think you can thank your wife for that. Something about not eating the frosting before the cake got baked."

Adam laughed. "That sounds like Martha."

"I also owe your wife my arm being as good as it is. She gave Raine herbs and directions for how to use them."

"That also sounds like Martha."

"Once I saw the hooligans show up here, I wasn't sorry she'd convinced Raine to put off... well the pleasures of the marriage bed. I wouldn't want to leave her with that kind of problem in case I don't make it through this."

"You made it through the war."

"I did… and then twice nearly got myself killed. I take nothing for granted anymore."

"I hope you don't have a death wish or something," Adam said. "I've seen that get many a man."

Jed looked back at him, met his gaze levelly. "Not that I know of, but I'd be a fool not to see I'm in a dangerous situation here. It wasn't good before. Grayson knows Raine is here now. I get the feeling he's taken on a personal vendetta against me which explained the shanghaiing."

"Any idea why he did that?"

Jed shook his head. "From the first time he saw me. There could be reasons, like my fighting for the South. Maybe jealousy over her. Maybe it's just his nature to be mean as a rabid dog."

"All right, I don't know what I can do to help you but will if I can."

"Probably Raine going back with you would be best. You could keep her safer than I can. I have those who hate Southerners, the Walpapi, and Grayson. It's hard to pick which is most risk right now."

"I'd put my money on Grayson, and she will decide for herself what she's going to do. She's a gutsy woman."

Jed smiled. "You should have seen her play that fish."

Adam chuckled. "So you watched?"

"I didn't want to let her go at all; but if she was going, I was going to keep an eye on her."

"A man after my own heart," Adam said with another laugh. "You do know though that women don't like a man trying to dominate them. Especially not the Stevens women."

"I just want to protect her."

"Sometimes they don't see it that way."

"I am trying to understand that."

Adam rose. "I guess I should head for bed. I need to decide tomorrow what I am going to do. If it's all right with you, I'd like to stick around a day or two."

"You are welcome, of course."

After Adam left, Jed sat in the dark, petting Ace and thinking. He had hoped if he put it together he'd know what to do about Grayson, but no answer seemed to work. The one thing he did know is if he didn't have a plan, Grayson would.

The next afternoon Jed was riding back from the upper pasture, tired but feeling good for the work when he saw riders entering the lower pasture. His momentary unease was relieved but came again when he saw it was the cavalry. So he'd meet this Captain Phillips. By the time he had unsaddled his horse, putting him in the corral, the men had dismounted and were sitting on the deck.

The captain rose and came to greet him. "I've heard a lot about you. I'm Randall Phillips," he said with the kind of smile Jed had seen so often in men who had known war—hard and calculating.

"Good or bad?" Jed asked as he tried to decide what he thought of the tall cavalryman.

"I try to decide that kind of thing for myself."

"I'm surprised to see you up this way." Not that he was. "We haven't seen much sign of the Walpapi."

"I've been a lot of places since I got here. The Paiutes are rustling cattle down on the Malheur. Sounds like you have enough up here that it might prove tempting to go out of their way."

"This country is pretty rough. Possibly it's seemed easier down that way without enough reason to come up for what they'd have to work harder to get."

Phillips' smile was short. "I suspect this war has just begun, Mr. Hardman. What you have seen might not be what you can come to expect. They are pushing back against those who would take their freedom."

Adam spoke up from the other side of the deck. "And do you blame them?"

The officer shook his head. "I'd be doing the same thing were

267

I in their position. However, I am not. It's my duty to secure this district." That hard smile reappeared. "And secure it I will."

"Would you gentlemen like something to drink?" Raine asked from the doorway. "I am afraid we don't have ice, but we made tea and it's cool."

Phillips' smile softened. "Very much."

"You should have gotten out of the military, Rand," Adam said his own smile laconic. "This one will be worse than the Rogue."

"The aftermath of that was worse. I think I know what to expect." He turned then to Jed with a telling look. "You were an officer in the Civil War, weren't you?"

"Is that a problem?" Jed asked.

"That war is over—at least for men like me. Now the question is how much former soldiers like you will support the federal government as it attempts to make this land safe for Indians and settlers."

Adam laughed. "One more than the other?"

Rand quirked a brow. "I have a job to do, of course. I try to be fair."

Adam moved to the edge of the patio. "I wasn't in the Civil War; so can't say about it, but I don't like how the country keeps pushing the Indian into smaller and smaller spaces. You wonder that they fight back?"

"I don't wonder. I take orders," Phillips said but smiled dryly. "I see you haven't changed, Adam. There is something encouraging about that."

Raine came out with a tray and glasses, which she sat on the long wooden table. Bernice brought more of the same, while Toddy came with a large plate of cookies, which the twelve soldiers happily set into.

"You've changed," Adam said with a faint smile.

"Good or bad?"

"Tough as nails. Are you still open to learning?"

Phillips shrugged. "When it makes sense or could make a difference."

"Not learning could be your death."

"I've faced that." Phillips smile was that bitter one as he bent for a cookie. "Thank you, these are good, Raine."

"I better wash up," Jed said. "Be back in a minute to listen to you two argue this out." He looked at Raine as she stood across the deck from him, her beautiful face, those somber big eyes watching him. All he could think was how much he wanted her and how far off that all seemed to be, moving farther and farther away.

Letting out a breath, he turned and went inside to the kitchen to wash off the dust, not wanting to watch how friendly Raine was going to be with the good looking captain.

"How were the cattle?" he heard her voice from behind him when he came out from under the water he'd pumped. He was surprised and pleased not only at her interest but that she hadn't stayed to entertain her old friend. Yes, he admitted to himself, he was jealous of the rugged officer.

"Looking good. For now, they're staying in the upper meadow. Nothing more killed up there." He took the towel she was holding for him and dried off his face and hands.

"Adam told me that he wanted me to come back with him."

"And you said?"

"You don't have an opinion on it?"

"Would it matter if I did?"

"Of course."

He resisted no longer as he reached out and pulled her to him. He tipped up her chin, met her level gaze before he brought his lips down hard on hers. When he felt her mouth open for him, he delved within, feeling her warmth and her equally passionate response as she pulled him to her, her hands up around his neck.

"How about what's outside?" he asked when she freed his lips.

"And what is that?"

"Your guests? Rand Phillips."

She laughed. "Oh you are going to get serious are you?"

"Want to go upstairs right now?" he asked calling her bluff.

She grinned and let go of him, moving back a few inches to study him. "Do you want me to go with Adam?"

"You know I don't, but the question is what is safest for you."

"No, the question is-- are we going to have a partnership or dictatorship?"

"Who gets to be dictator?" he asked leaning back against the counter and thinking this hardly was the conversation he had expected at this moment.

"Me," she said with a teasing smile.

"Then I'll settle for partnership... the kind we look out for each other though."

"Like you did the day I went fishing," she said with a knowing smile.

His mouth dropped. "You knew?"

She sighed and stepped back into his arms. "Yes, and Jei. You told me to be aware. I saw you and then knew I could relax and just enjoy fishing, which I proceeded to do. I am impressed that you didn't feel compelled to pull my big steelhead in for me."

He grinned. "Jei talked me out of it."

"Well, I'm glad you didn't. But I am not sorry you were there."

"And I'm glad you knew. I won't worry so much the next time you take off."

"Actually that happened today back down to the river, but Adam came with us."

"Us?"

"Bernice is determined she can learn to fish. She took her first lesson this morning."

"Sure she's not fishing for Adam?" he teased.

"If she is, it's a lost cause. He's still head over heels."

"And I don't blame him. I saw your mother, you know."

"The last day of my play?"

He nodded. "I watched you, saw Grayson coming up. I

thought he was your man and I held off contacting you then. I saw your family though. Fine looking people—especially your mother who is as beautiful as..."

Before he could say the rest of what he was thinking, ask her for more of a commitment, Toddy came in to the kitchen. "What are you two up to?" he asked. "We having them to dinner? The whole troop?"

"What do we have to feed them?" Jed asked as he let Raine moved farther away than he wanted.

"There is that side of beef hanging in the second root cellar. I could cut off a big roast or two or three." He grinned.

"Better do it then."

After Rand Phillips' men had eaten and bedded down in the pasture below the house, Raine and Toddy set about cleaning up the kitchen. Rand, Adam, Jei and Jed sat on the deck with a glass of whiskey each as the sun dropped behind the mountains. Jed looked around, but realized Josh was off somewhere with Bernice. Not much he could do about that.

"You have a beautiful home here," Rand said.

"Thank you. I feel fortunate to have it," Jed said.

"You own it before you left for the War?"

"Over two years. I never intended to be gone from it as long as I was."

"It surprised me I have to admit, considering your brother, that you were fighting to keep slavery."

Jed laughed. "You don't beat much around the bush, do you?"

"If I ever did, the War took it out of me," Rand said but smiled.

"I fought against someone taking my land, against those who would dictate what we must do. I didn't like the idea of a federal government controlling everything."

"In short me."

"Yes, you... or any like you."

"I like the military life, but I fought because I was ordered to do it. It's not a cause. It's duty. West Point was something in my path from childhood. From there, it's not easy to see alternatives—even when things get ugly."

"And they do get ugly," Adam said.

"If I didn't do this, who would?" Phillips asked. "Do you think this land won't have settlers, more and more? Do you think we can look the other way as innocent people are butchered one by one? This is a moral dilemma. I get that. It also though has to have a winner."

"God," Adam said with a laugh, pouring himself another whiskey. "I should have gotten you out of it after the Rogue. You're a career soldier for sure now."

"Maybe so." Rand shrugged looking back and studying Jed. "I hope you are taking the Indian threat seriously in terms of protecting what is yours."

"I take it as seriously as I see reason to. We've had no problem, and while I was gone, the predations were limited to what they, the wolves, bear, and cougar needed to eat."

"Are you understanding the problem is the joining up of the Shoshoni, Paiute and Bannocks? The battle of Godfrey's Mountain had five hundred warriors and armed. Chief Zeluawick was leading them in a concerted effort to move the whites out of their land. While the trouble down south has at least temporarily been quelled, it's moving your way." He rubbed his jaw thoughtfully.

Jed felt a chill. He hadn't anticipated anything nearly that large. What were the odds they really would leave a big ranch like his alone? "Not much I can do about it," he said finally. "I won't leave my ranch to be burned, my stock to be killed or taken."

"So you'd rather die with them?"

"If it has to be that way." He began to think how he could better fortify his buildings. How many men would he need to hold off a very large bunch coming toward them? He had good rifles, plenty of ammunition, but he needed to be thinking strategically. He had been more concentrating on the threat from Grayson.

"Adam," Rand said, "I know how you feel about the Indians, but Lt. Colonel McDermit felt that way too. He tried to befriend the Indians, and it didn't save him."

"He was killed in an attack?" Jed asked rolling a cigarette. It was looking like he hadn't left war as far behind as he had intended.

"No. He was riding past what he thought was a friendly bunch of Paiutes. One of them shot him dead. One shot. He lived four hours. You can't determine who is friendly and who is not is what I'm trying to tell you."

"Sounds like how Stonewall got killed," Jed said feeling morose at how a fluke could take a man's life. How did you plan for anything?

They smoked in silence for a while as they considered the problem they faced. Jed remembered the rest of his problem. "What is the military doing about the road agents? I assume you've been told about that."

Rand nodded. "It's being investigated."

"That helps a lot," Jed said with a laugh.

"It takes evidence for who is behind it, Mr. Hardman. When I have something, I will move to deal with them."

Jed had his doubts but said nothing.

"Where's Captain Montgomery stationed?" Adam asked coldly.

Rand smiled. "Still not your favorite person."

"Should he be?"

"No, well he's lost rank and lucky not to have been court-martialed out. He's at The Dalles serving in the Quartermaster's Depot."

"Such a shame. Couldn't happen to a nicer fellow."

"Not possibly the smartest place to put him given the thievery we've experienced."

"And he is involved?"

Rand shrugged. "Could be but not yet proven sufficiently."

Adam's smile was satisfied. "So he lost rank huh—private maybe?"

Rand laughed again. "We all lost rank when the War was over. I was up to a colonel but lucky to retain being a captain. He is now a lieutenant."

"Why the demotion? I mean for you?"

"Economics probably. Less pay. The War was costly, and they're cutting a lot of corners as well as decommissioning forts."

"Why aren't you fighting the showier war on the Plains with Custer?" Adam asked with one of those smiles Jed was beginning to like.

"You do keep track of things." Rand's answering smile was crooked. "I was there for a short time but requested this post or one at least in Oregon. I developed a liking for the Northwest when here... after I got over the initial—what the hell am I doing phase."

Adam laughed before his expression grew somber. "I have a concern about how safe this is going to be. I can't remain here as much as I'd like to. Martha will be worrying, but I am not feeling at ease leaving Raine. Martha is not going to like hearing her daughter is in danger."

Jed still wasn't sure what Raine intended to do. He knew what would be smartest, but the look in her eyes when they had talked made him uncertain as to her choice.

"Part of my crew are two Warm Springs," Jed said as he watched the smoke rise. The moon had just come up and was casting an eerie glow on the other men's faces. He supposed his also. "I wonder if they will feel safe to return."

"They might not want to leave their people," Rand agreed. "The Snakes aren't any friendlier to peace loving Indians than they are to whites. Right now they want to wipe any sign of us from their land."

"Again," Adam said, "I understand how they feel, but I'd have to kill them also to keep my own safe and protect my land. I wish there was a better way for men to resolve their differences."

Phillips looked then at Jed, met his gaze. "Sometimes there isn't and yet here we are, sipping a whiskey, smoking, when a year ago, Jed and I would have been trying to kill each other. Rather ironic, isn't it."

"You expect the Indian conflicts could end up the same way?" Jed asked with a touch of disbelief even if he wished it to be so.

"Once there is a clear victor."

"You expect there will be," Jed said laconically.

"Eventually. Hard feelings or not, this is a problem of land. It seems unlikely to be settled short of a lot of dying. I may not like it, but it's how the world has always operated. The military tries to make peace but again and again it's undermined by those who want control. What do you do about that?"

"Peace is found in a cemetery and sent there with a bullet," Jed said with some bitterness. Two of his brothers had paid the ultimate price as they had tried to secure their land. Just because it had always been that way didn't mean it should.

Raine and Toddy came out from the house. "Your talk sounds violent," Raine said as she settled near Jed.

"It does, doesn't it?" Rand said with a small grin. "I haven't brought good news, I fear." He repeated the gist of what he'd told them. "The best thing for you ladies to do is head back to the Willamette Valley until this whole thing is resolved."

Jed saw that Bernice and Josh had walked onto the deck hearing the end of the conversation. "I have nothing there to return to," she said. "Not to mention it might be as unhealthy as here. Here at least it's an if. There it's a definite."

"I am not going back with Adam either," Raine said

"It might be safer," Jed said.

"Someone once told me that no place is guaranteed safe," Raine said with a smile.

Phillips stared into the distance. "Perhaps I'll get lucky with some of my forays. The plan is to do sweeps and take any Indian we find with us to secure facilities."

"Prisons?" Adam said with sarcasm.

"We call them reservations," Rand said but his smile said the barb wasn't wasted on him. "Umatilla, Klamath, wherever they can be secured, fed and sheltered."

"For a people who rode free for thousands of years."

"They won't share."

"And so?"

"Those who won't go are considered hostiles, and we will kill them. I know it sounds harsh, but if you had heard and seen all I have, you'd see it's probably what it will take. Words won't solve this issue."

"The problem with what you just said," Adam said sipping his whiskey, "is the government will do two steps forward and then it'll be three back. About the time you think you have it worked out, there'll be a new treaty. That new treaty will get broken and back it all will go. In the meantime, you have to just follow orders —again and again."

Phillips chuckled with what seemed his first genuine amusement. "There you have it, and I admit it's true or has been too often. And I have to add that Superintendent Huntington is trying to work out a peace treaty with Paulina right now."

Adam whistled. "And not Ocheho or Weahwewa?"

"You have paid more attention to this than you claim."

"Until two weeks ago I was a sheriff. I had to pay attention."

"Wait," Raine said, "you quit being a sheriff. I thought you liked that job."

"I'd done it for over ten years. It seemed time for something different."

"What?"

"I'm not sure yet."

"You want a job as scout?" Phillips asked with no cynicism this time in his voice. "We could sure use you."

"And what would my wife be doing or my son while I did

that? I like you a lot, Rand, but the military..." He raised his hand twisting it from side to side.

"Well to answer your question, the problem is that they don't appear to be willing to talk to Huntington; so I am not sure if he can bring them in or even will try to sign the treaty."

"Not to mention," Adam added, "that the Paiutes, Modocs and Klamaths don't much like each other. You put them on one reservation and it's bound to lead to trouble."

"One step at a time, my impatient friend," Phillips said.

"This doesn't sound like a step," Adam said. "It sounds like a recipe for an extended war."

"It might yet be. I agree. I will just do what I am ordered."

"Damn the military," Adam said with a derisive snort.

"It's my life."

"It will let you down, Rand. You wait and see."

Phillips shrugged with cynicism. "That's how life often is whatever a man chooses."

With yawns, the others headed for bed as did Phillips to bed down with his men. "So where does that leave us?" Raine asked Jed as he rolled and lit another cigarette.

"Most likely we won't be the target of a big attack; but on the other hand, we could get hit by raiding parties who know of this ranch. And they do know of this ranch. The Shoshoni are most likely, and they are fierce warriors from all I've been told."

"The ones they call the Snakes."

He nodded.

"When we came West, there were some skirmishes with the Indians but nobody attacked us. It was all threats and bluster."

"I wish I thought this would be the same."

"You really want me to leave, don't you?" she asked knowing their future depended on his answer. If he wanted to keep her safe, bundle her in cotton batting, they would have no real chance.

If he had read her mind, he could not have answered better.

"No, I don't. If you want to stay, I want you here. I'll do all I can to protect this ranch, and if you stay, you."

She smiled then, putting out her hand to rub lightly over his arm. "That was the right thing to say."

He hoped it would be the right answer for her, that a fluke wouldn't take her from him. Life was too filled with uncertainties and things for which a man couldn't plan. He wanted her. Wanted her badly but when they said goodnight, he didn't ask her again to come to his bed. Maybe she would have said yes but he couldn't take the risk of getting her pregnant, not with so much uncertainty lying ahead. He still wasn't sure he'd be walking away when the dust cleared.

Lying in his bed, the moonlight lending an eerie light to his room, and his hand when he lifted it to stare at it. He remembered what it was like in the war. These were memories he had worked hard to push from him. Sometimes they came. The smoke, the noise, the smell of blood, of men groaning, screams in the night as men remembered or suffered from old wounds. War. How could anyone want one and yet here he was, having come to live in a country on the verge of yet another war. He wanted to sleep but wondered if he'd find it this night with his feeling of tension so high.

CHAPTER 20

Raine had decided when she entered her room that the cake was ready to be frosted. Not a particularly romantic way to think of what she intended, but she had stripped off her pants, shirt, boots, underwear and taken the nightgown she had stashed in her bag thinking maybe she would never use it. It hadn't after all taken that much room. When she had put it on, she knew what she wanted. She hoped Jed would agree.

She had never turned the key between the two rooms, but she knew he hadn't tried it. It had always been her choice. When she opened the door, he was lying with the covers over his lower half, his torso silvery looking in the moonlight.

"Are you sure now?" he asked huskily as she walked toward him.

"Are you the one with doubts?" she asked but didn't hesitate. She had seen that look in his eyes, the one she'd always looked for in a man, the one she'd seen when Adam looked at her mother or Matt at her sister. She had never seen it from a man she wanted until Jed. It was there now. She didn't wonder what he wanted.

He lifted her arms for her as she slid into the bed, under the covers and next to his naked body. "I just don't want to make you pregnant right now, not with all this hanging over us."

"You won't. It's safe... now." She moved over him and kissed him lightly on the mouth, savoring the taste of the tobacco and, as she ran her tongue along his skin, the masculine flavor of him. His hands ran through her long hair as she had left it loose and hanging long.

"God, I want you so much," he murmured, his hands going over her body, down her back to cup her buttocks. He ran his hands over them and then down her thighs, feeling her fingers exploring his own body. He was erect almost immediately and only hoped he could hold off his release until he had brought her pleasure. It wouldn't be easy. He had wanted this for too long.

She moved down his chest, licking and kissing as she followed the trail of hair to his belly and then below. Using her fingers, she caressed him, saw him grow even harder as she teased and played with him.

Lifting her, he put her beneath him and spread her legs as he went between them. Touching her lightly with his erection, he stroked down with his fingers over her breasts, teasing her nipples into hard little nubbins. If he thought she needed time to be ready for him, she knew that she had been ready for weeks. She reached up to take him into her.

When he thrust deep, she bit back the groan at how good it felt. Why had she waited so long? He hesitated a moment as though gaining control and then began to move, touching her all the places that most gave her pleasure. She felt the sensations growing, knew she wasn't far from her climax when she felt him surge and take her over with him.

Afterward she lay in his arms, as they stayed linked. He kissed her temple. "I love you so much," he whispered. "It makes me weak just thinking of how much."

"As I love you," she said. "And if someday I have your baby, I want that too. I don't want to wait long either, Jed."

"We won't, sugar," he said. "Just we have to know it's going to be safe for a baby to be here. For you to be pregnant. And I want this thing with Grayson settled."

"You won't go after him?" she asked feeling a cold chill at the thought.

"I won't have to. He'll come after us. It's only a question of when."

"Do you think he will send more men?" She ran her fingers along his arm, feeling of the scar from the bear attack. She didn't want him having more scars or worse.

"I don't honestly know. We just have to be ready for whatever comes. That's the tough part."

"I don't understand how. I mean he can attack anytime. We can't be ready all the time, can we?"

"No, but we can make this house more ready. I've been thinking about it. We need barricades outside, wooden shutters for the windows on the ground floor. We need it not just for him but for the Shoshoni if they come."

"What about when you are out with the cattle? They could attack you then and you'd have no protection."

"It's just staying alert to sounds and movement. I though won't be out until calving and this with Grayson should be settled long before that. When the snows come, I don't see him wanting to be uncomfortable. I also don't see him as a patient man."

She smiled then against the dampness of his skin. "But you are a patient man, aren't you, my love."

"When something is important, I can be." He felt her hands again beginning to explore his body.

"You are so beautiful," she said as she ran fingers over a muscle ridge on his belly. "Let me play with you."

He knew it wouldn't be easy, but he lay back and found himself being brought to the brink of a climax and then she would stop. When he tried to take charge, she asked again for this gift, and he lay back finding it to be one of the harder things he'd done.

"I want you to want me so bad," she whispered against his

belly. "I want it to be all you can think about, where you can't worry about anything but just feel me and how much you want me."

"God, you already have that," he said as she finally settled herself over him and took him to a place he had never been when they finally climaxed together.

When he woke later, she was watching him with that heavy lidded look. "Not enough yet?" he asked aware he was already erect again.

"Not nearly."

In the morning, Jed wasn't sure how much anybody in the house knew of what had changed. With the bedrooms in separate wings of the house, they'd have heard nothing. Was there something about the relaxed look on both their faces that might have told of their night?

Whatever the case, after breakfast, Adam went to the corral to get his horse. Raine had packed him supplies to get him back to the valley. He would ride as far as Camp Watson with the soldiers. "So I can tell your mother you are fine?" he asked as he tightened the girth of the saddle.

"Tell her the frosting is working now," she said with a grin.

Adam laughed. "I'll do that."

"If you decide you want to come our way," Jed said his own face a lot more at ease than she had seen it for weeks, "you'd be welcome to stay here. You know, since the homesteading act of 1862, this land hasn't been taken because of the distance and Indian risks. If you settled near us, it'd be a good thing for us all."

Adam considered that. "Other than the Indians, you mean?" he teased.

"That won't last forever." Raine put her arm around Jed's lean waist as she smiled up at her stepfather who was now mounted.

"I'll tell Martha. It'd be hard for her to leave Amy, Matt, the grandkids, and St. Louis."

"Unless they all wanted to come too."

"Move us all east?" he asked as he laughed at the idea.

"Could be done," Jed said. "I have ten sections. It would support several families if we expanded our numbers and could protect it. There is a need for beef and except the other side of the Cascades, we'd have the market. This land has more potential for like orchards. It hasn't yet been fully utilized but with enough of us, it could be."

"I'll talk to them. Not sure though. Martha seems to like it where she is."

"Well, I will be back to visit when I can," Raine said but didn't add when this situation is cleared up.

Before Adam rode off, the Kalama brothers returned. They had gone to the kitchen to get food and said nothing until Adam and the cavalry had left.

"Trouble is on the way," Joe told Jed as he took a big swallow of coffee. "The Shoshoni attacked some settlers near our reservation. Looking for easy pickings."

"I wasn't sure you'd be able to return."

"We like the work," Joe said, "but George, he might go back next spring to bring his woman with him here. You said we could."

"Yes, it'd be good. From what the military told me, we can expect trouble though. It could be dangerous some years to come."

Joe and George both grinned. "Could be we might like to get our licks in. We consider this ranch important to us. Ain't nobody gonna come rustling stock here or burning this house."

"All right then. And we can start figuring out where you want a cabin. We could start on this winter. With the freezes, we can cut the trees for the walls." He thought about it for a moment, then added. "You know that there are more dangers than Shoshoni that could show up."

"You mean like those two lowlifes?"

"Yes."

"We can handle it. We'll keep an eye out for you, check for tracks, and if it needs be, we'll fight alongside you."

Jei was listening. "You know I will do the same." He patted the butt of the revolver on his hip. "I wouldn't mind getting my licks in on Grayson if he shows up."

"I don't expect him to show up himself, not first anyway," Jed said. "We'll need to keep our eyes open—for white men or Indians. And first job will be falling trees for more cabins but also to form a barricade out front."

"A kind of stockade?" Jei asked. "I like that idea. It's a start anyway."

"The creek along one side and the mountain to our back where it'd be hard to come down fast in a fight, I think mainly we have to worry about what's out there." He gestured to the front pasture. "That and sneak attacks." That was the one that most worried him. It's the one for which you couldn't plan.

As Bernice and Raine made the dinner, with Toddy off to get supplies from Monument, Bernice said, "I should go. Not maybe right now, not when it's still unsettled with Russ, but I can't stay out here."

"It's not working for you with Jei?" Raine asked peeling potatoes.

"He isn't looking for anything with me. Probably not with any woman."

"He prefers men?" Raine asked thinking Jei didn't seem like the sort who would but she hadn't imagined Russ's proclivities either; so what did she know.

"No, not that," Bernice said with a laugh. "He's a trained warrior. A man who won't ever have a woman permanently cramping his ways and choices. A monk warrior with sex on the side, of course," she added with a laugh.

"Ah, well sometimes men change their minds."

"If so, it wouldn't be me. He'd be wanting a woman like you."

She gave a laugh. "Besides, I don't see marriage for me. I am too set in my ways. I'd always be looking at other men to add to the problem."

Raine looked over to try and interpret what she had heard in Bernice's voice. Since the blonde had her head turned down, she couldn't see her eyes.

"I have been thinking of something, Bernice. If we really do get this settled with Russell, well I have at least one business still in Portland." She assumed the leased one would be gone. "I asked someone to look after them but she's been more an aide than a manager like you were. Would you be interested in that?"

"You are joking?"

"Not at all. You said you liked the business end of what you did. This wouldn't be so different. Think about it. I realize if Russell is still there, it's not feasible or safe but if he isn't at some point."

Bernice smiled seeming to be speechless for once. "We couldn't actually be friends, could we?" she asked finally.

"If we didn't want the same man, maybe." She grinned at Bernice's chortle.

That night after making love, she lay in Jed's arms and told him about her decision regarding her businesses.

"You think you can trust her?" he asked not caring much except that Raine was making plans to be with him. There was a chance for them. If he survived anyway.

"It's hard to say, but you didn't want her involved with Josh did you?"

"I wouldn't do anything though to stand in his way if she's what he wants."

"I think that it's best if Bernice has an option. She is kind of like a big cat, you know for how she will act when she feels she has none."

He smiled against her hair. "Good judgment. All right then, if she takes it, that settles that. If Josh wants her, he'll have to speak up."

"You don't think Jei does?"

He shook his head. "Jei is hard to explain or figure out. He's not got his heart on Bernice though... if he has a heart." He kissed her temple.

"Or if she does," Raine agreed with a little laugh.

"When Toddy got back, he told me he had heard of an offer to buy our beef from Silver City."

"Where is that?"

"Too far and a little odd that it would even come up. It'd be beyond the Owyhee River. Even without this thing with Grayson, I wouldn't drive beef that far, especially not after what the captain told us. I just am trying to figure out from where the offer really came."

"You think a decoy."

"If so, not a smart one. Right now, sugar, the beef is the least of my concerns. I am going to leave them scattered in the hills again for the winter. This country is rough enough to make even the Shoshoni think twice about trying to round up many of them."

"So what is your concern, laird of this valley?" she asked teasingly as she ran her hand down the bare skin of his back to his buttocks.

"Ah laird is it?"

"Of course. Do you have a kilt?"

He smiled, his mind on anything but his kilt. "I do happen to have one."

"What do you wear under it?"

"You might have to find out someday.'

"I might."

"So you see me as the laird?"

"I do."

You can say that, the woman who twists him around her little finger with no trouble at all."

"You are my laird too."

"And you do anything I ask," he said with that husky tone to his voice.

"Within reason... maybe," she qualified as she began to see where this was going.

"You like to play. How do you like being played with?" he asked as he moved his lips to her breast, taking a nipple between his teeth as his hands delved down her body.

She swallowed hard at the sensations he was causing to grow. "Oh my," she said finally as he pushed her legs apart, and delved between her legs with his mouth and tongue.

"Don't move," he whispered, blowing on her most sensitive places.

"That's impossible," she said as she thrust herself against him. "I want you. And now."

"No orders, remember." He kept playing as she had with him the day before until finally he could hold back no longer. "Spread your legs, sugar," he ordered as he entered her with a hard thrust.

An hour later, still bathed in sweat, they lay with the moon now lighting the whole room. "You are so beautiful," he whispered. "I want you so much that I could do just this all day and night."

"You don't think you'd get tired of me and it after a while."

"Never. I could die this way."

"Don't you even suggest such a thing," she said with a little laugh.

"It'll be when I am old and gray. Won't that make it all right?" he teased.

"Not even then unless we can both die at the same time."

"Will you marry me again when this is all over?"

"And we have to wait for that? When will it be over anyway? I might be old and gray by then. And I want us to have a baby too, Jed. I don't want to wait forever on that either."

She fell asleep without waiting for an answer, but he lay awake considering what she had said. In some ways he had never felt so fatalistic about his own mortality. If he was killed, where would that leave her with raising a child? She'd have the money, of course, but it still would be hard. Was he being selfish to want to be there, to raise his own child? How could he ensure that would be possible? If he hadn't known it before, he knew it now. He couldn't.

Three mornings later, fixing breakfast, Raine was surprised that it was Bernice helping her and not Toddy. "Where is he?" she asked as she whipped up the hotcake batter while Bernice fried salt pork.

"Still in bed as far as I know," Bernice said. "Haven't you noticed by now that Toddy gets out of work whenever he can?"

That was true. "Could he be sick?"

"Not that I know of." Bernice looked a little green herself as she fried the meat.

"Are you all right?" Raine asked as she saw Bernice begin to gag.

"I'll be right back." Bernice ran outside and when she returned, she sat at the table.

Raine got her a glass of water. "Drink this."

"You might as well know," Bernice said with her hands holding her head. "I won't be able to hide it for long. I'm pregnant."

Raine dropped into the chair across from her. She felt a mix of shock and jealousy. She was supposed to be the one to get pregnant. Bernice had beat her to it. When Bernice looked up, her lips were pressed tightly together.

"How long have you known?"

"For sure? Maybe two weeks. I'm never irregular, but I thought maybe it was just that. Then I began to get sick in the mornings. I hoped to hide it and get out of here. Please don't tell anyone. I will go before it becomes obvious."

Raine let out the breath she had been holding. She walked to the stove, poured herself a cup of coffee and then sat down again. "Whose baby is it?"

Bernice gave a bitter little laugh. "Didn't you really want to ask if I knew whose baby it was?"

"I assumed you would."

"I've been pregnant before, you know." The blonde's eyes were filled with pain as she looked at Raine before taking another drink of the water.

"My god, I had no idea. I... did you lose the baby?"

"It happened twice and I did... you might say. I had the pregnancies terminated."

At that Raine had no idea what to say. She knew it was possible, of course. What did you say to such a statement? I'm sorry? Certainly not that, since it appeared Bernice had chosen her own course or had she had a choice? "Is that what you want to do this time?" Raine asked finally thinking it was unlikely she'd find such help out here. She herself had no idea how one might end a pregnancy-- even if she had been willing to tell her if she had known.

Bernice groaned and rose to stand at the sink. "We should fix breakfast. The men will be in soon. I don't want to talk about this with them here."

Two hours later with Jed having taken the Kalamas and Josh with him to move cattle a little farther from the ranch and then scattering them, Raine suggested she and Bernice take a little walk. Bernice nodded as Raine got her rifle. "We won't go far," Raine said.

After a few minutes, Bernice said, "You must not think much of me."

Raine shook her head. "I am just thinking of how this must be for you right now. Do you want this baby?"

"It wasn't much of a choice before or now," Bernice said with some bitterness. "I had no support. A madam can't stay in business pregnant or with a baby. I didn't even know for sure who the father might've been either time. Oh I knew the likely one, but he wasn't there to father a child. It wasn't part of the bargain."

"And this time?"

"It doesn't matter because he doesn't want to be a father either."

"How can you know he won't want to be? I am assuming you haven't talked to him."

She shook her head. "I won't trap a man that way. You might find this hard to believe, Raine, but I have learned a few things in my life. I've made mistakes, and I guess this was one. I don't want a man who resents me and hates me for why he has to be with me."

Raine considered that a moment. "But it will be his child also. Have you thought that might be important to him?"

"I doubt it," she responded with some bitterness. "To be honest, sex is something separate from a man. They don't even have to like a woman to have sex with her."

"You might as well tell me. Who is the father?"

"I can't."

"I know anyway."

"I doubt that."

"It's Josh, isn't it?"

Bernice turned away. "He's not it."

Raine knew she was lying. "Look, you might as well tell me because if you don't, I'll ask Josh if it's possible."

Bernice glared at her. "You wouldn't."

Raine stopped her and took hold of her shoulders. "You've changed a lot since you came here. Believe me now when I say, I would. I would not let you leave without him knowing and having a voice in what you do next."

Tears began to run down Bernice's face. "I might lose the baby anyway... after what I've done."

"Ah divine judgment huh?"

"Something like that." Bernice gave a little laugh. "I seem to be crying easier these days. Sorry. I don't like myself doing that. It seems manipulative."

"Bernice, I do not believe in divine judgment. I suppose if your terminations weren't done right, it might make you more susceptible to miscarriages, but it won't be any god doing it if that happens."

"One thing about being a whore," Bernice said with a bitter laugh, "you do get good medical care for such... inconveniences."

"And are pressured to do it also, I suppose."

Bernice looked at her through narrowed eyes. "I never pressured a girl to do that. I do have my ethics too, even if you don't believe that."

"You have to tell Josh and let him help you decide what you do next."

"He'll hate me. He'll think I did it on purpose."

"I might not know a lot about life, not as much as some, but I know one thing. He had a hand in what happened... as well as something else." She smiled when Bernice managed a weak smile.

"I can't believe I let it happen," Bernice said. "I should have thought. Should have... but I didn't. I just got carried away. Surprising as it might seem to you, I haven't done that often. Usually I know exactly what I'm doing, but he's so beautiful, so innocent in a way maybe I never was. When he wanted me, I wanted him as much. It wasn't... about the sex so much as something else."

"You love him?"

Bernice started to walk again. When Raine caught up with her, Bernice said, "I don't honestly know. What do I know of love? But I won't hurt him by trapping him that way."

"And it wouldn't hurt him if you were carrying his baby and left without telling him?"

"I hadn't thought of it that way. All right, I will tell him, and I don't have to tell him what I'll do about the baby, but I will tell you. If the offer is still good, when it's safe for me to go back to Portland, I will take you up on your offer. I won't raise a child in a brothel." She had pursed her lips together again.

"All right. And yes, it's still good, but let's see what Josh says first."

"Will you tell Jed?"

"The laird?" Raine said with a little laugh and at Bernice's look of confusion, she said, "It's what I've been calling him. Laird of this land."

"It does fit," Bernice said with a genuine laugh for the first time. "He's domineering for certain."

"Well this is something he can't dominate even if he wants to do so. I won't tell him until you have had a chance to talk to Josh. Perhaps it will be Josh who wants to do so."

Bernice looked disbelieving, but Raine felt certain she would at least tell Josh, and then what would happen, she had no idea.

CHAPTER 21

"So here we are," Russell Grayson said to Kirk Edmonton as the two sat at a private table at the back of the nicest saloon in The Dalles. "Now what? You've been pretty mysterious about this all. If you have a plan, why not tell me?"

"Because you have a knack for tipping your hand or going off half cocked. I wanted you here as backup just in case my plan didn't work."

"Well, let's hear it."

"What did you think of the men I hired to come with us on the steamboat?"

"Too smooth for my taste, but you think they can be trusted?"

"They know they are going with me on a little trip and that the pay is good. Added to it that it could involve some fighting. They may not look it, but they are all excellent marksmen."

Russell snorted with derision as he signaled for another whiskey. "Marksman doesn't mean killers," he said.

"They were in the Union army and hate Southerners. Help you any."

"It sounds a little more promising. The question is why you and not me? It's hardly your usual thing to go on hunting trips."

"Nor has it been yours. You hire it done with rough types that cannot be trusted and reveal what they are before a bullet is fired."

"And you're a writer."

"Ah but that's not all I am. I am one who thinks strategically. I plot out what must be done to keep a play interesting and in this case how we can get someone we want eliminated, while not being blamed."

"And your plan will do that?"

"I believe so."

"I don't like it."

"Because you want to torture Hardman. You want him suffering and not just gone." Russell nodded his head approvingly. "But that's not the long range goal is it?"

"I suppose not."

"What you want is the woman on your arm, a woman capable of thinking and looking beautiful. You want to present a façade to Portland that enables you to run for office and gain more power. Isn't that about it?"

"It has seemed within my reach. That is until he showed up."

"If he's dead, who will she turn to? She's vulnerable, naïve, and she will need someone to be with her, to keep her safe. Who but her friend who she misjudged recently. She will come back to seeing you as she did and realize it was he who put such silly ideas into her head that you weren't trustworthy."

"You honestly think it'd work that way?"

"It's the logical scenario. You can't have that if you don't do a clean kill. You were right from the start. I should never have suggested shanghaiing. It left too many places to go wrong. I will fix that by going there, and being sure that I or one of my men puts a bullet in Hardman's back."

"And you won't be charged with the murder?"

"Not how I will do it. He has no reason to distrust me. It is why it must be me and not you. I will do it when no one is around as though Indians did it. This is a wonderful time to have someone killed, and no one can prove how it happened."

"And my part on it is?"

Kirk sipped his brandy. "I am sure it will work; but if it does not, there can only be one reason. Hardman will stop me before I can kill him. I suspect he'll then head straight for Portland and you. He won't go over the mountains because of the snow up there. He will have to ride to The Dalles and take the steamboat. You will be waiting with your usual crew of unsavory men. You will finish him off before he knows what hit him."

"And what will have happened to you?" Russ asked with some concern finally in his voice.

"It would be dangerous for me, of course. But I don't believe he will figure it out in time. At the most, he will only know when he's dying, and then it'll be too late. Trust me, Russ. I can do this, and then we will comfort the widow and all her newfound wealth. We will pick back up life as it was."

Russ smiled. "It sounds possible."

"Not just possible, but probable. A virtual certainty." He raised his glass and they clicked them as a toast to the death of their enemy.

The next morning, Jed was out by the barns chopping wood when Josh approached him. "Got something to talk to you about, big brother," he said with a sheepish smile.

"Sure." Judd sank his ax into the chopping block, dried off his sweat with his sleeve before he threw on his coat. He had more work to do before he'd consider the pile sufficient. Where the hell was Toddy, who was supposed to be stacking it by the house?

"Bernice told me something this morning." He hesitated.

"Good or bad news?" Hesitations usually meant one or the other.

"Good. Just unexpected. She's pregnant."

Jed thought over what to say. He couldn't say he was totally shocked and yet it was unexpected at the same time. "And it relates to you," he said leaning back against the corral where Midas came over to bump his back.

"I am the father."

"You're sure of that?"

"I'd only take that from you because you are my brother," Josh said testily. "I know I am the father."

"All right then. And it's fine with you?"

"Does it matter?"

"Yes."

"Well, it's not like I planned it, but I do care for her. I certainly didn't expect to be a father right now, but I feel I can handle that."

"You getting married?"

"We hadn't talked that far. I told her I'd be responsible for the baby and her."

"All right," Jed said as he got the makings from his pocket and rolled a cigarette.

"I admit, she caught me off guard. I've had a little more time to think about it while I went for a walk, and I think it's good."

"If it's good with you, then it's good with me." He lit the cigarette taking a long draw on it. "You plan to stay here or should I say does she plan to stay here?"

"We could go back to the South, but it seems like an unfriendly place for a darkie making a white woman pregnant. Not likely to be easy on the baby either."

"That could be true pretty near anywhere, but won't be a problem if you and she decide to stay here. You know you're my brother, and it's my hope that this is your home as much as mine."

"If she's not scared to give birth up here, away from doctors, I think she'll stay at least until the baby is born." Josh walked around in a circle, obviously uneasy at the new found responsibility. "I want the baby, Jed." He met his brother's gaze. "I think it's like when I was born, and our mama took me in. I can pay something back now."

"Not a good way to look at it."

"How can you say that?"

"The word responsibility shouldn't be the first one that comes to your mind. A child is a gift of a sort. Something precious for you to help grow up and become an adult. I won't say it's from god or something but maybe just from life, part of the circle of life, the continuity."

"Kind of a philosophical bent from you."

"Raine's been talking about wanting a baby, and I've done some thinking on the subject. Does she know?"

Josh shook his head. "I don't know who Bernice told other than me. Give me some time I'll come up with a better way to see this. It was just a shock."

"It's a new start for her and you," Jed said drawing on the cigarette as he tried to find the right words. "When she got here, I'd have never figured there'd be a chance with any man that she'd make a good wife or mother. She's changed though, and I can see that. Is that change permanent? That's what I don't know. Raine seems to like her well enough."

"I didn't ask her to marry me yet, but I guess I should."

"If you love her or care for her enough, that would be good."

"Is that why you haven't married Raine? You aren't sure enough?"

Jed contemplated what he hadn't told Josh. It wouldn't likely make it easier for his brother to know his own doubts. "It's a dangerous time," he said finally.

"You have a premonition of dying? God damn it to hell, I can't lose you, Jed."

"Not that so much but recent events make a man know how easy he can be taken down."

"You better not let anything happen to you. I want you there to help me raise this kid."

Jed laughed and threw down the cigarette grinding it out with his boot. "Then I better be there." He reached out and hugged his brother.

"It's getting cold. Feels like snow soon," Josh said as he looked toward the dark clouds gathering over the rugged hills behind the home.

Snow wasn't a bad thing, Jed thought as he finished splitting the firewood. With enough snow maybe they'd have until spring to face whatever might be coming. Maybe.

The first light snowfall came the next morning. It didn't last long on the ground but was enough to remind Raine that she had things to do to make sure they were ready for winter. She had sent Toddy to Monument several times to buy extra supplies. Enough in case they had a long spell of not being able to get out. She had no real idea of what to expect in terms of winter weather despite Jed saying this area was warmer than one might expect.

Before he had gone to war, Jed had bought the newer kerosene lamps to light the house, which did a better job that the dirtier coal oil or less safe candles. With plenty of wood to heat most of the rooms of the house, if they didn't get attacked by the Indians, it all should go well until spring.

Jed had been concentrating on installing shutters on the downstairs window and had the Kalama brothers building barricades out in front of the house. They were intended to shoot from behind but also to slow a horseman from getting too close to the house or barns-- especially with torches. The cattle had been spread into the hills as had been their wont anyway. They'd fend for themselves through the winter, and she only hoped it wouldn't be a hard one.

She had hoped to get a letter from her mother, but so far no word had come as to their plans. Now that there was no need to try to hide her presence on the ranch, she had written asking about ideas for morning sickness—stipulating it was not for her.

She had time to gather information as to what she'd have to do when the baby came.

When Josh and Bernice had announced to everyone about the coming baby, the men had been supportive, Jed had smiled, said nothing privately to her about it, and only Jei had looked bemused. The men took the responsibility of helping with the house as a way to make it easier on Bernice as she adjusted to the changes in her body.

"My god," Bernice said as she looked down at her belly. "I can't believe it's already showing."

Raine was trimming the wicks on the lamps but turned to look. "Nobody but you would notice." She still had a hard time not feeling envious. If Jed was supportive of Josh and Bernice, he hadn't told her he was ready for such an event in his own life. Worse, he was currently making anything an impossibility by his restraint.

"What the hell was that?" Bernice asked running to the window to look toward the sound of gunshots.

Raine joined her and saw flashes of guns as riders approached rapidly firing toward the lower woods. From where they had been splitting logs, Jed and his men had come out from the corrals. Their own rifles were at the ready as they moved to the barricades in front of the house.

As the riders rode into barnyard, Raine saw Jed approaching them with a revolver in a holster at his hip. It wasn't in his hand. Looking toward the arrivals, she recognized Kirk Edmonton with four men she didn't know. She didn't like anything about this.

"What was that about?" Jed asked as Edmonton dismounted.

"We were attacked. Shoshoni, I believe," Edmonton said in an excited voice. "I had five men. One was killed." The others, who had arrived with him, were standing now watching Jed, their rifles still in their hands. The Kalamas, Toddy, and Jei had come beside Jed.

"What are you doing up here?" Jei asked. Which was the exact question on Raine's mind. She remembered her distrust of the playwright, but she had no proof. Why would he show up now and with so many men?

With no more sounds of shooting, Josh joined them from the barns. He also looked distrustful.

"I didn't realize you were here, Han Jei," Edmonton said looking at Jei with surprise. "I came out hoping to find Raine. I heard she had gone this way, and I was worried about her," the smooth talking man said as he looked toward the house and met her gaze. "Well, thank God you are here and safe" He smiled broadly.

"Put your horses in the corral. There are some oats in the barn. We'll talk in the house," Jed said in a terse voice, his eyes narrowed. "Josh, you, and Toddy keep an eye on the woods for movement in case there is something coming our way." His tone didn't indicate he didn't think there was.

"I think they were after us as easy targets," Edmonton said as he watched one of his men unsaddle his mount. "I heard there were Indians here, but thought we were beyond their territory when we got past Monument."

"Why would you think that?" Jed asked as he scanned the men with Edmonton.

"I heard it was mostly to the south that there'd been attacks. I was naïve, I suppose," Edmonton said. "I should introduce my party. Derek Whitman, Jeremy Barnes, Bill Jefferies, and Jacob Miller. I had asked them to come with me to assure my safety. I really though did not expect what happened. My, this is a dangerous place." He looked then again toward Raine who was studying him from the porch. "And how are you, my dear?" He then looked back at Jed. "May we ask for your succor?"

Raine saw the distrust on Jed's face but he nodded. "You will find food in the kitchen. Toddy, get them something." He watched as the five men went in. Raine came to where he stood.

"I saw no rifle flashes from the woods," he told her.

"So no Indians?"

He nodded. The Kalama brothers came up to him. "Want us to go check for sign, Boss?"

"No, in case there are Indians there." He didn't sound like he believed it. "Wait for morning."

"Can't we just tell them to leave?" Raine asked worriedly. She didn't like admitting strangers to their home—and even more didn't like Kirk showing up this way.

"I wish but not tonight. It's looking like more snow and too far to get back to Monument before dark. I don't know yet that there wasn't an attack. I can't ask them to leave in these conditions, not without a good reason." He looked at her then. "Do we have one?"

"Just that feeling I had that Kirk was too familiar with Russell, but he made excuses, tried to deny it being the case. I had no proof."

"Then we'll let them sleep downstairs and stay alert."

In the kitchen the men were eating when they entered. Edmonton smiled, but Raine saw that the man called Barnes surprisingly was glaring at Jed.

Jed poured himself a cup of coffee before he turned and looked thoughtfully at Edmonton. "So you got attacked? How many were there?"

Whitman spoke up. "I think fifteen but maybe more."

"And they followed you to the house before they turned and left?"

"Apparently," Edmonton said rising and taking his dish to the sink. "I have never seen Indians before. It's frightening. They hit Jerrod Gregory."

"Killed him?"

"That's what we figured."

"You didn't check?"

Edmonton swallowed with a regretful expression. "We ran for our lives. We were outnumbered."

"You can stay the night but then head back to Monument. We don't have supplies for more men up here this winter."

"Not very friendly," Barnes said his expression remaining frosty.

"It's friendly that I let you spend the night," Jed said. "We'll give you supper and breakfast but that's it." His tone brooked no argument, and although the men glared at him, they didn't argue.

"How about if you all get out of here while I start dinner," Raine said. "Build a fire in the fireplace please. It's getting cold."

"I had hoped to talk to you alone," Kirk said.

"There is no reason to talk to me alone," she said, "but after we eat, we can talk with Jed."

"I just wanted to assure myself that you were really all right up here."

"I am more than all right," she said. "Now get out of here and let me get to work. I need to expand my menu for tonight."

As soon as the men had left, Bernice came out of the pantry where Raine realized she had chosen to hide. "Why didn't you want him to see you?" she asked as Bernice set about helping her with the meal.

"I knew him. He was one of my customers."

"Kirk?"

"Yes. I thought maybe it's better he didn't know I was here. I never... serviced him, but he had a favorite, Violet. He came regularly."

Amazing what she realized she had never known about the world in which she thought she lived. "Well he knows about Jei anyway. Did you know any of the other four?"

She shook her head. "I didn't actually get a good look at them before I decided to hide. Probably I wouldn't though. A lot of men passed through my establishment."

"They will be gone tomorrow."

"I hope so. I don't like this. It makes me feel edgy."

Raine agreed with that.

After the meal had been consumed, praised, and then cleaned up, Raine went back into the great room where the men were sitting, three smoking along with Jed. They all rose as she entered.

"We so much appreciate your taking us in," Edmonton said again smiling. "I realize now how foolish we were to come this way without an announcement. I didn't expect the snow or the savages."

Outside she could see it was falling more heavily. It might have seemed pretty if she hadn't felt the uneasiness that this wasn't all it seemed with Kirk showing up as he had.

"I still can't imagine why you came, or how you knew I was here," she said trying not to let her suspicion show in her voice.

"I told you I wanted you to do my play. You know how a playwright is about that. I thought I could convince you to change your mind and come back."

"That doesn't explain how you knew she was here," Jed said not bothering to hide his distrust.

"I had been told you had been in Portland. I thought perhaps you had invited her to visit your ranch."

"Long way to come on a guess." A guess that made no sense.

Edmonton laughed. "I suppose. But I have always operated on whims. And this just seemed something I wanted to do. I really do want you in my play, Raine. It would be so perfect for you. Even some of the comedy you said you wanted next time."

"I won't be back, Kirk," she said. "This is my home now. I am sure you can find another leading lady."

"Not as good as you were." He looked then at Jei. "I am surprised to see you here, but I did hear you left town. I assumed you went with Bernice though."

"You come looking for me too?" Jei asked with a narrowed gaze and taut smile.

Edmonton laughed. "Of course not. Just surprised is all."

"We had a long day with more work to do tomorrow," Jed said. "You men can sleep down here. There are blankets in that closet.

Sorry but only two of you can use the sofas. The rug is pretty soft though. Better than hard ground anyway."

Raine rose to come with him as he went up the stairs. When they got to their two doors, she looked back to see Kirk watching with interest. She chose to walk into her own room and leave Jed to use his own door. She wasn't sure why. As soon as their doors closed, she locked hers and went to Jed. "Sleep in my room tonight, please?" she asked even though they had generally slept in his bed and never bothered to worry about someone seeing them go together.

"You didn't want him to know we slept together?" he asked as he walked into her room. He still wore his Colt on his hip.

"I didn't want him to know where you'd be sleeping," she said, "but it wasn't because of caring whether he knew we are lovers. I just don't feel comfortable about him being here, not any of them."

"Then we'll keep the adjoining door open and see if anything comes into the trap." He smiled, but it wasn't a smile of pleasure.

As they lay in the bed, entwined but not making love, she felt fear that she hated. She couldn't bear it if something happened to Jed. Not now, not when she'd finally found him. Was Kirk really connected to Russ and a danger?

"You think loud," he whispered against her hair.

"And you don't. I never know what you are thinking. That really irks me too, laird."

She could feel his smile against her skin. "How much does it irk you, sugar?"

"We can't make love with them in the house, with possibly someone here who wants to kill you."

"We can't? I thought I was the laird, the master of this land and you."

"You are except when it endangers your life."

"In this case you are right but more because it might endanger you."

"Don't think of me. Protect yourself," she whispered turning so that her lips were against his bare chest.

"You are not helping me to resist making love tonight," he said with a smile in his voice.

"I want you with me for years and years and years. I want the babies this muscular, strong body can make and that means you have to stay healthy and make me lots of them."

She felt his smile against her skin. The room was too dark for her to see him with the waning moon providing little light. It was much later, when the house had totally quieted down that she heard the sound of footsteps on the hallway outside.

Jed lowered her back to the bed and reached for his revolver. He rose naked to stand in the connecting doorway as his door opened and a form came in. The moon was lighting his room enough that she could see the glitter of a knife blade in a man's hand.

"That's far enough," Jed said as he leveled his gun. Rather than backing off, the man turned toward him. At the same time she saw the blade switch positions to throw, she heard Jed's weapon fire. The man staggered back. She knew he'd thrown the knife and looked to see if Jed had been injured. He was standing, but he reached to his shoulder and pulled the blade from it.

"You've been hurt," she cried as she ran to him.

"Stay behind me," he ordered and moved toward the man lying now on his floor. When he got to him, the man moved a little. "Why?" he asked as he knelt down.

"You're a Reb. That's enough reason." The man smiled sickly before his eyes went lifeless. Jed felt for a pulse. "He's dead." Outside she could hear running feet.

"Jed?" Josh asked.

"It's all right."

"The knife struck you," she said beginning to shake.

He nodded. "Nicked me. It's not much. Get on a robe and light a lamp." He was fastening his pants as Josh and Jei came through his door.

With light she could see it that it was the man she'd seen glaring at Jed earlier. Barnes.

"What happened here?" she heard Kirk Edmonton repeating again and again sounding on the verge of hysteria.

"You don't know?" Jed asked as he studied him through narrowed eyes.

"No idea. That's Jeremy, isn't it? What happened to him? God there's blood. Blood makes me sick." He moved away from the others and stumbled back down the stairs.

"Would you two take the body out of here?" Jed asked Jei and Josh. "We'll sort it out in the morning."

"You going to let them stay that long?" Jei asked looking from Jed to the dead man.

"I have to bandage your shoulder. You are bleeding on the floor," Raine said forcing her voice to sound determined and not show her terror. If Jed had slept in that room, if he'd been asleep when that man had entered, this night would have ended very differently. She could not afford to think of that. She just had to do what was required. Disinfect. Bandage the wound. Tomorrow. She'd think about the rest tomorrow.

He glanced down at the wound. "It's pretty much stopped bleeding. You were right," he added, "with where we needed to sleep. Let's finish the night here too."

"After I bandage your shoulder," she insisted.

"Yes, after you do that," he agreed with a slight smile. "Wouldn't want blood on your sheets."

She found no humor in that. "Is there a lot of pain?" she asked as she led him to the kitchen and poured alcohol over the wound, which she determined was shallow, before using strips of cloth to close the injury.

"Not bad."

"I don't think it needs stitches," she said trying only to think of what she had to do. She could not think of what had happened. When she had finished, she dropped into a chair to sit beside him. "What do we do about Kirk?"

"He leaves in the morning. I can't prove he had anything to do with this."

"I didn't," Kirk said from the doorway where he had evidently been watching them. He walked into the room looking from her to Jed and then to Jed's revolver now back in its holster on his hip. "It was clear he wasn't in his right mind."

"Edmonton, get out of my sight," Jed said through his teeth. "I'll talk to you in the morning." The man looked at him but turned and went back into the great room.

As she and Jed walked back up to her bedroom, she said, "I don't believe him."

"Neither do I."

As they lay together, he felt cold. "Are you all right?" she asked sensing his jaw was clenched. She put her arm over him, rubbing his uninjured arm to warm him up. He didn't answer right away, and she kept massaging his skin and muscles.

"I thought I'd done with killing when the war was over," he said finally with a sigh of clear regret.

"You had no choice."

"I didn't think I did then either. It doesn't make it easier to take a life."

She didn't know about that. Couldn't imagine what he had gone through with the war and even this when it was self-defense. All she could do was hold him to her and give him her warmth.

"Maybe I never should have gone back to Georgia. Maybe all this came out of that."

"Hate like that man doesn't come just from a war, Jed. You know that."

"Do I?"

"He has to blame someone for whatever has gone wrong in his own life. It's the way some are. When you're thinking more clearly, you will know that, when the shock of this is over."

"Will I know it? I had a choice about going to war. I could have stayed here, tried to convince you to marry me and maybe..." He sighed again. "I am being a fool. I can't go back and redo any of it."

"None of us can. You did what you believed was right."

"Thinking it doesn't make it so."

She had no way to argue with that. She wanted to bring him comfort but had no idea how to do it. "I love you. I love everything about you," she said finally. "I love that you are the laird. I love that you did go to war even though you never wanted to. I know it was a horrible thing, maybe worse than you expected even, but you walked into it because of who you are. I can't make it all right for you but just know my love is there for you."

He wrapped his arms around her. "I know... and I love you. I just wish... but not much I can do about that either."

It took a long while before she knew he slept, but she lay awake longer as she thought of what he'd said. She had her own wish that she could somehow find a way to heal him, the hurts, the pain he had felt and taken within. Perhaps she could share some of his burdens but most were those only he could lift from himself. Maybe she'd find the answer to helping him, but for now all she could do was hold him and hope worse didn't lie ahead.

CHAPTER 22

I n the morning, Raine was a little ahead of Jed, who was again wearing a cartridge belt, holster and revolver, as they came downstairs. She heard voices arguing in the kitchen, and if she hadn't already had her hand opening the door, she might've been tempted to listen, but it was too late. As the door swung open, she heard one man say, "Murder wasn't part of..." He stopped at her entrance into the room. Kirk looked up with a big smile. "How are the two of you this fine morning?"

Jed said nothing as he walked to the window and looked out. Raine saw a light covering of snow on the ground, but it had stopped.

"Good time for you men to leave. Right after breakfast," Jed said as she began to make coffee. Toddy had already gotten the fire in the stove going and apparently gone out for more firewood.

"I had hoped for longer to visit with Miss Stevens and convince her to become my heroine," Kirk protested with another of those smiles she had come to hate.

"I don't care what you want," Miller said. "I want to get the hell out of here before breakfast." Whitman nodded his agreement and Jefferies accepted a sack of biscuits from Raine. At the door, Miller added, "We are going now. We want no more trouble, and we won't be back."

"Good," Jed said watching through the window as he watched the three saddle their horses and ride out. When he sat at the table across from Kirk, Raine brought him a cup of coffee. He rolled a cigarette as he studied Edmonton. "You should have left with your friends," he said as he lit the cigarette.

"They were going to Canyon City next. I wanted to return to The Dalles."

"Anything special there?" Jed asked studying him through the smoke.

"No, just an easy way to get the steamboat back to Portland."

"Tell the sheriff in The Dalles what happened. We'll bury the man here unless you want to take his body back with you."

Edmonton rose and walked over to the stove, pouring himself coffee. "Heavens no, I don't. I didn't realize he'd do such a thing. He was certainly no friend. Did you, that is, figure out why?"

"No."

"He said nothing before he... died?"

"Would that be your concern if he had?"

"I suppose not. Dead is dead. Just so sudden and shocking."

"It often is."

"So he died without any last words?"

"None that should be of interest to you."

"I imagine this isn't new to you, having been in the war and killed others probably many times. What does it feel like to kill a man?"

Jed's eyes narrowed, his mouth tightened, and the tell-tale muscle in his jaw beat. "What makes you curious about a thing like that?" he asked taking another long draw on the cigarette.

"A writer's curiosity perhaps. It must be rather... well strange to realize you took a man's soul." He laughed. "Rather like a vampire, isn't it? Did you know that in Romania, they call them the strigoi?"

"What a ridiculous thing to say," Raine snapped stopping

from where she had been beating up batter for hotcakes. "Nobody takes a man's soul, and Jed did not choose what happened last night. That man came to kill him and could have when he threw that knife."

"Of course not," Edmonton gave an odd little laugh. "It is power, of course, to take a life. I imagine it must be rather exhilarating in an odd sort of way to have that power of life and death."

Jed stared at him saying nothing. Edmonton didn't wait long before going on. "I never have done such a thing. I shot at the Indians, of course. If they are human anyway, but doubt I hit any."

His intensity as he studied Jed made Raine feel it was as though he was contemplating a new plot. To Kirk, she supposed it was abstract not as it had been to Jed. She understood what the cost had been to him as she had held him through the night. For whatever Kirk's reasons, it appeared he was deliberately attempting to torment Jed. He couldn't possibly know the wounds Jed carried inside, and yet he was tearing at them, innocently or not.

"Is it easy to do?" Edmonton asked then. "I mean after killing so many I suppose it's rather old stuff to you."

Jed took a long draw on the cigarette. "You are going whether you have to be tied to your horse or not. And now."

"Of course, my good man. Of course. But could you... that is would you mind saddling my horse for me then? I don't really know how to do it."

"You seem an odd man to end up out in the wilderness," Jed said not rising. "You hire men to bring you, some of whom you claim you didn't know. The others desert you and you let them go while you cannot even saddle your own horse. What brought you here?"

"Concern for my dear friend, Raine, of course," he said before he grasped at his heart and groaned. His eyes fluttered as he gasped for breath.

Raine came over from the stove. "What's wrong?" she asked but Jed only watched without moving.

"My heart, I fear," Kirk said groaning now. "I can't... the world is going black." His head fell forward on the table.

Finally Jed rose and felt of his pulse.

"Is he... is he dead?" Raine asked staring in shock at the now still form.

"His pulse is strong," Jed said in a cold voice.

At that, Kirk lifted his head, blinking as he looked around the room. "I fainted. What happened? My stomach is hurting. I think... I am going to be sick."

"Interesting," Jed said with no sympathy.

"I am sure I'll be better in a bit. Could I just lie down in your great room for a few moments? It's likely all it will take."

"Toddy, help him in there," Jed ordered before he walked outside into the cold without a coat. Raine watched him go and grabbed her own and Jed's from the hook by the door. He was standing on the porch when she got to him and handed him the coat.

"A little cold out here," she said as he shrugged into it.

"Your friend is a lousy actor," he said.

She managed a smile. "I agree. How do we oust him?"

"I could tie him to his horse. It might take that."

"What do you think he's really up to? And he's not my friend. That's obvious."

"I have no idea. Maybe information for Grayson, but he came a long way, an uncomfortable way for a city man if that's the case."

"The other possibility?" She shuddered as she already knew the answer.

He pulled her into his arms. "It will be all right," he said against her hair as he kissed it.

"Promise?" she asked feeling like a child wanting reassurance.

"I wish I could." His voice sounded resigned, possibly fatalistic. She leaned back in his arms, and then pulled his head down for a kiss. When he would have made it an innocent one, she pushed his lips apart with her tongue delving into his mouth and feeling first his surprise and then ardent response as the kiss changed and became one of passion and need.

When they finally broke apart, she said, "We will make it right together. I promise you that."

When they walked back into the kitchen, it was Bernice at the stove flipping pancakes. She looked up. "I can't hide forever if he's going to stay."

"He won't be here long," Jed said as he left them to walk into the great room.

"He's a fraud," Bernice told Raine. "You both know that, don't you?"

"Yes, but we're just trying to figure out how to oust him."

Bernice pressed her lips together and then smiled. "Maybe I can help with that." She pulled the pan from the stove and followed Jed with Raine right behind her.

Lying on the sofa, Kirk was groaning. "I am so sorry to put you out," he was saying to Jed who was standing by the fireplace.

"You won't for long," Jed assured him feeding a log into the fire.

"Well hello, Kirk," Bernice said as she walked up to stand in front of him. Raine saw the shock on his face as his mouth dropped open. "Fancy seeing you here."

"I didn't realize you were also a guest," Kirk said uneasily as he looked to be trying to reconsider his options.

"Oh yes, for a few days. These kind folks took me in. I am just surprised to see you here. It's not where I generally saw you."

Kirk licked his lips. "I hope you are well," he said finally.

"Quite. I am just remembering the last time I saw you." She smiled then as Raine saw Kirk's uneasiness grow.

"I don't quite recall," he managed finally.

"You were sick then too... and then got well rapidly. I have a feeling you will now too, won't you?" The expression on her face was hard and determined.

He sighed and made an effort to sit up which looked as phony to Raine as the rest of what he'd been doing. "I do feel better."

"Toddy," Jed said without looking at him, "saddle Mr. Edmonton's horse, and Raine, would you put some food in a bag for him. He's leaving."

"I suppose I could... except I am not sure how to get back to Monument, and those Indians, won't they attack me again."

"If they ever did," Jed said with a skeptical smile.

Edmonton looked at him with amazement. "Of course, they did. Would you mind riding at least part way with me, just until I am close to the town."

Raine was shocked when Jed smiled and agreed. When he went outside to saddle Midas, she ran after him. "Are you mad?" she asked as watched him throw the blanket and then saddle over his horse's back.

"Would it be better to let him hide in the woods and take a shot at me?" he asked, tightening the girth.

"You think he'd do that."

"He's a coward, a coward with a taste for blood. Yes, he would do that."

"Saddle Fancy for me too and I'll go along."

Now it was his turn to look surprised. "Not on your life," he said with that tough smile that she had come to know meant no humor at all, "and I mean that, sugar. You will not come. You will not follow me. You will trust me on this."

"I don't want to lose you."

"You won't. Not this time."

God, she hated the way he said that, but she had no choice. She couldn't really follow him if he didn't want her alongside him. "I want to go with you," she tried one last time.

He threw the stirrup down and walked over to her. "That man came here to kill me. I want to know why. It is just possible that he will tell me if he thinks he's won."

"Before he kills you."

He smiled again that tough smile. "Yes, before he thinks he can get away with killing me."

"And what will stop him then?"

He pulled her into his arms. "I will. Now go back inside and don't worry. I can handle this. It's what I don't know is waiting, that's what I can't handle."

"Do you plan to kill him?" she asked more aware now of how hard killing would be on Jed if it was what he felt had to be done.

"Only if he tries to kill me." She saw it on his face that it was what he expected.

"If he doesn't try?"

"I will reluctantly let him go on his way."

"It's not what you expect though?"

"No."

"Please, at least take Jei."

"Sugar, listen to me and try to understand. It's what we don't know that's the bigger risk. I will be back." He took his bowie knife from his belt and slid it into his boot.

Edmonton walked out of the house with Bernice behind him, Jed kissed Raine lightly. She knew his mind was already elsewhere as he leaped into his saddle, showing no weakness in the arm that had been wounded.

"Bye bye now," Bernice said as Edmonton awkwardly mounted his horse. She waved as the two rode off. Looking back at Raine's face, the look that she knew had to show her fear, Bernice said, "Don't worry. Your man knows how to handle this."

Raine could only hope and pray that was so.

As Jed rode beside Edmonton, he had his hat pulled down as far as he could. The cold was growing, and the snow had begun to fall a little harder. He hoped none of it would prove a problem.

"Why did you come West?" Edmonton asked, teeth chattering a little despite a muffler and stocking cap.

"New start. I didn't want to work a plantation like my daddy.

Needed adventure I guess," he answered working to keep his tone neutral.

"You liked having slaves though?"

"I wouldn't know. Never had any."

"What do you mean?"

"My grandfather freed any slaves he bought, long before I was ever born. Our people worked for wages and if they wanted to leave, they left."

"Wasn't that unusual in the South?"

"Most folks in the South didn't own slaves. My people had been forced to leave Scotland after picking the wrong side of a war. They didn't like the idea of owning anybody."

"Choosing the wrong side appears to be a problem to your people." Edmonton smiled.

"Maybe so. They went to France and then to Georgia. Indirectly that's how I got this place."

"Related to Aubuchon?" His voice reflected more interest.

"Connected."

"You've been a lucky bastard, haven't you?"

"In some ways."

"Like with Loraine."

"That was luckiest of all."

"Or most dangerous." Jed glanced at him and saw the smug expression of a man who thought he had control. He looked up then to see if he saw any sign of the Kalamas. They were supposed to be out here looking for Indian sign. If they were, they were nearby.

"Walking down a street can be dangerous in some situations," Jed said as he looked at Edmonton and saw the smile that wasn't hidden.

"How far have we come from the house, do you suppose," Edmonton asked.

"Two miles maybe. Three to go to Monument."

"And we have to cross the river."

"You know we do."

"Do you know the best places to ford? Oh silly me. Of course, you do." The road led down to the North Fork. "So I can follow where you go, could you go first?" Edmonton asked with uncertainty in his voice. "I will try to follow."

Jed knew this was then the place and loosened his Colt in the holster where Edmonton would not see it. Midas took the river with no problem leaving the other man to struggle until he finally got to the other side. It was then that Edmonton said, "Drop your gun, Mr. Hardman. I do have mine pointed at you."

"What's this about?" Jed asked trying to put some surprise in his voice.

"The end of the trail for you. I want... well first, get off your horse."

Jed threw his foot over the pommel and slid off Midas giving him a bit of a slap to move him out of the range of the shooting that was going to happen.

"Drop your gun," Edmonton ordered and again Jed obeyed, letting it fall at his feet. The next order was the surprise. "Take off your coat and then your shirt."

Jed smiled even though he knew the situation wasn't funny. "Why?" he asked.

"Call it for my amusement. I don't enjoy hurting people as some do but I will shoot you in the arm if you don't do it. I am a good shot." His pistol didn't waver.

"You were there that night, weren't you? You and Russell both." he asked as he shrugged out of the coat, and then began unbuttoning his shirt. The air was biting cold, but the adrenalin coursing through his veins kept him from being more than absently aware of it.

"Yes, I came. I wanted to see, of course. I should have stayed away though. You are a very beautiful man, Mr. Hardman. Such a shame you will soon be a corpse."

Finally Jed stood bare-chested, contemplating whether this was when he should make his move as Edmonton said, "Russ wanted to torture, break your body. What a shame that would have been."

"You and he are partners, aren't you?"

"Silent, you might say," Edmonton said seemingly in no hurry to conclude his business. "Take off your pants too."

"There is a reason I should do that?"

"Same as before. With one addition. Perhaps I just want to see you naked or perhaps I know Indians take the clothing of their victims." He smiled then, and it was obvious he also wanted to extend the moment where he believed that he had all the control and time.

Jed wasn't averse to that. He bent as though to remove his boots. Instead he reached for the Bowie knife as he lunged to the left, hearing the shot and moving rapidly toward Edmonton who was now trying to steady a horse that was beginning to buck. Before Jed could throw the knife, Edmonton was tossed from the horse, landing hard on the back of his head as he crumpled to the gravel and rock beach.

Running to him, Jed, kicked away the weapon Edmonton's hand no longer could clutch. The dying man was staring up at him looking confused as he tried to move.

"You broke your neck," Jed said as he knelt and assessed what had happened. "You better make your peace with whatever you believe. You won't be alive in a minute or two. I can't move you, or it'd be less.

Edmonton stared up as he seemed to finally realize what had happened.

"Where is Grayson?" Jed asked thinking he was unlikely to get an answer.

"Waiting for you."

"In The Dalles?"

Edmonton smiled faintly. "With men. His pleasure is... different than mine... So beautiful. You are not a bad... sight for my last one," he whispered before the light went out of his eyes.

When Jed heard horsemen approaching, he grabbed his Colt before he saw it was the Kalama brothers.

"He dead?" Joe asked as he looked down at the prostate body.

"Yep."

"We saw what he tried but figured you'd handle it. If you hadn't though, George had his rifle ready."

Jed smiled at the quiet brother with the rifle still in his hands. "I appreciate that. I got all the information I was likely to. What'd you find about that fifth man."

"Injuns got him," Joe said with a faint smile and a glint in his dark eyes.

"Where was he?"

"Waiting in the rocks up ahead. Guess this one figured if he didn't get you, the other would. Fella wasn't looking for real Injuns at all."

"I take it no sign of the Snakes," Jed said as he holstered his gun, pulled on his shirt, buttoned it, and tucked it into his pants before he put back on his coat.

"Never been no Injuns... other than the ones got that guy. They snuck up on him and slit his throat."

Jed nodded with a grim twist to his mouth. "Did they bury him?"

"Don't wanta leave him for the critters?"

"Probably best not to take the chance. We don't want real trouble with the law, now do we?"

"Ah shucks. All right." Joe nodded toward George. "You pile a lot of rocks over him, got it?" George gave him a protesting look but rode off.

"What about this one?" Joe asked as he gestured toward Edmonton with his thumb.

"I'd been thinking we'd bury him and the one from last night in the ranch plot, but the idea is turning on me. I think we'll bury them in the woods with some markers. Anybody comes asking what happened to them, they can take the bodies back to wherever."

"Don't deserve no Christian burial," Joe said. "Looks like he was a real sick son of a bitch."

Jed nodded as he lifted the body onto his horse. Edmonton didn't deserve it, but he'd bury him anyway. At least this death would look like an accident if questions were ever asked. They weren't likely to be.

What he knew now though was he couldn't let Grayson go until the spring. This had to be settled. Raine wouldn't like it, but there'd be one after another coming for them. With Grayson waiting in The Dalles, he had some time to secure the ranch for Raine and settle this permanently. He hoped he could make her understand what he had to do.

Back at the ranch, Raine felt relief to see the Kalamas and Jed ride up but then realized another horse bore a body. "Kirk?" she asked as Joe led it beyond the barns.

Jed nodded.

"Did you kill him then when he tried to kill you?" She pulled him into the house to get warm.

He held his hands over the woodstove, took the whiskey she handed him. "He fell off his horse when it reared up at gunfire. It wasn't an animal used to guns going off, and he wasn't much of a horseman. The heaviness of his body, when he landed on his head, broke his neck."

She put her arms around him. "I am glad you didn't have to do it."

He hugged her to him. "Me too. I have enough on my conscience."

"But it's not over."

"Not yet. All right, enough of this, I need to do some work, what I had started before he arrived. I'll be back." He gave her rear a swat before he headed back outside.

Bernice sat at the table, a bemused expression on her face. "He didn't tell it all, did he?"

Raine had had the same feeling. "What makes you think that?" she asked anyway.

"Didn't you wonder what I told Kirk to make him so quick to leave?"

"Just that you knew he was a customer seemed enough. It wasn't?"

Bernice shook her head. "Kirk had odd habits. Twisted sort of things he wanted from the girls. Like tying them up or being spanked himself. He liked toys of all sorts."

"I guess men get off on that. Some men anyway," Raine said not wanting to sound so naïve to even imagine such a thing.

"He hurt one of them during one of his games. It was when I told him he wasn't coming back. He snapped at me and said he could do what he wanted. I said if he came back, Jei would deal with him, and he wouldn't find it so much fun. He just looked at me, with that peculiar look he could get, and said maybe he wouldn't mind. But he didn't come back."

"I realize I never knew him at all," Raine admitted as she put on water to make them each a cup of tea. It seemed to be one of the things that settled Bernice's stomach.

"People don't exactly brag about such. I just thought... the way I saw him watching Jed this morning, and when I was spying, that he had something twisted for how he wanted him."

Raine didn't like to imagine such a thing. The world Bernice had lived in obviously was one she had never let herself think about existing.

"Anyway that was just guessing. What I told him is I could make his, what some might consider more than peccadilloes, known if he didn't leave. In Portland, those things might be acceptable with some-- but not a successful playwright. I suppose he could have contemplated killing me, but I don't think he was by nature a killer."

"Yet he came here to kill."

"So it appears. It surprises me, but if he was working with Russ, I suppose I didn't know him all that well either."

"You do think they were partners."

"I do now. It seems an unlikely partnership, but it does appear that it's what it was."

"Do you think he and Kirk were lovers?"

"Frankly, I doubt it. Kirk liked beauty and innocence."

"I wasn't quite as innocent as he might have assumed by my refusal of him. You know Jed and I had actually met before he went to war."

"Ah, that rather surprises me. I thought of you as the type who holds out for a wedding ring."

She looked back at Bernice and laughed as she handed her a cup of tea. "I didn't really want to be married."

Bernice laughed with her. "You are in a rather odd situation here then for that attitude."

"Things change."

Bernice sighed. "I hope mine have but..."

"You're not sure."

"Nothing to test it yet."

"Do you er uh also like deviancy?"

Bernice shook her head. "Not at all but I like sex and often."

"I do too with the right man."

"Right man schmight man. If he knows what he's doing and has the right equipment, they're all the same."

Raine looked at her with shock and then realized by Bernice's smile that she had only said it to shock her. "You are too much," she said as she laughed.

"I will tell you one thing. If Jed is half as hot in bed, as Josh, you are a lucky woman. That man can go forever and his touch, ahhhh."

Raine grimaced. "Bernice, I am not about to discuss my sex life with Jed, not with you or for that matter anybody."

Bernice groaned. "That's what is making now so hard. I actually have been more celibate here than ever in my life. Josh hasn't touched me since I told him about the baby."

Raine sipped her tea as she thought. "Perhaps he fears it

would hurt you or the baby." It was a sore subject with her because since Jed had heard of Bernice's pregnancy, known she wanted one, he hadn't made love to her. It appeared he was determined not to leave her with a baby to rear alone if something happened to him. She was tired of his protectiveness. Where it came to women, he had a lot to learn. As she sipped her tea, she decided the coming night was where the lessons would begin. His willpower would only stretch so far.

CHAPTER 23

After they had eaten dinner, Jed said he was tired. It'd been a long day, and he was heading upstairs for bed. Raine followed him leaving the others playing a game of poker for matchsticks.

In his bedroom, she walked over to him putting her arms around him from behind as he stood looking out into the darkness.

"There is more, isn't there?" she asked as she reached up and began unbuttoning his shirt brushing his chest as she worked.

"I have to go after him. You have to see that after this."

She stopped and moved to sit on the bed, watching him in the lamplight. "To Portland?"

"From what Edmonton said when he still thought he could kill me, he won't be there. He'll be waiting in The Dalles—at least for a while."

"So once again you want to go walking into the lion's den?"

"Better than having the lion come here."

"Is it? I thought you had this all set up to stand off an attack?"

"I can't be here all the time and run this ranch. Now is when I can get him."

"And if I said I don't want you to go?" she asked.

"I'd ask you to understand. He can come anytime out here. He can keep hiring toughs. Some might come when I'm out with the cattle. I will have to take herds out. And then what if you are here, and they come?"

She knew what he said was sensible, but she hated the idea of him again riding into danger.

"That could happen anyway with the Shoshoni, couldn't it?" She tried another argument.

"It's less likely. They don't have a vendetta against me personally. If they show up, well, it's why we have the place fortified or will have it. Try to understand that I need to do this. Grayson is going to keep at it until he gets me. I want to get him first—because one reason he wants to get me is to get to you. I can't let that happen."

She sighed as she admitted to herself that he was probably right. "You will take Josh and Jei, of course," she said watching as he tightened his mouth and she knew he had no such intention.

"I need them here in case I am wrong or miss him on his way here."

"Joe, George, Jack and Josh would be enough here. Take Jei."

"I'll think about it if he wants to go. I won't ask him."

"Because it could get him killed," she said succinctly.

He nodded. "I don't want to argue with you," he said as he went to sit on the bed. "I just want you to understand why I have to do this."

"Maybe I could go with you and then become a decoy for him that would let you get him," she suggested as she reached over to unbutton his shirt.

He gave a short laugh. "I hope that was a joke."

"Make love to me tonight, Jed," she whispered as she moved to put her lips against his chest, kissing his nipple and then sucking as she pushed his shirt from his shoulders.

"Is it a safe time?" he asked.

"I am tired of wondering about that," she said. "I want you, and I want you now."

"You know how I feel."

"And you know how I feel." She left the shirt buttoned at the cuffs, holding his arms effectively at his side as she reached for the buttons on his pants. She unfastened and then pushed them down to bare his erection and thighs. "It appears you want it too," she said stroking him and heightening the effect.

"What I want and what's good are two different things," he said sucking in a breath as she pushed him back on the bed. She went to his boots and pulled them off, his socks went next before she turned to his pants and pulling, soon had him lying there nude other than the shirt cuffs pinning his arms. When he would have unbuttoned them, she stopped him by straddling his hips.

Fully dressed as she was, the thought having him naked and hers to play with was heady. She bent forward and kissed his bemused lips, pushing them apart and delving her tongue deep within his mouth. His response left no doubt that he was not going to resist her. Not tonight. She smiled and shifted to sit on his thighs, kissing down his body until she reached her goal and took it into her mouth. By then he was bucking under her ministrations.

"Do it," he demanded. His erection was hard and potent. She moved away, but before he could protest, she began stripping off her dress, slowly removing one garment and teasingly another to make the whole thing as seductive as she could possibly do.

"I might get pregnant," she warned as naked she came back to position herself above him. She saw he was no longer able to push her away and smiling, she lowered herself and took him within.

A few hours later when they awoke, his arms were around her, his lips in her hair. "I always wanted you and a baby," he whispered. "I just didn't want to not be here to raise it with you."

"You will be. I know it. And it might take us awhile to make a baby. Maybe we need to practice."

He laughed and kissed her again as he raised himself above her.

With morning, both of them in a considerably more relaxed mood, they came downstairs to smell bacon cooking. In the kitchen, it was Toddy at the stove. "Bernice sleep in?" she asked as she poured herself some coffee.

"Her and Josh," he said with a chuckle.

"What about Jei?"

"He's outside doing some kind of exercise thing he does. You've seen him. Not sure what it's called."

"Kung fu," Jed said lighting a cigarette.

"What is that?"

"Fighting technique. It is said to be superior to any other. From what I can tell when I've watched him, he's a master at it."

"Damn. Why hadn't I heard of it?" Toddy grumbled as he reached for the bowl of eggs he'd brought back from his last trip to Monument. With it being winter and hens laying less frequently, they were preciously guarded.

"Maybe you weren't interested in training to be a fighter," Jed suggested.

"Well there is that. I'm more a lover than a fighter," he chuckled.

"So where's your woman. Thought you'd had so many wives," Jed said as he sipped his coffee.

Bernice and Josh came into the kitchen arm and arm. "Beautiful day," Josh said smiling as he looked around the room.

"The truth," Toddy said as he cracked some eggs into a fresh bowl and began to beat them. "Is none of them wanted me because in the end I didn't want them."

"Not beautiful enough?" Raine asked with a grin as Josh poured himself some coffee.

"Not the right sex," Toddy said finally and gave them all a telling look.

There was a moment of silence before Jed spoke first. "So go find a gentleman friend. I don't have a problem with that."

"You don't?" Toddy said. If he had been hoping to shock everyone, he had failed as none showed any upset at the information.

"Jack's likely too old for you," Bernice said as she fixed herself tea. "The Kalamas have women."

"Both of them?" Jed asked. "I thought just George."

"Joe has one too. George though has a baby." Raine grinned at Bernice's span of knowledge. She certainly had a gift for gathering information.

"There has been talk of building them a cabin up here. A big one apparently," Jed said as he considered the new information.

Jei had entered from outside where he pumped and then drank a glass of water. "What's the plan for today?" he asked as he sat at the table lighting a cigar.

Toddy brought a plate of bacon to the table. "It's gonna snow hard soon," he said.

"You a weather expert?" Jed asked although it was lightly beginning to snow again.

"Sometimes. Wind's right for it. Cold enough. Big clouds to the north coming our way. Looks like snow to me."

"It sometimes bypasses our valley," Jed observed although his time on the ranch had only involved three winters and they'd each been different.

"How far off to Thanksgiving?" Josh asked. "I lose track of days up here. They all run together."

Jed had to think. Days had a way of getting away from him too, when it all revolved around physical work. "Maybe two weeks? I'll have plenty of time to get to The Dalles and back before it."

"Why are you going there?" Josh asked.

"Business."

"Want me to come along?"

"No, you stay here. Keep an eye on this place for me. In fact you all stay here."

"Not me," Jei said. "I go. I might not come back."

"My business might not suit you," Jed said as he blew out smoke, eyes narrowed as he watched Jei.

"I knew you'd be going soon. I'd have done it if you had not. We will go together."

"All right if you're sure."

Raine came to stand behind Jed's chair, her hands on his neck, twined in the thick hair that curled against his nape. She wanted to beg him not to go, but it wouldn't do any good.

"We'll get things in order here first. I want this place ready to withstand a full Shoshoni attack, although I don't expect one, not with the snow starting," Jed said.

Three hours later with Bernice and Raine in the kitchen working on making loaves of bread and cinnamon rolls, she heard the sound of horses and a wagon at the front of the house. When she went to the door, she stood in shock before she ran forward to throw her arms around her mother, Elijah and then Adam.

"Oh my Lord, what are you doing here?" she asked half crying and half laughing.

"Adam said we were invited," Martha said and then looked toward the tall man walking toward them. "And this is... Jed?" she asked without sounding as though she had any doubt.

Raine ran back to draw him forward with her arms around him. "Yes, this is Jed. And Jed, this is my mother, and Elijah is my brother."

"Glad to meet you, ma'am," Jed said as he put out his hand only to have Martha draw him into her arms for a hug.

"And I am glad to meet the man who finally convinced my daughter he was the one." She smiled broadly. She reached back into the wagon. "I hope you also have room for her." The crate had air holes and from the sounds, a very angry cat inside. "Her name is Heaven. She's getting old, but she's clean."

"She's welcome. Ace and Deucy will adjust to her," he said with a grin as he looked back at Martha Stone. "Not hard to see where Raine gets her beauty," he added. It was a mature beauty but perhaps more beautiful for it with thick black, silver-streaked hair pulled into a bun, lush lips and anything but a motherly look to her body.

Adam had thrown the reins to the team over the barricade out front. Joe was tied on behind. "I took you at your word that you wanted us to come."

"Good, and it couldn't be a better time," Jed said. "Glad you got here before Thanksgiving. We were just trying to decide how far off that was. We need to get ourselves a calendar up here"

"Two weeks. Eli and I saw a nice flock of turkeys on our way in. He and I will go back for them as Mama said she'd cook them just right, didn't she, Eli."

"She sure did," the boy said looking around him with excitement at the barns, corrals and wilderness that stretched beyond. "This looks like a big ranch. Big house. Nice place you have here, Mr. Hardman," he said politely.

"Your son's as good a shot as you are then," Jed asked as he ushered them into the house and to a fresh pot of coffee on the stove.

"He's better sometimes," Adam said with pride.

"What about Matt and Amy?" Raine asked as she handed her mother a cup of the tea that she'd been brewing for her and Bernice. Heaven was exploring the kitchen as Deucy looked at her suspiciously but didn't growl. Ace had gone out to inspect the wagon and new horses.

"They said they'd see how we like it and decide in the spring. I sold my house in Oregon City for a surprisingly good price. We have been talking to a land agent about what is available nearby to buy. It seems there is quite a bit of land. With so many wanting where they hope to find gold, this area is very available. Adam has the yen to be a cattle rancher, it seems." She grinned.

Raine felt so thrilled she could barely stand it. To have even part of her family near was the one thing she'd never imagined possible when she had decided to live on the other side of the Cascades. She knew she must be glowing with joy.

Bernice stepped forward then. "Remember me, Mrs.... er Stone?"

"I certainly do," Martha said with a friendly smile. "You are a part of why we decided to come now. Loraine wrote about her concern for your pregnancy and needing advice. I decided I might want to be here before spring if the baby is coming sooner than you expect." She looked at the broadening belly in front of Bernice. "And that does happen sometimes," she added with another smile.

"I really appreciate that, ma'am. I wasn't sure how friendly you'd feel toward me after... well after."

"It's been a long while. People change, Bernice. I understand that very well. I hope you are happy about the baby."

"Yes, ma'am, I am."

"Make that Martha," she said with another smile as she looked beyond her to Josh who had come to put his arms around her. "And you are the father?"

"And my brother," Jed said.

They introduced Martha and Elijah to everyone else. Elijah's interest was instantly drawn to Jei. "You look like a Chinese man," he said to everyone's laughter.

"I am that," Jei said. "A Mandarin to be exact."

The Kalama brothers came into the house to again be introduced and equally impress the youngest Stone.

"You and Adam are welcome to take my bedroom," Jed told them as they began to unload the wagon. "That is if Raine doesn't mind sharing."

She grinned at him nodding her pleasure at the idea.

"We brought our mattress and Eli's," Martha said, "with the bedsteads and bedding. Also what we hope will be enough food to get us through the winter to not stretch your supplies."

"We came by way of The Dalles," Adam added. "With the

spring we'll go back for the rest of the furniture and what Martha decides she wants when I build her a house."

"There are two rooms downstairs that might work for you also if you prefer," Raine said. "One is used as an office but I think we could work around that."

"Let me see it, as I'd rather not put you out," Martha said as she followed Raine for a tour of the house.

"Actually Jei and I will be off on a trip tomorrow," Jed said, "so this coming now is opportune for keeping an eye on the ranch while I'm gone."

When the women came back, Martha said, "The downstairs rooms will be perfect if we can set up the beds in them. For now I think Eli will be happier closer to us but later he might prefer in the other wing with the men."

As they began setting up the beds and carrying in boxes, Adam said, "From what the land manager told us, we can buy land adjoining yours with a good tract to increase the number of animals we can run. This is an area that will open up soon with the potential to sell beef around the state."

"You've been doing some planning," Jed said with a grin.

"Some."

"And the Indians don't scare you off."

"Might me but didn't Martha or Eli." Adam grinned. When they finished unloading the wagon, the two went out onto the deck to smoke. "You have a good place here to defend. If it ends up being a more difficult war than some predict, then we might need to stay close until it settles down."

"Who predicts it won't be difficult?"

"The latest opinion of government experts. They are cutting back on the commitment they have to the soldiers and the effort. The latest talk is treaty—not just here but across the nation. The soldiers already in the field will likely have a hard winter with less federal support."

"In my experience, that sounds typical," Jed said taking a long drag on his cigarette. "They might've been right if the tribes couldn't see that this area is getting filled up with whites. Where does that leave them? On a few small reservations. Likely, they know what happened to the ones down on the Siskiyous, getting shipped off to a land far from their own. They'll make a stand. It might be quiet through the winter, but I don't look for that to last."

They smoked in silence for a moment before Adam said, "Now about The Dalles. What's the real reason for that trip?"

"What makes you ask?"

"You wouldn't leave her now if there wasn't something going on big enough to get you off this place."

"Not your problem."

Adam shook his head. "Not the way I see it. You asked once if my wife was a witch. Not so much that, but she gets dreams. She had such a dream that told her Raine and you would need us, and we should not wait for spring. I take her dreams seriously."

Jed considered before he answered. "As a lawman you might not like hearing this."

"I quit-- remember."

"All right, I am going after Grayson. I have every reason to expect he won't let this go. According to the last man he sent to kill me, he's waiting in The Dalles right now. This is my chance to get him outside of Portland and in an environment where my odds are closer to even."

Adam took another draw on his cigarette. "How many you expect him to have?"

"If I am right and he's been behind at least some of the rustling, gold robberies, and murders along the Dallas Military Road, then I'd guess at least ten or twelve. Maybe more."

"And you expect to take them by yourself?"

"Jei is coming."

Adam considered a moment. The sun was beginning to sink in the west. "Your odds are not that great; you do know that. If you are right, he will be watching for you and with men who know how to kill and don't mind doing it."

"I figured that, but I consider my odds improved because while I know he's waiting, he will still be hoping his man succeeded, and I'm already dead."

"Tell me more about what happened."

Jed related the gist of it. When he finished, Adam whistled. "I will talk to Martha about it, but I am going."

"You mean ask her permission?" Jed asked with a laugh.

"I mean talk it over with her. When you've been married longer, you will know that pays off in the long run. Women have a way of seeing things we have missed."

"And if she says no?" Jed asked with genuine curiosity.

"She won't."

"I don't like you going. Raine shouldn't lose us both."

"Less chance of her losing either of us if I do go. And while I'm thinking about her, when are you planning to tell everyone you two are married?"

"You didn't already tell Martha?"

"I keep a confidence when there is a reason to do so. The reason in this case was to give you or Loraine a chance to do it. I think it's time, don't you?"

"I'll talk to her about it." He smiled. "You know, I actually might like having a father-in-law. New experience but not a bad one. And although I haven't heard much good about mother-in-laws, Martha might be the exception."

When Jed and Raine went upstairs to bed after assuring themselves the Stones were settled in their rooms, Jed opened one of his drawers and came out with a paper and small box.

She looked first at the paper that he handed her. "Our wedding certificate. Why now?" Then she opened the box and saw the plain gold band. She felt a shiver. "It's a beautiful ring."

He shook his head. "I bought this after the war. When I came home, I had every intention of immediately marrying you. Then when you had other ideas, I brought it with me back to the ranch.

I had not given up, sugar, not on us. I thought I'd be going back to Portland as soon as possible and try again to convince you to wear my ring."

"It's perfect." She had tears in her eyes. "Jed, why are you giving it to me now?"

"We are married. I love you. It doesn't seem we have more reasons now to keep our wedding a secret."

"And it isn't because you fear you won't live?"

He turned and looked back out the window into the darkness. "I want you protected."

She came to him and put her arms around him, her head against his back. "I love your back," she whispered, "So hard and muscular."

"But you didn't put on the ring." He knew there was pain in his voice at the possibility she was again rejecting a real marriage with him. Was she still unsure? "You still don't want me and it?"

"I want you both, but I want it when you aren't thinking you will die the next day."

"I don't necessarily think that." He couldn't deny it was a possibility. He might be killed, but he was determined he'd take Grayson with him.

"My darling, I want you and want us to be really married. I just don't want you to do this with some sense that you have taken care of your loose ends and can now take risks you'd not take otherwise."

He sighed. "I didn't think of it that way."

"Didn't you?"

"Adam said he hasn't told your mother. Don't you think she should know?"

"She probably already knows. She said she came because she knew that we needed them. She sees us as a couple."

"Adam wants to come with me. Maybe I should say no."

"You couldn't stop him."

He gave a short laugh. "Probably not."

She kissed his back. "I am going to wear this ring on a chain around my neck. I will keep it there, between my breasts. When you come back from The Dalles, I want you to put it on my finger."

"But if I don't come back…"

"Please don't say that. Don't think that way. I can't bear for you to think that way. You will come back. You are a warrior. You have survived it all, and you will again."

"When I do, will you marry me again? This time with your family there?"

"I will."

He turned then and took her into his arms. He tipped up her chin so that their gazes met. "I want you to know something. I have been married to you since I left Portland to go to war. You are the mate of my soul."

"I love you, Jed. I have loved you more than I knew was possible for a woman to love a man. I know you have to do this. I even understand why, but you have to believe you will live through it. Tell me you do."

"Your touch, the feel of you," he whispered against her temple. "It got me through the war, through more nights than you'll ever know."

"And it will again." She went to her jewelry and found the gold chain and locket he'd given her in Canyon City. She took them back to him. "Put the ring on this chain," she asked. When he had done so, she turned and let him fasten it so that the ring fell between her breasts.

"When you come back," she said, "then you will put the ring on my finger." She had forced a confident tone to her voice.

She was afraid. She could not deny that to herself, but she would not burden him with those fears. She could not stop him. Probably he was right. Russell would not give up and better to choose his fight than to have it be chosen for him.

When he bent and kissed her, she smiled against his lips before she felt his tongue delve into her mouth and all thought was gone, as they once again discovered each other.

Later as she lay in bed thinking this might be their last night together, she forced the thought away. There would be more. She had to believe that. If though, God forbid, he should be killed, she hoped she was already bearing his child. She would raise it there on his land and make his dream come true, as it had become hers. She finally understood her mother's words from so long ago. She had given up nothing and won it all. When Jed came back, and she could let herself dwell on no other possibility, they would have it all.

CHAPTER 24

"It will be bitter cold in the higher hills," Jed said. "Take two coats and a heavy scarf. We can expect to have two nights camping to get there." He was sacking the supplies they would need.

"I spent a winter in the Siskiyous. I came ready for whatever weather we had up here," Adam said leaning against the kitchen counter.

"It will be three days riding. Your horse up to that?"

"Joe's getting too old for a hard ride. What do you have I could use?"

"You're a big man. Let me think. How good are you with a horse that needs a firm hand?"

"Good enough."

"Then I have a gelding, Argo, that will do. He's green broke, and this ride will take him the rest of the way to being a good trail horse."

"Kind of a fancy name."

"From a constellation."

"Well, if he's not a stumble foot that sounds fine."

"I've taken him out in our hills, and he's good on rough ground, but my plan for the route will avoid the steepest hills." He sacked up enough coffee for two nights and figured he would buy more before they started back.

Jei, piling his coats and blanket on the table, caught the last of the conversation. "You think we can really do it with only two nights? It's quite a distance."

"We won't be taking the cavalry road but going on Indian trails. It shortens it considerably. I took cattle that way once."

Raine and her mother came in from outside. They'd been to the smokehouse. "Freshly made jerky compliments of the Kalamas," she said putting it on the counter. "Do you plan to cook and want bacon too?"

"Just coffee. Can't go without coffee," Jed said smiling.

"We made biscuits," Martha added as she went to the pie cupboard and brought out a big plate of them. "They should tide you over until you get to restaurants in The Dalles. That is if you aren't on the run by that time," she added teasingly as she sacked them.

"God, you know me too well," Adam said as he pulled her into his arms. "I will avoid being on the run as I plan to come back here for a full spread Thanksgiving dinner. Set Eli to getting the turkeys with the Kalamas. He'll like that."

She pulled his head down for a kiss. "He is going to run wild up here, which is pretty much what we counted on." She laughed at the surprised look on Jed's face. "Eli needed this. If he had stayed in Oregon City, he'd have gotten himself in trouble. He was already proving to be a chip off the Stone. He needed a challenge and this is going to provide it."

Jed laughed along with the others. "It will do that."

"I heard you say you might not come back," Martha said to Jei. "I hope if you decide that, that you will return sometimes. He is so counting on you to teach him I think it's called Kung fu, some kind of martial arts anyway."

Jei smiled. "Ah a young grasshopper, is he?"

"He is that," Adam said with agreement as Jed took three sacks of biscuits. He wanted them to each carry their own food in case they got separated. "Just enough to get there," he said as Raine came to watch him.

"Why?" she asked with that fearful tone returning to her voice.

"Because we can restock in town. Bring you back some candy if you want," he said bending to kiss her before he finished fastening the bags.

"You're all the sweet, I want," she said as she pulled him back for a kiss more to her liking.

"God," Jei said, "there is so much of that going on here that I don't think I can come back without a woman." His rare laughter joined theirs.

Elijah had come in from the porch with the two dogs following him. "You are going too, Papa?" he asked watching his father uneasily.

Adam nodded. "And you are going to look after this place, aren't you, Eli?"

He looked worriedly at his tall father. The two were so much alike for looks with Eli's hair the same coal black and his body already showing signs of the broad shoulders that he would someday have.

"In five days, mark it off on a piece of paper, go back with Josh or one of the Kalama brothers and kill us two turkeys. You can watch how they prepare them before hanging them in the cellar until it's time for Mama to cook them. Can you remember that?" He knelt in front of his son with his hands on the boy's thin arms.

Eli nodded. "You will come back?"

Adam grinned, the white teeth flashing against his swarthy skin. "Of course. And it will be a little over a week when I do, but I'll bring that candy your aunt didn't want. Some chocolate maybe?"

Eli smiled. "I'd like that."

"Good." He gave him a big hug, kissed Martha one more time, then followed Jei out to saddle their horses.

Jed bent to kiss Raine almost fiercely, feeling of the ring between her breasts. He smiled but when he would have let her go, she drew his head back, kissing him with equal fervor. "You will be back soon," she ordered.

He grinned. "Did not the laird say so?" When she laughed, he turned and looked down at Eli. "Watch out for our dogs, all right? Don't let them get in trouble with the cat."

The boy nodded stoutly and walked out onto the porch with his mother and Raine to watch Jed stalk across the barnyard to where Joe Kalama had already saddled Midas. He leaped into the saddle. Once he had decided he had to go, he wanted it over with as soon as possible.

As they rode out of the barnyard toward Monument and the route they would be taking north, he didn't look back. If he had felt fatalistic earlier, he no longer felt any of that. He knew he had a tough job ahead, and he was determined to get it done.

They didn't talk until they took the northern road out of Monument heading toward Heppner.

"You said you know this way well," Adam said. "Not much sign of a trail here."

"Which is why it's the best way to go. We will not likely meet other travelers unless it's an Indian."

Adam chuckled. "Was that supposed to reassure me?"

"Some. The main thing is Grayson won't know we are coming until we want him to."

On top, it was rolling grassland interspersed with tall pines as they rode toward Lone Rock, a community with a few homes. As they rode past them, no one paid them mind.

By late afternoon, Jed began to look for the place he had felt they could camp the first night. It was along Rock Creek, sheltered by high cliffs from what had become a cold and biting wind on the higher ground.

"We could go farther," Jei said.

"If we did, there are no places for a lot of miles that we can get out of that wind."

Adam didn't argue, unsaddled his horse and wrapped a scarf around his neck as Jed built the fire. Jei made the coffee, and they sat around the warming fire drinking it and eating biscuits, chewing the tough jerky.

"You have a plan in mind when we get to The Dalles?" Adam asked as he rolled a cigarette.

"Yes. It starts with not getting killed."

Adam chuckled. "A man after my own heart."

"You figuring whatever we do there will get us arrested?" Jei asked with a grin.

Jed lit his own cigarette, "it's a possibility."

"Grayson is a man with power."

"Who a lot of people know is behind a lot of the corruption in Portland," Adam said. "When I was there, I visited with the sheriff and he would give a lot to nail him for something."

"I don't plan to nail him. I plan to kill him," Jed said coldly.

"I figured as much," Jei said with agreement in his voice. "Maybe I should do it. You two have families."

"It's my job, and I will do it... assuming I live," Jed said. Then smiled. "If I don't live, then you do it."

Jei chuckled.

"You know I can't figure what you're doing mixed up in this," Adam said watching Jei through the smoke of his cigarette.

"You don't figure a Chinese for a gunman?" Jei said with a laugh.

"Just don't know why you'd have left your home, come so far."

"A lot of men have done likewise including you."

"It's not a strange land for me though."

"It is not for me either—now.

"Can you go home, that is if you ever wanted to?"

"Not if I wanted to stay alive. My family chose the wrong side in a battle between warlords. It was healthier to leave, spread out once we got to this land."

"So you do have family in the states?" Jed asked. He knew nothing about Jei's life, not because he wasn't interested but more feeling that he had no right to pry into another man's business unless it affected his.

"Father, brother, one uncle. Your country does not want our women to immigrate as you perhaps know."

"Did you have a woman back there?" Adam asked.

Jei shook his head. "If I had, she'd be with me—one way or another."

There was silence as they all stared at the flickering campfire into which Jed fed another dried limb. "I ask because of my son," Adam said finally. "He is fascinated by you and what you might know. He thinks you are a warrior, and he'd like to learn from you. I wanted to know if that would be smart from my end."

"Wise father. I might not go back to the ranch. There is not much there for me. After we kill Grayson, I could go back to Portland."

"And become a new crime boss?" Jed asked remembering the expensive office Jei had had in Portland. He hadn't really known how the man had gained his power or earned his money. Perhaps he should have had more interest.

"I did not make my money with crime," Jei said. He glanced at Adam. "And even without a retired sheriff here, I am telling the truth, not trying to hide something. I was a hired pistolero of a sort in San Francisco. It was lucrative. I was not a killer for hire though, rather a bodyguard, a protector."

"Which sometimes does involve shooting," Adam said not as a question. Jei nodded. "And it made you wealthy?" Adam concluded.

"Some but I was also involved with Pacific trade along with my family. I am not wealthy like Jed, but I have money sufficient to not need to stoop to dishonest means."

"If you come back to the ranch," Adam said as he threw his cigarette butt into the fire, "you could teach my son about honor as well as fighting."

Jei nodded. "I could. Your son looks like he will be a fine man someday. Like his father, perhaps."

"I hope so, or better than his father."

"All men wish that."

"It's a good goal," Jed agreed thinking about the possibility he might also have a son someday. The thought at one time would have worried him, but now he felt more ready for that responsibility—if he got the chance.

Raine, Martha and Bernice cleaned up after dinner. Looking at her morose nephew as he sat glumly at the table, Raine said, "Should we make some cinnamon cookies for tomorrow?"

Eli looked up with a bit of interest just as Heaven took a swat at Deucy who cowered back under the sideboard. Ace looked more than ready to deal with the cat before she called him back. "You three have to get along," she ordered in a stern voice.

"We should have gotten a dog," Martha said as she picked up the protesting cat and set her on her lap. "I was busy with the dressmaking and Adam seemed to be gone too much to properly train one. Your two are very polite dogs."

"Ace works the cattle," Raine said as she began to assemble cookie ingredients. "Deucy hides from them."

"How does he work them?" Eli asked.

"Well, rounds them up, makes them go where his master wants. He likes doing it and nips their noses if they don't obey."

"Even with those big horns?" Eli had more interest than he had yet shown.

"Even then. He's fast."

Toddy came in from outside. "Brrrr getting really cold again. Not gonna be a fun ride to The Dalles," he said standing over the stove to warm his hands.

"Adam had a winter like that down in the Siskiyous," Martha said as she got out the pans for baking cookies. "It was right after we got married." Raine realized they were talking to try and reassure themselves.

An hour later, they were sitting in the great room with Josh and Jack now back from feeding the two old cows who hung around the barn. "Anybody want to play some poker," Toddy asked. The room was lit by the kerosene lamps and warm with the fireplace putting out a lot of heat from the dry pine it was being fed.

"I don't know how," Eli protested and soon five of them were sitting around the table and playing for matchsticks.

Raine and her mother didn't join in and sat on the sofa by the fire neither wanting to say what they were thinking. Finally Raine spoke. "Have you heard from Belle? Even when I was in Portland I rarely heard how she is."

Her mother smiled. "I brought her letters. She's in New York City."

"Seriously?" Raine laughed. "Amy must be so jealous. She's the one who hoped to travel, to get a college education, and here it is Belle who did it all."

"I think Amy is still too besotted with Matt to mind. She just enjoys knowing Belle is happy, and she appears to be."

"Does she then live there now?"

She frowned. "Belle is vague about what she's doing. She seems to be a governess to the Chambers family. Mr. Chambers is serving in the some sort of government position, I guess."

"You guess?"

Her mother shrugged, and Raine laughed. "So then, perhaps it's a man."

"Perhaps. She certainly has never mentioned one."

"She has liked adventure."

"True and from a young age. Still it's as though she doesn't tell me all she's doing in the letters. Something more is... Oh I'm being silly. Would you like to read her letters?"

"I'd love to read them tomorrow." She sighed then and looked into the flames. "Do you wish you'd never come here?"

"Why would you ask such a thing? I am happy I came."

"But Adam is riding into danger for Jed's good."

"When I first came to love Adam I had to accept that he would be riding into danger sometimes when someone had a need. It's just who he is. I can't force him to change that. This time at least he's doing it for family." She smiled.

Raine pulled her ring out on the chain. "Jed and I are married. We hadn't told anyone because we wanted to be sure it was going to work."

"That was the only reason?" her mother asked.

"I wanted to be sure the cake was one I could frost." She grinned at her mother who gave a little laugh. "Jed has reasons to want to marry right away, but agreed to keep it a secret until I could be sure." When her mother looked puzzled, Raine added, " Did you know that a colored man cannot own property in Oregon?"

"No, I didn't. That's horrible. Why would anybody make such a terrible law?"

Raine shook her head as she put her ring back inside her dress. "I don't know, but he wanted to be sure, if something happened to him, that Josh's rights would be protected until the laws change."

"Did he make a will?"

"I don't really know. I didn't care. I don't want what he has. I just want him."

"I suppose if he did, it's in his office. But as you say, it doesn't matter much. He will come back and die someday a very old man." Raine felt comfort when her mother put her arm around her and cuddled her against her as she had so many times when she was a child. "You really believe that it'll be all right, don't you?" she asked wanting reassurance she knew no one could give her.

"I do feel that way, but I can't promise it," her mother said.

"They are doing what they must, and that's all that gives me comfort. I mean any man can be killed... or for that matter, woman. The Shoshoni could attack us here and maybe we'd be killed. I mean that's the nature of life. Even back East things can go wrong."

"So we go on. It would be nice to believe in prayer that worked," Raine said as she went to the fireplace and fed in a log.

"You can pray anyway," her mother said with a smile. "It cannot hurt."

"I can't do it when I don't do it all the time," Raine said. "It seems well hypocritical."

Her mother laughed. "My darling daughter, so practical, so ethical."

"Well not all that ethical perhaps," Raine said, but she also laughed.

"In comparison to me," Bernice said as she came to sit with them having tired of the card game.

"Am I?" Raine asked. "If I hadn't gotten involved with Russell, hadn't let him convince me I was creating a valuable business, would Jed be endangered now? Would any of them? I blame myself for a lot of this. I was so stupid."

"Naïve," Bernice said as she unconsciously rubbed her belly where the bulge was becoming more noticeable.

"You can't know that Russell would not have gone after Jed anyway just because of who Jed is and I don't mean Southern. Jed is a very impressive man, tall, muscular, handsome. Sometimes that's enough to cause one man to hate another," Martha said with a reminiscent look on her face. Raine knew what she was thinking about-- the hate Matt's brother had had for him.

"I guess so but still..."

"Fate is what it is," her mother said, "and who knows, perhaps it's all set out ahead of time."

"Oh my," Bernice said with a sarcastic laugh. "That sounds like religion, and we all know what religion says about women like me."

"We do, do we? You might try the Gospels sometime for that." Martha grinned and rose. "I should put Eli to bed. We can resume this conversation another day perhaps. It sounds like a good one, but he's yawning so much that I am sure he needs to go before stage two comes along where he goes into a mood that none of us want to see."

"I want to wait for Papa to get back," Eli protested.

"He won't be back for a week, remember," his mother said.

When Eli began to look as though he was going to cry, Martha said, "How about you sleep in my bed tonight? I might have a hard time sleeping too."

The child nodded and went with her without more protest. Raine dreaded going to her own bed, fearing she'd not be able to sleep. When she finally went up, she lay in Jed's bed, holding the ring, trying to find comfort in what he had touched, what he had given her as a symbol of his love.

He would be back, and they would have their own children. The laird would again rule over his land. She tried to feel him, to imagine where he was, how he was sleeping. As she imagined him, she imagined light around him, circling and protecting him. Perhaps that also was prayer. She didn't know why it would work or even could it but doing it gave her a sense of peace. He would be back and on that, she slept.

Heading west out of the canyon, the land was open and grassy with rock formations, juniper and a cold wind. The only pleasure in the hard ride for Jed was seeing Mt. Hood to the west.

At Summer Springs, they watered the horses and refilled their canteens before they dropped into rugged canyon country, crossing streams, avoiding lava flows and keeping a steady pace, walking the horses when the slopes looked at risk of a broken leg. When they reached the John Day River, they set up a camp on the east side. They would wait for morning to cross at the ford.

As they sat around the campfire that night, Jei said, "I think it's time for a plan."

"Well, I am guessing Grayson will have men posted on the Dallas Military Road as it comes into The Dalles. The kind of men he hires won't be eager to stay a long way from the saloons; so it's likely on the south edge of town, where the canyon narrows."

"And we take them first," Adam said as he rolled a cigarette. "I gotta give this habit up," he said as he lit it. "I keep quitting and then back to doing it again. It can't be healthy."

"Like you think tomorrow will be," Jed said with a hard smile smoking his own cigarette.

"It's not guaranteed not good like smoking has to be. Martha is always after me to quit. I already notice I don't have the wind power I used to. Getting old maybe." He chuckled.

"How old are you, Jei?" Jed asked as he studied the narrow featured man.

"You want it for my tombstone?" Jei asked with a grin.

"Just curious. And maybe you'll be the one carving mine."

"Well as it happens, I am thirty-five."

"Older than me but not by much."

"And younger than me," Adam said.

"We've all lived hard lives," Jed drawled as he leaned back against his saddle well aware that the next day was likely to determine the rest of his life—if there was a rest of his life.

"Warriors," Jei agreed. "From different paths but all warriors."

"And tomorrow we face mercenaries and one man who will do anything to win and doesn't care about what he does to others," Jed said.

"I am more concerned that we don't run into trouble with the law over this than that I get killed," Adam said. "I've faced down death many times, but being arrested not so much."

"I won't murder him," Jed said.

"Then the rest isn't a concern to me. It's just fate. A man's time or not."

"You a believer?" Jed asked Adam.

"In what? In flesh and blood and how life ends eventually. Yes. As to what happens after that, I don't think about it."

Jei grinned as he pulled a cigar from his pocket. "I was going to save this. It's my last until I get more in The Dalles. Might not matter tomorrow."

"What do your people believe about the afterlife?" Adam asked. "In case you happen to be the man telling my son about it."

"Buddha taught that man is born again and again until he figures it all out," Jei said.

"Reincarnation."

He nodded. "One word for it. It is a punishment of sorts. Man must achieve enlightenment, and then he is released from the endless cycle."

"You figure you lived before?" Adam asked.

"Perhaps. I do not say I remember such lifetimes nor think about them. Perhaps it's all as some say—dust to dust. I am fine with that being the case."

"Not like we have a choice in what it is—including whether it's heaven or hell as my mother believed," Jed said taking a long pull on the cigarette as he stared into the flickering flames.

"We do about how we live our life. That's all," Adam said. "When I was down on the Siskiyous, I was alone a lot and thought plenty about it. I knew what Martha believed, and it felt like I could talk to someone, and it helped. Then I got back and life got in the way of thinking about it." He laughed. "Maybe I only think about it when facing death."

"I didn't during the war. I just wanted to get through the days. Some say a man will when he faces death. I saw a lot of death, a lot of battles. I didn't think about it at all. I just reacted when the time came that I needed to."

"The true warrior," Jei observed. "A good man to go into battle with. Faces what he must and doesn't think beyond doing."

"The irony," Jed said, "is that whether you think that way or any other, death comes and it's like it did this summer for McDermit—not when we plan or expect it."

"This is fatalistic talk," Adam said with a laugh. "I hope you don't both plan to die tomorrow because I plan to live. I'd rather go into this with men who think likewise."

CHAPTER 25

When Raine rose in the morning, restless after dreaming of Jed all night with a mix of their making love and his lying dead in a street, she decided she'd had enough sitting around the house. Opening the drawer where she kept her pants, she saw an envelope lying on them.

Taking it over to the lamp, she read her name in Jed's fine hand. She felt a sense of dread as she opened it. Was this a will or his last words to her? For a moment her eyes were too filled with tears to read, but then she sucked in a breath, wiped her eyes and began to read.

'My darling, Raine, when I went to war I never wrote you, but I should have. I had some misguided sense that it would be unfair. I left you without the words I felt and should have said. Now I am going into an unknown that, yes, could be dangerous, but this is no attempt at last words. I intend to give you those when I am old and gray. Instead this is what I should have said, the words that are always filling my heart when I see you.

'I love you, my dear, but it's so much more than for your beauty or your wise mind. It's the whole package, all of the being that I have come to know intimately, who has challenged me and supported me and sometimes within the same hour.'

She stopped again to wipe away tears aware she was crying but couldn't stop. Finally she got control of herself and again returned to his words.

'When I return, and I will return, I want us to have the baby you wanted. I want us to make this into a good place to raise children, to grow beef, to live on a land that we have nurtured together. The fact that your parents have come here, that hopefully soon your sister and family will join us is only enriching the experience. Though I lost my own brothers in the war, I feel I am going to get new ones through your family.

'Trust me that I will do all I can to bring Adam back to your mother, to settle this in such a way that we can live here on our land in peace. And when I come back, remember to put on that nightgown, you know the one, on our first night, the first night of the rest of our lives.

'This is the letter that should have been sent before, from the man who loves you more than anything in his life, the man to whom you give purpose and strength.'

She sat holding the precious missive. Sucking in a breath, finally she put it back into the drawer, took out her pants and dressed with her own purpose. She would look over the land of the laird. She would have everything ready for him when he returned. And he would return.

She headed downstairs eager to get breakfast cooked, read Belle's letters and then head outside to do something, anything in the clean mountain air. Maybe she'd join the Kalamas when they rode out to check for sign. It was time she learned about tracking.

In the morning, Adam, Jei and Jed rode their horses across the John Day River and up onto a broad plateau before they again dropped down into the gravelly crossing for the Deschutes.

Riding at a steady pace, they came to the outskirts of The Dalles by late afternoon.

Halting their horses by a small stream to let them drink, Jed leaned forward on the pommel as he considered. "Where would you be if you were watching for someone?" he asked Adam as he studied the cliffs ahead. The entry into the town was through a heavily trafficked, narrow opening.

"They are likely to want to avoid jail," Jei said. "That is unless Sheriff Mason is on the payroll."

"Mason is sheriff here? Jess Mason?" Adam asked. When Jei nodded. "He's a good man. He and I worked together when he was sheriff in Albany. He's not crooked. He might though be getting old and that could make it easy for them to get things past him or maybe the town council ties his hands." He rolled and lit a cigarette. "You cannot believe how politics interfere with a man when he's trying to do that kind of job."

"Is it why you quit?" Jed asked rubbing his jaw thoughtfully as he considered the options especially the part where they didn't get killed.

Adam nodded. "Some of it. Town was getting more civilized, less need for anything beyond knocking on the door of some man who had just beat his wife and thought he was entitled to do it. I just got tired of it. Always arresting the same drunks. Not to mention Eli growing up and wanting to do things with youths we didn't see as good influences. It was time to move on. Your offer came at a good time."

"Back to the plan," Jed said. "Such as it is. There is a place right on the other side of this canyon. A bluff juts into the road a bit. It would be most likely for an ambush if they wanted to keep the person alive."

"You think Grayson wants you alive?" Adam asked.

"I don't know. The truth of this is none of it makes much sense. When I started this ride, after what Edmonton told me when he was dying, I thought getting to Grayson and killing him was the only way. I have to admit now I wonder if there is a choice."

"I doubt it," Jei said. "Even if Grayson gave up now for now, he would keep at it like a sore that he couldn't let alone. The man is a little crazy but maybe you knew that."

"Crazy in what way?" Adam asked. "I never met him, just heard about his dealings. He didn't sound crazy in them—just crooked as hell."

"There's probably a word for him. He swings between extremes. One day he'd be morose, depressed, the next time I'd see him, he would be on top of the world. When he's down, he'd be less dangerous than when he's up and thinks he can do and get away with anything."

"Great," Jed said, "crooked and crazy. I've known a few military officers like that. They usually ended up dead sooner than later—sometimes shot by their own men."

Adam nodded. "It sounds like a mix that should have taken him out of business a long while ago."

"I think, looking back," Jei said, "that Edmonton steadied him. I didn't know why, but now it seems obvious that he had someone there who could bring him a form of reality and even respectability. That's gone, until he finds another; so not sure how he'll be when he learns his support is dead."

"Back to my question... will these men be waiting to capture or kill me?"

"If they are there and we can take them alive," Adam said, "they would be witnesses after Grayson is dead—assuming he doesn't just surrender. Men like them will take any chance they get to lessen their own punishment."

Jed looked at Jei. "So what do you think? Kill or capture?"

"You thinking of using yourself as bait?" Adam asked with a frown as he smoked. "If so, I don't like it. Too many ways it could go wrong."

"My opinion is," Jei said as he stared at the cut in the road ahead. "Grayson will make it worth more to them if they can take you alive. You know what he wants and it's not a quick death for you." His smile was grim.

It fit what Jed believed also. "Then here is the plan. I will ride down this road as though I have no idea trouble awaits, but I won't start until you two have circled around and come in from behind. If they are where it seems most likely, you'll be in a good position to give them a surprise. I will be in front and not as unprepared as they expect."

Adam ground his teeth, but Jed appreciated the grit of the man that he didn't try to argue with him. It was the best chance they had if they wanted these men alive to answer questions and be witnesses to avoid the sheriff coming after them for the eventual shootings. He knew how it had seemed when he was in the hands of Grayson before. The man wanted his enemies to suffer. Grayson would be his own downfall. Step by step.

He waited an hour, giving Adam and Jei time to get in place, then began riding through the canyon, passing a wagon on its way to town. Then another heavily loaded and heading south. As he neared what he recognized as the spot most likely for someone to be waiting, he was only a little surprised to see Si Tubbs come striding into the road and blocking his way. He had a revolver out and pointed at Jed.

"Nice to see you, Reb," he said in a rough tone. Jed now recognized the voice as the one the night he'd been kidnapped.

"You still looking for work?" he asked pulling Midas to a halt as though he had no concerns.

"I have work now," Tubbs said with a laugh. "It's profitable too."

Behind them Jed heard sounds of a scuffle, then Adam's voice. "Sometimes what's profitable can prove dangerous."

Tubbs glanced around to see the tall man with a Colt in his hand, Tubbs' two henchmen with their hands in the air, and Jei behind them, also with a weapon.

"Odds changing a bit?" Jed drawled, as when Tubbs looked back at him, he now had his Colt pointed at him.

"It does seem that way," Tubbs grunted.

"Drop it. You know I'd like nothing better than to kill you, but I won't if I don't have to. I remember another night, all too well, and you don't inspire me to give you a second chance."

Tubbs dropped his revolver and within a few minutes, he and his two friends had been hog-tied to junipers far enough off the road to avoid being easily found.

Jei looked at Tubbs with somewhat of a disappointed look. "I really wanted to kill you," he said. "I remember you from Portland, and you don't deserve second chances."

Tubbs glared at him.

"So, boys," Adam said with one foot on a rock as he leaned forward looking down at their sullen faces. "Who wants to tell me where we'll find Grayson. Don't all talk up at once."

Jei grinned. "I can help you boys remember. I'm good at that."

Jed lit a cigarette and listened as two of the men remembered a lot of useful information. When they had all they were going to get, they gagged them.

"You better hope at least one of us survives," Jed said smiling. "Otherwise, you might never get out of this spot."

He turned then to his horse. It was time to face Grayson and however many men he had with him.

Raine came in from the barns feeling tired but surprisingly rewarded despite a long day in the saddle with the Kalamas as they pointed out various tracks that meant something to them, nothing at first to her, but she was learning. Some signs meant possible food. Others were predators. Fortunately, they had seen no unshod ponies or horse tracks that hadn't been theirs. The snow had disappeared leaving enough mud that tracks were clearly visible. Now, as with what her mother had been teaching her, all she had to do was remember the lesson.

In the house, dropping her coat, she was sweating because she's unsaddled Fancy and taken the time to brush her down. She hoped being tired would guarantee a good night's sleep. At the kitchen table, she saw a sullen Eli, Toddy, her mother, books and papers.

"What's going on?" she asked as she took a cup of coffee from Bernice who was in the midst of dinner preparations.

"School," Bernice said, "and I never liked it either."

"Eli," Martha said, "had the idea that leaving Oregon City meant no more school. He has learned otherwise today." Heaven was purring on her lap.

Raine grinned as she sipped the coffee.

"I wanted to go with you," Eli protested looking at his aunt for support. "I could learn more there than from books."

"Everybody needs schooling," Martha said with a set look to her lips that Raine well remembered.

The Kalamas came in throwing their coats over the hooks. "School? There going to be a school here?" Joe asked as he also took a cup of coffee.

"And I will be the teacher at least of history, geography, literature, and reading," Toddy said. "Finally I have a task suited to my skills."

"Hah," Bernice said from the stove where she had gone to heat up a frying pan.

"I like the idea of schooling," Joe said. He pointed at his brother. "George got stopped before he learned more than writing his name. You teach him too?"

"Certainly," Toddy said with pleasure etched on his round face. "We can run this at various levels."

"Have you ever taught anyone?" Raine asked thinking at least it meant she wouldn't have to do it. She agreed with her mother that Eli needed to have an education, but she also knew that a day in the outdoors had been wonderful for her own emotional health.

"Well not professionally," Toddy admitted as Josh entered

also from outside. He'd ridden to the higher meadows to check the stock and look for sign.

"I saw where riders had been up there," he said as he sat at the table, smiling as Bernice handed him the last cup of coffee and began to make more.

"They could be wild horses," Joe said. "How many?"

"I'm not as good at tracking as you, but I'd say five and more heavily loaded than wild. I don't think they were yesterday's. It looked to me as though other animals had crossed over after they went by. You'd maybe know better than me what that meant."

"Go by the pine needles," Joe said as he sipped his coffee. "If they are shiny, then been there awhile. Dull and likely turned over by someone or something."

"I didn't see that to tell. Sorry."

"If they passed by, it's not a concern, is it?" Raine asked.

"Not five anyway," Joe answered. His brother nodded his agreement. "They're looking for easy pickings. This house and us, we're not. It'd take more than five to be a problem. Maybe just looking at what's goin' on."

"See, that's what I should be doing," Eli protested trying again. "I could be an outlook."

Joe grinned and rubbed his hand over the boy's thick black hair. "You could if you did your school work first. Me and George, we're gonna get some of that learning you don't value."

Eli grimaced.

"He has too much energy," Raine said looking at her little brother with a grin. "Maybe he can help me put out some of the hay they cut last summer for the horses. After he finishes his assignments that is."

"Good idea," Martha agreed. "We can compromise some on this, son. You do the work and the reward is more work." She laughed, but Eli's mood brightened especially as the Kalamas took an interest in what Toddy was saying as he began explaining an assignment.

Raine went out for firewood to stoke up the fire in the great room. Kneeling by it as she fed a few small limbs to replenish the flames, she realized her mother had followed. They each carried in two loads. A few minutes later with the fire roaring, they sat quietly on the sofa.

"By now they are probably in The Dalles," her mother said finally.

Raine nodded. "What I hate is this not knowing what could be happening to him right now while I sit here by a fire. I know he's in danger, and I can't be there to help him."

"It is hard," her mother agreed.

"Supper is ready," Bernice said from the door and then disappeared back into the kitchen.

"I don't feel hungry," Raine said.

"It is important to eat. It's important to stay busy. What you did today was good. Keep so busy you fall into bed and sleep." She sighed and turned Raine to look at her. "That and stay confident that they will be back as soon as they can."

"I'm trying."

Russell Grayson sipped his brandy as he sat in the back of the cheap bar. It was not to his taste, but it was where he had seven hired men, planted as though they were customers. He had hopes that soon Kirk would show up with good news, but it was beginning to look worrisome. He thought, not for the first time, that Kirk had been right. He should have let this go at least for now.

There was always tomorrow. If Kirk didn't show up in a day, he'd go back to Portland. He'd wait for the spring, and he'd hire a marksman to go up to the Hardman ranch and kill him from a distance. This whole thing was beginning to seem stupid.

When he saw Lieutenant Montgomery enter the bar and head straight for him, he knew he should have gone the day before. Montgomery glared at him as he took a seat at his table. "I am being investigated," he said when he had gotten a whiskey from a garishly dressed girl who he dismissed with a wave.

"By whom?"

"The military, of course. They... Damn it, I should have never gotten involved with you. They will find me out and then I'll be court-martialed."

Grayson thought worse could happen but only smiled faintly as he sipped his brandy. He beckoned for Jace Walker to come to the table.

"You aren't listening to me," Montgomery said with a snarl. "I won't go down alone. I swear I won't."

"Jace, have you seen Si?" he asked the tall man ignoring the lieutenant's threat but quite aware of what he would have to do about it. His only debate with himself was how to do it.

Walker shook his head. "Trask and Bennett went out to spell him over an hour ago. They haven't come back. Somebody should have been."

Before Grayson could decide on what to do, the saloon door opened again, and this time it was a tall military officer with three enlisted men.

"Damn," Montgomery said as he tried to move back into the shadows, clearly a losing proposition as the officer headed straight for them.

"Mr. Grayson, I presume. I'm Captain Phillips." He looked over at Montgomery. "How convenient that you'd be here also, Montgomery. Running the Quartermaster's Depot not enough profit for you?"

"Just came for a drink," Montgomery said with what sounded like a weak voice even to Grayson.

"Join us, Captain. What would you like to drink?" Grayson asked smiling and giving his men the eye. If this turned ugly, the handsome Captain would quickly find he'd bitten off more than he could chew. Charges of corruption could be twisted to a dead officer's reputation and to his own advantage.

"I am here for questions, not drinks," the captain said, not sitting.

"Perhaps your men would like one."

"My men are on duty." Phillips' demeanor told Grayson this was not going to be easily handled. He rested his hand now lightly on his revolver. Not as he would have wished but still not impossible considering his own superiority of numbers, something the arrogant captain couldn't possibly assess.

Grayson considered options. In this part of town, a shooting might be explained away without consequences. A dead officer was not a pleasant thought, but it wasn't impossible that it could just be a tragic error in judgment on his part to have ventured into such a dangerous neighborhood. Before he could decide how to handle the killing, which would include Montgomery, the saloon door opened again.

As Jed walked in, the last thing he expected to see was Captain Phillips standing in front of the table where he had been told he would find Grayson. He glanced around the room to assess the numbers they would be facing. Seven men at the bar. Among them, he recognized Jace Walker. Most were probably in Grayson's employ. If they weren't, when the shooting started, they better hit the floor and not draw a weapon, or they'd be the enemy.

Adam beside him was looking only at the uniformed man sitting beside Grayson. "Montgomery," he said walking easily toward the table before he nodded toward Phillips. "What are you doing here, Rand?" he asked.

"That's an interesting question," Phillips said scanning over Jed and Jei before turning back to Grayson. "Originally I was here for some answers. Montgomery being here has made asking questions irrelevant. Now it's an arrest of William Montgomery and Russell Grayson for defrauding the United States government, theft, larceny and probably more as we get closer to a trial."

"You have no authority with civilians, Captain," Grayson said with a benign smile.

"I don't?" The handsome officer's smile had turned icy. "Perhaps you will find out about that, after I take your weapons and put you in our brig along with the officer on your payroll."

Grayson turned from him then, his eyes filled with malevolence as he centered his attention on Jed. "And you. What are you doing here?"

"Bad accident out at the ranch," Jed said hand poised over his gun, ready for whatever came next. "Man died."

Grayson's eyes showed his rage. "My friend?"

"Oh was he? His horse bucked and he landed on his head. Broke his neck. Real tragic. Of course, what he told me when he was dying, that added to the tragedy." He smiled then, the kind of hard smile he knew a man took into battle.

"You can't prove anything from a dying man and your word," Grayson snapped his own mouth tight, his eyes glancing around the room as though assessing his own odds.

"Now what do you think he might've said? Maybe that it involved you?"

"You murdered him, didn't you?" Grayson snarled. "He came there and your wife wanted to leave, and you killed him."

"That your scenario?" Jed drawled fully aware that Grayson likely had a pistol in his hand. The city man would have to bring it up to fire. He wasn't worried. He was accurate and fast when need be and this was need be time. He also was more familiar with what it took to kill than one, who had always hired it done by others. "You knew we were married, huh? Edmonton knew too."

"He did?"

"You and he lovers?" Jed asked goading the man to get him to do what would enable him to kill him. He no longer saw it as possible to let this go. One of them would have to die.

When he saw the light flicker in Grayson's eyes, he pulled his own revolver dodging to the left as he fired. Jei and Adam were also firing. Jed's first shot hit Grayson, at the same time he felt something strike his left arm. He twisted as he went down. Grayson fell backward.

On his back, now aiming toward the bar, he saw Jace Walker pointing his pistol toward him. He shot him between the eyes. He heard more firing coming from Phillips. Montgomery was now slumped forward over the table a revolver in his loosely extended hand.

For a few moments, there had been nothing but the flare of firing weapons, sounds of shots and smoke. Just as suddenly as it had begun, it was over. The room grew deadly silent except for a few groans.

Jed braced himself and rose from the floor. Jei was feeling of Grayson's neck. "He dead?" he asked knowing if he had failed, there'd be no second chance.

Jei nodded. "Whatever is over there, he knows it now."

Phillips felt of Montgomery's pulse. "He's dead too." His men were checking the other still forms. "This one's still alive," a corporal said.

"If you can find the town's doctor, get him."

"You are the last person I expected to see here," Adam said to Phillips as the captain sheathed his weapon.

"I wasn't expecting you either. I have a feeling it was lucky for me that you were. I thought you were in Oregon City."

"And I thought you were at Camp Watson."

"I was ordered to come up and question Russell Grayson, then arrest Lieutenant Montgomery. Finding them together I was about to arrest both-- assuming his minions didn't kill me and my men."

"That was a distinct possibility," Adam said with the kind of smile Jed had seen on men after a battle—a little shaky, a lot relieved, and aware of the fragility of life.

"Well, I told you I'd go after the road agents," he turned then to look at Jed who was now holding his arm. "You were shot," he said needlessly.

Adam sheathed his still smoking gun. "Damnitall, why'd you go and do that? Raine will blame me, you know."

"Just nicked," Jed said managing a smile and thinking he had had a lot of bad luck with that arm.

An hour later his arm had been treated, bandaged, and put in a sling by the local doctor. The wounded man was taken to the doctor's office for further care, the sheriff notified of the shooting, and Jed was sitting at a better saloon with his friends and the captain as they smoked and sipped whiskeys.

All too soon, Sheriff Mason was there and asking for the whole incident to be related to him. Five minutes later, he was sipping his own whiskey as he cut off a chaw of tobacco.

"Is this going to be a problem?" Jed asked watching him through the cigarette smoke.

"In what way?" the sheriff asked.

"I mean that we have to stay here for some kind of inquest or hearing, whatever happens when someone important is killed."

The sheriff shook his head. "I can talk to the judge tonight, but I don't see why. We knew what Grayson was but couldn't prove it. Those three men you delivered, they are talking plenty to get a lighter sentence themselves. I know where you'll be."

"What about from the military end?" Adam asked Rand.

"I can handle it."

"And Montgomery escapes the consequences by dying."

"Hard way to do it," Jed said with a smile and aware his arm was becoming more painful. "I saw that look on your face when you saw him. What'd he do to you?"

Rand answered. "It was down on the Siskiyous. Adam was teaching me the ways of real war versus the kind you learn in books. He and Montgomery disagreed on how to handle the Indians."

"He made my life hell," Adam said with a grimace. "If I believed in hell, I'd hope it's where he ended, but I don't. So he gets off without paying for any of it."

"Perhaps his life was paying for it," Jei said smoking a long cigar.

"So we can go home tomorrow," Jed said thinking he ought to feel more relief than he did. Maybe it was the aftermath of killing again. He hoped he'd had all of it he ever would; but given the Indian problems, that was unlikely—not for a few years at least.

"I have no problem with it. If I need you for anything, I'll let you know in the spring. If I was you, I'd get back to that ranch before winter gets a hold of that country."

"I was thinking of starting tonight," Jed saying knowing that would be foolish. "but likely am stuck 'til morning. I will have to buy a pack animal, extra supplies, and there's that candy I promised a certain little boy."

"You'd be smart to lay over an extra day," Adam said gesturing toward his bandaged arm. "I'd hate to have to explain how after you got shot, you rode off and then broke your fool neck when you fell off your horse." He gave a laugh helped on by his second whiskey.

"I am not in the habit of falling off horses," Jed said, "and I am going home tomorrow. Finally I feel like I have one and something there worth going back for."

Jei grinned. "Sounds like it's a good feeling."

"You have one too. Come back with us."

Jei shook his head. "I should go back to Portland and see what is left of my business there."

"How about doing that after Thanksgiving and staying with us at least until the winter is over. I can use you on the ranch."

"And Eli would be happier being so far from those friends if he had someone teaching him the arts of an Eastern warrior," Adam said smiling. "In fact, I wouldn't mind some training myself. Straighten out my back maybe."

Jei looked surprised but then smiled. "My family can deal with the rest of it. I will write them but yes, I'll come back—at least until spring."

"Is anyone likely to take over Grayson's businesses?" Rand asked. "Does he have family or something?"

"I doubt he has family, but with operations like his," Jei said with a humorless laugh, "someone else always comes along. Of course, we can hope for change. Blind faith and all that."

Rand looked then at Jed. "I will be heading back to Watson with supplies in the morning. Supplies I might add that I had to buy with my own money." He gave Adam a knowing glance. "The government has decided the Indian wars are over, but they are leaving us out there with little resources just in case. With your wounded arm, you should ride in a wagon with us at least half way."

Jed took a long draw on the cigarette. "Not a chance. I am in a hurry to get home. Adam and I have a Thanksgiving dinner to enjoy. You are welcome to join us, Captain, but I suppose you don't have the freedom being military and all."

Rand laughed, taking out a cigar of his own to smoke. "It has its moments and then again... doesn't. There are always reports to write, explanations to make for those who aren't here and have no idea what any of this is like. You three watch out for the Shoshoni as you go. Despite what the federal government claims, I don't believe this is over by a long shot."

CHAPTER 26

A s Jed walked out in the clear night air, his mind on getting
back to the ranch and the life waiting for him there, he
heard a familiar voice behind him. "Don't turn around."

He felt a cold chill. "What do you want, Jessup?"

"You just cut into a lucrative deal for me, Reb. Don't reach for
that hog leg. Put your hands up, or I swear I'll plug you right now
before I tell you why."

Slowly, Jed raised his hands thinking of the irony of this, as he
tried to reason out what he could do about it. Adam and Jei were
still drinking. Fast he might be, but not fast enough to avoid a
bullet in the back. It had come as he's so often thought—when a
man least expected it.

"This is going to make me a happy man if not rich," Jessup
said. Jed could hear the smile in his voice.

"You were the one who left the ranch, deserted it," Jed said
knowing it wasn't smart, but he felt suddenly angry that he was to
be cheated out of his happily ever after.

"I had better prospects. Those didn't pan out."

"And you can't stand up to me in a fair fight."

Jessup laughed. "I don't need to. I wish Grayson was still alive.

He offered two hundred dollars for you dead and five hundred alive. You know what he planned. I'm easy in comparison. It'll all be over in a flash for you. And nobody will know who did it."

When the saloon door opened suddenly, Jed lunged to the side. He saw the flare of Jessup's gun, but for the moment he hadn't been hit as he landed hard on his wounded left arm. He heard a second shot and realized it hadn't hit him either before he blacked out.

When he came to, he saw worried faces. Hands were running over his body to assess where he'd been hit. "What happened?" Adam asked. "You hurt anywhere I can't see in the dark?"

"I don't think so." He managed to get to his feet. Jessup's body lay a few feet away. "I am not sure what happened. Who shot him?"

"I did." He saw then for the first time Captain Phillips standing back a little from Jei and Adam. "I came out and saw what was happening. There was only time to shoot the dog."

"You saved my life. Damn."

"Damn?" Adam laughed. "You didn't get hit again. Isn't that good news?"

"Other than a bluecoat saving it," Jed managed to joke. "All right. All right, I admit it. I am grateful. Even if you were the man I thought Raine preferred."

Phillips managed a chuckle even though he looked a little pale himself. "I never even courted her. I won't say she wasn't temptingly beautiful. All those Stevens women are beautiful, but she never looked at me that way."

"Well, I owe you one."

Rand shook his head. "It was just luck that I decided to leave when I did to get a start on the reports."

"He didn't think anybody would know who did it. He thought he had plenty of time to gloat a little."

"They might not have," the sheriff agreed as he stood. "This kind of thing happens, and a lot of time we never do know. It's a violent time."

"I think I'll escort you to your hotel room," Adam said. "I don't trust you not to get in trouble. You sure your arm isn't bleeding again?"

"It's fine, and I'm fine. And a little shocked at both."

"Maybe I will go with you three," Rand Phillips said, "just as an escort to the ranch, of course, not with the intention of getting a home-cooked Thanksgiving dinner." He grinned. "I believe I will send the supplies to Watson with the sergeant."

"There's always receiving the gratitude of the ladies for saving Jed's life as an added bonus," Adam said grinning.

"Of course."

Finally, as Jed got to his room, stripped and lay in the narrow, hotel bed, he was near exhaustion but couldn't sleep. He kept coming back to how close it had all come again. He'd seen it so many times, just as the captain had said. It came when a man least expected it. And then likewise salvation from the same unlikely place. He had no answers for why or from where either came. He just knew that he'd be going home, and it so easily could have been otherwise.

Four days later, Raine was in the barn cleaning out a stall. She had buried her own fears into work that had her tired enough to sleep at night. She had to keep a positive view. If he didn't show up soon, she had determined she would ask the Kalama brothers to take her to The Dalles and find him—alive or dead. The length of time didn't mean he wasn't coming back.

When she heard a Rebel yell from Josh, she ran to the barn door and saw four horsemen and a pack animal. As soon as she realized one of them was Jed, she began running. He swung down from his horse and caught her up with one arm.

"Don't tell me you got hurt again," she laughed as she pulled his head down for a kiss.

"Just a nick." His kiss was passionate, and she met it with equal fervor.

"Whole or in pieces, I am so glad you're back." She kissed him again just for good measure.

"Hey, don't the rest of us matter?" Adam asked as Martha and Eli had now come out of the house and run down to where they were dismounting. He grabbed them both in his arms.

"Is it over?" Toddy called from the porch when Jei brought a pack animal to him to be unloaded.

"Yes," Jei said. "For now."

"What's that mean?"

Rand Phillips dismounted stiffly, "It means what it means. For now. You ever know a time when anything is really over?"

"I'm thinking. Hey, Captain , good to see you."

The Kalamas came out and took the reins of the horses back to the barn to unsaddle, water and feed them. Jed went with them.

"How was it?" he asked as he tended to Midas. "Any sign of the Shoshoni?"

"Ask your lady," Joe said grinning. "She's getting as good at tracking as me." He laughed at Jed's look of surprise.

Once they were all in the kitchen, fresh coffee was brewing, the story had to be told of what happened in The Dalles. Jed didn't feel like discussing it again and was glad when Jei and Rand took over the story. He walked into the great room and knew Raine had followed. Sinking onto the sofa, he patted the spot beside him.

She took the chain out from her neck, unfastened it, and handed him the ring. "Now, put it on," she said.

He laughed and felt a sense of happiness he hadn't known for years. "You are sure? No more obstacles, nothing standing in our way?" He smiled as he thought about all the ways he had imagined this moment, how it would be to put the ring on her finger. None had been as it was.

"Do I need to force you?" she asked as he took the ring from her and slowly slid it on the appropriate finger.

"I might like to hold out just to find out how you would do it," he said as he kissed the ring.

"I can think of a lot of methods I didn't used to know." She took his hand to her mouth and slowly kissed it.

"You know," he said as he enjoyed the quiet, the hearing of voices from the kitchen, "I had a feeling when I got to The Dalles that maybe I didn't have to go after Grayson. That I could turn around. That the whole thing wasn't making any sense. Then it all rolled out in the end where there was no choice."

"I still find it hard to believe how Rand came to be in it. That seems like... well fate."

He shook his head. "Surprising at least."

Rand, Adam and Martha had come into the great room and sat on the sofa opposite theirs. "It does seem as though it's come full circle," Rand said as he had apparently heard the last of what Raine said. "I remember when I first met Adam. I was a green kid barely out of West Point, my first time around Indians. His wisdom and steadiness got me through the Siskiyous."

"You have plenty of steadiness now," Adam said smiling.

"Experience and wars. They do teach something. Not all good."

"You had a core and strength even then," Adam said. "I've never told anybody but Martha about the trip you and I made, dead of winter and bringing what Indians had survived up to the north and a different reservation."

"Even given the nightmare of the more recent War, I still hold that to be a low point in my life."

"It was for me too," Adam said. "You gave me hope though when you told me it was possible there'd been letters from Martha and that Montgomery had destroyed them. It gave me hope that Martha would be waiting for me."

"I knew there had to be something more to it when you saw him," Jed said.

"It's true he took a real dislike of me, but what he did with the letters was what infuriated me."

"I don't suppose it matters if I tell you this now," Rand said. "Naturally I studied his files when I began seeing the potential for his connection to the road agents. He had the opportunity and his files said he had the character. When I realized he had to be involved, then it was a question of who else was behind it."

"How did he get demoted?" Adam asked.

Rand nodded. "After the Siskiyous, he got what he expected to be a cushy Fort Vancouver assignment, but he botched everything he touched. He was lucky only to suffer loss of rank and not to have been court-martialed. When the War came up, he didn't want any part of real fighting and was glad to stay stationed out here. With forts being decommissioned, his own demotions, I think that is when he must have met up with Grayson, who was always looking for people he could use."

"I just wish I hadn't been one of them," Raine said. "I was blind to his true nature."

"It was how he succeeded," Jed said as he pulled her tighter against him.

"You saw it right away."

"Well," he said with a teasing kiss on her hand, "jealousy helped that end."

Her mother gave a little laugh. "The ring is finally where it belongs, I see."

Raine turned her hand to see how the light caught the gold. "Yes, it is."

"Perhaps we can have a celebration of it when Matt and Amy arrive."

"You think they really will come?" Raine asked uncertain as to whether they'd want to give up what they had been building in the valley.

"To visit at least," her mother said.

"What about St. Louis?" Raine asked. "Would he come or stay in the valley alone?"

"Who is he?" Jed asked.

"Our wagon master coming west," Martha said, "and then a wonderful friend. He has so much wisdom."

"He'd certainly be welcome also. It isn't likely to be a safe time here though, not for some years."

"I wish your family here the best, however or whoever comes," Rand said as he got up to walk to the fireplace, feeding a log into the flames before he turned. "I most likely would have been killed if you three hadn't shown up when you did. I saw what was going down too late. It looked to me as though Grayson was trying to decide if he could kill me, my men, Montgomery, and avoid any accountability. He would have gone down but likely taken me with him."

"The world is better off with him out of it," Adam said.

"Not that there aren't always those to take his place," Jed said with a breathless laugh. "But I want to feel positive. Think ahead not behind. For now we have nothing but a real Thanksgiving to look forward to."

"And Eli did kill one of the two turkeys for the feast," Martha said as she pulled Adam's head down for a quick kiss. "We're trading off on work with studies and outside activities. So far, so good. Jei coming back will help."

"He's quite a young man," Rand said with a smile.

"Growing up too fast."

"I have a little brother who has done that also. I've only seen him a few times since he was born."

"How old is he?" Martha asked with interest.

"Let's see about twenty-four, I think."

"Is he a nice young man?"

"I don't really know him."

Martha smiled more broadly. "Maybe he'd be a possibility for Belle."

When Rand said nothing, Raine looked at his face and set lips. "You met her didn't, you?" she asked. "I think right after Eli was born you came to talk to Adam before you went east to the Plains. Wasn't Belle here too?"

Rand nodded as he walked back to the fireplace staring into the flames.

Raine watched him and suddenly saw something she had missed before. He had come that time, fresh from battles, barely twenty-four, handsome, strong, and certainly enough to stir any young girl's imagination. Especially one like Belle, seventeen and looking for adventure.

The hard expression on Rand's face discouraged further exploring that possibility. Had there been something more between them those many years ago? It would be impolite to ask.

Besides whatever her mother might wish for Belle, one thing she knew for sure about her strong-willed little sister-- Belle would be doing the choosing. Rand was too old for her anyway. Or was he?

She thought a bit. Eight years maybe. It would have been too much ten years ago, when Belle was still a girl, but now? She realized she was being silly. Belle was nowhere near, not likely to return to Oregon, nor would she want a cavalry officer if she did. She smiled. It was not her problem. Her problems had temporarily ended.

As the others headed back into the kitchen to check on dinner, Raine snuggled back against Jed. "Well," Raine whispered in his ear, "as for Thanksgiving dinner being all you have to look forward to..."

His smile softened as he turned back to her. "And what else might there be?"

"Oh maybe something you mentioned in that letter."

"You think we can go to bed early?" he asked with a gleam in his eyes, the look that she had always hoped to find and only had finally seen with him.

"I am sure of it," she said as she pulled his head down for a long and passionate kiss. "The laird is home—and what he wants is what he gets."

THE END

Thank you dear reader.

Please leave a review. Reviews are the life breath of writers ...good or otherwise.

A Full List and Summaries of Rain's books at:

http://romanceswithanedge.blogspot.com/